A Necessary Heir

A novel by

L.A. Hilden

© L.A. Hilden 2010

ISBN: 978-0-9829897-0-8

Also available in ebook formats at:
www.lahilden.com/

This book is sold subject to the condition that it shall not, by way of trade or otherwise, be lent, resold, hired out or otherwise circulated without the author's consent in any form other than this current form and without a similar condition being imposed upon a subsequent purchaser.

Any similarity between the characters and situations within its pages and places or persons, living or dead, is unintentional and co-incidental

Cover © Tony Szmuk 2010

Acknowledgments

I want to give my heartfelt thanks to my editor Michael McIrvin at Pro Editing. I want to thank Tony Szmuk at BeWrite Books for my website and book cover design. Without the two of you, my dreams wouldn't have been reached, so thank you.

Dedication

This book is dedicated to my wonderful husband who encouraged me to never give up on my dreams, and to my beautiful children who are my world. To my loving family and my caring friends, my life would not be complete without you. To my readers Diane and Jenny, thanks for your support and encouragement. May God bless and watch over you all.

A Necessary Heir

CHAPTER ONE
London, England 1815

"Bloody hell," Jackson cursed, looking about the cluttered room with a sense of utter exhaustion.

He stood amidst a pile of papers in his grandfather's unorganized study while one of the deceased earl's many solicitors rattled off expenditures. Jackson had stopped listening; his head hurt. The months after his grandfather's death had been pandemonium and he had quite nearly had enough.

"Augh!"

"I beg your pardon, my lord?"

"Nothing, Rolland. May we do this later?" He hadn't heard a word the man had said for the last fifteen minutes and it was pointless to let the solicitor continue.

"As you wish." Rolland gathered his papers into a neat stack, and with a bow, vacated the study.

No sooner had the solicitor left than knuckles rapped upon the door.

"Yes, what is it?" Jackson asked, his tone filled with venom in spite his attempt to control his frustration.

"A Miss Bodzin to see you, my lord," Townen, his late grandfather's distinguished butler, announced.

Jackson didn't recognize the woman's name. He waved his hand and nodded at Townen, indicating he was to show her in, all the while wishing he were four blocks away in the comfort of his own townhouse, far away from this house where he currently fumed, the house in which he was raised. It was not just the clutter and incessant solicitor nonsense, however. As he stood in the Waterford book-lined study, he could feel his grandfather's presence—and it was eerie.

Moreover, it was strange to stand in the very room where his grandfather controlled his kingdom. He could almost picture the old man near the white fireplace mantel, waxing poetic about the greatness of being the Earl of Waterford.

He gently inched the dark drapes aside, noting the scent of his grandfather's stale tobacco caught in the fabric, and looked out the front window. A milk cart was stopped down Park Lane and a small line of the area's maids stood waiting to make their purchases.

Jackson released the drapes and turned away from the scene when the door opened behind him. Townen ushered in a curly headed maid who quickly bobbed in what he supposed constituted a curtsy.

"Miss Bodzin, my lord."

Jackson nodded, motioning the woman into one of the chairs across from the desk as Townen left, closing the door silently behind him. Jackson thought he recognized her, and believed she came from the Sussex household, a family estate he hadn't visited in years.

"What can I do for you, Miss Bodzin?" The smell of cheap perfume wafted across the room. The cloying scent had him fighting back a choking cough.

The maid stiffened her shoulders as if preparing for battle. "I came for compensation."

"Ah, of course, and for what service are you owed funds?"

"Your grandfather and I…" Her voice faltered and then returned with a vengeance. "We were intimates, and your grandmother dismissed me without a reference!" She boomed out her words, and then she fell into great heaving sobs, tears rolling down her cheeks, her lower lip quivering.

If she expected sympathy from Jackson, she'd be sorely disappointed. It was a well-known fact that, despite his grandfather's advanced years, the old earl had still been capable of a licentious affair. There wasn't anyone in the household who wasn't wise to the man's debauchery, but Jackson presumed the women were willing participants, for the right price.

"How long did you *work* for my grandfather?"

"Five years."

Jackson decided to try to be diplomatic about this situation. "Five years is a long time to be set out without references. I shall see to it that you have one. Now if you'll excuse me, I have many other *important* matters to which I must attend."

The woman scowled, her tears now gone. "I do not plan to leave here without proper compensation," the maid exclaimed, her fists twisting on her lap. The toes of her worn walking boots dug into the expensive Aubusson area rug.

Five years was a long time. Money might rid him of the woman after all, and the rest of them who would come knocking be damned. He reached into the desk, pulled out a small velvet purse, and tossed the sack to her. "Goodbye, Miss Bodzin. Consider yourself paid in full," he stated with a calm he didn't feel. "We will not meet again."

She peeked into the bag. "I don't consider this proper compensation, sir."

Perhaps it was the mountainous tasks in which he had been engaged for too long, or perhaps it was lack of sleep or even grief, but whatever the reason, the maid's insolence proved to be his breaking point.

"Proper, Miss Bodzin?" His fist bounced off the desk with a loud thud. "I don't think there is anything about your dalliance with a man three times your age that's considered proper. I will not give you another farthing for conducting an affair with my grandfather, regardless if he promised you the moon! It's now time for you to take your leave."

The audacity of this woman to show her face in his dear grandmother's home was beyond contemptible.

"If you don't vacate my presence immediately, I will toss you out without your bloody reference." The woman didn't move. "Am I making myself clear, Miss Bodzin?"

"Perfectly, sir. I'm still not leaving without my money."

Jackson saw red. "It's...my...money! Townen!"

He heard Townen tripping over his own feet, and then the butler threw open the door and practically fell into the room. "My lord?"

"Remove this woman! She is no longer welcome at Waterford House."

"Yes, my lord." Jackson watched as Townen looked down into the ruddy complexion of the enraged woman before asking in a cajoling manner, "Miss Bodzin, if you'd please?"

Not a muscle moved as she sat defiantly, her back ramrod straight.

Townen tried again in a placating voice. "Miss Bodzin, allow me…"

"As I told his lordship, I'm not leaving until I get paid appropriately."

Townen threw Jackson the most helpless expression, clearly befuddled about how to proceed with the stubborn woman. Apparently the butler had never been presented with such a situation in his life.

"Simms!" Jackson roared. His large footman marched into the room, his mammoth size casting the area surrounding him into shadow. One had to admire the man's brawn, which was most impressive.

"My lord?" The giant passed him a crooked grin.

Jackson knew Simms' keen sense of observation had allowed him to measure the scene adequately with a mere glance, one of the burly man's qualities that had inspired Jackson to hire him. "Remove Miss Bodzin from the premises. See her into a hack and set on her way," Jackson instructed.

Simms peered down at the woman, anger now emanating from her frame with such heat Jackson swore he could feel it from across the room.

Simms did not bother to ask the woman to stand. He physically pulled her to her feet, tossed her belly down over his shoulder—amidst her screams of protest—and walked out the door, unmindful of the small fists pummeling his back.

"You should be taking notes, Townen."

"I daresay his method worked efficiently, sir. He must be useful to have around," the butler stated, his face taut with shock at the scandalous behavior he had witnessed.

"He is." Jackson gave the butler a crooked smile. The entire Waterford staff thought him a rascal, courtesy of his grandfather, who had regaled them all with tales of his exploits at some point or other, frequently exaggerating to get his point across. On occasion, Jackson found their sidelong glances a stellar reason to amuse himself. "That's not to say I have visitors thrown out on a regular basis." His tone indicated that he did just that.

"Of course not, my lord. I never meant to imply anything of the sort."

Jackson nodded.

"Will there be anything else, my lord?"

"No, you may go."

The butler bowed solemnly, then disappeared into the hall. Jackson turned to look out the window once again. He could see over the hedges, and he watched with some satisfaction as Simms deposited his grandfather's paramour unceremoniously into a hackney. He could not help but grimace ever so slightly when the woman tumbled to the floor. Thank heavens his grandmother was napping. The Dowager Countess had suffered enough grief, and Jackson was damn sure she wouldn't appreciate such women blatantly flaunting their association with her deceased husband.

The hack pulled into motion. The woman leaned her head out the window and hollered, a scene Jackson wished to avoid. He began to turn away from the window, but he noticed another conveyance pulling up to take the last one's place. "Now what?" He'd be admitted to Bedlam before he put his grandfather's estate, and mistresses, in order.

***

Abigail Gibbons' heart raced as she fidgeted on her carriage seat in front of the Earl of Waterford's town-home. The mansion's mere façade was overwhelming for a girl who had spent most of her life cloistered behind the safe walls of Lady Carlyle's Academy for Young Women. The gray brick structure had numerous smoke stacks that reached into the sky, and three huge white stone pillars helped form an impressive portico, giving the mansion an even greater aura of grandeur and importance. She knew it was ridiculous to let the home's size intimidate her, but she reasoned that such feelings couldn't be helped.

Her hands were clammy as she looked down at her faded black riding habit, the cuffs frayed, the hem torn in the back, and the bodice far too tight due to her chest's growth in the past five years. She needed clothes. She needed shelter. *Saints be praised.* She needed everything.

The Earl of Waterford's letter had been explicit. She was to put her things in order at school and come straight to his house to meet his wife, and together, the earl and countess would decide her suitability for the position.

Questions swirled in her mind. Were the Waterford's responsible for her education? Why else would an earl send for her? He was definitely no relation. Why offer her the position when they did not know her? To her knowledge, she'd never met them, and she was apt to remember if she was ever introduced to members of the gentry, since she knew so few.

Did they know she was a bastard? If not, would they toss her out when they found out? Why choose her? Why, why, why?

She wasn't going to get any answers hiding in this silly vehicle. She would no longer deal with the whys or what ifs, and she could not think upon her blatant disregard of convention by approaching a domicile without a maid in tow. She had come all this way, and moreover, she simply had nowhere else to go.

As the Countess of Waterford's companion, she would gain a modicum of respect from the members of polite society. At least she wanted to glimpse the glittering life her good friend Clarissa spoke of with enthusiasm. *You cannot get the assignment sitting here.*

The door on the house flew open, and Abigail watched as an older woman dressed in a black maid's uniform was being physically carried over some large man's shoulder like a sack of grain. Abigail leaned her head slightly out the window and saw the man dump the outraged woman onto the floor of the conveyance in front of hers. With a slight dusting of his hands, the burly man walked back toward the house, while the woman spat out some stinging obscenities before her conveyance hightailed it out of sight. What in the world was going on here?

Abigail looked up at the impressive structure yet again, now even more intimidated to approach the door. The man of mammoth proportions stepped up on the porch and turned to face the street. He stood before the door with his arms crossed upon his wide chest, guarding the front entrance. But even a man of such imposing stature would not keep her from her future.

Abigail opened the door, and the driver hopped down from his squeaky perch, probably relieved she had finally decided to emerge. She squinted to block out the mid-day sun while digging in her old leather reticule for some coins. She paid the driver from the funds the Earl of Waterford provided for her journey.

When the conveyance pulled away, she found herself standing at the end of the walkway. Sunlight gleamed off the row of windows lining what she assumed must be the front room, and so she couldn't see inside, but she felt as if someone was watching her. Valise in hand, she squared her shoulders, took a deep breath, and urged her feet to move forward.

Once at the porch, she smiled at the large man. Usually the simple gesture had the male population treating her amicably—her acquaintance with men was limited but it wasn't nonexistent—but the enormous man's glare only intensified. She decided not to dwell on this fact, however, assuming he must be of the same temperament as a guard dog, and hoped the earl would be more receptive. The door swung open before she could knock.

"Yes?" A man she presumed to be the butler gave her a once-over with his beady gaze, taking in her aged attire as she noticed the fine cut of his own stylish burgundy uniform.

"I'm here to see the Earl of Waterford," Abigail stated with what she hoped was a regal air. She held herself erect and let a warm smile play across her lips.

The butler's thin lips curled at the corners as he stepped back to allow her entry. "And you are?"

"Miss Abigail Gibbons. The earl's expecting me." She tried not to blush at the fact that she lacked a proper escort for a lady. Not that she was a lady born and bred, but she was taught to be one and conducted herself accordingly. Her hands shook in spite of her attempt to will them to stillness. She extracted the letter she had received from the earl and allowed the butler to read the summons.

She then folded her letter and placed it back into her pocket as he led her toward an arched alcove.

"Wait here," he instructed.

A set of double wooden doors stood to her right and a long hall to the left. A cozy parlor opened up before her. She consciously took in the scent of spent beeswax candles, noting the olfactory pleasure, which the less expensive tallow she'd grown used to lacked. The furniture in the parlor, a dark mahogany sofa done in navy flanked by two navy velvet chairs, looked heavy. Wallpaper of a soft shade of blue, tiny flecks of yellow slashed across it at various angles, covered the walls, giving the place a cheery atmosphere, unlike the dismal tattered papers of her mother's cottage. The butler noticed her avid curiosity regarding her surroundings for he cleared his throat to get her attention.

"I will inform his lordship of your arrival."

"I hate to impose upon you, good sir, but I must ask: Do you have a private place where I may freshen up first?"

"Townen?" The bellow echoed in the alcove.

The butler nearly jumped out of his skin. "Excuse me, miss." He gave her a hasty bow and ushered himself through the closed double doors.

Not seeing any place to change her attire, and not bold enough to go exploring without permission, she continued to survey the room. Two large crystal chandeliers, currently unlit, traversed the length of the room. Floor-to-ceiling windows cast rays of sunshine from the far end of the room onto a highly polished wood floor liberally covered with a decorative carpet. The table to her left held a vase of white roses, and Abigail couldn't help but move forward to inhale their scent. She was so nervous that her fingers trembled as she reached out to touch the softness of a rose petal. She then pictured the maid being physically removed from the house and took a deep breath to steady herself.

"Bring her here!" a voice boomed. The shout was loud enough to pull her thoughts away from the I-am-capable-and-reliable speech she'd practiced.

A second later, the butler hurried into the room, straightening his back and tugging on his tailored coat as if regaining his dignity.

"His lordship will see you now."

Abigail wanted to mention her change of attire, but the butler looked disconcerted enough. Not wanting to keep the earl waiting, she fell into step behind him.

Apparently she wasn't catching the earl on a good day—unless he was always so testy. The thought made her cringe. Perhaps he enjoyed barking out orders. She shuddered. What if he was mean-spirited? Oh, what was the matter with her? Perhaps the man was simply in a surly mood. Everyone has a bad day now and then. Besides, she told herself, he had sent for her.

A Necessary Heir

She reminded herself why she was here, of her dreams of travel. She had even allowed herself to dream that she might one day earn enough money to take a trip to Egypt. "A silly dream," she had warned herself even as she imagined great pyramids and swarthy folk bustling about crowded markets.

With no small amount of trepidation, she stepped inside the darkly paneled room and found herself facing the earl's broad back. She noted that his wide, strong shoulders held no signs of a stoop from his advanced years, and as a matter-of-fact, he appeared to have a full head of hair, blond hair to be exact. Completely thrown off guard because her expectations had been shattered, she stared in wonderment.

When the butler announced her, the figure turned.

Abigail inhaled. She was looking into eyes that were the most captivating shade of blue she'd ever seen. The man was a regular Adonis, from his cropped blond locks to his shiny black boots, his masculine form ideally presented in his formal yet snug attire. His breeches clung to him like a second skin, showing muscular thighs and lean calves, and the cut of his coat exquisitely displayed his broad shoulders and lean torso. *He must have a highly accomplished tailor.* She tried to gather her wits, flushing at her own thoughts.

The man moved closer, unnerving her as he inspected her from head to toe. "Well, I'll say you're much prettier than the last harlot I sent on her way."

CHAPTER TWO

Jackson looked at the lady standing in front of him, and for a fleeting moment, he was lost in her image. Long flowing brown hair with streaks of blond, where it had been kissed by the sun, cascaded around her petite shoulders. The silken, slightly curled strands were pulled up on the sides by silver combs shaped like lotus flowers. He thought for a brief moment about telling her why the Egyptians revered such a flower. Was this woman aware the lotus represented the passing of the day? Curiously, he wondered if she'd even care. He blinked away his train of thought. His mother had been much on his mind of late. He missed her. Clearly her love for anything Egyptian had rubbed off on him when he wasn't paying attention.

He continued his perusal of the young lady. Her clothing left much to be desired, her dress tattered, worn, and far too tight for her womanly figure; but her cheekbones were high, accentuating her deep brown eyes, which were bewitchingly ringed in gold. He observed all of this from a fairly good distance, and he realized at closer proximity, were the lady dressed in something more fashionable, she would be stunning. Of course her beauty was a moot point. Her sad attire spoke volumes as to why she was there.

"Leave us, Townen," he barked more harshly than he meant to. One thing was certain. He was bloody fed up with dealing with his grandfather's paramours.

The butler bowed and left the room, closing the doors behind him, but not before he cast the visitor a fleeting smile. Jackson thought this odd, for he was under the impression that Townen never smiled. He looked back to the woman, who seemed not to notice Townen's kind gesture. She was far too busy staring at Jackson. A frown furrowed her brow as she clasped her hands tightly in front of her. Her head cocked at

A Necessary Heir

a questioning angle. He hoped his presence intimidated her, and now that she had made it into the house to make her plea, she was having a case of nerves. Jackson did not plan to make it easy for her. He was more than disappointed that she didn't take issue with his insult.

"Miss Gibbons, what brings you to my door?" He kept his voice low and firm.

"I'm looking for the Earl of Waterford." Although her voice shook, it held a lilting melody that warmed his blood.

"I see." Jackson gave her a harsh grin. He crossed over to a table that sat between floor-to-ceiling bookshelves and poured himself a drink from a decanter. *This day seems to be getting worse and worse.* "Can I get you something?"

"No, no, thank you. Just Lord Waterford, if you please."

"Still having trouble believing I'm him, eh?" He lifted a brow, watching her over the rim of his glass, and downed a good portion of his brandy. *Could she not be aware of her lover's passing?*

Her forehead wrinkled as she shook her head no, sending soft curls bouncing through the air, and her lovely perfumed scent filled the atmosphere. "Are you the Earl of Waterford?"

"In the flesh." He performed an exaggerated bow.

Her shoulders straightened, and the uncertainty vanished from her eyes. She cast him a brilliant smile. He was sure her eyes sparkled. "Then I'm here to see you about the position of companion."

Jackson choked on his drink and slammed the glass down on the table as he covered his mouth. He'd initially believed her reasons for being here less than appropriate, but he was shocked that she had the audacity to admit it openly. How could his grandfather be so cruel to his grandmother by openly interviewing his next mistress under their roof? He tried to control his fury as the woman continued.

"I mean, I assume the position is still available?"

"Available?"

He pivoted on his heels to glare at her. "Listen here, Miss Gibbons. I may be new to my title. Nevertheless, I've been reared for this moment since I took my first breath of London air, and you and the many other lightskirts of your ilk are not getting a bloody farthing from me!" He felt victorious when she shrunk back. But after a moment's pause, she took a step toward him. *So much for intimidation.*

"Are you implying that I am a woman of loose morals?" The lady's golden-ringed eyes narrowed and he could almost feel the hostility emanating from them.

He thought for a passing moment that perhaps he was wrong, but no, he heard her say she was there to be his grandfather's companion. He knew his grandfather liked them young, but perhaps he liked them innocent as well.

"It was more than an implication." He took some menacing steps forward, his sense of indignation restored, and he stopped within inches of her. Damn, she certainly was pretty, especially with her features flushed.

The chit was obviously furious, and he would laugh at the spectacle of her tiny self on the verge of a violent reaction if he weren't so bloody sick of cleaning up his grandfather's mess.

"I will not stand here and take these insults." She clenched her fists at her sides.

He couldn't help being impressed by her fortitude. "There's the door." He nodded toward it, never taking his eyes off hers, which he now knew to be clearly a mistake for they were filling with tears.

Damn, damn, damn! A woman's greatest weapon is her damn tears.

She turned, but instead of marching to the door as he expected, she walked over to seat herself on the dark leather sofa. He heard her take a long breath then blow it out her pursed lips, a sure indication that she was struggling to gain her composure. Finally, she spoke. "You have everything all mixed up, sir."

Jackson held back a laugh. She couldn't have made her intent more clear. "Do I?" He sat in the chair across from her, leaning forward to rest his elbows on his knees in an effort to intimidate.

"Let us see if I have this right, shall we? It is to my understanding, and indeed I am now the Earl of Waterford, that you are seeking employment as my mistress." He smiled and sat back, finding the idea of her in his bed to his liking. He threw one arm along the seat back and awaited her answer.

She gasped, throwing a hand over her mouth. "Your mistress?" She swallowed audibly, her cheeks turning a deep crimson. "Heavens no, my lord. I assume the previous Earl of Waterford has passed away, and I am deeply sorry for your loss. I understand you must be grieving to have come to such an assumption. Therefore, I forgive you. I was summoned here to interview for a position as the Countess of Waterford's companion. I mean, assuming you are not married, for it's not your wife I seek. I mean, the lady in question would now be a dowager countess, but of course you know all of this. Although you seem too young to be her son and you don't look to me to be the marrying kind." She flushed yet a deeper red. "That is not to say you don't have any husbandly attributes. You just don't appear to be a hearth-and-home kind of man."

He could not believe his eyes, but she then turned yet a deeper crimson.

"I mean... I'll be silent now."

Jackson opened his eyes wider during her chatter, which to his surprise, wasn't the least bit condescending. When she locked her lips shut with a pretend key, he burst into laughter. She had managed to amuse him, pulling him out of his sullen mood with her ramblings. That she wasn't there to bed his grandfather, *thank the Lord*, had something to do with his lightened mood, to be certain. Nevertheless, he did find it bruising she'd been appalled by the idea of being his mistress. She reached into her pocket and extracted a letter, handing it to him with a delicate curtsy. He read it quickly.

"Miss Abigail Gibbons." He stood to take her hand. "I owe you my sincerest apologies." He used his most contrite expression.

Her head snapped up and she angled it slightly as she seemed to be examining him again. "Thank you," she managed to mutter.

"My grandmother is the Dowager Countess of Waterford. My mother holds the position of Countess of Hastings. And, no, I'm not married." He gave her the smile he used to charm the ladies, switching the topic back to his inexcusable insult. "What can I do to make up for my unforgivable conclusions? My only excuse… The woman who left before you arrived… I'm sorry. It doesn't matter. It's certainly not something I should discuss with someone of your virtuous nature. I should have been able to tell by the graceful way you carry yourself that I was wrong. Someone of your delicate sensibilities would find it distasteful…" Now he was rambling.

"I wouldn't say my sensibilities are delicate." She blushed once again, having regained her normal color only a moment before.

"I mean… Oh, nonsense! That's what this conversation is," she said in sheer exasperation.

Jackson found himself laughing for the second time today, both times because of this same young woman. He released her hand and sat next to her, and she moved over to what he assumed was a more comfortable distance for her. He was surprised that he had to fight the urge to take this woman in his arms and kiss her senseless. His body heated at the mere thought. What was the matter with him?

He found himself wanting to spend the remainder of the evening with this beguiling female, who was, to put it mildly, refreshing. "Come with me to the Bakersfield ball tonight?" he asked, knowing his invitation was less than appropriate given that they had just met, but for once, he did not care what might be appropriate. Truth be told, he found the multitude of ladies he acquainted himself with to be dull and transparent.

He was bored with their tireless flirtations and overly practiced manners, and Miss Gibbons had so lightened his mood that he was reluctant to let her go.

Of course, she was beautiful, but this need to be with her didn't have anything to do with her looks, at least that is what he told himself. Something about her stirred his blood, and it was true he had yet to find a woman who could accomplish such a task so effortlessly, but her presence was also somehow soothing.

Abigail didn't know what to think. The man literally went from insults to apologies to asking her out for the evening. *Ridiculous*. Even worse, she found herself wanting to accept his invitation. How she longed to be a guest at one of those grand parties Clarissa always spoke about with awe. But she couldn't escort him for it simply wasn't done. He was an earl and she was… That was the problem. She was well educated and a lover of Egyptology, but she was still illegitimate no matter what else might change in her life. At least she finally managed to say the word now without cringing, though it still hurt to watch others react when they were told of her origin. She turned her gaze away from the empty fireplace to the piercing blue eyes of his lordship.

"Surely you jest, my lord."

All right, perhaps she could have come right out and rejected his offer. But her body clamored to hear him reaffirm his invitation. An illegitimate daughter being asked by a handsome, titled man to accompany him had to be a rare occurrence. She basked in the warm sensation now filling her. Although she shouldn't, she couldn't help but picture herself on the arm of this intriguingly powerful man.

"On the contrary, I find you delightful and I never jest when extending an invitation to a delightful woman." His voice took on a sensual quality.

Her heart skipped a beat as tingles of excitement coursed through her. An earl, no, the Earl of Waterford found *her* delightful.

His smoldering looks took her breath away, turning her concentration on the matter at hand to cinders. She looked down to straighten her skirts in an effort to control her trembling, but her fingers shook as she patted down a crease in her faded, threadbare dress. *Wait a minute.* The realization that she was being played for a fool made her shoulders tense. How many times did her mother warn her about predators like the earl? And here she sat in a closed room with the man, and absent a chaperone. There probably wasn't even a Bakersfield ball this evening. He still thought her a harlot looking for her next meal ticket. The man believed she was there to keep his grandfather happy in the biblical sense, which was utterly uncouth of him, and now he wanted to have her in the old man's stead. *Disgusting.* She thought herself a fool for accepting his apology so quickly, and now this outlandish offer. Her at a ball? *Nonsense!*

She stood to leave. She wasn't about to be pulled in by his false flattery. "Good day, my lord."

He apparently didn't expect her departure, for he stumbled over his feet trying to get to the door ahead of her.

"Wait. Did I say something wrong?"

She glared at his boyish expression, which was all innocence. "From the moment I entered the room." She closed the door before he reached it, snatched up her bag from the foyer floor, and hurried across the street with hungry strides. She headed for a hack further down the lane, and once inside, she sank against the squabs with relief.

She bolted upright. "My job!" What was she going to do for employment? "I want the position," she said angrily, and then she glared down at her old gown. "No, I need it." Where would she go without this job?

It didn't take her long to decide what to do, for her options were limited.

She gave the driver instructions, and the vehicle soon stopped in front of Clarissa Mayfield's home. She knocked on the elegantly carved door and was ushered into a parlor by a wizened butler, his faded gray eyes gazing down at her attire in obvious contempt. "Lady Clarissa will be in shortly, Miss Gibbons." She watched him leave the room on wobbly legs that looked as dependable as twigs.

Abigail paced the long room along a plush red carpet, wondering what kept her friend. The scent of honeysuckle cascaded into the room from an open window, and songbirds sang in the spring breeze. Suddenly, harsh voices carried down the long hallway and into the room, the booming sound darkening the once serene atmosphere.

"I told you under no uncertain terms are you to associate with *that* girl!"

"She's my friend, Father," Clarissa's recognizable voice wailed.

Abigail's heart sank. She shouldn't have come. The last thing Abigail wanted was to subject her friend to Lord Loring's temper. She did not want to be the one to bring the man's vicious streak to the surface.

"Friend?" Lord Loring shouted in clear outrage causing Abigail to flinch.

"Yes, my friend," Clarissa continued bravely.

The sound of a loud crash echoed down the hall, and Abigail jumped, immediately heading for the exit. She would not allow Clarissa to suffer on her behalf.

"A bastard friend!" Lord Loring spat in disgust. "She's not suitable to clean your shoes, and I will not allow her kind in my home."

Abigail made for the open parlor door as the yelling grew louder, turning to see Clarissa staring down at the remnants of a crystal vase as she reached it, delicate irises scattered amongst the shards of glass and water.

"Please do not punish your daughter for our association, my lord. I'm leaving."

"Good, at least one of you has an ounce of sense. Show yourself out, and don't darken my doorway again."

"Yes, my lord." Abigail sent her friend a sorrow-filled frown as she mouthed, "Sorry." She hurried out the front door, which the old, now smiling butler conveniently held open. Thankfully, her driver had waited, and she hurried inside the interior of the vehicle shaking with rage and hurt, her illegitimacy looming over her head like a merciless black cloud.

As she grew older, she perfected the art of withholding her tears, but now she barely held them back as she considered her paltry options. Her acquaintances in London were limited. She remembered her mother mentioning her Aunt Nottingham, but her aunt now resided behind the walls of Bedlam, the poor soul. But Aunt Nottingham had a son. What was her cousin's name? Oh what did it matter? He was no more likely to allow her admittance into his home than Lord Loring.

There seemed no choice. As much as she dreaded going home to her melancholy mother, she would do so. Better to be there than sleeping on a park bench, which seemed to be her only other alternative.

The hack was about to pull away when Clarissa came running out of the house, a harried maid following in her wake.

Before Abigail could question what her friend was doing, the door was thrown open and Clarissa leaped inside, her maid following.

Adjusting her peach skirts, Clarissa moved over to allow her maid ample room and looked up with a sly smile, fixing a few strands of her blond hair, which had loosened from her coiffure in her hurried dash.

"What are you doing?" Abigail asked. She was well aware of her friend's adventurous nature, but openly defying her father seemed too much even for Clarissa.

"I'm running away."

"What? You can't!"

"Surely you can see I jest, Abby."

Clarissa waved her hand through the air. "If you haven't yet guessed, I'm taking my friend to the museum, where there happens to be an Egyptian exhibit." She paused, worrying her bottom lip between her teeth. "I'm sorry if my father upset you."

"Oh, I'm fine." Abigail shrugged.

How many times did Clarissa hear her say those three little words?

Clarissa gave her hand a gentle pat of understanding. "Of course you are."

"Won't your father be angry you left with me?"

"What he doesn't know can't hurt me. After his tantrum, which wore him out, he retired to his room, where he found renewed energy and continued his tirade with my mother. She'll simmer him down. She always does." Clarissa shrugged to indicate this a common occurrence.

"I see." Abigail smiled in sudden glee. She'd dwell on where she was going to sleep later. There had to be inexpensive lodgings somewhere in the city, but an exhibit of Egyptian artifacts was not to be missed for the world. "Are we really going to an exhibit?"

"Yes, we are." Her friend grinned and gave the driver directions.

They spoke of the weather and other mundane topics on the way to the museum, not wanting to discuss anything of a personal nature in front of the maid, but all the while Abigail's thoughts were on their destination.

When they arrived, they paid the driver, and the ladies strolled into the museum, making their way to the section housing the ancient artifacts and following the signs to the Egyptian exhibit. Clarissa's maid trailed them at a distance, allowing them to speak freely.

"All right, what happened?" Clarissa prompted. "I was surprised when the butler announced you. I thought you'd be sipping tea with the Countess of Waterford by now."

"It was ghastly. I don't know where to begin."

"Well, at least try to give me the details," Clarissa said. "I am anxious to know everything."

"First, the Earl of Waterford has passed on to the hereafter, leaving the new earl in charge of my destiny."

"Jackson Danvers is now the Earl of Waterford?"

"Is that the awful man's name?" She shuddered. Abigail should have known Clarissa would know him. She seemed to know everyone.

"Yes, although I've never met him. Is he really awful?"

"The worst. He actually believed I..." Abigail paused, finding this harder to say than she imagined. "He thought..."

"What, Abby? You're killing me with your hesitancy."

"Very well. He thought I was there to become his grandfather's latest paramour, and when he realized I was still interested in the position..."

Clarissa gasped. "He didn't."

Abigail nodded. "He did. He believed I would willingly become his mistress instead."

"The beast!"

"He's unquestionably so. Although I've grown accustomed to such insults, for a woman of my ilk has to deal with these gruesome assumptions, still I was taken aback by his behavior."

"I should say. How dare he categorize you as a lightskirt. I hope you slapped him soundly for the grievous insult to your character." Abigail smiled at her friend's quick defense of her. Clarissa's loyalty was always incomparable.

"Trust me, I wanted to. Nevertheless, I couldn't. I needed the position. Besides, I assumed I'd be working for his grandmother and not in his presence, and thus, after I explained matters, I ignored his misconception—until I realized he was still set on his course to make me his mistress."

"No," Clarissa hissed.

They stopped in front of an ancient sarcophagus to stare at the captivating hieroglyphs that were believed to help the dead on their journey to the afterlife. Abigail turned to study a plaque depicting Khons-in-Thebes wearing the side lock of hair said to represent youth. "He then had the nerve to ask me to a ball. Me, can you imagine?"

"A ball?" Clarissa asked, sounding intrigued. "Which ball?"

"A fictitious one, I am sure. I mean, look at my attire, which is hardly fitting for traveling the streets of this city let alone traversing the length of a glittering ballroom."

"I hate how you always underestimate yourself, Abby. I've been to a few galas, and you have more class in your pinky finger than all the debutantes summed together." Her friend cocked her head sideways. "To what ball did the earl invite you?"

The ladies moved over to examine a small statue of a goddess whose form was a pregnant hippopotamus with a crocodile back. The talisman served as protection for mother and child.

"Ugly, don't you think?" Clarissa asked.

"Indeed," Abigail agreed. She thought the teeth on the figure were frightening. "I believe he said Bakersfield."

"He invited you to the Earl of Bakersfield's gala?" Clarissa exclaimed loudly, causing curious heads to turn in their direction.

"Are you telling me he was sincere?" Abigail whispered.

Clarissa took Abigail's hand and led her to a nearby bench. She prevented her maid from following with a single hand gesture. "Of course he was sincere, Abby. You seem to forget that you're not a troll." The ladies sat.

"No, just illegitimate."

"And lucky to have it so. How I wish I were in your position. I know you don't believe me, but I'd rather be illegitimate than subjected to my father's temperament."

"I was horrified when I heard the vase shatter." Abigail agreed with her friend that a tyrannical father was not to be wished for, but only to some extent. It was impossible for Clarissa to understand what life is like when you're shunned for the circumstances of your birth.

"Pish!" Clarissa exclaimed, dismissing the matter with a wave of her hand. "The same vase is replaced on a weekly basis. Our housekeeper buys them by the case, which I believe, my father is well aware of because he never hesitates to send them sailing across the hall."

Abigail smiled at Clarissa's nonchalant tone. "Do you believe the earl earnest in his invitation?" She couldn't help but hope this true. Knowing a wellborn gentleman was partial to her did wonders for her self-confidence. A handsome earl fancied her. Who could have imagined?

"I do."

Abigail fought to control the flutter of butterflies at her friend's response. Trying to remain aloof, she shrugged. "Perhaps you are right and I assumed the worst. I'm still sure the Earl of Waterford would not appreciate knowing he even *almost* escorted someone like me to an earl's ball. It is good I left when I did. I only wish I had secured the position. I didn't even get a chance to meet the dowager countess."

"My mother claims she is a no-nonsense woman who is kind and well liked by all."

"Unlike her grandson. The bounder cost me my future."

"Sounds like both of you jumped to some illogical conclusions. Perhaps you should try to speak with him tomorrow. Now that you know his invitation to the ball was sincere, it stands to reason the man is not as averse to you as you assumed."

Abigail couldn't help smiling at the thought. The Earl of Waterford found her delightful, at least if her friend Clarissa's estimation could be trusted. She gloried in the warming feelings this knowledge evoked in her body. "Come. Let us continue our study of the sarcophagus."

***

"What do you mean you dismissed my companion? I gave you no authority to do so." The recently widowed Dowager

Countess of Waterford crooked a finger accusingly at her grandson. "I want her back, now!"

Jackson groaned inwardly. Bloody hell! What else could go wrong today? As if he didn't have enough to contend with, he soon found himself on his steed riding through various London thoroughfares and parks on a mission to find Miss Abigail Gibbons. Blast the woman for walking out on him. He even offered to find his grandmother a replacement, but Grandmother Margaret was having none of it. She wanted Miss Gibbons, which meant he would find her.

His grandmother's furious voice roared in his head as the wind whipped against his face and his horse continued its brisk pace. He turned down another lane, his eyes darting around at every woman wearing black.

"Your grandfather assured me that Miss Abigail would make me a suitable companion," his grandmother had stated.

His thoughts turned dark at the silliness of this mission. How the hell would his grandfather know if Miss Abigail Gibbons would get along with the dowager if the old Earl of Waterford had yet to meet the woman himself?

Jackson nearly gave up on his search when he caught a glimpse of faded black skirts and, he noted, the same lovely brown hair dancing about the lady's petite shoulders. He glanced at the woman's companion, a pretty blond in an elegant peach confection who had her arm linked through Miss Abigail's as they exited the British Museum.

Jackson blinked in amazement. He seriously never actually expected to find the chit and had already devised excuses to give his grandmother upon his return. But there she was, looking as breathtaking as ever, laughing at something her companion said. It occurred to him that, given London's vastness, God had placed her in his path intentionally. He immediately dismissed this notion as ridiculous.

He jumped down from his mount, tossing the reins to a nearby museum lad. Putting on a winsome smile, he approached the ladies. He'd grovel if necessary; he did not plan to disappoint his grandmother.

CHAPTER THREE

"Miss Abigail Gibbons." The Earl of Waterford bowed deeply before her.

Abigail's eyes widened in surprise. Her stomach fluttered as she took in his handsome appearance. *Where did he come from?* His wind-ruffled hair made him appear even more attractive. Who would have thought such a thing even possible? Then she remembered her earlier irritation with him. "Lord Waterford." Her tone was harsher than she intended. If she wanted her job, it occurred to her, she had best try to be personable. "May I introduce my friend, Clarissa Mayfield."

"The Earl of Loring's daughter?" the earl asked, bowing to Clarissa.

"Yes." Clarissa gave him an elegant curtsy.

"A pleasure to make your acquaintance. I'd appreciate a private word with Miss Gibbons, if you don't mind." Abigail noticed his domineering attitude shining through his courteous words, which he tried to cover with a smile. "I believe I owe her a slew of apologies."

"Indeed." Clarissa smiled at Abigail. "I'll find us a hack and wait for you inside."

Abigail nodded, too stunned to speak. Why was the earl here? Had he followed her? A thrill of delight coursed through her limbs at the thought.

"Shall we?" Jackson held out his arm.

She thought the wellborn of London might call her manners childish, but Abigail refused to place her hand upon him. Just because he was a member of the gentry didn't give him the right to trample upon her sensibilities. "Am I to assume this is a chance meeting, my lord?"

He dropped his arm, and she noticed irritation sweep across his features before another forced smile appeared as if by magic upon his lips. "Meetings between men and women are rarely by chance, my dear. I have been looking for you since you rudely stomped out of my grandmother's home."

She smiled with sugary sweetness. "Is this when you make your apology, my lord?"

He laughed and her breath caught in her throat. *Oh, botheration! Why does this man have the ability to make my body stop functioning properly?* She tried hard to force her expression into one of nonchalance, fighting off her feelings of stunned adoration. He held out his arm again, and she unthinkingly followed his cue, hoping he wouldn't notice her body quivering.

He led her to one of the benches beneath the shade trees lining the front of the museum. She was grateful to sit down and release his arm. Noticing Clarissa and her maid were tucked away in a waiting vehicle, she returned her attention to the earl. Every few seconds she caught a glimpse of Clarissa watching them.

"I admit I'm confused as to why I'm apologizing, since I had done so, before you got yourself in a snit and left."

The man stated seconds ago that he owed her an apology, and now he was backing out of it, indeed was being insulting again. *Predictable.* "You're not very good with apologies are you, my lord?"

"True, Miss Gibbons. I never find need for them."

"Then you're a lucky man," she told him, leaving out the "or an accomplished liar" line that she wanted to say. "I believe most normal people do unfortunately find themselves apologizing on occasion. We can't all be infallible." He did not reply, so she said, "Very well. I apologize to you for my hasty departure. I'm afraid I misconstrued your intentions this morning."

"And which intentions were those?" He crossed his ankle over the opposite knee, leaning in closer to her.

She blushed, fidgeting on the bench to move further away so their legs wouldn't touch. "The invitation to the ball. I…" *How to say this without sounding like a complete dunderhead?* "I thought your invitation artificial."

Jackson ran his large hands through his blond waves, causing the thick locks to stand on end, which she found charming. "Is that what happened?" he asked, and she wondered if indeed he was completely unaware of her reason for flight. After all, she thought, there were many reasons that could have sent her on her way.

"And here I thought my earlier assumption regarding your character was to blame, for which *I am* greatly sorry."

She could see in those stumbling blue eyes of his that he meant what he said.

"My request that you accompany me to the ball this evening still stands."

"And my answer still has to be no, my lord." He looked ready to object, and she added, "But I thank you for the invitation." To know he was sincere made her feel as light as a feather, lifting her spirit like nothing else she could imagine.

He exhaled audibly as if dealing with her was as difficult as dealing with a lame horse.

"Very well. You don't wish to accompany me this evening. Does this mean you are refusing the position as my grandmother's companion?"

"You mean I can still have the position?"

"My grandmother wishes for your companionship. In fact, she ordered me to find you."

For some reason she could not find, his answer felt like an arrow to her heart. What did she expect, that he would beg her to take the job just so he could be near her? Yes, in a way she had hoped he would. She knew she really needed to get control of her fanciful thoughts. There would never be anything between her and the earl, she reminded herself harshly, but she smiled nevertheless for her future had just opened up before her again, and she was grateful.

She must have remained silent for too long, for he asked, "Do you still want the position?"

"Yes, yes I do. Nonetheless…" She hesitated. She didn't want this man to have any authority over her. She would not share his bed for the position. Indeed, she wouldn't put up with his highhanded behavior.

"Yes?" Exasperation hummed in the undertones.

"Will I be working for the dowager?" Her voice turned downcast. "Or for you?"

The earl's mirth was obvious as he bent in laughter. "She will be your employer," he managed to say, and he gave her a crooked grin. "You may find her harder to deal with than I am."

"I should hope not!" Abigail's face scrunched up as she turned four shades of red. "I mean, that is to say, I…"

"Relax, Abigail. I take no offense. You are not the first to find me overbearing. Some might even say I'm domineering."

She couldn't help smiling, for he had described himself perfectly. She felt that, somehow, he could read her thoughts and knew she was itching to add to his list of faults. She wondered why this realization so obviously amused him. "Am I missing some adjectives, madam?"

"Quite a few, my lord, but I'm not apt to point them out."

His grin widened and his blue eyes locked with hers. She felt an odd tingling sensation spread through her limbs. She deemed herself cowardly, as she was the first to break the trance by looking down at her hands folded on her lap. *I cannot fall for an earl. I cannot fall for an earl.* She repeated the words in her head as if in an enormous effort to remember what was, and more importantly, and what was *not* in the realm of possibility.

Jackson could feel lust deep in the morrow of his bones, and knew, even if the lady denied such feelings, which he was sure she would, she was definitely attracted to him as well. The air hummed with electrical currents between them, and it took all his discipline not to kiss her breathless right now. He tried to concentrate on the task at hand. "I had hoped you could start your position right away. My grandmother is looking forward to meeting you."

Abigail looked at the vehicle where her friend awaited her. "I... I mean, Miss Loring and I have plans to visit Vauxhall this evening."

If such was the case, why does she sound nervous all of a sudden? "I see." He took a calming breath. *Does this damnable girl want the position or not?* "May I ask about your escort this evening?" He told himself curiosity was to blame for this query, but he couldn't help wondering if his question had more to do with the possessiveness he suddenly felt regarding this young woman.

"Clarissa and I will escort one another. Although I'm sure her maid will accompany us as well."

"I will not allow you to do something so foolish. Vauxhall is not a place for young ladies, especially without a gentleman escort," he scolded.

She appeared surprised by this news. "Are you offering your services?"

Am I? He pictured slipping off with her down one of the garden's dark walks, one of the unlit paths known for romantic romps. *No, definitely not.* The last thing he needed was to spend more time in this tempting woman's company, not at a ball, and certainly not at Vauxhall. Those bow-shaped lips of hers had him imagining the most wonderful fantasies. His blood was rushing to all the wrong parts. She was to be his grandmother's companion. She was an innocent who deserved his respect. He couldn't tumble the chit to the ground and have his way with her. Or could he? *No, I can't.* "No, I'm not. I'm insisting you return with me to Waterford House or you can forget about your position." Even he could hear the frustration and overbearing undertone of demand in his tone.

Miss Gibbons leaped to her feet in outrage. *Perhaps I could have phrased that better, but hell's teeth, it is hard to think when the only thing on a man's mind is seduction.*

"You, sir, are impossible. You claimed I would be working for your grandmother. You've no authority over me, and thus giving me an order is utterly untoward."

When her hands came to rest on her hips, he knew he had definitely approached this all wrong. Nevertheless, the cart was already moving, so to speak, and he decided he might as well continue. "True, Miss Gibbons. Nevertheless, until my grandmother meets you, I get to decide which people are allowed an interview with her." He knew his tone was unmistakably domineering now, and that he needed to appeal to her sense of understanding, that he needed to reason with her. "Perhaps I should explain." He noticed one of her serviceable black shoe's jut forward to tap impatiently on the cobble stone walkway. "Anything you do. No, I should say, *everything* you do will reflect on my family. This being the case, I forbid you to go to Vauxhall this evening."

"You are the most dictatorial man I have ever met!" He watched her face flush red in anger.

"I believe I already admitted to such a trait." He smiled, finding her quite arousing when angered.

"Ugh!" She turned and marched to the waiting vehicle. "Add impossible to that list, my lord," she said over her shoulder before she stepped into the hackney and slammed the door shut.

"Be that as it may, Abigail. I'll expect you at Waterford House at half past the hour." He was shouting as the carriage got underway. *Damn, she is exquisite.*

He turned to the lad holding his horse, flipped him a coin, and swung up on his stallion's back. "Blasted women, never know what is good for them."

***

"Saints be praised, Abby. He is splendid, is he not?" Clarissa all but crooned as their hired hack set off at a brisk clip into the din of street vendors selling their wares on the busy thoroughfare.

"If you prefer the tyrannical type," Abigail answered irritably, banging her head against the back of the hack's squabs and sending dust floating through the air. Unfortunately she was only too aware how her heart still raced from the encounter.

Clarissa laughed. "You're smitten!"

"I am not!" Abigail protested too quickly. *I cannot fall for an earl.*

"Are too." Clarissa held up her hand before Abigail could protest again. "There is no sense in denying it, my dear. I've never seen your eyes light up so. He is magnificent though, all brawn and sinew. Did you notice the width of those shoulders? There was definitely no padding there." Clarissa waved her hand in front of her face as if Lord Waterford's mere image made her faint.

Abigail scoffed, "I'll admit he is good for the eyes. Happy?" She couldn't sit there and let Clarissa continue to compliment the odious man. Abigail was already attracted to him to an unreasonable degree, and discussing his attributes made matters worse. "Do keep in mind he has put a halt to tonight's festivities."

"Most likely for the better. We shouldn't attend the gardens without a proper escort."

"Then why were we going?" Abigail asked aghast.

"You were sad. I wanted to cheer you up." Clarissa's eyes widened as she clasped Abigail's hand. "And the plan possessed the makings of an excellent adventure."

Abigail laughed and reached across the carriage and hugged her friend. "You are the best, Clarissa, and I daresay, someday you'll find your great adventure. If necessary, I shall help."

"I can only hope you are right. And believe me, I won't forget your offer of assistance." Clarissa clasped the cross that hung around her neck in her hand, and Abigail knew her friend was praying to make her dreams of adventure come true. When she was done with her short prayer, her eyes opened and she passed Abigail a sly smile before asking, "Do you think the Earl of Waterford has taken up residence with his grandmother?"

"Good heavens, I hope not." Abigail couldn't imagine what it would do to her if she had to see the earl on a regular basis. Her mind didn't seem to operate appropriately with him near. But she couldn't dwell upon these thoughts at the moment. Her meeting with the dowager was far too important to let thoughts of this man interfere. Nevertheless, she couldn't help wondering why the dowager was so eager to meet her. Why did she send her grandson on a mission to find her?

The carriage rolled to a stop in front of Waterford House. The Earl of Waterford passed by seated on his mount and circled around to the back of the house to hand his horse off to a stableboy, but not before he gave Abigail an inappropriate wink that made her body quiver with excitement.

"Ooohh!" Clarissa exclaimed. "He makes me wish I was seeking a position at Waterford House."

Abigail couldn't help but laugh. "Do stop. You're making me more nervous than I already am."

"Sorry," Clarissa said.

Abigail knew she was not the least bit contrite. "Yes, I can tell."

Clarissa opened the door when Abigail made no move to do so. "All right, off you go."

"You're enjoying this, aren't you?"

"Indeed I am. Now don't forget to keep me informed. Perhaps we might meet at Hyde Park on Tuesday?"

"That sounds splendid." Although still days away, Abigail experienced an acute sense of relief to know her friend wasn't going to abandon her to face her new life in London alone, regardless of how Lord Loring felt about her.

"You had better get moving. The earl is on his way to retrieve you."

Abigail looked out the coach window to see the crystal blue eyes of the earl watching her with such ferocious intensity that she found it hard to swallow. "So it appears." She gave her friend's hand a squeeze for courage and alighted from the vehicle, but she immediately turned back in a panic. "Wait, perhaps you could come in and sit a spell?"

"Sorry, Abby. I must go before my mother begins to worry. I was remiss in telling her about my trip to the museum. Try to relax. All will be well."

"I wish you could give me a guarantee."

"Guarantee for what?" The earl's seductive drawl sent tingles down her spine as his eyes seemed to study her face. She could feel herself flush under his gaze. She turned her eyes to her friend, beseeching her without words to stay.

"Right. Good day, my lord," Clarissa crooned. "A pleasure meeting you." She winked at Abigail, causing her to give into nervous laughter as her bag was dropped to the ground and the carriage moved on its way.

"Miss Abigail." The earl picked up her bag and then held out his arm to escort her inside.

Remembering his condescending behavior moments before, Abigail ignored his outstretched arm, snatched her bag from him, and turned in a huff. She marched up the walkway and through the door, which the butler held open with a welcoming smile.

"Miss Abigail Gibbons, a pleasure to have you return to Waterford."

"Thank you, Townen." She sailed into the house with her bag in hand. "A place for me to change, if you please." She wasn't about to greet Lady Waterford in anything other than her best dress.

"As you wish, miss."

"Take her to her room, Townen." The earl came in behind her with a smile, and Abigail cast him a questioning glance. Did assigning her a room mean she had the position even before she met the Dowager Countess of Waterford? Her new life was about to begin, and she allowed herself to feel a moment of happiness and relief, until the earl issued his next order, reminding her of her prickling discomfort in his presence.

"I'll see you in the sitting room in thirty minutes." He bowed and left the foyer.

Abigail followed sedately behind the butler, anticipating her next meeting with the incorrigible man who set her heart ablaze.

***

A short time later, the butler escorted Abigail into a candlelit sitting room. A cozy fire was burning in a white marble hearth to remove the late afternoon chill from the chamber. She was glad to have a moment to collect herself, for her nerves were rattled. She felt like she was standing on a cliff waiting for the wind to take her over the edge. Would she soar like an eagle or plummet to her doom? For the hundredth time since she learned about the position, she prayed she would meet with Lady Waterford's approval.

Smoothing her hands down the blue silk of her dress, her best attire, she regained some of her confidence. She had left her hair up in the lotus combs, afraid the earl would come fetch her if she took too long readying herself. The man was clearly used to getting his way. Thankfully, she wouldn't have to answer to him.

At that moment, the devil himself sauntered into the room as calm as you please, but in far more casual dress than she had seen him previously.

As if his formal attire wasn't enough to make her blood simmer in her veins, the way he looked in his buff breeches and partially unbuttoned white shirt had her clenching her hands into tight fists. *You'd think he could at least button up for my benefit.* He gave her a crooked smile, and she realized he had left his shirt undone purposely. What kind of gentleman would behave this way? She turned her gaze from the small expanse of neck and chest in view and instead met those blue eyes of his. *Clearly a mistake.* The power of his gaze had her clearing her throat uncomfortably.

"Tea, Miss Abigail?" His eyes traveled down the length of her body, sending a shock of liquid heat through her. Never had a man such a profoundly incapacitating effect on her. In her nervousness, she giggled, which caused him to look at her with a crooked brow.

"Something amusing about tea, Abigail?"

"Uh, no, my lord." She could feel her face heat up in embarrassment. "Tea will be fine."

"Mrs. Rhodes." The earl stuck his head out the door to order a tea service, from the housekeeper, Abigail assumed.

"Yes, my lord," a robust woman replied. The woman had appeared in the doorway and was now casting a quick glance in Abigail's direction, who smiled in return.

The earl closed the door in the woman's face. The sound of dangling keys hanging from the large metal chatelaine on the housekeeper's hip could be heard as she moved off into farther reaches of the house, taking the sound with her.

"My grandmother will be along shortly. Have a seat." He motioned toward a cream-colored sofa.

Abigail was all too happy to sit down. His presence made her unsteady on her own two feet. In truth, it disheartened her to find herself attracted to this man, an unattainable earl. For *heaven's sake*. What happened to her unerring sense of self-preservation?

He took a seat across from her, and she could smell his manly scent mixed with expensive cologne. He smelled clean and utterly wonderful, and again she cursed her senses. Of course she noticed how his shirt opened even further with his seated position, and from this vantage, she could see the curly blond hair that likely covered his entire chest. How she longed to run her fingers through the springy mass. She found herself imagining the expanse of his chest. The man had the physique of an Olympian god. From the smug expression on his chiseled face, it was apparent he knew his effect on the female population, and indeed, on her.

"Should I button up, Miss Abigail." He gave her a wicked grin. "I'd hate to offend your delicate sensibilities."

What utter nonsense. A gentleman of proper breeding would never ask a lady such an outlandish question. Her mother had warned her often about men of his ilk, good-looking, smooth talkers who thought they could have whatever, and whomever, they desired. Abigail's experience with men was limited. Her mother's advice was all she had to go by. "Do you feel your attire offensive, my lord?" She kept reminding herself of his title and how far out of her reach he was.

Jackson laughed, a deep masculine sound that vibrated up her back and increased her heart rate. "My grandmother is going to love you."

She made no comment, hoping his conjecture true. "Speaking of the dowager, my lord. I have something I need to tell you." She paused, trying to allow her courage to build. Speaking about her illegitimacy was never easy for her.

"Go on." He waited for her to continue.

"I was thinking about what you said earlier." His brow tipped upward as she gently bit down on her bottom lip. Garnering courage, she went on to explain, "I was thinking about what you said regarding how the things I do will reflect upon your family. I think it only fair to tell you that I'm a bastard." She waited for the loud dismissal that usually followed this admission. When there wasn't one, she continued, "I would hate for people to think negatively upon your grandmother because of my lack of a father."

"Are you saying you came into this world by an act of Immaculate Conception?"

She smiled at his uncanny ability to make light of a situation that had served to torture her throughout her life. "Not likely, my lord."

"I see." He crossed his hands over his chest, contemplating what she had told him.

That was it? He has nothing else to say? No shriek of outrage? No look of disgust? Nothing?

"Are you awaiting my reaction?"

Abigail gave him a hesitant smile. "I usually do get one, my lord."

"I told you earlier that your employment is my grandmother's decision. Your parentage, or lack thereof, is her concern, not mine. I can tell you this…" He leaned forward to look deep in her eyes. "If my grandmother wishes for your companionship, no one will question her. She has enough clout in this city that most in polite society will not dare malign her good name, at least not to her face, or they may find themselves on the outside of said polite society looking in."

"I see, my lord," Abigail answered calmly, although her relief at this news was great. She felt her eyes fill with useless tears and blinked them away.

Jackson shrugged. "Perhaps you do, but I should forewarn you, Abigail. My grandmother is not the easiest woman to get along with. She's not as judgmental as my late grandfather, but don't think for a moment you can run roughshod over her."

"I would never dream of doing so, my lord." His insinuation offended her, but she tried to cover her irritation with a smile. Bugger the domineering, handsome man, he was going to be a problem, she just knew it.

Jackson sat back and watched the enigma sitting across from him. He admired this woman's courage. Not many women—or men for that matter—would be so forthcoming with such a harsh truth about themselves. He could actually see her relax when he gave no reaction to her lack of parentage, and he couldn't help being impressed by her integrity.

The sad truth was that the majority of people he associated with would have tossed her out of their house without a second thought. Jackson never viewed such matters as fair. After all, Abigail, among countless others, did not choose to be born into this world outside the bonds of wedlock.

Unfortunately, his country was filled with people who didn't feel they had a proper place in this world. He couldn't imagine having to live with such a stigma, and he found himself feeling sorry for Abigail, even though he sensed pity was the last thing she'd want. Although they had just met, he felt he now understood Abigail. Recalling his harsh words toward her this morning made him regret how unjust he'd been. "I want to again apologize for my abominable behavior this morning, Abigail. My assumptions were inexcusable." He marveled at how easily he fell into addressing her on a personal level. Saying her name allowed him to feel closer to her. She didn't appear to mind, but then she was "my lording" him to death. Even more bizarre, he understood why she was being overly deferential.

"And for your behavior in front of the museum?" she asked.

He recognized her rigid tone and grinned. "My behavior in front of the museum was exemplary, and I am not the least bit contrite."

To his delight, she smiled that beautiful smile of hers, which he deemed bound to make any man's heart pause. Her bewitching brown eyes with their golden rings met his in merriment.

"Pray tell me, Abigail," he asked, "what do you find amusing?"

"Just that I knew your answer before I even posed the question."

He returned her smile. "Then why ask?"

"Strictly for my amusement, my lord."

He laughed in sheer astonishment at her wit. This lovely young lady was incomparable. He wondered if she had any past romantic relationships. Would she consider one with him? After spending some time with her, he doubted she'd be interested in the position of mistress. She had balked at the mere notion this morning. Yet his mind couldn't stop imagining how perfect sex could be between them. Tea came and they were silent as the housekeeper exited and Abigail busied herself with pouring.

He noticed how efficiently her slim fingers went about pouring tea, and how her pert breasts peeked enticingly above her overly tight bodice when she leaned slightly forward. He told himself that any man in his right mind would have noticed such a chest. He imagined flicking his tongue over her nipples until they puckered and ached for his attention. To run his tongue over her bow-shaped lips, to delve his... He felt the sudden need to get control over his baser thoughts, which were not the thoughts of just any man, but his own thoughts, and they were bordering on lewd. Abigail was to be his grandmother's companion, and as such, she deserved... well, better thoughts. She did not deserve to be lusted after by a man who couldn't seem to keep his ardor in check around her. It was rare, but he felt himself flush with embarrassment at his mind's lascivious wanderings.

He also found himself again watching the rise and fall of her chest with each breath she took. The silence stretched out before them. She seemed to be focusing on something over his shoulder. He believed she felt the same intense feeling of desire when their eyes met, which was most likely the reason her gaze remained fixed behind him.

Say something. Although he had charmed ladies out of their clothes since his youth, and even convinced government officials to see many things from his point of view, at this moment, he found himself so befuddled that he couldn't concentrate on so much as creating a respectable conversation.

"Your clips!" he shouted, nearly scaring the lady out of her skin. He hadn't meant to shout, but he was overwhelmingly thankful he thought of a suitable topic of conversation.

"My combs?" She pursed her lips together in confusion.

"Yes, the lotus flower. Are you familiar with Egyptian history?"

Again, the musical sound of her laughter filled the room, causing him to feel pleased with himself. "I see I'm still entertaining you."

"Indeed, my lord."

"Care to explain?"

"Very well." She shrugged, placing her hands in her lap.

The depth of her cleavage increased and he suppressed a groan. "Egyptology happens to be my passion. I've had many classes on the subject, participated in many discussions, and attended numerous lectures—all in an effort to understand the ancient civilization better. I love trying to decipher hieroglyphs, although I admit I'm not adept at it. These combs were a gift to me, one I treasure. I wish I could have told your grandfather how much I admire them. I have often wondered since if he knew about my love for such things. Did you know that the last king of the Fifth Dynasty, King Unas, had the walls of his burial chamber covered in hieroglyphs to ensure his well-being into the afterlife?"

Jackson was struck mute. She was a student of Egyptology? When did his grandfather send her this gift? More importantly, why? How well did the old earl know this woman? He recalled she had said that she never met the man and didn't even know of his death until today.

"I'm sorry. I've bored you. You have the same glossy-eyed look my mother gets when I ramble on about such things."

"You have not bored me. I'm just stunned. I too enjoy Egypt's history. My mother is honeymooning in Cairo this very moment. Like you, she has a passion for the land's past and the history of the pharaohs who once ruled there. As a matter of fact, my Christian name is Jackson Sethos Ramesses Danvers."

Abigail laughed so hard tears came to her eyes, and he smiled.

"I must admit you have piqued my curiosity about my grandfather. Are you sure the two of you never met?"

"I'm as sure as any person could be, my lord. I tend to remember the people I meet, and they usually fall into two categories."

"Which are?"

"Those who don't accept me and those who do. I believe your grandfather fell into the latter category. For whatever reason, he sent these beautiful combs to me, and I'm most appreciative. However, I never met the man."

Why would his grandfather send a girl he never met hair combs? Jackson sensed he was missing a great many pieces to this puzzle. "My grandmother expected your arrival at Waterford House, and indeed, you say that my grandfather arranged for your journey here. Do you know why?"

It was at this point that the door opened, and with a swish of black bombazine skirts, the Dowager Countess of Waterford entered the room. The tall, willowy woman gave Jackson a warm smile, seemingly happy he had successfully returned Miss Abigail to her.

Although her hair was void of any color but gray, she carried herself like a woman half her age, with a regal bearing others tried to emulate. Jackson held her in the highest esteem. "I have found Miss Abigail Gibbons for you, Grandmother."

Abigail immediately stood. "Lady Waterford, it's a pleasure to finally meet you."

His grandmother turned toward Abigail and Jackson was surprised to see the smile slide from his grandmother's face as she sucked in a breath. He watched as her silvery blue eyes met Abigail's brown eyes.

"I'm terribly sorry about your husband's passing, my lady," Abigail said.

Jackson's grandmother turned to him with her arm outstretched. Panic filled her face. Her skin lightened and her eyes shuddered as she blinked and swayed. "Grab me, boy. I'm going down."

CHAPTER FOUR

"She fainted," the Earl of Waterford exclaimed in sheer astonishment.

Abigail was having the most difficult time holding the lady up so she didn't crash to the ground. She saw the dowager's eyes gloss over and knew the lady wasn't jesting. "A hand, my lord," she huffed, trying to hold the woman's frail body away from the floor. She peered up at the earl from her stooped over position.

"Oh yes, sorry." He scooped up his grandmother as if she weighed no more than a stone and placed her on the sofa. "I've never seen... I mean, she's never fainted in her life, which is a fact she's proud of, continually going on about how other ladies drop away on a ballroom dance floor, but never her. She fainted, huh. Should I send for the doctor?" He placed a hand on his grandmother's wrinkled cheek. "Do you think she's ill? Smelling salts, do you have any?"

Clarissa claimed Abigail babbled when she was distressed, and Abby was discovering that apparently his lordship suffered from the same affliction. "Please sit, my lord. Your grandmother is fine." With purposeful strides, she crossed the room, gave orders to the housekeeper, and returned to the dowager's side.

She gently patted the older woman's cheek in an effort to bring her back around. The housekeeper shuffled in, waving the smelling salts in the air as she went. She passed them to Abigail, who swiped the vial back and forth beneath Lady Waterford's nose. The dowager sputtered, her nose wrinkling in protest, as her eyes fluttered open in confusion.

"You're all right, my lady," Abigail tried to reassure the woman.

"Grandmother?" Jackson stopped his insistent pacing to approach the sofa.

Abigail helped Lady Waterford into a seated position.

"Are you all right?" Lord Waterford asked.

The dowager's eyes grew clear as she nodded to him, and then she turned toward Abigail. "First of all, Miss Gibbons, when someone says 'you are all right,' that is a pretty sure indication that one isn't, all right."

Abigail nodded. "Of course, my lady."

"Are you all right?" Jackson asked again. Abigail noticed the paleness of his complexion and the concern etched on his face.

"Yes, dear. I'm fine. I can't believe *I* fainted." She turned to Abigail. "I've never fainted before."

"So I've heard." Abigail smiled in understanding, assuming the loss of her husband was sure to have some adverse effects.

"Fresh tea, Mrs. Rhodes," the dowager ordered. The housekeeper bobbed before leaving the room.

"What happened, Grandmother?" Jackson knelt on the floor in front of the dowager to take her hands in his.

"I'm not sure," she answered, continuing to study Abigail and, paying only the least attention to her grandson.

Abigail groaned inwardly under such scrutiny. Lady Waterford didn't like her. Why else would she be staring at her in such a manner? Her chance for a future was slipping away faster than the ocean tide, yet again. "I'm terribly sorry if my appearance upset you, my lady. Would you like me to leave? I could come back another time." She held her breath awaiting the response.

"Heavens no, dear. I daresay my husband is responsible for my fainting spell."

Jackson cast Abigail a bewildered expression. Evidently he didn't understand his grandmother's meaning.

"Miss Abigail, perhaps we can conduct your interview later. I think my grandmother needs to rest."

"Stuff and applesauce, my boy. I'm perfectly fine." The dowager straightened further, her gaze still on Abigail. "Please, dear. Come sit by me."

Abigail cast a questioning look at the earl, who looked a bit perplexed but nodded for her to do what his grandmother instructed. Without another moment's hesitation, she sat next to the dowager, who immediately took her hands, tilting her head to the side as she continued to look at Abigail from every angle.

"Jackson, I need you to leave us," the dowager quipped, her eyes never leaving Abigail's face.

"Leave?" the earl all but croaked, apparently not used to being dismissed so lightly. He even looked to Abby as if she should verbalize a reason for him to remain.

"Grandmother, you just fainted. I shall stay."

"You will do no such thing. Miss Abigail is to be my companion. I wish to speak to her without you present." The dowager's eyes finally left Abigail as she took a moment to glare at her obstinate grandson.

Jackson grunted in disapproval. "I'll be in the hall."

"No, you will go to the study and get your work done." Lady Waterford smiled to take the edge out of her voice. "We'll be fine, dear. I promise. I won't be fainting again."

With complete reluctance, the earl left. Abigail was in awe at how well the dowager handled him and wished she possessed half the talent to handle the man proficiently.

Lady Waterford expelled a sigh of relief. Abigail couldn't help wondering what the woman was thinking.

"Now then, my girl. How have you been?"

"I've..." Abigail's brow wrinkled in an expression of complete mystification. The dowager acted as if she knew her and they were renewing a past acquaintance. "I've been well, madam."

"Stuff and applesauce, child. Please, I need to know. Where have you been?"

"I was here earlier, but..."

"No, I'm well aware of your earlier meeting with my grandson. I'm grateful he found you. What I want to know is where you were before you came to Waterford House?"

"Oh." Abigail smiled. The woman still had a firm grip on her hands. "I was attending Lady Carlyle's Academy for Young Ladies."

"You're educated?"

This sounded more like the interview she expected. "Yes, my lady. Some would say overly."

"I see." She freed one of Abigail's hands and reached up to cup Abigail's chin, angling her face in a different direction. Abigail thought the behavior odd, but made no comment. "Your parents, who are they?"

"I'm not proud to say that I am illegitimate, my lady." Her body grew rigid as she awaited the inevitable reaction.

A calm voice of understanding asked, "Are you saying you are unaware of your parentage?" The old woman reached out to touch one of Abigail's brown curls.

The tenderness in her expression had Abigail, who was amazed at how this woman was stirring feelings she long since closed the door on, choking back her tears. Abigail had packed her tears away when she was about ten, refusing to allow her sorrow to show. She would not live her life regretting her lot in this world; she had declared herself stronger than that.

But under this woman's knowing gaze, she believed she could open up her heart and spill out all her heartache and longing, her longing for a life not tainted by the circumstances of her birth.

She felt comfortable with the dowager, as if they had known each other for their entire lives, and yet they just met. She smiled at the thought. They were kindred spirits, of that she was certain, and suddenly Abigail knew that no matter what she said to Lady Waterford, the dowager would not scorn her.

"My mother's name is Delores Gibbons, and she resides in Norfolk." She could feel her cheeks flush as she blurted out the rest. "She is unaware of my sire's identity." That bit always sounded awful. It definitely didn't paint her mother in a positive light.

The dowager seemed oblivious to Abigail's discomfort. "Delores Gibbons." She rolled the name off her tongue as if trying to remember it. "Why do you not live with her?"

Abigail tried to think of a suitable response, one that would not make her mother seem even more horrid. In the past, her schooling always served as her excuse, and Abigail realized she couldn't come up with even one plausible answer beside that one, and even more unusual, she found she didn't want to. Moreover, she did not want to tell falsehoods to the dowager. So, she fell back on her familiar excuse, which was at least partly the truth. "I've been at school."

"I'm well aware of your age, dear. You could have quit the schoolroom years ago, so why didn't you?"

Abigail gave her a dainty shrug. "There aren't many places where people wish to welcome me into their midst."

Fire flashed from the dowager's soulful eyes. "Including your mother?" Anger practically vibrated from the older woman's form.

"No, I'm always welcome at home. My mother loves me despite my flaws." Abigail felt comforted by the woman's obvious support.

"As she should. I, however, will not allow you to speak of yourself as flawed. You are a treasure and should be cherished." She brushed some hair back from Abigail's face. "I want you to know you will always have a place with me."

Stunned by the sentiment, Abigail remained silent. For this woman to welcome her as a companion in spite of her status as bastard was one thing, but to disregard her lack of a sire and still welcome her "always" was more than surprising. Before she could thank Lady Waterford for her kindness and understanding, the woman posed another question.

"Why didn't you return home?"

There was no help for it. Aside from Clarissa, and her mother's neighbor, no one knew of her mother's need to fortify herself.

"Trust me, dear." The dowager smoothed a hand over her cheek. "Whatever you tell me won't leave this room."

Abigail nodded. It felt right to entrust this woman. "My mother enjoys strong spirits, my lady." It hurt to say those words. Why did her mother have to drink excessively?

"And you feel you are to blame?"

Did she sound guilty when she admitted her mother's problem, or did this woman, because of her keen insight, have her entire life figured out without Abby having to say much of anything? "Yes," Abigail choked back her anguish. "I believe my being in residence makes her drink more."

"Why?"

A great question. How many nights did Abigail lay awake in bed listening to her mother's cries, wondering how she could help? It crushed her to learn that leaving her mother actually served to help her. Love lost was the only reasonable explanation. It pained Abigail greatly to see her mother under constant affliction. She gave the dowager her best educated guess. "I think I remind her of something, someone, lost. I believe she truly loved my father."

"But she claims not to know his name?"

Abigail knew from the dowager's tone that she didn't believe the assertion. *What was this woman's saying? Stuff and applesauce.* The truth was that, Abigail didn't believe such nonsense either. Nevertheless, she never forced the issue with her mother. The mere mention of her unknown sire caused her mother great distress.

The dowager patted her knee. "Then it is your mother's problem, not yours."

"I suppose, but nevertheless, my constant presence doesn't help her state of mind."

"Well it helps mine." She smiled, giving Abigail's cheek a light pinch. "Very well then. Your position her is settled. You, my dear, will remain with me."

"Truly?" Abigail's face lit up with happiness. "I will be a good companion to you, my lady."

"I know you will." The dowager had difficulty getting to her feet, and Abigail helped her. "You'll be like family."

Abigail helped the dowager right herself, making sure the older woman gained her balance before she released her. "I'm honored. Thank you, Lady Waterford. I promise I won't let you down."

"You could never do so, my child."

"Can I ask you a question?"

"Naturally."

"Do you know if it was your husband who so generously paid for my education?"

The dowager nodded as she walked to the door. "Ah, dear, I believe it was."

Abigail wanted to question why he would do such a thing for her, but the dowager hurried across the room with amazing speed for a woman her age, apparently indicating a need to exit the room, which in turn indicated this wasn't the right time to ask.

Lady Waterford opened the door to find Mrs. Rhodes approaching with a teacart. "You're too late, Beatrice. Just bring it to my room."

"Yes, my lady."

***

Jackson came out from the study at the sound of his grandmother's voice. "Did you hire Miss Gibbons?" His gut clenched at the thought of her not doing so. He didn't bother to wonder why. Clearly he had found a woman who piqued his interest. Nothing else could explain this strong pull toward her that he felt. However, although his attraction for her was undeniable, that still didn't explain his reasons for wanting to see her smile, for wanting to protect her. Indeed, he wanted her to belong to him—only him. *Hell's teeth, I haven't even known the woman for a full six hours. What kind of spell am I under?*

"I have." His grandmother's mouth pinched in anger. "Your grandfather is lucky he is dead or else I'd kill him with my own bare hands." Tears suddenly streamed down her face as she turned on her heel and marched away to her room, which was located on the first floor so she didn't have to traverse the steps at her advanced age.

Perplexed by his grandmother's sudden vehemence and obvious upset, he stalked into the parlor to put the blame for his grandmother's anguish exactly where it belonged, on Miss Gibbons' lovely shaped shoulders. She was standing by the mantle staring into the blue flames of the fire. "What did you do to her?" he demanded.

Abigail spun around at his accusation. "I beg your pardon?"

"As you should." He made his way toward her. Enamored or not, he wanted to shake her silly. "What did you do to upset her?"

"She was upset?" Abigail frowned. "She appeared fine when she left."

"Well, she wasn't." He barely suppressed his desire to shout his words at her. How dare this woman cause his grandmother even an ounce more upset. "Tell me, Miss Gibbons, why did she hire you?"

She gave him a dainty shrug. "I believe our conversation went well, and she decided we suit each other just fine. She is a wonderful woman, my lord."

He eyed her steadily, deciding if she was being truthful. He believed she was. "You better hope she finds no fault with your companionship."

He noticed the gold rim around her brown eyes blaze and knew he had angered her, which suited him fine because she angered him first. "I can assure you that I was nothing but honest with your grandmother. I daresay we have already formed a bond for which I couldn't be more grateful. Don't you have a home of your own to go to, Lord Waterford?"

Saucy wench. He gave her a cynical laugh. "I will be in and out of Waterford House for some months with all the work that needs to be done here. I will be watching you, Miss Gibbons."

"As you wish, my lord." He watched in stunned awe as the bold woman turned with a swish of blue skirts, and without a backward glance, fled the room. No woman ever walked out on a conversation with him regardless the topic, but instead of finding such behavior irksome, he found himself slightly pleased by her bravado.

***

The Dowager Countess of Waterford entered her room, and snatched the dark basket from beneath her bed before roaring at Mrs. Rhodes to bring in her tea.

"I'm right here, my lady."

"Fetch me my husband's private financial reports. I don't believe Jackson has gotten around to looking those over yet. They are in the wooden box marked 'personal' on the bookshelf in the study. Bring the box to me. I wish to see them straight away."

"Yes, my lady." Mrs. Rhodes slipped out of the room to do as bid.

Although Lady Waterford believed she knew why her husband felt it necessary to pay for Miss Gibbons' education, she still needed to see the proof of his treachery. Her head began to throb from the thoughts filling her mind. "He couldn't have possibly done something so horrible," she told herself, knowing the plot growing in her psyche was exactly the kind her husband would have put into motion.

She lifted the lid on the basket and pulled out the miniature of her dead son.

"Blast you," she cursed her dead husband. "How could you do such a thing to her, to us?" She actually knew the how's and why's, but that did not stop the tears from falling down her aged face as she ran a finger over her son's portrait.

"I'm so sorry, my love, but I promise you that Mama will make things better."

***

The next week and a half passed by quickly for Abigail. She and Lady Waterford forged a bond of friendship Abigail never dreamed possible. Her employer was a kind and understanding woman who never hesitated to tell Abigail exactly what she thought, and Abby found such open conversations a treasure. Aside from her mother and Clarissa, no one in this world seemed to have the conviction to say what was on their minds.

She finished penning a letter to her mother, informing her of how happy she was to be in her current position, when a knock on the door penetrated her train of thought.

"Yes?" Abigail folded her missive and sealed it with a dab of hot wax.

"It's me, miss." Sophie, Abigail's assigned maid, came in the room carrying a tray for luncheon. Sophie was another welcome addition to her new life. Although it felt odd to have someone at her beck and call, Abigail was inclined to admit she enjoyed having someone assist her.

"I'm ready to go when you are, miss."

Abigail smiled. "A quick bite and I'll be ready. If you could post this for me, I'll meet you down in the foyer in ten minutes."

"No rush, miss." Sophie set the tray down on a nearby table, took the letter, and left the room.

Abigail would have liked to slink out of the house through the servants' entrance in the kitchen to meet her maid, thus avoiding the Earl of Waterford. But as soon as the thought occurred to her, she deemed such an act cowardly. She refused to shy away from his presence. True, the earl had shown himself to be an overbearing man, but it was her reaction to him that concerned her the most. She couldn't think straight with him near. Her head filled with dreams and hopes of a future with a man who wasn't accessible to her.

He had an uncanny ability to irk her, while drawing her closer at the same time, which made no sense. Her troubling thoughts about him were new and unfamiliar. She'd never felt attraction in any form, and now that she did, she had chosen someone completely unsuitable for her. She did not know if she should be more annoyed with him for his effect on her or with herself.

She had skillfully avoided running into him the past couple of days or so, but she knew her luck wouldn't last, considering how often he appeared at her new residence. It seemed inevitable they'd run into each other again, and although her heart soared to the heavens at the thought, her mind told her to avoid the temptation calling to her. Such a path would only lead to heartache, her heartache.

After eating a few bites of her meal, she checked her appearance in the mirror, giving her cheeks a pinch for color. The dowager insisted she wear the latest styles and fashions. Abigail adored the navy morning dress with its ivory fur collared pelisse, far and away the finest garment she ever owned.

She pulled on her white gloves as she descended the stairs, hoping the earl would continue his work in the study and not hear her slip past.

"Abigail, dear."

Her heart stopped and then resumed its normal pace when she realized it was the dowager beckoning her.

She walked into the parlor. "Yes, my lady?"

"I could use your judgment on something."

Abigail happily obliged. She made her way over to the sofa where her employer sat. Lady Waterford busily smoothed her fingers over some fabric samples. "How can I be of assistance?"

"Which of these do you prefer?" Lady Waterford held up a copper swath of fabric beneath Abigail's chin and then swapped the silky square with a dark brown velvet swath. "As

I thought, the copper brings out your eyes splendidly. You know, there are few people who have eyes as beautiful as yours, my dear, as unique."

Abigail watched in confusion as the dowager's eyes swam with tears, as they often did when they were alone together. She wished she understood why. "Are you all right, my lady?"

Her employer gained her hand and gave her fingers a gentle squeeze. "I'm fine, dear. I believe I'm getting more sentimental in my dotage. You know I care for you a great deal, Abigail."

"And I you," Abigail admitted.

"If you have no objection, I thought I'd have some more clothes made for you, gowns, specifically. Do you like the copper?"

"It's exquisite."

The dowager looked at the swath of fabric in her hand. "I agree. You will outshine all the ladies at the ball."

A ball? Abigail tried to swallow back her terror. She believed it would be best if she just blended in with the background here at Waterford House, but she didn't express her thoughts, knowing she'd suffer the dowager's censure for such a comment. Lady Waterford never allowed her to speak negatively about herself. Nevertheless, the more people she met, the more likely the truth of her unknown parentage would surface. She wanted to save the lady from the viciousness she came to expect. Calmly, she asked, "When is the ball?"

"A few days hence."

An actual ball. She had always dreamed of attending one, but at this moment, she wished the event further away, preferably a decade. It was easy to pretend she was worthy when she was with the Dowager Countess of Waterford, but the very thought of herself at a ball scared her witless.

The old woman obviously read the alarm on her face, for she said, "Try not to fret, dear. Nerves are expected before your first ball. I promise I'll be there for you every step of the way. Of course, due to my current state of mourning, I'll be sitting quietly to the side of the festivities."

Abigail smiled at the older woman's effort to put her more at ease. Obviously, Lady Waterford realized Abigail had misgivings about being accepted. One of the most amazing things about her employer was how she treated her as an equal, a wonderful, and yet unusual, feeling. Abigail vowed to do whatever it took to make this woman proud of her. Clearly, this entailed attending a ball or two. Well, she had always wanted to experience a grand ball, at least once. "You are too kind, my lady. But if you're not yet ready to reenter society, I'm sure the ball can wait."

"Stuff and applesauce. I'm tired of sitting around twiddling my thumbs. It's bad enough I'm donned in black. My husband always hated the color on me for it washes out one's complexion. But you deserve to be treated with respect, and you certainly are entitled to an official season."

Abigail blinked her eyes and a buzzing sound hummed inside her head. She knew she was not in the least entitled to a season. The dowager seemed to forget that people like her didn't partake in such pursuits, which were for the young debutantes with strong bloodlines looking for the perfect title into which they might slip and ultimately grow old. Marriage wasn't an option for Abigail, at least not in Lady Waterford's circle of friends. And yet, hearing her employer praise her made Abby almost feel worthy. Tears filled her eyes, but she refused to give into the sadness filling her. She couldn't change her lot in this world any more than she could change the weather, but she definitely could not allow herself to give credence to the dowager's grand illusions, even if she wished to.

Lady Waterford stood and pulled Abigail toward her for an embrace. "My sweet child." Abigail smiled at the endearment and the comfort she felt in this gentlewoman's arms as she rubbed her back. Her uneasiness over the coming ball was eased some by the unerring support of this woman whom she had come to love like a grandmother. She never had a grandmother before, and this relationship felt astoundingly right. "I think you underestimate my reach of influence," said the dowager. "I promise that you *will* get the life you deserve." She backed up and gave Abigail's face a motherly pat. "All right, off you go or you'll be late for your engagement with Lady Clarissa Mayfield. You should invite her for tea sometime. I'd really like to meet this lady who stands by her friend so admirably."

"She'd be honored, my lady."

"Then I'll see you at dinner." Without another word, the dowager departed with her swatches, passing them by the window's light for examination before she left.

"She's amazing, isn't she?"

Abigail spun around as the earl's warm timbre washed over her like a gentle breeze. His well-built frame filled the doorway. It seemed impossible, but the earl had become even more breathtakingly beautiful in a few short days. He was dressed casually in buff colored breeches, which clung to his body and pulled at her line of vision. His white shirt was unbuttoned at the top, his gorgeous face etched with a crooked grin, and his wavy blond hair looked like he had combed his fingers through it a dozen times until it lay in irresistible disarray. She found herself wanting to run her own fingers through the unruly mass.

The dowager claimed her grandson was working hard lately. From his unkempt but still beautiful appearance, Abigail would have to agree. For all his natural splendor, she could see the lines of fatigue around his eyes. "She is an original, my lord."

This man's nearness made her feel light-headed and her stomach fluttered with those uplifting butterflies again. Never had a man's presence affected her so completely, but then, no man had ever stared at her with such blatant hunger. Although he'd yet to move, his eyes called to her, inviting her to join him in carnal pleasure, which she could only begin to imagine. Flustered, she said, "If you'll excuse me, Lord Waterford, I have an appointment to keep."

"Yes, of course." He smiled at her and her palms actually started to sweat. "I wanted to thank you for making my grandmother so happy. Since your arrival, she no longer hides herself away in her room, and for that, I will always be grateful, Abigail."

She didn't know what to say. She gave him a small smile, and with a nod, fled, hoping her sanity would return with her flight.

***

Jackson watched Abigail hail a hackney and disappear from his sight. Every instinct told him to fetch her back. She appealed to him in every sense of the word, and she was kind and loving to his grandmother. In fact, the two women, so obviously comfortable in each other's company, acted as if they had known each other for years. Indeed, those were his grandmother's exact words when he asked her how they were getting along.

Abigail was a lovely woman inside and out. Her outer beauty held his interest in a way he recognized, but Jackson wanted Abigail in a way he never imagined possible. He dreamt about her at night and thought about her all day. It was becoming clear the lady was in his blood. He could not dispel her image from the back of his mind no matter how hard he tried. But it was her innocence that drew him to her and he couldn't help but admire her inner strength. He was sure it was difficult dealing with the harshness society threw at her, and yet she seemed to rise above such ignorance. Although she didn't appear to need any, he felt himself wanting to help her feel some kind of acceptance. There was no denying his grandmother's clout in high society, but even his grandmother's influence only reached so far and he wondered just how much the old woman could accomplish in that regard.

Abigail had looked so pretty just now, dressed in her

navy frock, a vast improvement from the tattered black garment she arrived in. She appeared to have gone through a transformation both externally and internally. She held herself with more poise and spoke eloquently when spoken to. He was also aware his appearance set her aflutter, which fueled his unquestionable need to have her.

"My lord, the Earl of Everett to see you."

"Show him into the study, Townen." He inhaled the remaining scent of Abigail's lilac perfume before he turned with a sigh to visit with his friend. He hadn't seen Alexander since his grandfather's funeral, but as busy as he had been of late, it was impossible to visit any of his usual haunts.

Although he missed his grandfather, he did not miss the continuous lectures the old man gave him. There weren't many days that went by that his grandfather didn't mention how honored and grateful Jackson should be to have the title and the lands being left to him. In fact, Jackson appreciated his place in the world quite a bit. He did just about anything he wanted as a member of the privileged class, and he unremittingly celebrated the station his grandfather never allowed him to forget. The bulk of this revelry was conducted with his good friend Alexander.

He entered the study to find his friend already seated, his legs outstretched on a nearby hassock and, a drink in his hand. "Alexander, good to see you."

Green eyes turned to Jackson. His friend, dressed in his best attire was likely stopping by after parliament. "I figured, if I wanted to talk to you, this was the place to find you. I stopped by your house twice last week, and it seems you're spending all of your time here. Am I to assume your grandfather left you with a mess?"

"An accurate assumption." Jackson motioned to the bottle of spirits and Alexander poured him one.

After passing the drink to Jackson, Alexander set his own glass down. Placing his hands behind his head, he arrogantly tossed his black hair out of his face and grinned like a child who made his way out of the kitchen with a handful of treats.

Jackson's brow raised in curiosity. "You have something to tell me?" He circled around his grandfather's desk and took a seat.

"Is it obvious?"

Alexander laughed like a man in love. *Wait a minute, could it be?* "It is."

"As it should be. Congratulate me, my friend. I'm getting married."

"You're what?" Jackson felt like he was punched hard in the gut. He downed the rest of his drink in one gulp. It seemed all his friends were entering into the state of matrimony lately. Abigail's lovely face traipsed through his mind uninvited and he felt a shiver of longing he could not deny rush through him.

"I know it comes as a shock."

"Yes... I mean, no. That is, I thought you were going to wait a few more years. It doesn't matter, however. You found a wife; splendid. What is this paragon's name?"

"Her name?" Alexander reached into the pocket of his waistcoat and extracted a piece of paper. "Her name…? It's here somewhere. Ah-ha, here it is: Miss Kaitlin Snow. An American name for my soon-to-be American wife."

"You're marrying an American?"

"Kaitlin is an heiress, and yes, I shall wed her."

"Excuse me, Alex, but I was unaware you were short on funds."

Alexander laughed. "I'm not. But one can never have too much money."

"Have you even met this woman?" Jackson asked, confounded his friend would enter into the marriage state for additional income.

"Not yet. She's to arrive in a few months."

"You're committing yourself to a woman you've yet to meet? This doesn't sound at all like you."

Townen knocked on the open door as Viscount Kentworth stepped around him and walked into the room. "I agree. I believe our friend's brain is addled."

"Julian, welcome to the party." Jackson gestured to a chair. "Care for a drink?"

"I thought you'd never ask." Julian sank into the chair. "Pray continue. I'd like to hear what Alex has to say."

"I don't mean to call you superficial, Alex, but a woman's looks have always been of utmost importance to you." Jackson gave Julian a glass of brandy. "What if your intended looks like the arse of an old nag?"

"Yes." Julian considered their friend. "Do you know anything about her, Alex?"

Alex shrugged. He surely expected his motives to be questioned. "She's an American heiress with golden hair and eyes bluer than the ocean. She's educated and her companion happens to be English, which means she's familiar with our ways. I'm told she is much sought after because of her beauty."

"And you don't think her wealth factors into the equation?" Jackson asked acerbically.

"I suppose she was the one to supply you with this information?" Skepticism rolled off Julian's tongue. It was a known fact that Julian held some trust issues when it came to the opposite sex.

Another casual shrug from Alex caused Jackson to grit his teeth. How could his friend enter into marriage so blindly?

"Her father wants her to capture an English title, and I'm willing. It's as simple as that."

"Nothing about marriage is simple," Julian quickly pointed out. He missed getting leg-shackled himself when his fiancée disappeared a short time before the ceremony was to take place. Jackson knew this fact still bothered Julian greatly.

"Nevertheless, we're not getting any younger, gentlemen," replied Alex. "It's time I procure myself a few heirs."

"If you're going to start talking about offspring, I'm getting another drink." Jackson grabbed the snifter and poured himself a hefty dose.

A Necessary Heir

"Fill me up too." Julian held out his glass.

"May as well give me a refill, and then we can toast to my good fortune. Both of you are gaining in years. Perhaps I could arrange for her to bring along a couple of her heiress friends?"

"No thanks," both men said in unison, which set Alexander to laughing.

Jackson lifted his glass. "To Alex's future wife and his progeny. We wish you a lifetime of happiness." The men raised their glasses as one and downed the contents.

"Thanks." Alex swung his legs off the ottoman. "I'm off."

"Where too?" asked Jackson.

"To share the good news with my mother."

"You haven't told her yet?" Julian questioned.

Alex gave them both a wicked grin as he stood. "I thought I'd bounce it off my friends first. Jackson is far stuffier than my mother."

"The hell I am," Jackson protested as he walked toward his friend to see him out. He considered himself the least stodgy person he knew.

Alex laughed at Jackson's contrived look of hurt, then clapped him on the back. "I'll see you soon."

"Count on it." Jackson gave him a nod. "I daresay your mother will be thrilled by the news. She'll finally be able to hand the job of coddling you over to your wife." Jackson patted Alex on the back good-naturedly.

"Amusing, Jackson," replied Alex.

"And accurate," said Julian from the doorway.

"Although, the majority of the debutante's you've danced with this season will be most disappointed to find themselves bested by an American," Jackson assured him.

"Now there's an amusing thought," Julian commented.

"Another bonus, I suppose." Alexander bowed and left. Jackson could hear him telling the butler about his engagement and the congratulatory remarks Townen issued. One thing was certain. Alex appeared to be genuinely happy, which Jackson deemed good.

"So on that note, how about another round?" Julian questioned.

"Definitely." Jackson refilled both of their glasses.

CHAPTER FIVE

Abigail smiled and nodded helloes to people she didn't know as she made her way through Hyde Park looking for Clarissa. A slight spring breeze breathed life into the air and appeared to put everyone in a pleasant mood. Her maid Sophie followed closely behind, stopping as Abigail found her friend and they hugged in greeting.

"How are you faring at Waterford House?" Clarissa asked as she took Abigail's arm and led her to a secluded bench beneath a large English Oak. Their maids conversed a short distance away.

"Better than I could have imagined. You must meet Lady Waterford. She is so genuine and wonderful. We have already grown very close. I'm really happy there."

"And?" Clarissa hedged.

"And what?" Abigail mocked with a knowing smile.

"I swear I will pinch you if you don't tell me what has transpired between you and the earl."

"There's nothing to tell. He did take dinner with us once," she said, and Clarissa groaned, obviously not satisfied with this tidbit of information. "Aside from that one dinner, I've hardly seen him since I moved in."

"And here the gossips say he's been spending every waking moment at his grandmother's."

"I'm sure he does, but I've never ventured into the study to check," Abigail answered insouciantly.

"So you're avoiding him." It was a statement, not a question, but Abby still answered.

"As much as possible. There is no reason for me to fawn over the man when nothing can ever come of it."

"Perhaps you underestimate the earl?" When Abigail rolled her eyes skyward, Clarissa continued. "I'm serious, Abby. Not all men would frown upon your lack of parentage."

"You are most likely correct, but none of those accepting types are from the gentry," she said with a sigh of defeat. "I must think logically where the earl is concerned, and indeed, where my future is concerned. He and I are from two different worlds. You, of all people, know those two worlds, and the inhabitants thereof, don't mix."

"All I'm saying is on occasion the impossible has been known to happen." When Abigail started to object, Clarissa held up her hand to interrupt her words. "For example, are you aware that the Marquis of Glasbourne married his children's governess? Or that the Earl of Arlington married his housekeeper? Such things are done, Abby. There are some who disregard social restrictions when dealing with matters of the heart."

"I had no idea of such happenings, but what has me even more puzzled is that I never knew you were such a romantic."

"I'm not, really. People in my position usually marry for social standing and money, and I have no intention of doing anything else. Nevertheless, I want to make you aware that there are those who will happily marry for love, regardless of the circumstances."

"Good afternoon, Lady Clarissa." A dark haired gentleman with intelligent brown eyes smiled down at them. Clarissa made the introductions and the man, a viscount, bowed. "It is a pleasure to meet a friend of Lady Clarissa's. Will you be attending the opera this evening, my lady?" he asked Clarissa.

"I daresay I must, my lord. My mother would be completely heartbroken otherwise," replied Clarissa.

"Well you can't have that. Perhaps we can talk again later, since I too plan to attend."

"I will look forward to it," Clarissa answered with a sweet smile.

"A pleasant afternoon to you both." The viscount bowed and then disappeared beyond a stretch of trees.

"He was nice," Abigail said, jumping at a chance to turn the tables on her friend, she wanted to discuss Clarissa's love interests, for she was too confused about her feelings toward Lord Waterford to put her thoughts into words.

"According to my father, the good viscount gambles too much." She shrugged, then said, "But no man is perfect."

Abigail's perfect man flashed before her eyes. His skin was bronze, his smile warm, hair blond and tousled, eyes the color of the early morning sky, and his understanding insurmountable. It seemed impossible to keep the Earl of Waterford far from her thoughts, though she had her sincere doubts about that last qualification, his understanding, even as it occurred to her. "You've obviously been traversing the ballrooms since your come out. Has there been anyone who has caught your eye?"

"Unfortunately, no. I wish there were. Nothing would make me happier than to marry and quit my father's house."

"Speaking of your father, I do hope he hasn't been harsh with you because of my visit."

"My father is rarely kind, Abby, but no, he hasn't mentioned you. He assumes, since he said I was to avoid you, that I have dutifully obeyed his demand." Clarissa cast her friend a saucy smile and then easily switched topics. "My mother is planning to buy me a new wardrobe, which I'm excited about."

"That sounds splendid. I can't wait for a viewing. Lady Waterford bought me some new clothes as well."

"I've noticed. Your dress is lovely, by the way."

"Thank you; so is yours."

"This was one I left in my closet from the last time I was home." Clarissa plucked at the mauve skirts.

The ladies fell silent for a couple of minutes while they watched a group of children playing next to the Serpentine, its calm waters shimmering with brilliance in the rare sunshine.

"I'm attending a ball on Friday."

"Truly?" Clarissa clapped her hands in glee. "Which one?"

"I didn't think to ask." She was nervous even contemplating going to such an event, but she knew Clarissa would be excited. Her friend truly believed people would view Abigail without a care about her illegitimacy. Abigail wasn't so trusting of such an occurrence happening. Her mind dwelled on all the things that could go wrong, like being turned away from the door, or worse, being ignored and whispered about by all.

Her friend knew her well enough to know she was scared to death. "Well, regardless of which ball, I shall be there. Please send me a message when you return to Waterford House."

Hearing Clarissa state she'd be there for her was heartening. Nevertheless, she would not subject her friend to ridicule by Lord Loring or any other members in society who chose to snub her. "But what if your father…"

"Saint's be praised, Abby. I'm not going to let you attend your first ball without me. Besides, there isn't anything my father can say or do to prevent me from being your friend. We swore to be friends for life. I'm not going to break our vow. Now forget my father. He doesn't attend such functions anyway."

"I just don't want you to suffer because of our association."

"Balderdash! Association? We're friends, Abby. That will never change."

"You are the best friend, Clarissa." Abigail gave her a tight hug. She truly was lucky to have such a wonderful confidant. She doubted she could have made it through so many years of schooling without Clarissa by her side.

"I should be going. We shall do this again and soon. Make sure you send me the information regarding the ball." Clarissa came to her feet, shook out her skirts, and called to her maid.

"I shall. Lady Waterford would like to have you for tea."

"A splendid idea."

Abigail smiled. "Good. I'll see you soon."

"You certainly will." Clarissa turned back to her friend with a serious expression. "Will you promise me something, Abby?"

Abigail stood with a raised brow. "Of course. What?"

"If the earl is interested in you, which I firmly believe he is, promise me you'll give him a chance?"

"The earl will never wish to wed himself to someone of my birth."

Clarissa huffed. "Promise?"

Abigail smiled. There was no point in denying a promise when such an event would never happen. "Very well. I promise if he asks to wed me, I shall say yes."

"Abigail Gibbons, the Countess of Waterford. You have to admit it has a certain ring." Clarissa spun around and walked away, and with the click of her fingers, her maid fell into step behind her.

***

Abigail returned to Waterford House to find the man who dominated her thoughts saying farewell to one of his friends. The earl took a moment to introduce her to Julian Bancott, Viscount Rathemore, an attractive man with a crooked smile and glazed eyes. She quickly surmised why his eyes were thus when he bowed over her hand and his breath assailed her nose. He nodded at Jackson and stumbled out the door.

"Your friend appears to be well in his cups, my lord. I hope you are faring well?"

Jackson sauntered toward her like some predatory cat and she fought the urge to back up a step. His sudden nearness was causing prickly sensations to course through her limbs. She was thankful there weren't any servants in the area to witness her telling blush.

"I am faring well enough, my sweet." He ran a finger down her cheek, and she flinched in reaction to the bold caress, the path his bare finger took leaving a heated trail of sensation. "How was your visit with Lady Clarissa?" he murmured near her neck. She heard him inhale as he took in her scent.

Abigail couldn't help enjoying the heat radiating from his masculine frame, the smell of bourbon mixing with his cologne all but drowning her conviction to steer clear from him. He was too close. She took a small step back. "It went well, thank you." Her voice came out in a whisper. "I shall return to my room now."

"Now?" He swayed forward to run his finger down her cheek again, and she inhaled deeply. This was the closest they had ever been and she fought the urge to touch his cheek in return.

"You're inebriated, Lord Waterford." She tried to sound stern and disproving, but her voice came out in a panted breath when his hand slid down her neck to encircle her throat.

"I am, my little butterfly."

Saints be praised. If she was smart, she knew she'd run to her room, but his blue eyes held her in place and her desire to be near him prevented rational thought. She couldn't leave him in the hall. What if his current state upset the dowager? "Come with me," she ordered in the no nonsense voice she occasionally used on her mother.

"I'd follow you anywhere," he crooned, and he leaned toward her with lips puckered. Self-preservation now took over and she jumped back. Taking his hand, she led him back into the sanctuary of the study, softly closing the door behind them.

"Has your grandmother seen you like this?" She immediately let go of his hand. Physical contact didn't seem like a good idea.

"Not today." He swayed into her, and she pushed him toward the sofa. He fell back with arms flailing. Abigail turned her head to avoid laughing at his dramatics. His facial expression was indeed priceless. *You'd think he was falling off a cliff, for heaven's sake.*

Once seated at a cockeyed angle, he gave her a boyish starry-eyed look. His smile was lopsided as he patted the cushion next to him for her to join him. She ignored the gesture. "Do you indulge in such behavior often?"

"And to which one of my behaviors are you referring?" He slurred a bit and laughed at himself.

She crossed her arms over her chest. "Drinking, my lord."

"Ah, then, no. I usually don't over imbibe. Time for me to ask a question. Do you always have to look so fetching, Abigail?"

Although the compliment sent a shiver of excitement down her spine, she knew not to take the flattering remark to heart. Her mother often said and did things while under the influence of spirits that she did not mean. Then, in the morning, she'd apologize for everything, like the words that cut at Abigail's heart were never spoken. "Why were you drinking?" She found most people had a reason for getting deep in their cups.

"A celebration. My friend Alex is getting engaged." His tone was somber.

"And this upsets you?"

He grunted. Looking at her like she was daft. "On the contrary. I'm thrilled for him."

"I see." She certainly didn't understand why anyone would ever want to be in such a condition, but she also knew she would help him the only way she knew how. "Lie down on the sofa, my lord. I'll have you feeling better in no time."

"Am I dreaming?" he asked in a drunken whisper. He eagerly laid himself down, passing her a wolfish grin.

"Why would you think so?"

"You've often joined me on this sofa in my dreams." He held his arms out to her.

She knew it was the alcohol talking, but she was also aware that people could be brutally honest when under the influence. *Does he really dream of me?* She definitely dreamt of him, even when she was wide-awake. She said nothing to his comment, but she couldn't help from giving the sofa a second look. "I'm going to the kitchen to make you something suitable to drink and to fetch a cool cloth. I'll return as quickly as I can. Please stay put. I don't wish your grandmother to see you in this state." Examining his position on the sofa to make sure he wouldn't roll onto the floor, she tossed a nearby blanket on him and headed for the door.

"Abigail?"

"Yes?"

"If I'm dreaming, please don't wake me." Abigail saw his eyes close before she dashed out of the room.

Thanking her lucky stars that the kitchen staff wasn't anywhere to be found, she scrambled around the kitchen mixing her infamous tonic for those who have over imbibed. She had taken care of her mother so many times in this condition that it was second nature to her now.

Hurrying out the door with her bundle, she crept into the study. *Saints be praised! The man has divested himself of his shirt.* She suddenly felt faint. He was temptation personified. His sculpted chest was lightly sprinkled with hair, which tapered down beneath the blanket, his physique indeed impressive, all sinewy and bronzed. He had muscular arms she wished she could feel around her, and she noted his black lashes fanned over his lean clean-shaven cheeks. His breathing was heavier than normal, but it remained even. Again his cologne wafted through the air as he threw an arm over his head and she squeezed her eyes shut to ward off his overpowering image. Building up some courage, she reopened her eyes, but they automatically focused on his chest again. She found herself wanting to lift the blanket to peek at his lean stomach and beyond, to follow that trail of hair. Closing her eyes again, she hoped her sanity would return. At the moment, she wanted nothing more than to curl up on the sofa next to him so his powerful heat could seep into her.

She tried to gain control of this new yearning, that was starting to feel like a need, but she didn't know how. She wanted his strength and support, and she wanted his love. *Oh dear, to admit these things, to use that word, even if only in my mind.* She was even wondering what it would be like to marry a man like the earl. He possessed an unspoken aura of mightiness and power. And now he was practically lying naked in front of her.

Admittedly, this was the first male chest she ever had the pleasure of viewing, but she couldn't imagine any of the others in the world looking any better than this. She blinked away the image and tried to concentrate on the task at hand. Surely, she could manage this.

She told herself she was acting as his nurse, and as such, she needed to remain indifferent. With a calming breath and her eyes averted from his glorious chest to his too handsome face, she moved closer.

Shutting her eyes tightly to ward off his perfectly chiseled image, she bravely opened them to find his penetrating blue gaze upon her. If he *had* lucid thoughts at this moment, he probably thought her mad, or that she kept getting something in her eyes. She laughed to herself.

Placing her items down on a nearby table, she determinedly set to her task by dampening a cloth and then placing it on his forehead. Before she could turn back for her special tonic, he grabbed her hand and pulled.

With a yelp, Abigail landed across the nude chest she had just been so brazenly admiring. "Lord Waterford, release me at once," she shrieked, taken back by the suddenness of his attack. She tried to push up on her arms, but he collapsed them with an elbow, causing her to lie upon his chest again.

Then he feathered light kisses across her cheek and toward her ear, sending shivers of pleasure dancing over her skin, and she forgot about freeing herself. The damp cloth fell to the floor. "I don't wish to release you, my love, anymore than you wish to be free."

He was right. Being held in his embrace felt remarkably good, and oh so comforting. For a girl who grew up without such sentimental embraces, his caress moved her like a Shakespearean play moves its audience. She allowed herself another brief moment of contact even as notions of self-preservation raged a war in her head. *I shouldn't be allowing this.* "This is highly improper, my lord. I'm afraid I must insist you let me go." *But not yet, please not yet.*

"You're worried about proprieties, my sweet?"

She nodded. "As you should be." She told herself to pull away. In his condition, she could easily escape. But she didn't want this closeness to end—ever.

"Where you're concerned, I'm more than willing to throw caution to the wind and let nature take its course."

Nature? Did he mean sex? Saints be praised, I have to get up. She refused to follow in her mother's footsteps and allow a night of passion to ruin her life. That path led to heartache and a lifetime of grief. She jumped up, pushing against his muscled chest. He sat up with a moan and grabbed his head, which was most likely pounding.

She could no longer remain to help. She was in jeopardy of losing her heart and her innocence to the Earl of Waterford. She snatched up the cloth and tonic and thrust them at him. He gave her an odd look, but he took the proffered items just the same. She fled before he could grab her again, which she noticed, he had tried to do.

***

Jackson finally managed to pull himself together and make it back to his house. It was early morning when he received a summons from the Waterford town house asking for his immediate return.

Sexual dreams about Abigail caused him a restless night. He was finding it increasingly bizarre that he was so caught up with this particular chit. Besides her beauty and impertinent manner toward him, what did he know about her? Nothing. So why this overwhelming fascination? Granted she was extremely kind to his grandmother, which he had secretly witnessed countless times. He had watched them interact and realized their friendship was something they both needed. At times, he was even jealous of the bond they formed so quickly.

And it would be considered sheer folly not to acknowledge that he returned to Waterford House daily since Abigail moved in precisely because she was there and he hoped for the opportunity to see her.

Perhaps he simply liked her. She was courageous and strong against the ill-treatment she suffered from society. She was loving and gentle with his grandmother, and brassy as hell with him, but he was coming to understand why.

Abigail was attracted to him, this he knew. Like most ladies, she would not allow herself to act on impulse, for to do so would mean ruination.

Nevertheless, Abigail's reasons were even more complex because she was born on the preverbal wrong side of the blanket. She would not want to give into her baser desires and wind up in the same dire straits as her mother. He understood these things, but he nevertheless wanted her terribly.

And he wasn't so drunk last night that he hadn't sensed her reluctance to leave him. Just thinking about how perfect it felt to have her breasts pressed against him instigated an erection. He wanted her with a fierceness he hadn't thought possible. He enjoyed their verbal squabbles and their lingering glances. He thought it uncanny how they always seemed to know what the other was thinking. He never felt this kind of intense connection with anyone. Even if he couldn't have her in his bed, he did not want her to leave—ever.

And why was a little voice inside his head telling him to marry her? Perhaps he was more foxed than he thought. Or perhaps he wanted to feel happy like his friend Alexander. He certainly felt elated in Abigail's presence. *A sign of sorts?*

Women had been literally throwing themselves at him since he came into manhood. He continually reminded himself that he had plenty of time to obtain himself a wife, but he had yet to meet Abigail, and now these attempts to sooth his agitated mind when it came to marriage failed him utterly. "Abigail," he said her name aloud, and then he cringed at the lovesick croon of his voice.

***

"You know I usually sleep away the morning hours, Grandmother." Jackson sauntered into the frilly sitting room stifling a yawn. "The reason for my summons?" He briefly wondered if Abigail shared the news of yesterday afternoon's encounter, but he dismissed the thought almost immediately. Abigail wouldn't tattle.

This morning it took a good hour for his stomach to settle and his head to stop hammering, and it took another hour for his valet to dress him. Now here, he couldn't help wondering where Abigail hid herself. Would she avoid him now that she witnessed him deep in his cups? *No, she'll avoid me because she's even more afraid of the chemistry between us than I am.*

"Stuff and applesauce, Jackson. Have a seat. I hate when you tower over me." His grandmother placed her teacup back in its flowered saucer, motioning to the chair across from her. The Dowager Countess of Waterford was never one to mince words.

"Something amiss?" Jackson eyed his grandmother curiously.

"I'm afraid I have a bit of a headache." She dramatically put the back of her hand to her head.

Jackson leaned forward in concern. "Is it serious? Would you like me to send for Doctor Pierson?"

"No, nothing so dire. I believe some sleep would help."

"You're not sleeping well?"

"Not lately, no. But I'm sure that, with your help, I'll manage."

"Very well. How can I help?"

"I planned to take Abigail shopping to extend her wardrobe today, but with my throbbing temples, I'm afraid our outing isn't possible." She eyed him shrewdly.

"You know I deplore shopping," he thought to mention.

"Of course, my boy, but I find myself in a bind, and who else would I lean on for help. Besides, you have exquisite tastes. Abigail could use your guidance as well as your friendship."

Friendship? He knew he'd have a damnable time thinking of Abigail as a friend. Lover? Yes. Friend? Definitely not. To refuse, however, would upset his grandmother, something he strived not to do. What's more, his heart raced at the mere thought of accompanying Abigail. *It would be a boon to spend the day in Abigail's company.* "I'll go."

From the look she gave him, it was clear she knew he'd comply. "Somehow I knew you would," she said under her breath.

"Pardon?"

"Nothing, dear. It's this headache."

Like hell it was. Apparently, his grandmother had decided to take over his mother's role as matchmaker. Although he thought his grandmother would have insisted—as she had many times in the past—that he choose a lady from the finest lineage. But he knew how close Abigail and his grandmother had become and assumed this the reason for her encouragement. Funny, he thought, but he found himself in the mindset to let her succeed with her meddling.

Grinning as he stood, he leaned over to kiss her cheek. "I hope you feel better soon. Now where can I find your companion?"

"I believe she's breaking her morning fast on the balcony."

He scrunched his brow, considering the many balconies of this house. "Which one?"

"Most likely the one off her chambers. If you could please be a dear and fetch her for me."

His follow-the-rules grandmother was sending him into Abigail's private sanctuary? She must truly be tired. But he wouldn't gainsay her. With a hasty grin and a quick bow, he went to search out Abigail. He couldn't wait to see her reaction when she found him in her room.

As Jackson entered, Abigail's maid frowned, her face a stark mask of confusion as to why he'd enter a lady's private domain. Too intimidated to comment, she smartly shuffled out of the room, and Jackson casually closed the door behind her.

He hadn't been in this room for many years, but he remembered exploring it in his youth. He traveled across the carpet of rose and cream, noticing the canopy bed had yet to be made. The pillow still held the indent where Abigail had laid her beautiful head. His body hardened at the mere thought of her lying disheveled on the bed after a thorough session of love making with him.

"Sophie, I could use some more tea." Abigail's lovely voice carried into the room from the balcony doors, where sheer white curtains billowed into the room caught on a cool breeze.

Jackson stepped out onto the verandah, noticing how a light fog hovered above the ground below. The scent of brewed tea mixed with a hint of Abigail's sweet perfume filled his senses. She had been reading the paper but looked up at his approach. The look of surprise on her face was mirth provoking, and he couldn't help but smile. His appearance seemed to have taken her breath and obviously her voice. "Surprise." He couldn't help himself.

"My lord?" She inclined her head. "Why are you here?" she asked with more than a hint of indignation in her tone.

"My grandmother had me fetched. You look lovely this morning, Abigail." *Surely an understatement.* She looked good enough to eat dressed in a simple burnt orange dress that accentuated her eyes. The sun glinted off the blond highlights of her brown tresses, which were pulled up on the sides and in the back by pearl combs. Her eyes were wide at his sudden appearance.

"Thank you, but I believe you know that is not what I meant. Why are you here in my room, or rather, on my verandah, to be more specific?"

He crossed his arms casually across his chest, enjoying the heat that bloomed in her cheeks. "Actually the house is mine, but that's neither here nor there."

"You're stalling, my lord."

Yes, he was, he had to admit. He enjoyed provoking her.

She read him well. "Am I?" He walked to a chair and spun it around to straddle it.

"An explanation, if you please."

"Yes, right. The reason for my presence in your chambers." He shrugged. "My grandmother asked me to come and get you."

"She sent *you* to *my* room?"

"She did."

"I can hardly fathom such, my lord."

"Are you accusing me of dishonesty?" He acted taken back by the comment, but the truth was he just liked to watch her redden in frustration. At the moment, her fingers were drumming steadily on the paper she placed on the table.

"Are you being dishonest?"

"You wound me." He dramatically placed a hand to his chest, and he was rewarded with a hint of her lovely smile.

"I hardly think so. Nevertheless, I find it shocking that the dowager would send you in here."

He found his grandmother's request odd as well, but he didn't comment in that regard. "She seems to have developed a headache."

Abigail stood. "She's ill?"

"Not in the least." Jackson chuckled when he thought about his grandmother's poor acting skills, which earned him a scowl from Abigail. "She claims she needs more sleep."

"I see." He watched in adoration as she worried her lower lip between her teeth. A simple gesture he was coming to find endearing. He wished she'd nibble on him in such a fashion. Her troubled expression touched him in a way he hadn't expected, however. It was evident she loved his grandmother, and he had a feeling that when Abigail Gibbons loved someone, it was completely. He felt himself yearning for such devotion from her.

"I assure you, she is well. I'm to do some shopping with you in her stead."

"You and I are to go shopping together?" She didn't sound at all happy at the news.

"We are," he said flatly, meeting her gaze with challenge in his own, allowing her to realize he would not be swayed. He meant to spend the day with her. He held back explaining his own distaste for shopping let alone the admission that the only reason he was doing this was to spend more time in her company.

He watched the rise and fall of her chest and heard her all but sigh with resignation when she exhaled. "Very well." She stood and walked inside. "If you'll wait for me downstairs, I'll join you in a moment."

He wasn't about to let her back out of their day together. "No. I'll remain," he said in his most authoritative voice as he followed her into her chamber. "There's no need to dawdle."

"Actually, there is." She turned with disdain, the gold around her dark eyes sparking to life with her agitation. Abigail apparently wasn't a woman who enjoyed taking orders. "You will leave my room this instant," she stated calmly, but he noted that her fists were tightly clenched.

"I wish to leave the house now, Abigail. I have other more pressing matters to attend to today."

"Good. Then you go and take care of those matters, my lord. I am perfectly capable of shopping on my own."

"And upset my grandmother? I think not. You look ready. Fetch your maid and we'll be off."

"I'd prefer to fetch a hammer so I could pound on that obstinate head of yours."

"I'm not sure I understand what all the fuss is about." She was growing angrier by the second, and now her annoyance was no longer amusing. *Did she have to be so bloody difficult?*

"Then allow me to enlighten you. For one thing, I don't like to be ordered about—ever." This he already construed. "My other reason is no concern of yours."

"I disagree." He opened the door and stood in the threshold.

"Of course, you disagree," she huffed. "Fine! If you *have* to know why I wish for a few moments to myself, it is because I need to relieve myself before we depart. Are you happy now?"

A blush infused her cheeks that made him feel like a lowly cad for insisting on an explanation. "I only wanted to know why I was being waylaid, not to detain you in such... I'll meet you downstairs."

He shut the door behind him, but he heard her shout, "Ooohh, that man!" Although he knew this was Abigail's first foray into employment, she wasn't at all as biddable as one would wish for an employee to be. In truth, she was the sauciest woman he'd ever had the pleasure to meet. He grinned to himself. This was turning out to be a most promising day.

***

Abigail adjusted a few pins in her hair as she tromped about her room. How dare Jackson walk into her room and then act so cavalier about the entire matter, like it was an everyday occurrence. Perhaps he was used to going in and out of ladies' bedrooms, but she had yet to have ever found a man in hers before today. It was unnerving. But Jackson's entire demeanor was unnerving. When she saw him, she remembered how wonderfully intoxicating it was yesterday as she lay across his warm body in the study. The image had been affixed in her brain the entire night, until she finally fell asleep near daybreak. She'd never forget the way his fingers slid down her cheek in a soft caress or the moment he said he dreamt of her. She sighed at her memories.

He was easily the most handsome man she had ever met, but he was also easily the most domineering. She noted how he showed no signs of yesterday's drinking. If anything, he appeared more self-assured.

Abigail didn't know what to do about this man who made her reason flee the moment he was near. *How does one remain unmoved by such charms all wrapped up in a breathtaking package?* It took every ounce of willpower she possessed to fight off the attraction she felt for him, and although she admonished herself that she shouldn't, she found herself wanting to spend the day in Jackson's company. This knowledge angered her further.

In the end, she purposely dawdled, making sure the autocratic man knew she wouldn't be bullied. Although, when she met him in the lower hall, he acted as if her delay hadn't upset him in the least. *Bugger him.*

"Grandmother went to nap. Are you ready?"

Abigail looked behind her to find Sophie waiting patiently. "Yes, I believe so."

He held out his arm with a smile, and she took it. Jackson had left his vehicle at home and had instead rode over on horseback this morning. So he decided they'd take Lady Waterford's fancy equipage. Sophie sat next to Abigail, allowing Jackson to take the seat across from them facing the rear. Her blood seemed to turn to liquid fire in her veins because he appeared intent on staring at her the entire ride to Bond Street, where the dowager's dressmaker, Madame Bouchard's boutique was located. To keep control of her fluttering emotions, she fixed her gaze out the window.

They entered the opulent dress shop a short while later. Sophie immediately took a seat by the door to wait, and Jackson approached Madame Bouchard, a French woman in her fifties who evidently tended to favor bathing in perfume. The dowager had informed Abby that this particular modiste was well known for her eye for fashion and knowledge of trends. She seemed very business-like. Abigail watched as the lady nodded her head at everything Jackson said. And just what was he saying? Abigail couldn't guess.

After intently listening to Jackson, Madame Bouchard walked over to Abby and circled around her like a hawk eyeing prey. She clucked her tongue, held out Abigail's arms, and then disappeared into the back room.

"Where's she going?" Abigail asked, unsure how these matters were conducted. In the past, she had relied on the seamstress who visited the school to see to her limited wardrobe. She had no insight as to the inner workings of a fancy boutique. The few dresses she had in her possession, the dowager had given to her already made.

Jackson shrugged while taking a seat on a flower-upholstered sofa. He looked a bit odd sitting there in all his masculine glory on a sofa so utterly feminine. "I imagine she's pulling together various fabrics to complement your beauty."

A warm pleasure filled her at his compliment. Not many minutes later, Madame Bouchard reentered the room followed by two younger girls bogged down by weighty fabrics.

"Place them on the table, girls," Madame Bouchard ordered as she walked up to Abigail. "The earl's informed me of your desire for an extensive wardrobe."

"I do need a few dresses," Abigail admitted, feeling awkward. The dowager had already purchased her some clothes, and she did not wish to appear avaricious.

Jackson saw Abigail fidget uncomfortably when she answered Madame's question, and so he said, "She also requires some riding habits, day dresses, a few ball gowns, and any other fripperies you deem necessary, madam. Money is no object. I want her to be the envy of all the other ladies in London." Truth be told, Jackson didn't feel new clothes were necessary to achieve that end, but he wanted Abigail to know she was worthy of everything his money could buy.

From the sofa, Jackson then watched Abigail pose as colorful fabrics were draped across her in rapid succession. Occasionally, he was gifted with a glimpse of a shoulder, a hint of her calf, and even for a brief second, a sliver of thigh. He leaned back, putting his arms behind his head as a pillow. Shopping was going splendidly.

***

Abigail tried not to notice Jackson's hooded stare as she allowed Madame Bouchard to work her magic, a most difficult task to be sure. Nevertheless, she remained intent on pretending his ogling didn't rattle her. In truth, she felt like she was going to melt into the floor.

Shopping took several hours, and they had made their way to many more shops before Jackson decided to call it quits. They then sat under an awning at an outside café eating a light repast. The look of relief on Jackson's face was evident, and of course, she didn't miss his comment under his breath before he sat: "Thank goodness that's over."

"I don't know why you insisted on coming if you detest shopping." Feeling flushed, Abigail flicked open the ivory fan looped around her wrist and rapidly fanned her face. It had been a long day, especially for her, since she was the one being poked, prodded, and ogled.

"You can't guess?" His brow grew lopsided with his inquiry. They were both exhausted, but in the past few hours, they never lacked for conversation. Indeed, they were comfortable together.

"I know you didn't wish to upset your grandmother, but I also know you are not the kind of man to do something you don't wish to do."

"You know me that well already, do you?"

"Yes, I think I do."

"Would you believe I agreed to come today so I could spend time with you?"

She tried not to sputter her tea and slowly swallowed. She felt the blush rise into her cheeks. *Did he truly want to spend time with me?* He had indicated as much, and the sheer joy she felt consumed her. Her heart fluttered as she valiantly tried to come up with a witty rejoinder to remove the spell he cast upon her with his smooth words.

"No, I wouldn't." *All right, that wasn't witty in the least, a response fit for a child actually.* And yet it was all she could think to say. She couldn't let herself be drawn in by this man. If she didn't gain control, she'd be falling in love before she could blink.

His hand came down over hers where she had been nervously thumping her fingers on the table. "You need further convincing?" He cast her a devilish smile, causing her to snatch her hand from beneath his. Such intimate contact would be delicious fodder for any watchers. The mere feel of his hand upon hers sent her mind spiraling out of control with far too many *what ifs*.

What if he was serious?

What if he really wanted to be with her?

What if she had untainted bloodlines?

Stop it, stop it, stop it! she scolded herself. *He's not for you! He can't be! He's an earl!*

She took a deep breath at his question, her tongue feeling dry regardless of the quantity of tea she consumed. She stood. "I think we should go. I doubt your grandmother thought we'd be gone this long."

"Ah." He remained seated, his head cocked at a questioning angle as he studied her. "I've scared you with my candor?"

"Highly unlikely, my lord," she said with the haughtiest voice she could muster while struggling for a manner of nonchalance. The mere hint of a possible future with him made her completely unbalanced.

"Very well, Miss Abigail. Let us be off."

"Yes, my lord." She nodded, suddenly feeling deflated that their day together was coming to an end, but she thought it prudent to leave before she threw herself at him.

CHAPTER SIX

Abigail stood next to the dowager as they slowly made their way up the steps of the Drury Lane Theatre. The crowd of people was incredibly thick, which made their ascent slow moving. The crush wasn't helping Abigail's already frayed nerves, and yet, she had to admit that excitement hummed through her veins too. This was to be her first actual play. She'd read *Romeo and Juliet* several times. What young lady hadn't? But the prospect of actually seeing the scenes played out made her giddy with anticipation, so much so that she wanted to charge through the crowd. Thankfully, she refrained from doing anything that silly, but only barely.

Finally seated in a plush red velvet chair, she took a moment to peer over the dowager's private balcony at the sea of people below. "Thank you for bringing me here, Lady Waterford."

"Thank you for escorting me, my dear."

Abigail smiled. "It's what we companions do."

The dowager patted Abigail's knee. "You know, you are much more to me than a companion, Abigail. There's no one else I'd rather have escort me."

"You wound me, Grandmother." Jackson parted the red privacy curtains and walked into the box, then bent down to kiss his grandmother's cheek. It felt to Abigail like he consumed all the oxygen with his appearance. Abigail gave him a small smile while her insides did flip-flops of exhilaration. He looked splendid in a bottle green velvet coat with black waistcoat and trousers. His cravat was elaborate, bright white, and tied to perfection. His blond locks were resting on his shoulders, indicating that he was due for a cut. His mesmerizing blue eyes twinkled in merriment.

"Jackson, my boy. What a pleasure. And here I thought you avoided the theater," the dowager commented, casting him a look that held some sort of secret understanding. Lady Waterford seemed to find his appearance here in their theater box amusing, though Abby could not understand why.

"I thought to give the theater another chance." His eyes fell on Abigail. "Are you enjoying yourself, Miss Abigail?"

"So far, my lord, but the play's yet to begin."

"Then there's still time for me to make my escape."

"Stuff and applesauce, my boy. You wouldn't have attended if you had no intention of staying. Take the seat next to Abigail. I can't see the stage from here anyway."

"Yes, ma'am," he said in military fashion as if it was an order, which for the most part, it was.

Abigail turned in her chair to query the dowager once she reseated herself. "Then why do you sit here?"

"Because these seats are the best," the dowager said airily and with a wave of her hand in front of her as she indicated the box.

Abigail smiled and then turned back to glance around the room to find dozens of female eyes staring in their direction. "Do you have a female following, my lord?"

"Very amusing, Abigail." Jackson smiled at some of the women and even nodded at a few. "Most are probably merely surprised to see me seated in a theater box."

Abby shrugged, pretending the attention he was receiving from the female population wasn't irksome in the least. "I was only making a simple observation, my lord." Indeed, the mass of females now looking this direction had not been staring before his arrival.

"There are as many male eyes admiring you, my sweet, but then who could blame them? You are the loveliest creature to ever grace London."

Her heart picked up its already brisk pace. He certainly knew the right things to say. "Doubtful, my lord, but thank you." Although she did notice the attention of a few males, she assumed they were just curious as to who she was and how someone like her had use of a private box.

The lights dimmed and the play began, and thereafter Abigail's gaze remained riveted to the stage. When the first act came to a close, the roar of applause was deafening. She stood clapping with her delight for such a talented group of performers. "Simply wonderful!"

"I'm glad you're enjoying the performance," the dowager replied with a hand-covered yawn. Abigail noticed the dowager seemed tired lately, but she assumed the sleepless nights were due to her mourning the loss of the man she loved. "I think I'll go fetch myself some lemonade."

"Nonsense, Grandmother. I'll fetch you a beverage." Jackson stood.

The dowager got to her feet and waved him off. "That is not necessary. You keep Abigail company. I won't be but a minute." She disappeared beyond the curtain before either of them could protest further, her maid following dutifully behind her.

"Do you think she's feeling well?" Abigail asked, watching the gentle sway of the red velvet curtain as it moved back into place.

"Why do you ask?" Jackson turned back to take the seat beside her.

"She still seems…well…tired."

"I've noticed," he said. "She's had much on her mind lately."

"Yes, I agree. Her adjustment to her present circumstances can't be easy. I'm sure you are right and with time she'll be able to sleep better."

She could smell the light scent of his cologne. He took her hand, and she all but jumped at the contact. "Thank you for caring so much about her."

"Think nothing of it, my lord. I love her as if she were my own grandmother, which I never had. I'm most grateful." She didn't want to pull her hand out of his grasp. She could feel his heat seeping through her glove, the subtle power of his fingers as he gently caressed the back of her hand with his thumb. *All right, that's enough.* She pulled her hand back and noticed the disappointment on his face. *Saints be praised, did he expect to hold my hand throughout the rest of the night?*

The curtain parted behind them and Abigail turned with a smile to greet the dowager.

But it wasn't the dowager. Instead, the dark exotic beauty who played Juliet on stage only moments before stood there staring at Jackson with a pout on her full, reddened lips. Why was the actress in their box? Was this a normal occurrence? From the look of surprise on Jackson's face, she would have to guess not, which meant the woman was there to see him. The seductive glance she slid his way spoke clearly the woman's intentions.

"Jackson, darling, it has been an age. I've missed you." She closed the distance between the two of them and pulled Jackson up out of his chair by his collar and into a tight, perfumed embrace.

Jackson appeared stiff and flustered, awkward in a way Abigail had never witnessed in him before. He stepped back clumsily, clearing his throat. "Miss Spritewater, allow me to introduce my grandmother's… I mean, allow me to introduce Miss Abigail Gibbons." Abigail stood with her shoulders back and her head held high.

"Miss Gibbons." The actress hardly spared her a glance before her heated eyes raked down Jackson's fine torso.

"Miss Spritewater," Abigail responded automatically, wondering why she suddenly felt angry, and yes, even jealous. Now jealousy was a feeling she knew well. Longing to be legitimate had a way of making one feel that way, and unwillingly, she'd often been envious of others.

But this was an altogether different kind of jealousy. She actually wanted to scratch the irritating woman's eyes out for looking at Jackson—her Jackson. *Oh, Saints be praised, when the devil did that happen?* She wanted the Earl of Waterford to be hers…forever.

"Promise me, my darling, that you'll come backstage after the show. It's been far too long since we spent any..." Miss Spritewater paused to see if Abigail was paying attention. Abigail pretended amazement by the activity going on below. "It has been ages since we spent any quality time together," the woman finished with a subtle moan as she ran her hand down Jackson's arm.

This woman has to go. Now!

"I'm afraid that isn't possible tonight, my dear. I'm here with my grandmother," replied Jackson.

"Oh pooh!" The lovely black haired woman thrust out her bottom lip again, which looked ridiculous.

Abigail turned completely toward them. Time to take action. "Your performance was wonderful, Miss Spritewater. I imagine it difficult to memorize your lines so masterfully. I'm sure your time is limited, and although we appreciate you gracing us with your appearance, it would probably be best if you returned to the show for the next act. You're excused."

The woman eyed her, and for a moment, Abigail thought she'd protest being dismissed, but instead she gave Abigail a dainty shrug and focused her attention back on Jackson. To Abigail's astonishment, she ran one of her fingers across Jackson's lips, made some kind of moaning sound, and then left. Jackson's face lit up with a red-faced grin.

Completely shocked by such behavior, Abigail retook her seat. She didn't want Jackson to know how much the woman irritated her, but her hands were trembling with her emotions and she hid them in her lap, deep in the folds of her gown. Perhaps she should have gouged the woman's eyes out in an effort to make herself feel better.

"You're awfully quiet. No comment about Miss Spritewater?"

"I don't think a woman like her deserves further comment, my lord," she answered hotly.

"Are you sure?" He spoke right in her ear, sending shivers down her spine as his breath caressed her neck.

Thankfully, the dowager returned, saving her from further comment. "Was that Miss Spritewater I saw coming from *my* box?"

"Yes, my lady," answered Abigail. "It seems the actress is on friendly terms with your grandson." *And now I'll have to watch the shameless woman on stage for the next hour.*

"Is she now?" The dowager took her seat without further commentary.

Abigail regretted her words the second she spoke them. The last thing she wanted to do was act jealous over a man who in no way belonged to her. So Jackson bedded an actress, most likely a legion of them. It was no concern of hers.

***

Jackson felt incredible. A grin remained fixed on his face as he sat next to Abigail. Her body shook with jealous rage—he saw it and felt it even at a distance—and truthfully, seeing her in such a way made him happy. After all, to be jealous, one did have to care about the person, didn't they? Yes, jealousy resulting from her attraction to him was unquestionably a logical conclusion for her agitated behavior. His night at the theater had just paid off in spades.

This realization, however, came with a further realization, this one discomfiting. He too felt jealousy, and because of Abigail. He wanted to knock out every man who even dared look in her direction. Irrational, yes, but then love usually was, and it was this last notion that made him most uncomfortable. He was surely falling for the fair Miss Abigail. He welcomed the thrilling sensation but the word made him nervous. She made his body quake, his manhood throb, and his heart soar. And to think he wasn't even looking for a wife. But he knew how he felt and what he wanted. His life's course seemed suddenly revealed. No woman had ever made him feel even remotely like this, like he could lasso the moon, cure world hunger, do anything with her near.

Although, truth be told, there was no reason for Abby's jealousy. He'd not spent time in Miss Spritewater's bed in years, but then Abigail didn't know this, and he wasn't about to enlighten her. He wanted her to admit her feelings for him.

When the play ended, Jackson insisted on seeing the ladies home. Once there, he decided he very much wanted to go inside and spend more time with Abigail, who had yet to smile but artificially since her introduction to Miss Spritewater.

"It's still early, Jackson. Come inside for a nightcap," his grandmother said when he assisted her out of the vehicle.

As he expected, once they were inside, his grandmother went off to bed, leaving him alone with Abigail. They were in the drawing room and he crossed to the black lacquered table to pour himself a drink. Abigail went to sit on the sofa, and all he could think of was what a perfect place to lay her back and have his way with her.

"Can I get you something, Abigail?"

"Just some water please, my lord."

He could still hear the anger in her voice, although she was obviously trying to hide it. "Did you enjoy the play?"

"Yes, the play was nice. I should thank you for attending. I never would have met the lead actress if not for your presence."

Yes, definitely jealous. He bit back a smile. Perhaps an apology was in order. Although it was no fault of his that Miss Spritewater sought him out. "I'm sorry if Miss Spritewater's presence upset you." Her eyes flared. Obviously an apology was not the way to go about this.

"Excuse me?" she said with a raised brow, which he knew coincided with her anger. He remembered the look from the first day they met and he accused her of being his grandfather's mistress, which seemed like an eternity ago. Well, he wasn't stupid enough to repeat what he said, especially if she was going to be so downright hostile.

"What you need, my dear, is a restorative." He splashed the amber liquor into his crystal snifter.

"Don't presume to know what I need, my lord."

Damn, she's even angrier than I thought. "I would never do so."

"Being controlling is part of your nature, my lord."

Jackson crossed the room and sat across from her. "Does it make you feel better to insult me? If so, by all means, pray continue."

That had her blinking at him. She must have realized she was acting the shrew because she smiled. The simple gesture caused his heart to race and his hands to sweat. She was lovely. "I'm sorry, my lord. I don't know what's come over me."

"Jealousy, plain and simple." He thought the words but remained silent.

"It's been a long day," she exclaimed by way of explanation. When he still didn't speak, she threw up her hands. "Very well. I admit to being somewhat bothered by Miss Spritewater's appearance. I know that's completely irrational, and I shouldn't have been bothered but..." She paused as if formulating her thoughts, then said, "I was."

"Why did her presence bother you?" He knew he was pushing his luck, but he so wanted her to admit she liked him and was jealous of the attention the actress laved on him.

"I don't know, my lord. It just did. I think I'm tired. I should turn in. You are capable of showing yourself out. You have certainly been in and out of here often enough lately. Not that I've been paying close attention to your comings and goings, it's..." She bit her lip to silence herself, then said, "Your grandmother may wish to go shopping on the morrow. And I have any number of correspondences to write..."

He held up his hand. "Whoa, Abigail." She was talking quickly. "You're rambling."

Her mouth closed with an audible snap. "So I was. Another sign of fatigue, I should think."

He knew nervousness usually gave rise to her talkative tongue, but he didn't correct her. "Then I shall take my leave and wish you a pleasant evening." He walked to her, taking her soft, gloved hand in his and bringing it to his lips, wishing he'd the right to remove the glove and kiss all the way up her arm. He blew a warm breath into the glove, hoping to leave her dizzy with anticipation for their next encounter. "Good night, Abigail."

"Good night, Lord Waterford," she whispered.

Jackson couldn't help whistling as he took his leave.

***

The next afternoon, Abigail sat in the cozy drawing room she had come to favor. She had just finished penning a letter to Lady Carlyle at the academy, informing her about her newfound happiness with her current employer, when a rapid knock came from the open door.

She knew who stood there before she looked, so in tune with his presence she seemed to be when he was near. She tried to keep her face stoic as she gently set down her pen and turned to him. He stood in the threshold looking so beautiful it was mind numbing. Her heart fluttered. "My lord?" she said with such calm control she almost smiled to herself. It was quickly becoming his habit to seek her out whenever she found private sanctuary.

"Are you busy?"

She snatched up her pen to break the spell he'd so easily woven over her. He walked toward her, and she didn't dare look at him, for she knew those penetrating blue eyes were focused on her. The pen snapped in her fingers and she set it down. She looked up to see if he heard the snap. He did. He smiled; she blushed. "No, I was finishing my correspondences."

He clapped his hands together and then rubbed them together greedily. "Then we can begin our lessons."

Lessons? The first lesson she needed was one instructing her on how not to fall in love with this man. She had no idea what kinds of lessons he was referencing, but the ones that came to her mind were scandalously wicked. She teased, "Are we to conjugate French verbs, then?"

"Nothing so tedious. Something far more pleasing." He gave her a devilish wink and held out his hand. "Come with me."

"Where are we going?" She placed her hand hesitantly inside his, marveling at its warmth and strength.

"It's a surprise."

His so-sure-of-himself smile had her pulling her hand back. To be alone with him would be a colossal mistake. She didn't even know where he was taking her. Perhaps to one of the vacant rooms upstairs? She grew warm. What was the matter with her? Where did all these wanton thoughts come from?

"Do you trust me, Abigail?"

She did. More than she ever trusted anyone. Without reserve, she placed her hand back into his. He smiled, and with a gentle pull, led her from the room. They traversed the hall and continued up the stairs, his boots echoing over each wooden step, the sound vibrating up her frame with every footfall. *Oh good heavens, what am I doing*? Where was he taking her, to her room to ravage her? Nonsense, she wasn't thinking clearly, but his silence, along with his crooked smile, had her imagining him holding her in his arms. He was naked.

"Please cease your fidgeting, Abigail. I'm not going to ravage you in one of the rooms up here."

Devil take it! How did he always seem to know the direction of her thoughts. It was unsettling as well as embarrassing. Before she could come up with a response, he said, "After all, we are under my grandmother's roof."

He gave her his flirtatious wink again.

She gave him a stressed laugh. "The thought never entered my mind, my lord." She kept her gaze firmly ahead.

"Are you sure?" he whispered in her ear as he turned down a hall lined with ancestral pictures. Windows flanked the other wall, casting light upon the Waterford ancestors. "This is my grandfather." So he was giving her a history lesson.

Abigail stood back to admire the entire portrait, when her back hit the opposite wall, she stopped. The picture was mammoth. The late earl clearly felt himself important to warrant a picture of himself of such magnitude, a portrait that dwarfed the rest.

"This was one of the ways he made sure his legacy—or at the very least—his image, carried on."

Abigail studied the painting encased in a gold etched frame. "Is this a fair rendering of him?" she asked, wondering if the man in the portrait was as domineering and powerful as he appeared.

"Yes. He was as fierce as he looks." Jackson stepped next to her to look at the portrait from the same perspective.

"Not to offend, my lord, but he is near to snarling." She snickered at her observation and Jackson laughed.

"Ornery as ever. He wanted the portrait done quickly, but he hated sitting for it. My grandfather was never one for patience."

She continued her perusal of the late earl. He was depicted in the prime of his life, not a hint of gray touched the canvas. His hands were militantly behind his back as he stood tall, and his snarling expression only served to highlight his aristocratic features. He looked formidable and every inch the proud man she heard about. "Aside from the obvious personality traits you share with him, I don't see a resemblance in you. I assume you take after your mother's side of the family?" He cast her a sideways smile at her teasing comment.

"Not really," he answered, pulling her further down the corridor to show her a picture of his mother. The woman's smile practically lit up the hall. She was beautiful, and kindness shimmered in her eyes.

"I'd say you're wrong, my lord. You seem to share her generous nature." She thought she heard him grunt in response as she moved over to study another portrait, this one a portrayal of Jackson's father. Chills danced airily on her skin when she looked into a pair of eyes similar to her own, the brown orbs ringed in gold. She didn't know anyone else who shared the unique trait.

"You and my father have similar eyes," Jackson noted as he lovingly traced a finger along the frame.

"Possibly the reason your grandmother fainted at my appearance. She misses her son a great deal. We've talked about your father on many occasions. It must be hard for you to have never known him."

"No harder than it is for you, I imagine."

She pondered that. "I don't know, my lord. I do assume my father is alive somewhere." Here insinuation was clear: whereas his father was not, so he hadn't even a glimmer of a chance to build upon a relationship.

"Do you have any clue as to his identity?"

"None." She shrugged and ambled over to another section of the family tree.

"Someday I'm going to have to have a talk with your mother."

"Trust me. I've tried, bidding her to tell me of him until I was blue in the face. She claims not to know his identity." Although Abigail in no way believed such nonsense, there seemed very little she could do to get her mother to give her that vital piece of information.

"Hmm."

"This is lovely, Jackson. Thank you for showing me. It's nice to be able to put faces to the names. Your grandmother speaks highly of your mother. When is she to return?"

He shrugged as he stared at the portrait of his mother. "When she's had her fill of ancient history, I presume."

"In that case, she may never return." She thought of her own future trip to Egypt, knowing it would take her a lifetime to get her fill. He gave her a worried glance and she smiled. "I'm teasing, my lord. I can tell you miss her."

He smiled. "Indeed. My mother has a calming demeanor. I think the two of you will get along splendidly."

A lovely thought. Abigail walked over to look up at the young woman with flowing auburn tresses. She found it unique that her hair wasn't pulled up but left in wild disarray about her shoulders. "Your mother's very pretty."

"Yes, she is," he agreed.

"Can I ask you a favor?" She spotted a miniature on the wall and went to look at it. It was of Jackson as a boy of about ten. He was adorable: golden waves cropped short above his shoulders, his blue eyes twinkling. He stood proudly with his little legs showing beneath his short pants. The family dog sat on its hindquarters at his feet looking up at him in adoration.

"Of course. What is it you wish?"

She was suddenly nervous. But she realized with the ball tomorrow night, he remained her only hope. "I would like you to dance with me."

"Now?" he asked, his eyes watching her with staggering intensity.

"If you wouldn't mind. I'm to attend a ball tomorrow, and to be perfectly honest, I've never had a man as a partner before."

"I would be honored to be your first." Abigail got the impression he wasn't referring to dancing and felt herself blush to her roots at her sinful thoughts.

He laughed, grabbing her hand. "Come with me. The music room is around the corner."

Abigail laughed nervously, allowing him to tug her down the hall at breakneck speed. "Why are we hurrying?"

He gave her a smile, slowing his gait. "I wouldn't want you to change your mind."

"I'm hardly in a position to do so. I really want to make your grandmother proud of me." Although, as his grandmother's companion, she'd likely be sitting beside the dowager all evening, she also knew her employer was persistent about getting her way, and in all probability, she'd insist Abigail dance.

"I believe you already have. I spoke with her earlier, and she is excited about your first foray into the social whirl."

"I noticed." She tried to remain calm, but nervousness assailed her. She really wanted to meet the dowager's expectations. "That is why I want to do all I can to assure I have everything right."

"I'm touched you care so much for my grandmother. It seems my grandfather finally did something right."

She peered up at him in question.

"He brought you to us."

She couldn't speak. That had to be the sweetest thing she ever heard. He led her across the smooth expanse of wood floor to the center of the music room, which had wainscoting along all four walls. The walls were pale red in color with painted gold pictures depicting various instruments in the center of the squares. A black grand piano was by a set of French doors that led to a small stone terrace.

"I hope you don't mind the lack of music," he said.

"Perhaps you could sing a tune?" Abigail laughed when his features scrunched up in distaste.

"I think we'll just have to improvise. My singing voice is abysmal at best."

"Mine as well." She gave a dainty shrug, feeling awkward with the entire situation. She gave him a shaky smile, all the while ignoring the little voice inside her head screaming, *"Danger! Call off the lessons before they even begin!"*

He pulled her into his strong arms. His scent assailed her senses. Her stomach somersaulted as she fought for a pose of self-assurance.

"Does my nearness affect you, my sweet?"

Yes, it does, blast you. She backed up to the appropriate position for the waltz. "Not anymore than my nearness affects you, my lord." *Two can play this game.* In truth, she loved taunting him as much as he did her.

"In that case, your lessons should prove interesting. You know, Abigail…" He began to move her gracefully around the room, leading her effortlessly into the steps of the waltz along the smooth expanse of the gleaming wood floor. "I have been told I have many other gratifying skills. Someday I will school you in other private matters as well."

It wasn't a question, more of a promise, and Abigail's blood heated at the thought of some very intimate and pleasurable lessons. Her body quivered at the feel of his hand on the small of her back, but she wisely decided not to respond. She was playing with fire after all, and she had no desire to come out of this scorched.

As he continued to dance her around the room, she tried to relax, a nearly impossible task when he seemed intent on making their bodies touch on various turns. But this was a dream come true, a mere moment in time she planned to keep with her forever. For right now, she was dancing with the man she *could* love.

"You move like an angel." They continued to move about the room, both oblivious to their audience.

***

The Dowager Countess of Waterford stood near the double doors watching her strong grandson lead Abigail around the music room.

Tomorrow, Abigail would attend her first ball, and regardless of the older woman's period of mourning, the dowager planned to enjoy every second of this momentous occasion.

She watched as they slowed, their gazes locked, and then with a smile, she turned and made her way down the portrait gallery, stopping in front of the late earl, her William. Her husband's image towered over her, and she placed her hands on her hips as she glared. "I'm having a difficult time accepting all you have done. Nevertheless, if Jackson ends up with Abigail, I will be grateful a happy ending has come from your mess."

She turned away from her husband's arrogant pose. Perhaps, as the years passed, her husband realized what a mistake he had made and knew he had to right the wrong he had created. She found she couldn't hate him, because, unfortunately, she understood why her husband acted as he had. No one knew the old earl better than she.

Jackson and Abigail made a lovely couple, she thought, and it wasn't going to take much effort on her part to bring those two together. She could see caring in their eyes when they looked at each other. If her husband were alive, he'd be crowing about this turn of events.

Although she was thrilled with what she witnessed, she knew the truth would have to be told, but only the Lord knew what would happen in the aftermath of such news. She really wished she had some evidence to back up her beliefs. She knew her son had been completely devoted to his wife, which meant her suspicions were correct. There was no other logical explanation.

She'd certainly do whatever she could to protect them from the nightmare her husband set in motion.

***

Abigail sat in her room looking out the window at Park Lane below. Rain danced down the windowpanes and trailed across the glass. Her mind swam with images of Jackson leading her around in a waltz. The connection between them was extraordinary but also terrifying. Worst of all was the fact that the connection left her with an unending sense of false hope, for she now wished more than ever that the earl was hers.

He almost kissed her in the music room, but they were interrupted when his Herculean footman arrived and called him away. She noticed his reluctance to leave her, and it took all her will not to grab him and beg him to stay, to make him finish his descent upon her lips. In the end, sound reasoning made an appearance in her head, however, and she thanked him for the dance instruction before hastily excusing herself.

She rested her head against the cool window and stared off into space as thoughts of what could never be made her want to weep in angry despair.

Why didn't her mother marry her father? Who was he? Was he a member of the privileged class? That would certainly explain her mother's silence on the matter. Abigail often thought of the father she never knew. She pictured him warm and kind, like a true father should be. He'd make sure his daughter married the man of her dreams. He would make sure Abigail had Jackson for her own. A tear slid down her cheek.

How different her life could have been if she was born within the bonds of matrimony.

One can always dream. She sighed, wondering if Jackson would be attending the ball tomorrow. Most likely not, or he would have mentioned it earlier, but when she pictured herself at a ball, she saw herself on Jackson's arm. These pining thoughts couldn't be helped.

She didn't know how long she would keep her position as Lady Waterford's companion, but the thought of leaving and never seeing Jackson hurt her as much as the thought of him marrying another, which was an honor bound eventuality. "An heir and a spare," seemed a commonly used phrase in high society, where titles were coveted and bloodlines were cemented for future generations.

She gave up her vigilance on melancholy and went over to pull a piece of vellum out of her drawer. She'd pen a letter to her mother and tell her about her first official step out into grand society.

CHAPTER SEVEN

I'm not going to be sick. I'm not going to be sick. I can do this. I have to do this for the dowager. More importantly, I have to do this for me.

How many times in her youth did she envision dancing in the arms of an attractive male while circling the highly polished dance floor amongst an array of glittering gowns and glowing candles? Too many times really. Her stomach lurched and her fingers trembled. "I'm not going to be sick." Abigail repeated these words over and over during the hour and a half it took Sophie to ready her for the grand event, but nevertheless, her stomach twisted from the worst case of nerves she'd ever experienced. It felt like she was holding precariously to a cliff waiting for the ground to give way beneath her.

"You look stunning, miss." Sophie's face lit with excitement while Abigail was having a hard time feeling anything but dread.

Abigail gave her a shaky smile. "I appreciate all your help. I couldn't have achieved such artistry with my hair. Thank you, Sophie." Abigail moved her head in the mirror, to view the crystal pins strategically placed, the light reflecting off them like diamonds. It really was a masterful creation.

"Always at your service, miss." Her maid curtsied. "You better hurry along now."

Abigail gave her a firm nod and headed gracefully toward the stairway. *I can do this.*

Head held high, she tried to pretend her hands weren't shaking like the Countess of Glausbury's pet poodle. She held on to the banister and made her descent.

The dowager, dressed in a gauzy black ensemble and looking elegant and refined, fitting for her station, awaited her at the bottom of the staircase. Her face lit up in open delight as she gazed from Abigail's slippered feet, along the smooth flowing lines of her copper gown, and up to the crystal gems and copper satin decorating her chestnut tresses. Abigail had to admit, she'd never felt this beautiful, but when the dowager's eyes filled with tears, she rushed down the last few steps and took the woman's hands in hers.

"It's beautiful, and I love it. Thank you, my lady." Abigail had thought she should wear black, because the house was in mourning, but the dowager insisted that, since she had never met the earl, it was best if at least one of them could enjoy wearing colors. The copper, not overly bright or too light-colored, suited Abigail perfectly.

The dowager freed her hands to fish a handkerchief out of the reticule around her wrist and dabbed at her eyes. "It is even lovelier than I imagined. You, my dear, are breathtaking." Tears continued to stream down her wrinkled cheeks. "How I wish your mother could see you." She daintily blew her nose and stuffed the cloth back in her pouch. "I'm turning into a virtual watering pot lately."

"Quite all right, my lady. I'm feeling a bit emotional myself." Surely an understatement, but she had no desire to upset the dowager further.

"I understand." The dowager linked her arm with hers and led them toward the foyer. "I remember my first ball like it was yesterday." She looked sideways at Abigail. "Yes, I said yesterday. I have an excellent memory. Anyway, I remember being scared witless, but don't you worry. I will be by your side. If you feel overwhelmed by the atmosphere, you let me know. Try not to let hurtful, ill-mannered people spoil this night for you. People of my acquaintance can be either kind or vicious, the path they take influenced by many factors. Your birth will affect some ignorant people, but the determining factor is how well you comport yourself. If you carry yourself with the ease and dignity you do here, then I daresay we will be able to get you a marriage proposal as well." When she stopped her words, Abigail almost sighed her relief—the dowager was indeed scaring her to death. And now she spoke of marriage, a concept Abigail hadn't really given much consideration until Jackson entered her life. "You are a lovely, intelligent woman. Any man would be honored to have you for his wife. And regardless what some of those empty-headed fools say, you'll always have a place with me."

If Abigail wasn't nervous before, she now felt faint. She knew the dowager was only trying to guide her on the right path, and she was grateful she had come to mean so much to the woman for the feeling was mutual. And even though Abigail assumed some rumors about her past might circulate, she still didn't know if she was ready to handle such belittling. One can never be sufficiently prepared to have an entire ballroom criticize one's very existence. Her nerves were getting the better of her. A buzzing sound filled her head. "I think I need to sit for a moment."

"Yes, of course, dear. I'm sorry. I hope I didn't upset you?"

"No, it wasn't you." Abigail tried to smile but failed.

"Don't fret. As I've said, I've done this before, and so I do have some idea as to your emotional state. Now take some steady breaths."

Abigail wanted to point out that, although Lady Waterford claimed to understand her predicament, she couldn't possibly understand what it was like to be illegitimate. But to voice this would upset the kind-hearted dowager, which she didn't want to do. Abigail suffered distress enough for both of them.

"Grandmother."

Saints be praised! The Earl of Waterford is here? Just when Abigail thought things couldn't get worse, the forbidden man of her dreams sailed through the door to knock her even further off kilter.

"Ready?" Jackson asked her, as if he would be joining them this evening. She almost groaned her complaint. How could she act composed and unfettered when the object of her desire was joining them? He looked exceptional in his elegant black attire with white cravat. His blond locks, which were slicked back tonight, had a devastating effect on her already overwrought nerves, his poised grace an added reminder of his social standing and her own lack of pedigree.

"I need to fetch my wrap. Jackson, please tell Abigail she has nothing to fear." With a flash of black skirts, the dowager disappeared down the hall, leaving Abigail alone with a rapid beating heart and a man who was giving her a smoldering smile. The air between them felt charged with electrical currents. Time seemed to still as their eyes met.

"You're nervous," he said, boldly sweeping his gaze over her, pausing at the gentle swells of her breasts that peeked over her fitted, and in Abigail's opinion, constricting bodice.

She nodded in the affirmative. "I didn't know you were joining us, my lord."

"Grandmother thought my presence would be beneficial."

"Truly?" she asked to be difficult. She knew having an earl at her side would only be to her advantage, but she couldn't help teasing him. Having him near did indeed bolster her confidence, however, regardless of the other, less welcome effects he also had upon her.

He laughed. "You know, some women actually welcome my company."

She was sure countless women would go out of their way for this man, but teasingly, she asked, "Would they?"

He laughed harder. "Indeed." When he gained control of his mirth, he held out his hand to help her stand. "Come, look in the mirror." He positioned her in front of him as he made her face the mirror in the hall. "What do you see?"

A gorgeous man with eyes that hypnotize, whose breadth surpasses the mirror's frame, whose scent debilitates my senses, whose voice sends shivers of desire down my spine. Bother. How she would have loved to lean back into his chest, to take in his heat, to feel his strength.

"Abigail?"

"Yes, Jackson?" She stared into his eyes through the mirror. He smiled at her use of his Christian name. This was the first time she had used it, at least to his face.

"I asked you to describe what you see." His hand brushed the nape of her neck and prickles of pleasure almost had her moaning in response.

"Yes. Right. What I see." She looked back into the mirror at him. "I see a man who, despite his domineering and controlling demeanor, is the sweetest, gentlest, most understanding man I've ever met."

She smiled when she saw him blush and fidget uncomfortably behind her. It seemed fair to know she wasn't the only one affected by their encounters. He cleared his throat, causing her smile to widen. Did she render him speechless? An uplifting thought, that she had the power to affect him as much as he affected her.

He leaned down toward her neck. "Thank you," he whispered in her ear, before straightening. "All right, now try again. Concentrate on yourself this time."

Evidently, this madness wouldn't stop until she responded how he wished. She huffed and looked at her reflection. "I see a woman trying to be something she's not. I see a fraud." Her eyes began to fill with tears, but she rapidly blinked them back.

"Would you like to know what I see?" His strong hands rested on her shoulders, and she felt like she was going to melt into a puddle at his feet. She couldn't speak. She just stared into his eyes reflected in the mirror and gave him a tiny nod.

"I see a beautiful woman who, despite life's unfairness, has picked herself up and made something of herself."

"I'm only a companion, Jackson, not the Prime Minister. I have no idea of my lineage."

He laughed. "You don't even realize how special you are. You are a strong, courageous woman. I feel lucky knowing you." His warm bourbon-scented breath caressed her cheek.

Special? He thought her special. Heat crept into her face. "Well, thank you for that. I do feel a bit better."

"If the mirror isn't working, I can always distract you a different way." His strong fingers squeezed her shoulders as he turned her toward him. "You don't have to be apprehensive. I promise you that I won't leave your side."

The sincerity in his words caused her to lean toward him in comfort. She couldn't help but wonder how long he'd stay by her side when the snide comments about her tainted blood circulated within his circle as common knowledge. But he smelled so good, too good, earthy, and manly with a hint of musky cologne. He leaned down to brush his lips against hers; she lifted herself up on her toes, welcoming the kiss. But before his lips touched hers, a voice came from down the hall.

"All right, my dears, I'm ready." The dowager came toward them and they quickly pulled apart from their near embrace.

Fastening on her pelisse with trembling fingers, Abigail gave Lady Waterford a smile, refusing to allow herself to be disappointed at her untimely arrival. The Earl of Waterford had almost kissed her, again.

"Are you going to be all right?" He whispered the question in her ear, sending more heated thoughts through her mind and more tingles through her body.

"With you by my side, I cannot possibly fail." She smiled and he winked at her.

"That's my brave girl. Come on then. Although it may be fashionable, my grandmother hates to be late." She felt bereft as he walked away from her to take his grandmother's arm.

His grandmother swatted his arm away. "Tend to Abigail. She's the one who needs our support."

"Of course, Grandmother." He looked back at Abigail as the dowager bustled out of the house.

He held out his arm. "I shall give you all the support you need, my sweet." Abigail nearly swallowed her tongue at his husky tone.

"Thank you, my lord."

"There is no need for gratitude. My motives are more selfish than you realize."

Her brow raised in confusion as she wondered what in the world he was talking about. "How so?"

He shrugged. "It seems second nature to support the woman you wish to wed." With those momentous words, he laughed at her speechlessness and led her to the carriage.

***

Was he serious? The Earl of Waterford was considering marriage to her? In what dream world was she living? Wherever it was, Abigail wished to never awake. She hardly spoke a word in the carriage, her mind far too busy playing back the events that had occurred in the house. Lady Waterford kept casting her reassuring smiles with every mile they traveled, but Abby felt more discomfited than she had perhaps in her life.

Abigail couldn't fathom why an earl would wish to pursue her, and not just any earl, but the devastatingly handsome Earl of Waterford, who had a brief moment ago claimed a large portion of her heart.

No one had ever made her feel so beautiful and yet independent and competent at the same time. With him by her side, she felt like there wasn't anything she couldn't do. She dared to look at him sitting across from them, his face as stoic as if he hadn't just made a stunning pronouncement to her. But as she watched him, she detected a smile lurking beneath his stoic visage. *He is glad he shocked me, the beast.* Well, his statement certainly took her mind off the ball, that is, until she heard the dowager announce,

"Here we are." Lady Waterford peered out the window at the line of vehicles.

Abigail's nerves were now in a frenzy again. She looked out at the overwhelming sea of people as they slowly shuffled their way toward the Duke and Duchess of Bayberry's London manor, a large rectangular structure with gas lanterns lighting both sides of the expansive stone entranceway.

Although etiquette dictated that the earl should escort his grandmother, the dowager immediately shooed him toward Abigail and hustled up the steps on her own.

Abigail tried to ignore all the curious stares and quiet whispers about who she was as she tightened her grip on Jackson's arm and he led her up the steps. They greeted their hosts at the top of the stairway, and then they proceeded up the wide wooden staircase inside that led to the ballroom.

The room was spectacular, just as Clarissa had described such places, but the experience was even better because she was on Jackson's arm. It felt right having him beside her, like she could take on the world if necessary. His presence filled her with newfound strength, and yes, the word he had used to describe her earlier: courage. With the poise befitting a queen, she walked into the spacious room. Dozens of white pillars lined the length of the room, each topped with an extravagant display of colorful blooms, their flowery scent along with the various colognes perfumed the intoxicating air. She listened to the constant din of voices and couldn't help but smile: she, Abigail Gibbons, was at a real life ball. The sheer tumult of the atmosphere made her euphoric, as if she had walked into a festive fairyland with her handsome prince.

"I see you like what is before you," Jackson commented to her as they followed his grandmother to one of the cozy sitting areas.

"It's amazing." Abigail took in their surroundings with awe.

"You're amazing."

She blushed at the compliment. "You better watch your charming tongue, my lord, or I may begin to believe you are seriously courting me," she teased, not being able to stop herself from seeking reassurance about the sincerity of his admission that this was the beginning of a courtship.

He stopped, and she paused to look at him. "I've never been more serious in my life." He held her gaze for a breathless few seconds before leading her over to stand beside the dowager and some of the other aging matrons.

After several greetings and introductions, Jackson excused himself to fetch them some beverages. Abigail was thankful to sit and sort through her thoughts as the dowager socialized with her friends. *The Earl of Waterford is seriously courting me? How can this be?*

She didn't get far into her contemplation when Lady Waterford dismissed herself from the circle and came over to sit beside her. "What do you think?"

"It's magnificent and somewhat overwhelming." She watched a group of elegantly dressed couples dance the reel.

"You'll get used to it." The dowager nodded at some passers-by. "As I predicted, you are turning the gentlemen's heads." The woman puffed up with pride and Abigail smiled.

She looked around to find that her employer's words rang true. Men were indeed looking at her, and some even passed by numerous times to stare and nod in her direction, but she looked away.

"You shall dance," the dowager announced.

"Dance?" Abigail had hoped this wouldn't happen. Although she would never forget the magic of dancing with Jackson yesterday, she hadn't really planned to do any dancing tonight. She was here to serve as a companion, not to have her first debut for heaven's sake.

"Well of course, dear. I daresay there are many entertainments to be had at a ball, dancing is most essential. You do know how to dance?"

"Yes, but... That is, I've never done so in a public arena."

"No worries. Jackson is an excellent dancer."

She was well aware of the earl's talent on the dance floor. She was beginning to see that the man had many talents, including his unerring ability to understand her situation and make her feel more comfortable. Even if his intentions toward her were false or short-lived, she'd never forget his support this night.

She saw the object of her affection coming toward her and leaped up in excitement to find her friend Clarissa on his arm.

"Look who I found." He gave her a warm smile and she fought back the desire to throw herself into his arms and hug him for his thoughtfulness. He obviously knew Clarissa's presence would put her more at ease. Her heart expanded with warm feelings she wasn't yet ready to inspect.

"Thank you, my lord." She gave him a wide smile to show him how much his gesture meant. He winked in understanding and then departed as she introduced her friend to Lady Waterford. Clarissa was gracious to the older woman, and they immediately struck up a conversation about the people they knew in common.

An hour later, Abigail was having the time of her life. Everyone she met was kind, and she didn't notice a single critical eye. As the orchestra struck up the first waltz of the evening, Abigail found, as Clarissa also found, she suddenly had her own group of admirers. The men were witty and the conversations were kept light, mostly comments about the weather and such, but it was heady to have so much attention. She was sure a large portion of this attention was due to the fact that Clarissa was introducing her as a friend, leaving out her employment status with Lady Waterford, a deception Abigail was more than happy to go along with.

"Excuse me." Jackson's gruff voice could be heard among the crowd of males, and she immediately turned in the direction of his voice. He looked perturbed, but as he drew closer, he smiled at her before sweeping her an elegant bow. "I believe this dance is mine."

Abigail felt her nervousness grow, but absent the ache in her stomach from previously. No, this pain was that of longing, the desire to be near him.

"You're still nervous?" he asked, finding them a position on the dance floor and placing his hands in the appropriate positions.

"Not about the ball."

"Are you implying…" He pulled her closer than propriety dictated, murmuring, "Are you implying that I make you nervous?"

"You know you do." She pulled back slightly. He grinned and then led her effortlessly into the waltz. She spun, she laughed, and she prayed the dance would never end. With the music playing and his comforting arms around her, she was able to shut off the blur of the world around her and concentrate solely on him, on this man who took her breath away with a seductive glance, who appeared to accept her for who and what she was.

Jackson wanted to protect her from censure. He cared about her. Her heart expanded with feelings for him. It didn't matter if they were butting heads over his behavior or staring at each other with longing in their eyes. She realized for the first time in her life that she felt whole. She, Abigail Marie Gibbons, had fallen for the Earl of Waterford. *Dear Lord, what is wrong with me?* Where was her well-developed sense of self-preservation when she needed it most? Oh, why did the earl have to be the man for her?

If he was seriously courting her, and she believed he was, could she really marry an earl? She did not truly wonder because she thought she wasn't deserving of him, but society would certainly view their marriage with distaste. *And what of Jackson and his set? How will he feel when the people who claim to be his friends shun him, as they certainly would, because he married me?* She'd seen it happen repeatedly throughout her life. If a person chose to befriend her, that person could say farewell to a goodly number of the population, and that fact kept people away from her. In truth, no one was willing to accept the consequences that came with an association with her, except for Clarissa. And now the dowager. *And Saints be praised, now Jackson.*

Just dancing with her could wreck the image he held in high esteem. It was clear in his countenance that he enjoyed his life and this atmosphere. He appeared to be in his element. She couldn't take this away from him; she wouldn't. She cared about him too much to hurt him that way.

What a sad thought. She could never marry the Earl of Waterford.

She had been walking away to protect people her entire life. Clarissa was the only one to come back to her. She pushed those sad thoughts from her mind and concentrated on the moment. She didn't have many such moments in her life, those to keep with her all her day, and she absolutely wanted to enjoy this one.

The dance was magical and she hoped it would never end. At that thought, the music slipped away and Jackson led her back to his grandmother. *Drat!*

"I think I'll go to the ladies retiring room for a moment," Abigail informed the dowager upon her return. She needed a moment to compose herself. Jackson's sweet attendance was addling her brain.

"I'll show you the way," he said, and he offered her that well-muscled arm of his again. She happily took it.

At the doors of the retiring room, Abigail released him. "I only need a moment."

He leaned casually against the flower-print wallpaper. "Take your time, my sweet."

She knew she looked flustered by his endearment, and when she heard him laugh, she cast him a saucy smile and entered the room. *The bounder is trying to rattle me.* She entered a room adorned with many full-length mirrors. A circular velvet sofa monopolized the center of the room and she walked around it to go behind the mirrored partition to the water closets.

As she made rights with her clothing, she heard a gaggle of females enter.

"Can you believe she is Lady Waterford's companion? The old woman must truly be off her rocker to hire someone of such base origins."

Abigail felt a pain in her chest start to ache.

"Most likely it's dementia from her advanced years," another woman responded.

A third voice entered into the fray. "What is the earl's excuse?" The woman's voice was filled with obvious disdain, and Abigail felt herself shrink.

"Oh come now, Cynthia. I'm sure the earl is only trying to appease his grandmother. His grandfather did pass away recently."

"Well, it's unseemly. Besides, they are supposed to be in mourning."

Abigail remained hidden, although at one point she wanted to rush out and ask them why they thought themselves above others, but she knew the answer: pedigree, pure and simple. Lineage was all that mattered to these well-dressed butter heads. She also would have loved to have seen their shocked faces at her sudden appearance, but she wasn't ready for their scornful stares and hateful words. She had heard enough. Clearly, no matter what she did, or how she behaved, or whom she married, she would never belong anywhere. Not in the ballroom nor the schoolroom. A heavy weight settled in her chest to replace the ache.

"At this point, it's likely half-mourning, but it still seems wrong," she heard one of them say.

"Appalling," spat another as they left the room. Abigail heard the door close behind them and the soft drone of music.

Once the disparaging women left, she departed to find Jackson.

***

Jackson leaned against the wall, his booted feet casually crossed at the ankle. He nodded and gave the occasional greeting to those who passed him, his thoughts not on the ball but the woman in the room behind him. Abigail thought him sweet, gentle, and understanding; no one had ever viewed him in this manner. The compliments roared through his brain riding a constant wave of euphoria. He couldn't help being touched by her kind words, which only further proved his initial thoughts on the matter of marriage. Abigail Gibbons was definitely the lady for him.

He remembered how often his grandfather stressed the importance for a man to beget "an heir and a spare" while young. Of course, Jackson knew marriage was an eventuality. He just never really thought much about the selection process until he met Abigail, a temptress who conquered his thoughts everyday and hardened his cock every night. He never thought to find a woman who would monopolize his mind so completely, never so much as imagined a woman like Abigail. She challenged him with her words, and in turn, made him a better man for it. Thoughts of Abigail put a spring in his step and a smile on his face. In fact, he had to acknowledge that the humdrum that was once his life changed the moment they met.

"Ladies." He nodded at a group of women entering the retiring room.

He hoped Abigail was enjoying her first ball. As for himself, he was having the most splendid time. It made him feel magnificent to have an intelligent and caring woman on his arm. She took his breath away, and she obviously had the same effect on a good share of the other gentlemen in the room as well. He was inclined to notice. His heart raced with exhilarating excitement whenever she came near, and so he could not exactly blame them. He couldn't explain the depth of those sensations, however, and he never wanted these feelings to end.

He watched the Mandelin sisters, who had previously entered the room as he stood there, hurry away, hiding their faces behind their fans' and whispering. He couldn't help noticing the condescension in their eyes as they each glared at him in turn and then pointedly ignored him.

Society can be so cantankerous. He wasn't sure what prompted their nasty looks, but when he overheard two men making their way down the hall, he picked-up on the words "bastard" and "unfit company." He wasn't sure they were referring to Abigail, but he would have bet all he had they were. *What is wrong with people?* Didn't they realize Abigail was innocent of any wrongdoing? He felt his temper spike, and he was about to go over and give the so-called gentlemen a piece of his mind when his life's purpose sashayed out of the retiring room looking stunning. Abigail. The men were quickly no longer even a memory. He noted his abrupt change in demeanor and told himself to tread slowly with her. He certainly didn't want to frighten her off with his desire to be near her. But then he forgave himself, for he couldn't help wanting to caress her, taste her, and make love to her until her toes curled. The effect was not so much one he allowed as one he could not hold off with all his willpower.

As she approached, the first things he noticed were her stiff posture and the frown etched on her lovely face. He couldn't prevent his anger. He saw red, for he knew what must have transpired within the retiring room now. *How dare these pompous people think themselves above Abigail?* But some part of him also understood their pretension, their arrogance. He'd been blessedly born to the same life of privilege and prestige, and he had heard this nonsense all his life. Yet he saw Abigail in a completely different light. He saw a woman striving for acceptance in a world that deemed her unfit. *It isn't fair, damn it!* Abigail didn't deserve such harsh treatment. To hide his anger, he gave her a lazy smile. She tentatively took his arm. *What happened to the carefree woman who entered the ladies retiring room a short while ago?* He wanted to ask, but he didn't for he knew the answer. The Mandelin sisters. Clearly those uppity ladies said something to hurt Abigail.

"Exactly as I expected," Abigail exclaimed airily. As much as she tried to hide it, he could see the anger vibrating within her petite frame.

"What did those harpies say to upset you?" The silence stretched and he noticed how she trembled. Wisely he took her back across the ballroom and out onto a stone balcony, vacant due to the chill in the air.

She released his arm and walked to the balustrade. As she stared off into the distance at the nearby homesteads, he walked up behind her, fighting the urge to pull her back against him for comfort. Instead, he settled for being next to her and placed his hand on top of hers. "Do you want to talk about it?"

"Talk about what, my lord? Shall we discuss the vileness of people who believe themselves above me?" she asked, and she turned away as red heat seeped into her beautiful features. "Or shall we discuss the fact that I will never belong?" She turned toward him again with fiery eyes. "Perhaps you'd like to discuss the social hierarchy and how people like me have no place in it? We could always discuss how people like you..." She poked her finger into his chest. "Cannot marry someone like me? Or how my hopes and dreams for any kind of future are pointless!" She went to poke him again, but she must have realized she was attacking the wrong person because she stomped her foot in vexation, let out a frustrated sigh, and went back to staring off into the distance.

"Feel better?" He put his hand back atop of hers on the balustrade.

"Not yet," she admitted, looking down at his hand upon hers.

"You know it doesn't matter what they say."

"Doesn't it?" she asked, looking deep in his eyes.

"Not to me."

She threw her hands up in the air, dislodging his from their offer of comfort. "If you believe such nonsense, you're disillusioning yourself! These are your friends, my lord. How would you feel if they found out you were interested in courting me..."

"I am courting you," he interrupted. He'd be damned if she thought she could chase him off.

"Well you can't. I won't allow it. Just as I have to quit being your grandmother's companion. I will not allow my tainted blood to allow the two of you to become the subject of gossip and ridicule." She began pacing back and forth in front of him. He could not help but note that she looked incredibly fetching in the moonlight with her ire up.

"So you want to quit your position and run from my courtship because of some bloody puffed up fools who think themselves above God himself?" He grabbed her shoulders to prevent her from moving. "Look at me, Abigail." Her eyes met his. "You are not a quitter. I won't allow you to shrink from the world. I'm sorry if you have a tough time of it. I'm sorry those disdainful women said something to upset you. I'm even sorry for the circumstances of your birth. I'll tell you what I'm not sorry about. I'm not sorry for the attraction between us and I'm not sorry my grandmother hired you. The fact is, I'm grateful. You have made my grandmother the happiest I've seen her in years. You have made me feel..." He paused, having a difficult time putting his feelings into words. He tilted her chin up to make sure he had her complete attention before saying, "Special."

Tears filled her eyes, but as he had come to notice, his brave girl blinked them away. "I will not let you go now that I found you. I don't care what anyone says or how they react." He ran a finger down her cheek. "You are mine."

He brought his lips down upon the ones he craved. He felt her stiffen, and then her hands were fisting his black coat and pulling him closer. She slanted her head to allow him better access to her sweet mouth, and he took whatever she willingly gave. He plucked at her mouth with delicate kisses, sliding his tongue out to glide it across her bottom lip, nipping it with his teeth. To his utter astonishment, she repeated the motion. Her delectable tongue sliding across his lips caused him to grow hard at an alarming rate. *This innocent is a seductress*. He ignored his arousal, giving into his need to taste her. Just one taste, he told himself, and he'd pull his raging desire back under control.

His tongue slid into the warm recesses of her delectable mouth. Her hands were everywhere, moving across the expanse of his clad chest to circle around his neck and pull him even closer. He deemed this how a kiss was supposed to be, hot and passionate beyond his wildest dreams.

As their tongues danced together, he pressed his leg between her thighs, rubbing his leg against the soft mound of her woman's flesh. His control was slipping, and his erection was begging for an introduction as he moved his hips against hers. He moaned into her mouth. He wanted to lift her skirts and take her standing up against the balustrade, but he knew such a move would be beyond foolish. They moaned in unison, and she pulled back, dazed. Her fingers went to her kiss swollen lips in what he assumed was amazement. He was thoroughly amazed himself. The powerful feelings he had for her surpassed logical reason.

"I'm… I mean, that was…" she stammered, and he smiled at her loss of speech.

"Yes, it definitely was." He took her trembling hands in his. "You're perfect."

Decision made. He could not live without this woman. And there was no way he was going to let her slip away, even if she felt it for his own good. Without a qualm, he dropped down onto one knee in front of her, noticing a tiny tear making its way down her lovely face. "Marry me, Abigail. Make me the happiest man alive. I promise I'll treat you like a queen. I'll slay your dragons. I'll silence the ignorant. But I can't live without you. I promise I will make you happy. Say yes." He knew he sounded like he was begging, but he didn't care.

"But you don't love me."

"Who's to say I don't? What I feel is beyond description, defying my ability to put it into words at every turn. I do know one thing that is easy enough to find words for: I never want my time with you to end." It hurt him to know that the insults she had borne had made her feel unworthy of his attentions. "You make me feel invincible. You make me feel gentle and understanding, and trust me, I have never been known for these attributes before." She laughed. "Do you trust me to take care of you, Abigail?"

She nodded her head, yes, and he held out his hand to her. "Then trust me to make you happy." She seemed to hesitate for a painstaking second, but when she placed her hand in his, his heart soared and he swooped her up, spinning her around in a circle.

She laughed when her legs caught flight in the air. Excitement thundered through his veins. It was sheer delight to know he had found himself a wife, and this awareness that he had found his mate filled him with a wholeness he never realized existed, filled a lack he never recognized until it was no longer part of him. Abigail was, without a doubt, the woman for him. Indeed, he felt the luckiest man alive.

He slowed the spinning and she slid down his body to stand on her feet. "Thank you."

"For what?" he asked.

"For accepting me." She looked up at him adoringly.

He tucked her hand around his arm. "Let's go share our news."

She pulled back in alarm. "We can't, Jackson."

"What do you mean, we can't?"

"You don't understand. If you think associating with me earns you contemptuous comments and loathsome glares, think about how your peers will react if you marry a bastard."

"Stop it! Stop it this instant!" He hadn't meant to shout and felt terrible when she flinched. "When will you realize I don't care what anyone else thinks?"

"They know about my tainted blood. You didn't hear those ladies in the retiring room. If you marry me, doors now open to you will close."

He shrugged, trying to think of a way to convince her of his sincerity. "I still don't care. When I'm with you, nothing else matters. If they can't accept my choice of a bride, they can all go hang."

Abigail stared at the defiant and handsome man in front of her, who moments ago promised her a lifetime of happiness. The fight was leaving her. It was hard to defend her position when winning this argument meant giving up something she so desperately yearned for. He was her dream come true, and yet he really didn't understand the full scope of what would occur like, she did. Yes, she'd accept his proposal. She'd be a fool if she didn't. She wanted him as fiercely as he appeared to want her. She just didn't want to see him hurt. She knew how it felt being on the outside. *Oh Lord, please tell me I'm not making a mistake.* But how could something be wrong if it felt so utterly perfect, even in spite of the consequences?

"Come with me. Trust in me. I will make everything all right."

At present, she thought the man completely daft for even thinking he could somehow make others accept her, but with one look at his adorable, determined face, she was lost. When he was near, she felt invincible. After all, she was going to marry the Earl of Waterford. "You're sure you want to do this? I mean, we certainly don't have to make the announcement now."

"And give you a chance to back out?" He grabbed her hand. "Not on your life." He gave her a quick firm kiss. Unlike the bone-melting embrace they shared a few minutes before, this kiss was secure and reassuring. Perhaps he was right and there really wasn't anything they couldn't overcome, as long as they were together.

Gathering her courage, she gave him a wide smile and took his arm again. "Let's go shock these people into awareness."

"That's my little spitfire." He winked and led them into the glittering ballroom, stopping in the center of the dance floor among the swirling guests.

"What are you doing?" She tugged to pull her arm back, but he wouldn't allow her to escape.

"I'm making our announcement."

"Are you mad?" Already she found people watching them most curiously.

"What did *you* have in mind?" he asked.

"I thought we'd start with your grandmother and allow the news to circulate on its own."

"A fine plan," he admitted, "but there would be no attendant shock." Her eyes widened and he laughed. She knew why he was making this a public pronouncement, and it made her heart swell with love. This was the way he would show her that he wasn't ashamed of who or what she was, his way of showing the members of so-called polite society that he didn't care what they thought.

This is social suicide.

"Perhaps we should forgo the shock factor?" She had to try one last time to change his mind.

He looked down at her, a sly smile playing upon his perfectly shaped lips, his expression telling her he was going through with it no matter how much she protested.

"Ready?"

She gave him a shaky smile and nodded.

"Very good." He waited for the music to die down and then addressed the crowd. "Lords, Ladies, and Gentlemen, I would like a moment of your time." The throng went silent. Abigail's body quaked with nerves, but she held on tightly to Jackson's arm. "Miss Abigail Gibbons has consented to be my wife, and I…" He looked deep into her eyes for several mind-numbing seconds. "I have never been happier," he said, and her eyes misted with tears. He kissed her then, in front of everyone, amongst the gasps and barely contained shrieks, a slow and soft kiss that left her stunned, tingling, and longing for more.

All the guests were talking at once. There was no applause, only censure, whispered comments, and some louder than a whisper: "I can't believe it." "How could he?" and even, "But her bloodlines are beyond the pale." The murmurs could be heard from every corner of the spacious room, or at least it felt that way to her.

"What do you think, my dear, shockingly scandalous?" His brow was cocked up in evident amusement as he looked at her.

"Saints be praised, I believe we will be the talk of the town for months to come."

"Possibly even years."

"Undoubtedly." With an infectious smile, he kissed her again.

Suddenly he was pulled away from her and they looked into the heated gray eyes of Lady Waterford. "We are leaving, Jackson. Now." The dowager turned on her heel and marched toward the door.

Abigail's heart broke. She never thought the news would upset the dowager. She had believed Lady Waterford thought of her, if not as an equal, at least fondly.

"Seems we have raised my grandmother's ire."

"I'm sorry, Jackson."

He shrugged as they followed behind the silent, erect form of Lady Waterford. "Don't be. I'm certainly not."

CHAPTER EIGHT

"Grandmother..." Jackson tried to explain his behavior, but the dowager held up her hand to halt his speech.

"This can wait until we are home. I'm not ready to discuss it."

Abigail sat quietly next to the dowager in the black carriage, wishing she could disappear into the squabs, or at least extinguish the swinging lantern, the light from which distorted the occupants' features and made them look sinister. Or was that just her imagination? The dowager's lavender cologne could not cover the thick apprehension hanging in the air of the compartment. An uncomfortable silence filled the confined space as the vehicle rattled over the cobblestones down the lane toward Waterford House.

Abigail kept squeezing her hands restlessly on her lap, still in shock at what occurred. She was engaged to the Earl of Waterford. The thought rattled her brain, but so did the echoes of their condemners.

When he announced their betrothal in such a public manner, she'd been touched and proud of his motives. She knew he did it for her. He knew the outrage the crowd would spew forth. He was proving he didn't care what they thought, proving he cared for her so much that he was willing to share the snide comments she'd become accustomed to receiving. His brave gesture was the sweetest thing in the world, and she loved him with all she was. A life with Jackson had become the possible dream.

She paused in her reflection to look at Lady Waterford whose attention remained fixed out the window in contemplation. Sadly, Abigail's happiness would cause the dowager grief for this announcement would affect her socially as well.

Abigail thought the dowager was angered upon hearing the news, but on further examination, she realized the dowager wasn't mad at all, merely pensive. But the silence was unbearable. She wanted to apologize to the older woman but didn't know where to begin. Everything was happening too quickly. She never dreamed she'd attend her first ball, become engaged to Jackson, and set the room on its ear with their announcement all in the same evening. She wondered if Clarissa had been in the ballroom, but if not, she knew her friend would have had to have caught wind of the news by now.

Just because his grandmother didn't wish to speak did not mean Jackson had to remain mute, and that realization made her uneasy. *He is probably having second thoughts after witnessing the crowd's reaction.* She wouldn't be surprised if he called the whole thing off as soon as they returned home. She realized the two of them fit, be it wrong or right, they were meant to be, and so she fervently hoped not. She felt the rightness of them together with every fiber of her being.

Looking up at him in the dim light, she felt her tense muscles soften like butter. He'd been watching her the entire time. The look he sent her was predatory, definitely male. Thinking about their passionate kiss earlier, in combination with his steamy gaze now, sent blood rushing to her face. Did he know she thought of the kiss? He continued to stare and she stared back challengingly. He glanced at his grandmother and then swiftly back to her. Hungrily he licked his lips like a randy beast. Oh how she wanted to be the one to tame him. Her hands grew clammy, and while she had the courage, she too looked at the dowager to make sure her attention was elsewhere before boldly proceeding to drag her moist tongue against her lips in return. *Two can play this game.*

She noted that his face didn't redden in embarrassment, but instead, became rigid as if he was fighting to keep himself away from her. She smiled at the power she wielded over him, stifling a laugh when he shifted uncomfortably in his seat. His mouth tipped up in the corners with an insidious smile. She knew he was thinking wicked thoughts, and her body warmed to molten lava under his hooded gaze.

Then Abigail felt her face flush and knew she was likely beet red. She hoped the dim lighting hid this fact. She swallowed and quickly averted her eyes to stare safely out the window.

Never had she felt such relief at reaching her destination as she did when the expensive vehicle rolled to a stop in front of Waterford House.

Calmly and quietly, they all entered the house. Townen walked into the foyer to take their cloaks and various articles one felt obliged to carry when navigating London's social whirl.

"I'll see you both in my sitting room," Lady Waterford announced before disappearing down the hall.

"I think we're in trouble." Jackson winked as if they were two children in for a lecture because they pilfered cookies from the kitchen.

Abby smiled at his ability to make light of the situation, which she noticed was a habit of his. She was overjoyed he wasn't calling a halt to their nuptials. "An astute assumption, my lord."

He cast her a crooked grin. "I have my moments."

Yes, he certainly did. And every moment with him was like a slice of heaven.

"Will the two of you get in here," the dowager's voice echoed down the hall.

"Ready?"

He held out his hand and she clasped it tightly in hers. "No," she stated as they made their way into the dowager's private domain.

Abigail was surprised to see Lady Waterford already in her satin burgundy robe. She sat on a divan, patting the cushions on each side of her. *Wishing to separate us?*

Abigail hoped this wouldn't be difficult. She'd come to love the dowager dearly. Jackson appeared to be contemplating the release of her hand, finally he let her go, nodding at his grandmother with a spark of mischief in his eyes.

Abigail took a place on the dowager's right while Jackson sat on the other side. Once seated, Lady Waterford let out the long breath she was evidently holding.

"Much better." The dowager turned to smile at her, and Abigail felt her shoulders relax some. But she still trembled inside. The dowager took one of her hands and then turned to her grandson.

"What you did at the Bayberry's gathering this evening was deplorable."

"I know, Grandmother, but..."

The dowager waved his comment away. "Let me finish, boy."

"Yes, of course," he replied.

The dowager waited a moment before speaking again. "Your announcement this evening shocked everyone, including myself. The way you took over the ballroom floor was unforgivable. I will now have to pay a call to the Bayberry's tomorrow, if just to defend the actions of young love, but I daresay this gala will be all the buzz. Which I'm sure the lady of the house will appreciate..." She paused. "Now where was I?"

"The ball," Jackson answered, and he was rewarded with a scowl.

"Don't interrupt, dear. Not only have you made us temporary outcasts, but you have now thrown more undue attention onto my sweet Abigail. It will take years for me to fix all the ruffled feathers, and some, I'm afraid, will never understand the situation."

"I know, Grandmother. I'm sorry, but..." Jackson failed to get more out before the dowager spoke over him.

"Nevertheless," she bellowed with a smile, "I happen to know why you behaved as you did." She looked briefly at Abigail and then back to her grandson. "And I've never been prouder of you."

Abigail laughed when Jackson's eyes widened in confusion. The gorgeous man didn't have a clue why his grandmother was proud rather than outraged, but Abigail knew. The dowager was impressed by Jackson's fortitude to brave whatever high society had to dish out. He had made a stand, and he made it for Abigail, and so this really must be love. Jackson Sethos Ramesses Danvers loved her. And she loved him right back.

"I've watched you grow from a puny little boy..." The dowager grinned in a teasing manner. "Into the strong capable man you are today. I know your grandfather heaped many arrogant, opinionated words of wisdom upon you, and yet you've risen above your teachings to become a decent and honorable man. You thumbed your nose at society this evening, a daring, even a bold move, something my husband wouldn't have done for me or for anyone else." She turned to Abigail. "There wasn't anything more important to my William than his birthright. The earldom was his everything. No one understood this better than I. When the doctor informed him that I would not be able to have another child after Marshal was born, my husband was crushed. In time, he came to see that the family seat would survive. He had one son. One would have to be enough."

She swiveled back to Jackson. "Your grandfather loved your father completely. When he was taken from us, a part of your grandfather died too—the hopeful part." She paused. "Here I am blubbering on about an heir and the two of you are not yet married."

"You approve of my asking Abigail to marry me?"

"Indeed I do," said the dowager. "I think it's splendid the two of you have found something special in each other. It's as it should be."

Abigail held in her emotions. The dowager approved of their marriage, which seemed too much to hope for. *How is this happening?* Her life stretched out before her in a kaleidoscope of colors. Children tugging on her skirts with dirty hands while her glorious husband took them for rides on his back, and even the chaos it was said to be when one had a house full of children—it all sounded splendid. Suddenly, Abigail imagined a bevy of children; a big family would be a joy. She was going to have her happily-ever-after with the man she loved. Yes, she loved Jackson, for nothing else could define this giddy feeling of rapture.

"I want you to know that I love you both very much." She took Abigail's hand and placed it in Jackson's upon her lap. "Now that this is settled, I want you both to pack."

"Pack?" they said in unison.

The dowager laughed. "Yes, pack. We, my dears, are off to the country. One cannot drop such astonishing news and hang about for the backlash. I will smooth things as best I can later. For now, it's best we not stay. People can be vicious and I will not put Abigail through an ordeal, or you either, dear Jackson. Now, I will post the banns in all the papers tomorrow. Jackson will need to procure a special license before we depart. Unless you wish to have an extended engagement?" she asked Jackson, who adamantly shook his head no.

He appeared to be struck speechless by his grandmother's unerring support.

"As I expected." She stood and their hands fell away.

"I bid you both a good evening then." She turned back at the door, her focus on Abigail. "You'll love the Waterford Estate, my dear. There is a quaint church near the village that will be perfect for the ceremony." Abigail nodded her agreement. She didn't care where she married, as long as she could have Jackson.

When his grandmother departed, Jackson took Abby's arm and escorted her out of the room. She soon found herself ensconced in the study with him. Her eyes went immediately to the sofa where she had once lain in his arms.

"Do you believe that?" Jackson stood to walk over to a sideboard and poured himself a drink. He gestured with the bottle toward her, and she declined the spirits.

"She's an intuitive woman," replied Abigail. All she could think of was that they were alone. Engaged. And alone.

Those dazzling blue eyes met hers over the rim of his glass. "Hmm," he said. "She didn't used to be this agreeable."

She watched him sip his drink and suddenly wished it was from her lips he quench his thirst. Her tongue automatically darted out to moisten hers. "Did you wish for her to forbid our union?"

He casually drained his glass, placing it on a table. With deliberate slowness, he made his way toward her, his gaze traveling down her frame and then slowly back up to lock with her eyes, which were surely round with anticipation. He finally reached her and her hands itched to touch him, but she fought to remain steady and in control. She knew what he wanted, what all men wanted, and she wasn't the least bit hesitant to give it to him. She was finding her lust difficult to manage. *Stay focused. Look at his shoulder or something. Break eye contact. Damn it, break eye contact!*

"When the word union comes from those sweet lips, it makes me think of all the ways I could pleasure you." He leaned in to place a delicate kiss at the base of her throat. She swallowed. Her heart raced, her stomach fluttered, and her nipples hardened. Her mother's words filtered through the sexual haze absorbing her mind. "Whatever you do, my darling, please wait until you are wed before you enjoy the pleasures of the flesh." She suddenly realized the conflicting emotions her mother went through when faced with temptation. This was a difficult feeling to fight off when her body screamed, *Yes, take me now!*

She nervously licked her lips and heard him groan. "We will be married soon enough, my lord." She leaned forward to prevent herself embarrassment as she whispered, "But I can't wait to see what pleasures await me."

When she pulled back, he cupped her face between his strong hands and brought his warm, intoxicating lips down upon hers.

It didn't take long until they were both pulled into a sensual frenzy: tongues delving, hands roaming, and murmurs of pleasure rending the air.

He pulled back in a huff. "Off to bed with you, Abigail." His voice shook with the raw emotions consuming them.

She lowered her gaze to the bulge beneath his breeches and felt herself blush to the roots of her hair. The domineering earl was back in full force. She couldn't help smiling at his evident desire, which was exhilarating as well as empowering. "I'm going, my lord." She reached the door and cast him a saucy grin. "This is far from over."

"This, my sweet, is only the beginning." He went to move toward her again. "You have until the count of three, and then I can no longer be held accountable for my actions."

With a squeal of delight, Abigail dashed out of the room.

***

The Waterford staff had finished loading the trunks on the second carriage, which would carry the servants traveling with them, when an elegant black vehicle came to a stop in front of the house.

A bright yellow parasol alighted first, and Abigail's face lit up in a warm smile when the parasol shifted, allowing her to see Clarissa. Her friend was dressed in a lovely canary yellow ensemble to rival the sun. Her sky blue eyes were squinting as she adjusted to the blinding light of the day. She hurried over to Abigail with her maid following smartly in her wake. "Thank goodness I caught you. Where are you going? Why are you leaving?"

Abigail linked her arm through her friends. "Come inside for a spot of tea and I'll explain."

"You definitely have much explaining to do. The gossip has been traveling faster than my brother Patrick's fine stallion."

"I'm sure it has." Abigail led the way into the parlor and sent Mrs. Rhodes for some tea and cakes.

When the door closed, Clarissa let go of her arm and spun on her heel to face her. "You said 'yes' to his proposal?"

"I did." Abigail smiled. "I did make you a promise, after all. Besides, I am madly in love with the earl."

"Oh, Abby, that's wonderful. I'm very happy for you." Clarissa hugged her. Her excitement was so contagious that they both gave a shout of glee.

"It's hard to believe really. I never thought I would be this happy. Yet here I am. Life is wonderful. Jackson is wonderful."

"I told you there was something between you two. I sensed it."

The tea arrived and Abigail poured them both a cup, offering Clarissa a lemon cake as well.

"So where are you going? Are you eloping to Gretna Green?" Clarissa nearly bounced on the edge of her seat cushion with exuberance. Abigail knew better than anyone how her friend longed for some dashing adventure to pull her away from her life and into excitement.

"I'm afraid it's nothing so adventurous. But we do plan to be wed at a church near the Waterford Estate."

"Oh, truly." Clarissa clapped her hands together in happiness. "This is the best news ever, Abby. I tried to find you last night, after the earl made the announcement, but you disappeared."

"The dowager thought it best we depart straightaway."

"An intelligent decision. The audience was quite set on their bottoms afterward."

"You mean cursing me for taking one of their own away from them?"

"Some, perhaps. We can't expect to enlighten the ignorant. Nevertheless, many close to the Waterford's rejoiced at the news."

"Really?" Abigail asked skeptically.

"Yes, really." Clarissa laughed in merriment. "I can't believe you're getting married. This is splendid."

"Now you need to find a spouse so we can try to time our pregnancies together."

"You mean you're..."

"No, no, no. Definitely not. I mean we haven't... Well, you know what I mean."

"I do." Clarissa grinned. "Saints be praised. Are we talking about our future children? I would love to join you on the road to marital bliss, but there is just one problem: I've yet to find a man I deem proper husband material. With any luck, I will find such a man soon, however." She laughed.

"I wish you could come with us," Abigail stated.

"Me too. Nevertheless, as much as I wish to, I'm afraid I won't be allowed to attend the wedding. My mother plans to take me shopping for the next few weeks. She has many activities planned." Clarissa took off her necklace with a diamond encrusted cross. "Wear this and know I am with you in spirit."

"It's lovely. Thank you. Imagine, when I return your necklace to you, I will be the new Countess of Waterford. It is hard to fathom."

"Not to me." Clarissa smiled as she got to her feet. "Now give me a big farewell hug and promise me you won't stay ensconced in the country for too long."

"I promise."

Clarissa's eyes misted with tears. "I love you."

"And I love you. Now don't cry. I won't be gone forever."

"The unattached you will be." Clarissa dabbed at her tears with a lace handkerchief she fished out of her reticule. "Remember, Abigail, you deserve happiness. You deserve to be treated with respect. Your lack of a father does not define who you are but enhances your strength and ability to achieve your dreams."

Abigail was too choked up to respond, and so she only nodded. After a kiss to both of Abigail's cheeks, Clarissa left. Abby sat down and fastened the necklace. She was going to miss her friend.

Abigail remained in the parlor contemplating the turn her life was taking. She did deserve to be happy as Clarissa said. The majority of her life had been passable at best. But she had the power to change it. With Jackson empowering her, she couldn't fail. He was the right man for her, and they would be blissfully happy together.

The man of her every thought then strolled into the room as if on cue, wearing casual traveling attire and carrying a smile to rival Clarissa's. He walked with purposeful strides toward her, and when he was at her feet, he dropped to one knee, raked his fingers through his blond hair, and then reached into his inside coat pocket. "I've something for you."

"It wasn't necessary to get me anything, Jackson."

"I disagree, and as my soon-to-be queen, you must have gems." He opened the small box he held. "I'd be honored to put this on your finger as a token of my esteemed devotion."

Abigail stared down in awe. There, in the folds of black velvet, was a stunning heart-shaped ruby surrounded by brilliant diamonds on a silver band. "It's resplendent, Jackson. I've never owned something as lovely, or I suspect, as expensive." *Should I tell him it is too much?* No, he wouldn't want her to do that, and the truth was, she loved it. Looking down at the dazzling ruby, she gave him a watery smile. "I promise to treasure this and you forever." Her smile widened as he slid the precious and weighty gem on her finger. Her eyes filled with tears, making her vision blur.

Still holding on to her hand, he gave a gentle tug and she tumbled onto the floor in front of him. Then he pulled her toward him for a lingering, heart-melting kiss, a kiss filled with warmth, affection, and even understanding. "Promises I plan to hold you to."

"You've made me the happiest woman in the world."

"Trust me, you've yet to witness happiness, but I promise you, I have every intention of making your statement factual."

"Stuff and applesauce. You aren't supposed to be making vows before the ceremony. And what are the two of you doing on the floor?" The dowager stood in the doorway with a proud smile. She did not allow the embarrassed couple to answer her question before posing the next. "Are we ready?"

"I went to the Doctors' Commons this morning. The Archbishop of Canterbury was most accommodating." Jackson patted his breast pocket. "So yes, the special wedding license is procured."

"Then let us be on our way. I'd like to arrive at the estate in time for dinner. I don't plan to stop at any of the crass inns along the way. The fare is inedible."

"I shall endeavor to make our arrival at the designated time, Grandmother." Jackson stood, helping Abigail to her feet. "Shall we, my sweet?"

She took his hand, marveling at the ring sparkling on her finger. "Yes."

About four hours later, the coach drew down a long oak-lined drive to the Waterford Estate. Manicured lawns and expansive gardens monopolized the landscape until they turned down a bend in the road and Abigail looked up at the Waterford family seat in admiration. Beyond a doubt, this was the largest home she'd ever seen, really more of a mansion with red brick and gray stone accents.

"How many rooms are there?"

"There are twenty bedrooms, my dear," Lady Waterford informed her. "Most of them are on the second and third floors."

"It's magnificent!" exclaimed Abigail.

"I've always admired it," said the dowager.

Jackson had refused to leave his favorite stallion back in London, and so he had ridden alongside the coach for the journey. As they drew closer to the estate, he came up beside the window. Abigail couldn't help admiring how powerful he looked upon his horse. He was a natural in the saddle, unlike herself, who'd only had her bottom on a horse once in her life, and then only for a short time because, the horse nearly bucked her over the stables. Since that one unfortunate attempt at riding, she kept her distance from the hairy beasts. She smiled, remembering Clarissa's mirth at her folly. "Your home is magnificent, my lord."

"*Our* home, my lady. And thank you." He set his steed in motion to alert the stable lads of their arrival.

"We have plenty of horses if you wish to ride," the dowager informed her.

"I had an accident once, one I don't care to repeat, but I thank you all the same."

"I have never been partial to animals myself, but if you wish lessons, I'm sure my grandson would happily oblige."

"I'll keep that in mind." Abigail looked back at the house to see the servants filing out like a swarm of bees from their hive.

"Stuff and applesauce," the dowager complained. Her posture stiffened as she looked at the line of her staff.

"What is it, my lady?"

"It's Fitzroy, my butler, the man who's supposed to be in charge during our absence. I had asked him to replace the maid to his left, and yet I see he has failed to do so. Remember, my sweet girl, don't let servants go unwatched for too long. There is no telling what mischief they will achieve while you're away."

"And the maid is unsatisfactory in her duties?" Abigail posed the question, realizing with trepidation that, as the new lady of the house, such duties as having the maid fired would fall to her when she was wed.

"Actually, the widow Foxworthy was close to my husband, although that is not why I dismissed her." She leaned in closer to Abigail as if somehow they could be overheard in the vehicle. "The truth is, I don't care for her daughter. She has a habit of shamelessly draping herself all over my grandson."

Abigail nodded, trying not to let jealousy of yet another woman seize control of her. "Then you are correct. She really must go."

"Precisely," said the dowager as the vehicle came to a stop. The driver barely had time to put down the steps before Lady Waterford shoved open the door and marched toward Mr. Fitzroy. The man seemed to shrink in the dowager's presence.

Abigail slowly descended the steps, taking in her surroundings and drinking in the fresh country air, allowing the sun sinking below the horizon behind the house to shine upon her face.

Not seeing Jackson, and assuming he took his horse to the enormous stables around the corner, she followed the dowager.

"I'll have a word with you, Fitzroy." The dowager's finger waved near the butler's face before she continued on into the house.

"Yes, milady." The man's shoulders seemed to droop as he followed behind Abigail.

"In my sitting room," the dowager ordered in a strict voice, a tone Abigail had never heard from her before.

The butler bowed his head and obeyed.

"I won't be long, Abigail. Feel free to explore the house. Jackson should be in momentarily."

"Yes, my lady." Abigail was about to turn away when a thought struck her. "Lady Waterford?"

The dowager turned. "Dear?"

Abigail walked closer so the butler couldn't hear her words. "Can I watch?" Lord, that sounded terrible. "I mean, soon I'll be expected to handle domestic responsibilities, and the truth is, I have no knowledge as to how I am to attend to these matters. Not that I want to hear you scold him. It's just that you're all but seething with authority at the moment, and I'd like to learn how."

"Enough, dear. Stuff and applesauce but you do tend to rattle on at times."

"Sorry." Abigail smiled meekly.

"No, I am. Of course you don't know how to run a household. It was remiss of me not to realize it. Please, join me."

Abigail watched in utter fascination while the dowager brought the butler to task and ordered her instructions to be carried out immediately. Poor Mr. Fitzroy apologized profusely, and once dismissed, he couldn't seem to get out of the room fast enough.

"And that, my dear, is how it's done."

Abigail applauded. "Bravo!"

Laughing together, they vacated the sitting room and entered the hall to find Jackson entangled in some woman's arms.

Abigail was sure steam came out of her ears. She stopped to look at the dowager. "Miss Foxworthy, I presume?" she asked with a hiss.

"Indeed," answered the dowager.

"May I?" She didn't say the words she longed to include in her interrogatory: *rip her hair out, sock her in the nose, beat the wench bloody*. Her body vibrated with possessive rage.

"Take her to task?" asked the dowager.

"Yes."

"By all means, my girl. Give it a go." The dowager waved her off and stood to watch her protégé at work.

Abigail approached with a calm dignity. Copying the dowager's earlier posture by trying to look down her nose, she interrupted them with a clearing of her throat. She was not one to let her anger get the best of her and so her voice came out surprisingly calm but unmistakably firm. "Miss Foxworthy."

"Yes," the blond, large breasted woman purred, running a hand up the Earl of Waterford's chest. Abigail noticed Jackson's smile as he tried to release himself from the woman's grasp. *Perhaps I should rap him on the head, hard, first. He enjoys these jealous tantrums and the wretch is amused by this situation.*

She dismissed his smile and focused on Miss Foxworthy. "You are to unhand the earl and pack your belongings. Your mother will be joining you. You're both to report to Lord Jennings' estate posthaste." She had heard the destination in the dowager's instructions to the butler.

Jackson was finally able to back up a few steps as the woman released him to turn on Abigail.

"And who are you?" The insolent maid had the audacity to step closer to her in an effort of intimidation. Little did this woman know that Abigail was not easily cowed. Jackson actually laughed. Apparently, her fiancé knew she would put this brazen woman in her place.

"I'm soon to be the lady of this house, and you are now trespassing. I will have you gone from my presence this moment or I will have the authorities personally remove you from Waterford lands. Do you understand, Miss Foxworthy?"

The girl's eyes narrowed toward her, then with a huff, she turned and fled up the servants' steps.

Abigail smiled triumphantly when the dowager and Jackson complimented her mastery and calm demeanor.

***

The weeks flew by in a blur of enjoyment. Jackson took Abigail on numerous tours of the estate. She met the tenant farmers and their families, and she believed, just about every person who lived in the nearby village. Everyone she met appeared joyous when told of their upcoming nuptials.

The country was spectacular. Abigail loved the clean air, the never-ending hills of green, the well-groomed gardens, and even the livestock that dotted the landscape as far as the eye could see. She was happy here, although all these things paled in comparison with her sheer joy at being with Jackson.

He was the most thoughtful, caring man she ever had the pleasure to meet. It still boggled her mind that she was going to be his wife. They had shared many ardent encounters since reaching the Waterford Estate, but each time, Jackson showed self-restraint, pulling them back countless times from their raging passions before they were consumed by need. These feats of strength endeared him even more in her heart, for she noticed how difficult it was for him to push away and she knew he did so for her sake.

Although waiting for their wedding night was what she truly wanted, it remained a difficult task for them both. With her domineering man in control of the reins, it was looking like they might actually make it—the wedding being only three more days away. But Abigail found herself growing increasingly impatient for the night when she could truly show Jackson how much she loved him.

Currently, she stood dressed in a pale blue riding habit that hugged her curves, and her hair was tied back with a simple blue satin ribbon. A light summer breeze blew refreshingly in her face while she watched Jackson in abject terror. He was busy harnessing and saddling a dapple mare, and she decided, given the mare's seeming spunk, to keep her eyes on his broad back and not on the beast. Jackson stretched and reached beneath the horse's belly, his muscles tight and defined, even through the white lawn shirt he wore casually buttoned. A patch of sandy blond chest hair was exposed to her view today. The horse nickered as Jackson cinched a leather strap beneath its girth. "She seems overly large, my lord. Perhaps you have a pony I could ride instead?" Abigail said when her focus returned to the horse because it had sidled several steps to the left.

He laughed at the look of panic she knew was on her face. "No ponies."

"I fail to see the humor. This could be the last time you see me alive. I told you I'm scared of the beasts. Don't you have one a bit smaller? Or better yet, I could practice with the saddle draped over the fence."

"Come here, Abigail. Sunflower's as meek as a lamb."

"And ten times larger, no, twenty."

He laughed again, noticing she hadn't moved a step in his direction. He made his way toward her with a smile and wrapped one of his strong arms around her waist. He appeared to find her fear amusing. She told herself she was being silly, that this was only a horse and people have been riding the monsters since the beginning of time. Besides, Sunflower looked to be a more docile creature than the stallion Jackson rode, even if she did prance sideways a bit on occasion.

Jackson leaned toward Abby to kiss her neck and whisper in her ear, which sent chills coursing down her chest and arms. "Where's your unswerving courage I admire?"

She glanced up at him. *My, but he is handsome.* "You're enjoying my trepidation far too much, my lord."

"And you're making too much out of a silly ride upon a horse. Come on, Abigail. I'll be right here." He shuffled her grudgingly forward.

"All right, but if I get hurt, it's your fault."

He put a hand to his chest. "I will take sole responsibility."

"Great. Sole responsibility for my untimely demise. Very well, give me a boost please."

She thought he'd cup his hands so she could step up and place her bottom on the saddle, but instead his powerful hands curled around her waist and he picked her up and easily placed her in the seat. She felt like she was towering over him from this vantage, and her fear increased. The horse suddenly sidestepped, causing Abigail to shriek. She remembered being told when she was younger that the hairy beasts could sense a person's apprehension, and she knew this creature must now be sensing her trepidation in heaps. Thankfully, Jackson still had a tight grip on the reins and easily settled the animal.

"Perhaps this isn't such a good idea. I mean, it's a beautiful day, and you did promise me a walk. We could turn it into a picnic. I could make us some lunch. Yes, lunch is a splendid idea. Help me down and I'm off to the kitchen."

He eyed her curiously. "Are you really petrified of riding?"

"I would define my feelings as more unease, than being petrified. Is it important I learn?"

"I did think you'd enjoy riding off with me into the sunset, or maybe racing through the wildflowers while the wind steals your breath, or perhaps even escaping to a nearby glen to enjoy the delights of the flesh. But if you're sure you don't want to do those things…" He sighed. "Then I'll help you down."

What he offered sounded like pure bliss, all things she very much wanted to do with him, especially the delights of the flesh part. She bit her lower lip and nodded her head that she would give it a try. He passed her the reins. She gave them a jiggle and brought them down lightly upon the horse. She eyed her surroundings. A walk around the large oak a little in the distance would be plenty for one day of lessons, she decided, but Sunflower was clearly not in the walking frame of mind and she set off at the most bone-jarring pace. Abigail's teeth rattled and she bit down hard on her lip.

"You don't want to trot, Abigail. It's not a smooth ride," Jackson hollered.

Abigail bounced uncontrollably in her seat and cringed when she tasted blood on her lip. Her bottom, as well as her organs, felt like they were being shaken to pieces.

"How do I stop her from trotting?" Her voice came out in a stuttering of words.

"Increase pressure on her flanks with your heels."

The horse continued to rattle her to death in spite of her squeezing it as directed. "She's not listening," Abigail yelled in sheer agitation, wondering again why she had agreed to do this. Then she remembered Jackson's coaxing kisses were responsible for her agreeing to ride the beast. *The cad knows he can get me to do anything that way.*

"Then give her a kick."

He wants me to kick the horse? And just how angry will that make the animal? She just knew she'd probably find herself bucked into the tree. *Bother. That would hurt.* A stick to the eye would not be good before her wedding. But the pace was giving her a headache, and so, without a second thought, she raised her heel and connected with the mare's side. She grabbed the mane of the horse with her one free hand and they were off. *This is pleasant.* The horse's gait was smooth, with long effortless strides, which brought the wind whipping against her face. She heard Jackson's whoop of excitement behind her and smiled triumphantly. "I'm doing it. I'm riding a horse," she cheered.

Sunflower slowed before she turned her around the tree to head back to Jackson. Once around the turn, Abigail placed her heels to the horse's side and kicked lightly. Sunflower skipped the rough going trot and galloped, leaving Abigail feeling exhilarated and happy. She slowed in front of Jackson, the trot making her gnash her teeth, but the horse quickly settled into a walk and she felt relieved.

"Well?" Jackson held up his arms to her with a pleased smile and she slid off the horse into his embrace.

"Absolutely splendid! The wind whipping in my face, the speed, the great power of the beast under me—invigorating! I felt powerful. Does that sound silly?"

Jackson fished a handkerchief out of his pants pocket to dab at her injured lip. "You're a horsewoman in the making, but it appears your first lesson wasn't without incident. I'm sorry you hurt yourself."

"It's not your fault. I shouldn't have been biting my lip."

"True, but I did claim responsibility for your safety. I insist on making reparations." Jackson watched his soon-to-be wife look up at him with those enticing golden-rimmed eyes of hers and was lost. To see her jubilation on the horse was an aphrodisiac to his soul. She was such a beautiful, caring, and courageous woman that she humbled him. And to think she felt herself not worthy enough of him, when in truth, she was too good for him. He realized how lucky he was to have fallen in love with the right woman and he moved closer and took Abigail's bottom lip into his mouth, running his tongue across hers, his hand sliding down from her slim neck to graze one of her nipples.

Abigail pulled back, her eyes darting toward the house and then the stables. "Someone could see."

"Then they'd see a man whose need has far surpassed his self control. I'm having an increasingly difficult time waiting until our wedding night, my love."

"As am I." She leaned into him, inhaling his scent as she ran her hands up the contours of his chest. His arousal was immediate. "I think we could…"

The very words of her surrender threatened to make his erection a permanent condition. He pressed his fingers to her lips to prevent her from speaking. He knew full well she was giving in and about to say he could take her to his bed, but he wouldn't allow himself to give into his longing. She deserved to have a wedding night. He would wait for her sake. It was the honorable thing to do.

Although he questioned the solidity of his honor when she took one of his fingers into her hot mouth and sucked. His breath seized and he hissed as he backed away from her. *My soon-to-be wife is temptation incarnate.* She'd been throwing those kinds of provocative invitations at him since they arrived in the country. He found her sexual gestures amusing and extremely erotic. Soon he'd show his wife *exactly* how much she inflamed him. "You wait, my dear. I intend to make you beg for me, so you get a taste of the devilry you're plying."

"Promises, promises," she teased, turning for the house.

"Where are you going?" he asked, falling into step behind her, unable to keep his gaze from the gentle sway of her hips.

"To bathe. I smell like horse."

"May I watch?" he quipped, coming up behind her to nibble on her neck.

"If you can stand the heat."

He laughed. "The heat I can handle; you, on the other hand, I can't. I'll meet you in the parlor in an hour. I believe Grandmother wanted to go over some of the wedding plans today." He winked and turned away to march back toward the stables.

"Where are you going?" she asked.

"I'm in need of a cold plunge in the lake."

She laughed, knowing he had needed dozens of these freezing dunks since their arrival. "Then I'll see you soon," she said.

As he watched her disappear inside the house, a smile lit up his face and he cut down a trail toward the lake. Coming to the country was a marvelous idea. He couldn't think of a better place to make Abigail his wife.

CHAPTER NINE

The dowager sat at her desk going through a stack of her deceased husband's papers in an attempt to prove her suspicions correct. So far, she had failed to turn up a single shred of evidence in spite of having gone through a great many documents. Her back hurt from sitting hunched over her desk, and her eyes watered from squinting to read the fine, and an in many cases, faded print, but she would not give up. There was far too much at stake. Her family deserved the truth.

A knock at the door had her standing up with a needed stretch. Merta, her personal lady's maid stood at the door with a brown package wrapped in twine.

"This package arrived for you, milady." Her dark skinned servant placed the parcel on the desk.

"Who's it from?" The dowager retrieved her reading glasses.

"Your husband's solicitor, milady."

"He sent me a package now? Stuff and applesauce, I've been asking the man for months to get me information regarding my husband, and he'd yet to supply me with anything. Now he suddenly has a package he pulled out of thin air?" she huffed as she untied the strings and removed the paper wrapping. She stared in stunned dismay at the many letters in front of her. The hair on the back of her neck tingled. Herein was the truth. The evidence of her husband's perfidy sat before her.

Recognizing William's penmanship, she dismissed her servant with a nod, and then she shuffled through the letters dated six months before her husband's death. The top letter was addressed to her. There was also a letter to Jackson and another for his mother, Stephanie. When she reached the last two letters, tears fell from her eyes, her hands trembled, and a sob escaped her constricted throat. Her William had done the unthinkable. The name Abigail Gibbons, in neat script, multiplied before her tear-filled eyes. The last letter was addressed to Delores Gibbons, the woman Abigail called mother. She removed the letter addressed to her from the stack and tucked those addressed to the others safely into her top drawer until she decided what to do. "You have yet to read the letter addressed to you, old woman," she reminded herself. "Perhaps you are jumping to the wrong conclusions." But even as she said it, she dismissed the notion as nonsense.

With trembling fingers and a heavy heart, she opened her late husband's letter.

My Dearest Margaret,

If you're reading this, it means you are safely ensconced in the country and I have surely departed this world.

I hope this letter also finds you happily reunited with our granddaughter. I know it may not help, but I am sorry for keeping her from us. I had to do what I thought was best for our family. I needed a male heir, and when the opportunity presented itself, I took it. I don't regret my decision, for I did what needed to be done. I want you to know that I've never forgotten about Abigail. I always made sure she was provided for.

That being said, I now leave the matter in your capable hands. Perhaps you can bring the two kids together. I believe she and Jackson would suit one another. He needs someone like her, and our granddaughter deserves to have the respect due to someone of her birth. See, my love, even from the grave I still try to subject my will upon those within my care when I was alive.

I know this is much to absorb, and if you decide my work must be undone, I've enclosed letters to each person I affected with my desperate plan to procure an heir. I'm sorry if perhaps my overly heavy-handed strategy has caused everyone grief. I know you, my supportive wife, understand the motive behind my deceptions. I could not allow my wife to lose her home anymore than I could allow my title to pass to my nephew's son.

Know that you, my darling, are with me no matter where I am.

*All my love, your husband,
William.*

The dowager dropped the letter and gaped at it in horror. Her husband had done the inconceivable, traded their son's precious daughter for Delores Gibbons' bastard son. Tears poured down her wrinkled cheeks and she shook with her cries as she stared at the truth in front of her. Her body filled with hopeless despair.

William knew she could never in good conscience keep something this important from Jackson. Even if he wasn't her blood, Jackson would always be her grandson, the treasure of her heart.

The thought of how this news would affect him staggered her. His title would be ripped away and given to Grayson Mathers, a second cousin, who happened to be one of Jackson's close friends.

Then there was the matter of Jackson living his entire life in someone else's shoes, the matter of how to deal with his current mother not to mention the biological one he had yet to meet, not to mention the matter of his bastardy and the unknown identity of his sire.

And the Dowager Countess of Waterford couldn't forget about Abigail. She too had been living in a world of lies, all fabricated by a controlling grandfather. It thrilled her to learn Abigail was indeed her son's daughter. She had indeed fainted upon their initial introduction because of the likeness Abigail shared with her son.

Although she felt upset for Abigail's past, Jackson was the one who worried her the most. He would not take any of this well. He would lose all he held dear. Her eyes swam with tears and her head began to pound as she tried to decide what to do.

Perhaps she could share the news with Abigail and see if her bright granddaughter had any ideas on how to relate this life changing news to Jackson. Two heads were certainly better than one. The dowager suddenly felt inadequate to determine, let alone to handle, the consequences all on her own. This turn of events, though she had suspected it since she met Abigail, was too momentous for even *her* to handle. She needed to talk with someone and her granddaughter was the logical choice.

She couldn't help wishing she knew who Jackson's biological father was. Blast William for not finding out. With the truth revealed, hopefully such information would soon come to light. She hoped so for Jackson's sake.

A sickening feeling settled in her stomach. Would her family overcome this?

***

Lady Waterford found them ensconced in the parlor laughing over a chessboard set up before the bow window. She walked into the room with a smile, their closeness making her heart lighter than it had been moments ago. Since coming to the country, Jackson and Abigail were inseparable: where she found one of them, the other was surely close by. Two halves of a whole was how the dowager liked to think of them. They were happy together. Surely, their love would see them through the most difficult of hardships, which this news would be. "I never thought chess to be amusing," she said, entering the room.

Abigail smiled at her. "I assume it's not for practiced players, but I'm just learning. I can't seem to remember the moves different chess pieces are allowed to make."

"It takes time, dear," she said.

"How's the wedding planning coming along, Grandmother?" Jackson asked. She smiled at how impatient the handsome devil was to make Abigail his bride.

"I know you wish to handle everything, my lady, and I do appreciate it, but if there's anything I can do to help, you must tell me," Abigail insisted.

The dowager sat wearily down on a plump eggplant-colored sofa. The truth was eating her up inside. She felt weary, as if her body was going through the motions of life while worry sapped every ounce of energy within her. Nevertheless, planning the wedding would hopefully help to keep her sane. "The wedding plans have been a breeze, my dear. You've approved of all the décor, food, ceremony, and etcetera. Now we just have to wait two more days. You had your dress fitting?"

"I did. The gown is spectacular," Abigail said happily.

"I've hired extra help for the banquet and everything is proceeding well. Tomorrow will be a busy day of preparation." She paused in thought. "There are a few things I'd like to discuss with you, Abigail, when you have a moment."

"I believe my chess lesson is finished for today, if you'd like we could…"

She didn't finish her sentence and the dowager groaned when she realized why. They could hear the front door open and voices fill the hall. So much for handling this *before* things became chaotic.

"It appears we have guests." Jackson stood from his seat next to the chessboard to see what all the commotion was about. Before he got to the door, it swung open and in walked the dowager's daughter-in-law, Stephanie, now remarried and looking regal and happy—that is until her gaze fell upon Jackson and her lips pursed in clear disapproval. The dowager groaned inwardly at the sight of another family member whose life was about to change courtesy of her husband.

***

A Necessary Heir

"Mother." Jackson walked over to place his lips on each of her sun-kissed cheeks. "Lord Hastings." He shook hands with his new stepfather. He was happy to have his mother home. He didn't like the idea of getting married without her by his side. "I assume the wedding trip went well. Egypt still houses a fair number of artifacts? Or did my mother convince you to bring the bulk of the country's priceless treasures home?"

His mother didn't even smirk at his jest. Her face was affixed in a stony visage as she looked over his shoulder at Abigail, who seemed to shrink under the close inspection, and Jackson hurried to make the introductions.

His mother shooed him away as she approached Abigail. "Come here, my dear. Let me look at you."

Jackson watched his mother warily, her odd behavior puzzling to him. He assumed she'd be thrilled to hear about his upcoming nuptials. She'd been pestering him to wed for years now, and for his part, he never gave her any encouragement that he ever would marry. She took Abigail's hands in hers and gazed mutely at her lovely face.

Was she going to speak? Or just continue staring at Abigail with that all knowing gaze of hers? Abigail fidgeted under the steady scrutiny, and Jackson decided to intervene.

"Abigail is my intended, Mother. We are to be married at the village church in two days."

"She's well aware of your engagement," Lord Hastings intoned, he too watching his wife quizzically. "We traveled at breakneck speed to make it here in time."

"I wasn't about to miss my only child's wedding." His mother continued to examine Abigail like a rare Egyptian artifact. She pulled Abigail close for a hug and then set her back. "It's a pleasure to meet you, dear."

"Likewise, my lady. Your son speaks highly of you."

"As I do him." She smiled adoringly at Jackson and then turned to his grandmother. "Margaret, a word with you in the sitting room, if you please."

Jackson noted that his grandmother seemed dejected and

resigned at the same time, but he didn't have time to ponder her peculiar behavior before she stood and, with a shake of her skirts, left the room.

Stephanie turned back to her husband. "I will be up to rest shortly, my love."

Lord Hastings passed his wife a questioning look, which Jackson interpreted to mean, "We will discuss what is bothering you later." Then Hastings walked up to Abigail. "You will make a fine addition to our family, Lady Abigail." He bowed over Abigail's hand, and with a smile, exited behind the dowager.

Dressed in a creamy green traveling dress with her brown hair pulled up and pinned behind her head, his mother then turned to Jackson. "I don't appreciate being the last to find out about your nuptials, young man. And the gossip circulating about the two of you in town…" She sighed. "Well, it doesn't bear repeating." Her gaze went to Abigail. "Regardless of your birth, dear, I'm happy as long as my son is happy. This is a love match?"

"It is, Mother."

"Very good then." She smiled at Abigail before leaving the room.

"That didn't go as I pictured," Jackson said with a shake of his head. His mother was acting out-of-character and he didn't know what to make of it. Perhaps the long journey and the mad dash home was the explanation. If he didn't know better, he would have thought his mother had taken an instant dislike to his bride, and yet he thought he noticed a warmth in her eyes when she looked at Abigail. No, the long journey had to be the reason for her bizarre behavior.

He watched Abigail squeeze the tears back into her eyes, refusing to give into the sadness evidently engulfing her. He noted that, although she could prevent the tears from spilling, she couldn't control the trembling her body made due to the tide of emotions coursing through her. This had Jackson crossing the room and taking her into his arms.

"She hates me." Her voice shrank at the admission.

"No, she doesn't, my sweet; she doesn't even know you. I admit she's acting odd, but she did rush home to find me happily engaged to the woman I love."

"You love me?" Those lovely gold-rimmed eyes of hers met his and he grinned like a lovesick adolescent. He was surprised he hadn't told her of his love sooner.

"With all my heart."

"I love you too, Jackson. You're my dream come true. I just want your mother to like me."

"You make me happy, and my mother is sure to love you as I do. Well, perhaps not like I do." He laughed, trying to make light of the situation as he pulled her closer to breathe in the scent of lilac and the essence of Abigail. This impulse caused a rush of need to pulse through his body and settle in his groin. He backed up a step to put a safer distance between them, but at Abigail's forlorn expression, he felt compelled to reassure her. His mouth came down softly over hers, and soon his reassurance turned possessive and fervent. He felt her arms circle around his neck, her fingers playing with the back of his hair, as their tongues danced heatedly around each other. His arousal pulsed and he wanted nothing more than to sweep her up in his arms and carry her to his bed so he could finally make sweet, passionate love to her. As his erection pushed into her delectable thigh, he heard her groan, felt her surrender, and ripped his mouth away. "I'll see you at dinner."

"But…" Abigail's lips were red and swollen from their heated encounter.

"Go, Abigail." His fists clenched as he tried to think of something to counter his pulsing arousal. *Dead puppies. A man's head on a pike. The odorous smell of the Thames on a hot summer's day.* Anything to keep him from making Abigail truly his before they wed. *Looks like I'm heading back to the cold lake again.*

***

Lady Waterford sat in a chintz-covered chair drumming her fingers on the arms in nervous agitation. Stephanie was irate and Margaret didn't blame her. She had taken one look at Abigail and suspected the truth—or at least part of it.

This was a nightmare.

Margaret had no idea how her lovely daughter-in-law would take this news, but she knew it wasn't going to be easy for anyone involved. She silently cursed her husband again as she waited for the ax to fall.

Stephanie sailed into the room like a thundercloud, slamming the door behind her with a loud boom.

The dowager held up her hand, wanting to speak first. "I know what you're thinking…"

"Truly, Margaret? Do you truly know what I am thinking? How could you? I leave for a few months and return to find my son engaged to…to whom? His bastard half-sister? Sweet Jesus, Margaret. What were you thinking? Not only do I have to learn that my wonderful husband was clearly unfaithful to me, a thought I admit that I've never considered, but to bring his bastard home with you, to introduce her to Jackson. Hell's teeth, Margaret, they are in love. They can't marry each other. This is a disaster. It's unthinkable. It's incest. It's…"

"Not true," the dowager finished. "I know you have questions, dearest, but I can explain." At least she hoped she could. This was such a convoluted mess she didn't know where to begin with the explanation exactly. She'd start with her husband. She picked up a bell and ordered her housekeeper to fetch the letter addressed to Stephanie from her bedroom's desk drawer, and then she sat back to wait.

"How can it not be true? She looks just like him, Margaret." Stephanie's eyes filled with tears.

"Not exactly," the dowager responded, knowing someone had to remain level headed about this.

"She has Marshall's eyes!" Lady Hastings exclaimed with vehemence.

"I know, dearest. Please calm down. I don't want them to hear you."

Stephanie took a needed breath and pushed her words out through clenched teeth. "Then explain to me, if you please, what that woman is doing here?"

"I'm getting to that…" The housekeeper rushed back in with the letter and passed it to the dowager before she hurried back out the door, closing it behind her. "It's my hope that this will answer your questions."

"And who is it from? The girl's mother?"

"It's a letter from William." Stephanie glared at her in confusion.

Lady Hastings snatched the letter and took a seat. She broke the wax seal and read.

My dearest daughter-in-law Stephanie,

If you are reading this, then I am surely gone and my wife has found it fitting to follow her kind heart. Truly, I didn't expect differently. Leave it to my Margaret to make sure all is put back in order.

Perhaps you've now met your daughter. From the letters I received from her school, Abigail Gibbons is a bright, courageous young lady. She deserves to have her mother back. The two of you have missed too many years together.

I'm rambling when I should be apologizing. I took the girl you gave birth to and switched her for Jackson. I needed an heir and you needed a babe to love. It seemed the ideal situation at the time.

As I've grown older and watched from afar as my granddaughter grew up, I also became wiser and realized my error. You were in and out of consciousness after giving birth. I should have kept both children and insisted you had twins, but my mind was fixed on an heir and Jackson was the logical result. He's a fine man, one whom I'm proud to call my grandson.

I'm sorry if my news upsets you, but you and Abigail have been given a precious chance to get to know one another. Treat her well, Stephanie. She needs your love and guidance.

Your esteemed father-in-law,
William.

The paper fell to the floor. A heart-wrenching sob tore from Stephanie's throat while tears slid down her cheeks.

The dowager ambled over to pull the younger woman into her arms. "There, there, my girl. You let it all out."

"How could he do this to me, Margaret? How could he do this to her? That poor girl in there has suffered horribly from his cruel manipulating. Where was his concern for her need for love and guidance years ago? She's a woman grown." Tears ran down her daughter-in-law's face, her body shook, and her eyes took on a scary blank stare. She was obviously both heartbroken and angry.

"I don't condone William's actions, Stephanie. I was horrified and angry as well. But I don't believe it was his intention to be cruel."

"What he did was inexcusable! I can't believe this! He took my daughter from me! He took my life! He took her life! Then he twisted them to suit his own purposes!" She hiccupped as tears continued to run down her face. "I will never forgive him. She raised her fist and waved it in the air while looking at the ceiling. "Never!" she vowed.

The dowager continued to rub her back. Wishing there was something, anything she could say to help Stephanie cope with her loss. But really, there were no words. "She's found her way back to us."

"Yes." Stephanie gave her a watery smile, swiping at her tears with her handkerchief. "She has, hasn't she? She's beautiful."

"Like her mother," the dowager responded, causing Stephanie to burst into a fresh round of tears.

"This is so unbelievable." She fell silent. "Oh Lord, what about Jackson? This news will destroy him."

"He's a strong man, Stephanie."

"Strong, yes. But this still has the potential to send my son into a downward spiral. Is he illegitimate? Who are his parents? How long until he loses his inheritance and everything he holds dear? This is preposterous. I can't even handle the implications of this news. How can we expect him to?" She hiccupped, gratefully took the fresh handkerchief the dowager handed her, and then quickly blew her nose. The tears kept coming.

"With the love and understanding of his family by his side, along with the unwavering love and support of Abigail, he will see the light at the end of the tunnel."

"The light? He's been living a lie his entire life. If William were still alive, I would beat the stuffing out of him. The man deserves to burn in hell for this. How dare he destroy the lives of others to suit his purposes? It's beyond selfish and…and… it's disgusting, that's what it is. The scoundrel! How could he not know how wrong he was? Knowing William, he didn't care. All he ever cared about was his precious title, and to hell with the rest of us!"

The dowager understood Stephanie's anger. She had the same anger hammering in her own breast. What her husband did wasn't fair to anyone, but now the only thing left to do was fix it.

"Oh Lord," Stephanie sobbed. "What are we to do? You have not yet told them?"

"I think we wait until after the wedding," the dowager answered. She'd spent sleepless nights trying to come up with answers when she had only suspected Abigail was her granddaughter. "Then Jackson will realize all is not lost because he'll have Abigail. True love will overcome. And they do love each other madly. You should see them together, Stephanie."

"I don't seem to be able to see anything clearly at the moment," Stephanie responded numbly as Margaret helped her to the sofa and sat beside her. Stephanie bent at the waist, retrieving her note from the floor, and then placed it in a pocket of her traveling garment. She took out another handkerchief from the same pocket to blot at her face.

"It may take time, but things do have a way of working themselves out."

"I can only pray you are right." More tears leaked from Stephanie's pale face. "He took my daughter from me, Margaret. I had a girl, a beautiful baby girl." A quick knock sounded on the door and it opened.

"I'm sorry to interrupt, Lady Waterford, Lady Hastings, but you said there were a few things you wanted to discuss." Abigail stood at the door, concern evident on her pretty face.

Both women stared at the lovely girl with brown tresses highlighted with blond streaks, which brought out the unique, golden-rim around her tawny eyes that were so much like her father's. She had the smile of an angel, the poise of a queen, and a heart to heal Jackson. The dowager instructed Abigail to shut the door and have a seat. Once her granddaughter settled herself on a cushioned chair, Stephanie burst back into tears.

***

"Are you all right, my lady?" Abigail cast concerned eyes upon Jackson's beautiful mother, who appeared to be having some kind of breakdown. *Saints be praised, the woman disapproves of me and now she is sobbing uncontrollably, most likely wishing me far away.* "If this is a bad time?" Abigail began to rise, thinking perhaps she should give Lady Hastings time to get used to the idea of her son's wedding.

"This is the best time, my dear," the dowager stated, and Abigail settled back into her seat. "There's someone I wish to introduce you to." Lady Waterford went on in such a sad tone that Abigail felt sweat forming on her brow. She suddenly wished she had not intruded and worried that the dowager was losing her mind, for the woman had just watched Jackson introduce Abby to his mother.

"Not like that," Stephanie scolded while dabbing her handkerchief at more tears.

"I'm sorry if our news has upset you, Lady Hastings," replied Abigail.

"She called me Lady Hastings." Another unladylike sob came from Jackson's mother and anguish cut at Abigail's heart.

"Tell her, dearest," the dowager exclaimed with tears in her eyes.

Abigail fidgeted in her seat. *Would someone please tell me something! What in Hades have I walked in on?* Now both women had tears streaking down their faces and she was hard-pressed not to join them. If Lady Hastings were to forbid her marriage, she was sure to follow their example.

But they remained silent, staring at her through watery eyes. "Stuff and applesauce, what is it?" she asked.

The dowager laughed gently at Abigail's use of her saying and then began to cry harder. Finally, Lady Hastings stood. "Come here, Ab-i-gail." More tears cascaded down her cheeks when she said her name. Abigail came forward, wondering if the woman planned to attack her for her upcoming nuptials to Jackson, but she bravely walked onward, prepared for the worst.

When they stood nearly toe-to-toe, Abby noted they were the same height and even shared the same hair color, though Stephanie's was beginning to gray on the sides. Abigail blinked and found herself pulled into Lady Hastings motherly embrace. She smelled of exotic flowers, and Abby found her touch comforting, and she relaxed into the embrace with unbelievable relief. *Perhaps she doesn't hate me. But something is definitely wrong.*

"Tell her," the dowager ordered with a sniffle.

Lady Hastings led Abigail to the sofa where the dowager was sitting. "Please sit. I'm sorry, but I'm afraid this is complicated, and the truth is, I fear your reaction."

"You have nothing to fear from me, my lady."

The dowager took one of Abigail's hands in hers as Lady Hastings dropped down to her knees in front of her. "Such a sweet, beautiful lady you've become."

"I'm very proud of her," the dowager thought to add. Ringing the bell to her right, she informed the housekeeper to fetch a letter addressed to Abigail in her desk drawer.

"This is about a letter to me?" Abigail asked, this endless stalling driving her mad. Whatever Lady Hastings had to say, Abigail really wished she'd be done with it. "Who from?" Abigail didn't know if she really wanted to know the problem. After all, whatever it was had caused these two women a great deal of sadness.

"Your domineering grandfather," Lady Hastings said with more than a touch of hostility.

Abigail felt claustrophobic with their hovering and stood to walk over toward the windows so she could think. "My grandfather? I assume you mean my maternal grandfather, but he was deceased before I came into this world and so he couldn't possibly have written me a note. As for my fraternal grandfather, since I don't know who my father is... Is that it? You found out the identity of my father?" She continued to gaze out the window toward the stables as she thought aloud.

"Yes and no, dear," the dowager responded.

"I can't take much more of this," Abigail huffed, turning back toward the women.

"Again, I'm sorry, my dear. There's no easy way to say this... Your grandfather is the late Earl of Waterford." Lady Hastings swept across the room to stand beside her. She took Abigail's trembling hands in hers. "I... I am your birth mother."

Abigail shook her head in confusion and denial. Did this woman just claim to be her mother? Was this all some kind of twisted tale to prevent her marriage to Jackson? "Are you telling me that I am engaged to wed my brother?" The thought chilled her to the core and her stomach churned with dread. This wasn't happening.

Tears began anew as Lady Hastings tried, but failed, to speak.

"He's not your brother," the dowager stated from her place on the sofa. "He's no relation to you."

Abigail sighed in relief. "He's not?" She blinked in puzzlement, fixing her gaze on the woman claiming to be her mother. Her heart resumed a normal pace. "He's no relation to you?"

Lady Hastings sobbed, dropping Abigail's hands and turning away. "He's not my son," she admitted with a shaky voice.

"Remember when I told you how desperate my William was for an heir?" the dowager questioned, patting the cushion next to her for Abigail to sit, which she did. The entire tale was jumbling her up inside. Suddenly her mother wasn't her mother. Although the mysterious funds for her schooling suddenly made more sense.

Pulling her emotions back under control for what seemed the millionth time, Lady Hastings came to sit on the other side of her. The housekeeper returned with a letter addressed to Abigail. The servant made a quick retreat out of the room after her delivery. Lady Waterford immediately passed the missive to Abby.

"This is the letter from my grandfather, the Earl of Waterford?" This all seemed so surreal. *My grandfather is the Earl of Waterford. Delores Gibbons isn't my mother. Lady Hastings is my mother...* She repeated the statements to herself in an effort to understand, but none of this made sense.

"Yes, dear," answered the dowager.

"Do you wish to read it in private?" Lady Hastings asked, her face etched with concern.

"No, I don't think so. If you don't mind, I think I'll go sit by the window to read it. I would like you both to remain in the room. I feel a bit out of sorts. This is far too much for my mind to grasp right now. Can I ask you a question…Mother?"

"Yes, my dear, anything?"

"Am I still illegitimate?"

"Goodness gracious, no, child. Your father and I were married a few years before you were born. We loved each other deeply. Ours was a love match."

"But what about Jackson?" Abigail couldn't fathom where this left the love of her life.

"I believe the letter will explain everything you need to know." The dowager nodded downheartedly.

Abigail stood with her letter, walking numbly to the chartreuse cushioned chair by the bay window to sit. Her fingers shook as she broke the Waterford crest's wax seal. She couldn't believe she was about to read her deceased grandfather's words, and the fact that they were written specifically to her was even more astounding.

My dearest granddaughter Abigail,

I'm sorry doesn't begin to explain how much I regret what I've done to you. I took you from your loving mother and switched you for a strapping baby boy who could carry on the Waterford legacy. Although I'm ashamed by my actions, I truly did what I thought was best for everyone involved. I couldn't bear to see my title leave the immediate family, nor could I bear for your grandmother to be tossed out of her home.

I've been watching you your entire life. I assuaged my guilt by making sure you were educated so you could make a good-match in the future. I sadly admit that I underestimated the stigma your illegitimacy would bring you. I should have chosen a married woman to foster you. Nevertheless, Delores Gibbons loved you, and the truth is, that's all that mattered.

Even if she can't pull herself out of the depths of her own sorrow, you were her life.

Abigail went to the next page, realizing that, if her high-handed grandfather were to have his life to live over again, he still wouldn't hesitate to rid himself of her for a male, which hurt.

Regardless of the measures I could have taken, I apologize for the burden you carried for being born out of wedlock. I feel it important to tell you how extremely proud I am of you. Your courage, my dear girl, is remarkable.

Was that supposed to make her feel better? It was his fault she had to live with such infamy.

I have now returned you to your rightful place, to the bloodline of which any English woman would be proud. I do hope with the passing of time you will come to understand why I did what I did. Most importantly, I wish to say, Welcome Home, my darling granddaughter, I love you.

My heartfelt love and devotion,
Your Grandfather William.

The man was mad. He loved her? What a mockery of love. He took her life, took her from her real parents, a mother and a father who where happily married and in love, and from her grandparents. She could have had him and the dowager. But he chose not to love her. He chose money and power over loving her. He chose his title.

Abigail crunched the papers in her hand. Eyes burning with unspent tears, she stood to say something to her mother. But a buzzing sound echoed in her ears. Her vision blurred. She could hear their concerned voices through a haze before she fainted.

***

At the shout for smelling salts, Jackson came running out of the study where he had been going over some financial reports. He hurried past the servants and into the ladies sitting room. "What's going on? What happened? Did someone faint?"

"Yes, dear. It's Abigail. But she's all right now," his mother said with tears in her eyes.

Abigail was lying on the sofa, and she sat up at the sound of his voice. Her careful coiffure was mussed, the silky brunette strands falling around her face in gentle waves. He crossed the room to pull her into his chest. Relieved she was well. "What happened, love? Are you all right?"

"You're smothering me, Jackson," Abby said with a smile that held his heart. He had never felt such intense love in his life. The mere thought of her being ill caused him pain. He realized he couldn't picture his future without her. So if he wanted to smother her with his love, then by God, he would. He gave her another tight hug just to be difficult and was delighted to hear her laughter.

"All right, my love. You've made your point."

"Now what happened?" he asked.

Abigail gave him some kind of helpless shrug, as if she was one of those women prone to the vapors when he knew she wasn't. It was most peculiar. "Really, I'm fine. Pre-wedding jitters, I suppose."

He cocked a brow. "As long as it's not cold feet?"

"Never, my lord."

"We were planning your big day, son. As you can see, your intended is fine. It takes much out of a lady, the planning of such an event." His mother spoke from somewhere behind him.

"She needs to rest." He stroked his hand over Abigail's chestnut tresses, pushing some strands away from her beautiful face and tucking them behind her ear.

"We only need a few more moments of your time, Abigail," said his grandmother.

"Yes, of course." She gave Jackson a gentle push and shifted herself into a seated position on the sofa. "You go, my love. Perhaps when I'm done here, we can go for a walk to the ruins you told me about."

"If you are sure you're all right?"

"I am." She kissed his cheek. "Thank you for being such a wonderful man. And thank you for caring about me."

"You anchor me with your love. I was certainly not this wonderful until I met you." He leaned close to whisper, "I highly doubt anyone finds me wonderful but you, and for that I'm grateful." He stood and helped her to her feet.

Looking at the fake smiles plastered on his mother and grandmother's face, he shook his head. His gaze fell to his mother. "All is well in here, Mother?"

"Of course, dear." He could have sworn she had looked like she'd been crying. He was well aware that women could get sentimental at times. He was sure his mother was remembering the special day she spent at the chapel near the Waterford Estate, the day years ago when she had married his father.

He turned to give Abigail a quick kiss. "If you need me, or the planning becomes too tedious, holler and I'll come running to sweep you away from these two wedding planners." He winked at her, gave a smile to the others, and left.

Abigail watched the door close behind him, and she had to bite the side of her fist to keep from crying out in anguish. Understanding of just how devastating this mess would be for her beloved struck her with such force she felt the impact like a blow to the chest. The import of her grandfather's letter filtered through her mind, and tears she had not allowed since her youth dropped from her lashes. "Jackson's illegitimate," she said to her mother through a watery haze, knowing how it felt to be in his position. Her heart ached with the knowledge of her past, which was in some sense the knowledge of Jackson's future. Lady Hastings crouched at her feet and took Abigail's fisted hands to her chest.

"I'm afraid so, my child."

"He's going to be devastated by this news." Her bitter sadness turned into abject outrage on Jackson's behalf, and she stood up from the sofa, no longer able to remain seated. Lady Hasting stood with her and put an arm around her shoulders. How dare her grandfather commit such a heinous crime against two innocent babies? "Jackson's not going to be able to cope with this!" she said hysterically. "His whole life has been a lie!" She turned out of her mother's comfort to stomp around the room, venting her overwhelming anger. The betrayal she felt was choking her, and soon Jackson would be served a heaping helping of that same betrayal as well. "But he loves being an earl," she wailed. "He loves overseeing his lands, and he loves the prestige he receives in elevated circles. Saints be praised, he even enjoys the numerous routs and balls he feels obligated to attend! This news will surely destroy all his hopes for a future. I know this! Being born outside the bonds of matrimony has followed me like a black cloud my entire life. What if he calls off our wedding? What if he feels he is no longer worthy of me?"

"Then we shall hold off telling him," her mother said from her place by the sofa.

"Not tell him?" Abigail asked aghast. "He needs to know. He has the right to know. He has a right to meet my…I mean, his mother. And she has a right to know she had a son, not a daughter. And then there's Jackson's unknown sire. It is imperative we find out who he is for Jackson's sake, for it is more important for a man to know. I really can't believe any of this is happening. I get the taint of my birth washed away, but that same taint is passed on to the man I love."

"I agree that he needs to know his roots," said the dowager. "However, I think this news should wait until after your nuptials. Jackson would call a halt to the wedding if his ancestry were to come to light sooner. Of this, I have no doubt," the dowager stated.

"He can be most obstinate once he sets his mind," her mother added. Abigail couldn't help herself from looking at Stephanie in wonder. This woman was her mother. As peculiar as the realization was, it also felt right somehow.

"But how can I keep something this important from him?" Abigail all but wailed her question. Her relationship with Jackson's was built on trust. She trusted him with the news of her birth and with all that she was, and he in turn had trusted her with his heart, even admired her ability to see through all his arrogant bluster. She would do anything to prevent his heart from breaking, but she saw no way around it. She would have to tell him, but not yet, as her mother and grandmother had suggested. She couldn't lose him before she even had him. Even her new family was in complete agreement on that score. He'd just have to understand that she kept it from him because she loved him, that she was waiting for his sake. As his wife, she could help him sort through this mess. As a rejected fiancée, she'd have no ground to stand on. She'd tell him after the wedding and guarantee their happiness before he, in his despair, prevented it. With her love, she'd see him through this betrayal and spend the rest of her life making sure he knew how important he was to her.

The dowager sniffled. "It's only for a couple more days. Surely we can all conduct ourselves appropriately until the time comes and we deem him ready for the news."

"Daughter." Lady Hastings smiled at that. "I know you don't want to keep this from him and I would never ask you to do so indefinitely. Even so, I agree it would be best to wait until after the ceremony, preferably days after. But he is to be your husband. Margaret and I are willing to let you decide the time."

"I don't want to ever tell him." But her mother was right—she would because she had to. He trusted her to be honest. She would tell him when the time was right, if there ever really was such a time, which she doubted. *Love will see us through this mess my grandfather set in motion. Won't it?*

"You are a strong, courageous woman, Abigail. I'm proud to call you my daughter. I know you will do what is right when the time is appropriate."

"And if you need us, we're here, always." The dowager came over to kiss her cheek and then left in search of her rooms, announcing that she was in need of a nap.

Lady Hastings stood staring at Abigail in wonder. "I'm glad we have found each other. I know it will take time for us to adjust to being mother and daughter, but I'm looking forward to getting to know my lovely daughter better." She kissed her cheek. "I have much to explain to my husband, but if you need to talk, I am here. I promise I will not allow anyone or anything to part us again." With those words, Abigail was left alone with her troubled thoughts.

***

Jackson hugged Abigail to him as they made their way upon his horse to the ruins he promised to show her. He relished the way his body hugged hers as his arms circled her waist to hold the reins in front of her. Her bottom bounced in stride with the horse, giving him a distracting erection, so preoccupying his mind that he nearly missed his turn.

She had, of course, balked when he insisted they ride together, her being new to the saddle. She preferred to walk. But after her brief bout of unconsciousness earlier, he wasn't taking any chances with her health. Besides, he was enjoying this experience with far too much enthusiasm. Perhaps he'd forget the idea of teaching her to ride; this arrangement was suddenly preferable.

His passion for her increased every day, and now he literally felt like he'd explode if he couldn't have her soon. As a gentleman, and knowing it important to abstain for his bride's sake, he controlled his hunger and waited. But he knew he had waited until his lust was so out of control that he'd have a damnable time being gentle when the time came. However, he reminded himself that, to judge from their countless amorous embraces, his sweet Abigail was just as passionate as he. She was a match for him, and he knew without sampling her that she would far surpass any of his wicked dreams. The thought made him ache below and he pulled her tighter against him.

He could smell the sweet scent of her hair as she rested her head back against him in contentment. He smiled. His entire life felt right with Abigail part of it. He had goals and purpose. Before they met, he had thought himself happy carousing the streets of London with his friends, drinking until the early morning hours as dawn streaked through the sky. The reality was his life lacked meaning and purpose, but now he could envision a future—their future and even their children's futures. He had never thought much about a family of his own, and now he couldn't stop thinking about it.

Abigail snuggled closer into the folds of his coat and he kissed the top of her head. Life didn't get better than this. He couldn't wait to make her his wife.

"This is lovely," she exclaimed, looking out at the long grasses swaying in the breeze. Insects hummed a soothing song and bits of twigs occasionally snapped under the horse's hooves. "We're up so high. I've never been able to see so far off in the distance. Thank you for bringing me."

"I'm glad you are enjoying it. I promise to take you riding often in the future. Are you comfortable?"

"Mmm Hmm. Very." He noticed she shut her eyes. He continued to lead the stallion off the path to a trail that cut through some brush. Ten minutes later, they came around a bend and he stopped. Abigail's eyes lazily opened and squinted while she accustomed herself to the slowly descending sunlight. She blinked in surprise at the sight before her. The ninety-foot high tower, which was very impressive even in its ruined state, always awed people.

"Most of the structure is gone, all except the tower. It was built in the 12th century and converted to a castle in the 15th century by Lord Riverdale. I used to play here often in my youth."

"And were you the gallant knight in shining armor come to rescue your lady love?"

He laughed at her romantic notion, just one of the many things he loved about her. "No. I was a dragon slayer who came to kill the two-headed dragon. You see, he was casting havoc on the surrounding area by breathing fire down upon the villagers." He puffed out his chest.

She laughed. "Were you a successful dragon slayer, my lord?"

"The best in the world. No one aside from myself was brave enough to take on a two-headed dragon."

"You certainly do sound brave. Did you not have any friends up to challenging this dragon?"

"None that could best me at sword play, and indeed, even in childhood, to the victor goes the spoils, but in this case, the victor got to scale the tower and kill the dragon."

"You climbed this tower?" Abby looked up at the imposing structure.

"I tried but never did make it, all the way to the top. Fear of crumbling rock kept me a safe distance from the ground."

"I can imagine."

"There's a perfect place around back where the grass has grown between a couple of collapsed walls, a splendid place for a picnic, I should think." He hugged her. "I can't wait to see what you've prepared."

"I hope I don't disappoint," she said.

"That, my sweet, you could never do," he murmured near her ear, gently nibbling her neck. She sighed in surrender. He pulled her forward and they continued around the structure to where the vegetation had grown up the sides of what remained of the walls of the building, creating an oasis around a grassy knoll in the center. Birds flew to and fro singing to each other among the deep green vines.

"You're right, Jackson. It's perfect. You're perfect."

Her sweet words touched a chord in his heart, and he kissed the top of her head. "I love you," he said, looking at the verdant nature surrounding them. He'd always found a special comfort here and was glad she appreciated this place's wild beauty. He slid off the back of his mount, flinching at his ebbing erection. Wasting no time, he grasped her waist and set her on her feet. Then, untying the basket and blanket, he passed them to her and secured the horse's reins on an outcropping of rock. He then spoke to his horse until his desire faded to a more controllable level.

He entered under a canopy of vines to find Abigail sitting peacefully on the blanket unloading an array of goodies from the basket. He could watch her all day. She found joy in even the most menial of tasks. As he walked closer, she looked up at him, casting him that enchanting smile of hers, her golden-rimmed eyes sparkling in the late afternoon sun, which also served to highlight the blond streaks in her thick brunette tresses. *Damn, she is exquisite.* "Need some help?" He came down to sit beside her.

"I'd prefer to serve you, my knight errant," she said like a meek serving girl who was eager to please.

"Then do so, wench," he teased, kissing the end of her pert nose. He watched her pop a grape off a vine before offering it to him from her fingers. He took the grape making sure his lips brushed her fingertips. "Keep it coming, woman. I'm far from satisfied." He smiled with wicked pleasure, knowing she knew he wasn't referring to food.

Her cheeks flushed becomingly. "Then allow me to remedy that, my lord."

She continued to feed him cold bits of smoked fish, chunks of cheese, and pieces of bread she dipped in a special sauce she had personally prepared. She spoon-fed him some plum pudding she made and he groaned in pleasure.

"I could definitely get used to this." He laid back to relax, folding his arms behind his head as a cushion. "Aren't you hungry?"

"No. Besides, I must see to my lord's appetite first."

"I'm quite full, thank you. Now, eat." He sat up. "No, allow me." He began to feed her as she had him, his desire sharpening each time her delectable lips clasped on a piece of fruit or her lips slipped down the spoon. At times, he could have sworn she was being purposely seductive. The vixen didn't realize the fire she had blazing inside him.

***

Abigail tried her hardest to keep all of the day's revelations far from her mind, but she was having the most difficult time behaving normally. She prepared a picnic for Jackson with the hope of freeing her mind from her troubled thoughts, but it hadn't helped. Although her smile came easy whenever she was in Jackson's presence, she still found some moments when she had to force her lips to curl up. *Why did this have to happen now? We are so happy.*

The weight of the knowledge she carried was taking a toll on her. She felt her silence on the matter as a kind of betrayal to him. She tried not to think, tried not to dwell on things she couldn't change, and to concentrate on the wonderful man beside her. She fully intended to tell him at the most opportune time. Now, was simply not that time. What words would she use to tell him of his supposed grandfather's treachery? The heartless machinations of her actual grandfather weren't easily explained away.

The unrelenting cloud that had followed her throughout life was shifted to Jackson. She wasn't sure how he'd weather the news without losing himself in the process.

Saints be praised, this is truly a disaster. She was reeling from the fact that her life was made up of falsehoods, but at least her changes born of the day's news had been positive. She was no longer a bastard. She had noble bloodlines. She even had another mother, a kind-hearted mother to care about her. And of course she couldn't forget her newfound grandmother. Abigail now suspected Lady Waterford had fainted upon their initial meeting because she surmised the truth.

Nevertheless, Abigail knew that her life could very well turn upside down when Jackson learned of his lack of title, money, position, and she feared, his self-worth. These facts were completely unfair and undeserved, and yet, she knew it was too much to hope that his reaction would be mild. Could he bear such news with understanding? She doubted it. What man would? She wished the truth hadn't been revealed. Her soon-to-be husband was a proud, in-control kind of man. He was sure of this world and his place in it and she found it unlikely that a man so used to having his own way was going to stay hinged when his life was completely knocked off kilter. One thing she knew for certain—he'd be furious.

She watched him stretch out on the blanket beside her completely at ease, his hands behind his head and his ankles crossed. His sandy colored lashes formed a perfect crescent on his lean cheeks. His relaxed expression told of his positive outlook on the future, their future. She sent up a silent prayer for God to see them safely into that future.

Jackson claimed she had steered him from the life he considered routine. He insisted that she was the spark he was missing. With a simple smile, she could feel his love wash over her like an ocean tide. Abigail had found the man for her, and come hell or high water, she was going to keep him. She would not let her dead grandfather wreck the best thing that ever happened to her.

She watched the birds fly overhead, bits of sticks clamped in their beaks as they went about fortifying their nests. How she wished she could build a shelter around Jackson. She was so lost in her guilt-ridden thoughts that she didn't even notice Jackson running his fingers down her arm.

"Are you all right, sweet Abigail? You seem a million miles away. You aren't worried about the wedding are you? No second thoughts?"

She turned to him with a warm smile, swallowing the guilt of keeping something monumental from him. "Second thoughts about marrying the love of my life? Absolutely not, my lord. Now that I have you, I'm not about to let you go."

He gave her arm a tug and she willingly fell across him. Kissing her firmly on her lips, he pulled back to say, "Good, because I'm not about to let you slip away."

She ran her hand down his face, her heart aching for the hurt she knew he'd soon feel. Why couldn't this discovery remain buried with her grandfather?

"Are you ready to head back to the house?" he asked, leaning up on one elbow. She imitated his position as they lay side-by-side looking into each other's eyes.

"If you are."

"If you don't wish to sacrifice your virginity within the ruins, I believe we should go."

She kissed him, quickly sitting up to put the empty containers back into the basket.

"You are sure nothing is troubling you?" he asked.

Abigail realized she was going to have to work on perfecting a stoic expression. Apparently her troubled thoughts were too close to the surface. "I'm fine, Jackson. I can't wait until Saturday."

"Me either." He stood, offering her his hand. She grabbed the basket as she rose to her feet. "Especially the evening." He ran his hand possessively down the curve of her bottom and gave a little squeeze, sending a surge of desire shimmering through her body. She couldn't wait for Jackson to make her his in every way. The mere thought of sharing his bed made her heart race and her mouth go dry. The pull between them was undeniably captivating.

"I'm quite looking forward to the night myself," she told him. "I do hope it's all we have built it up to be," she teased lightly, and he gave her bottom a firm smack.

"Minx." He laughed as he picked her up and placed her onto the horse. After securing the basket and blanket, he swung up behind her.

With a sigh of happiness, she settled against him, allowing his warmth and masculine scent to wrap around her like a protective cloak. When she was in his arms, it was harder to dwell on the wrongs dealt to them in the past, and much easier to lose herself in the wondrous feelings of being loved by Jackson.

The future she envisioned for them was bright and filled with promise. Love and laughter would surround them. It had to.

Trying to keep her mind fixed on the positives, she leaned her head back against his chest and listened to the steady beat of his heart, taking comfort in it. She closed her eyes and concentrated on the rhythmic sound. The wind kissed her face as his scent mixed with the animal smell of the horse and made her mildly woozy. The even drone of insects filtered around them as they made their way back to the Waterford Estate. At some point, she drifted off to sleep.

Jackson knew the moment Abigail drifted into slumber; she turned in his arms and nestled her cheek against his chest. The sensations he felt having her cuddled up next to him made him proud and protective of the woman who had captured his heart.

Not wanting to wake her, and enjoying the feel of her in his arms far too much, he circled around a large portion of the estate before finally making his way to the stables. He shushed the stable boy as he tossed him the reins, then he slowly slid to the ground with Abigail tucked in his arms.

Entering the foyer, he noticed his mother rushing down the hall. At the sight of Abigail in his arms, her eyes widened in alarm. "What happened? Is she all right? Did she faint? Oh, dear heavens, did she fall off the horse?" His mother put a hand to Abigail's cool cheek. It warmed his heart to see her caring for Abigail. He knew the two of them would get along splendidly. Whatever Abigail and his mother discussed earlier had obviously created a bond between them.

"She's fine, Mother," he whispered. "She's asleep. With all the wedding plans and fittings she's had to endure, it is little wonder she's exhausted. I need to take her to bed."

"You'll do no such thing, young man. I'm not going to allow you into her room. Now hand her to me. I'll see her safely tucked into bed." His mother held out her arms, gesturing to take his burden.

Jackson gave her a puzzled look. "She's not a child, Mother. And I don't believe you can carry her, at any rate. She's too heavy for you. Now please stop being silly and step aside. I'm not about to take liberties on her person until we are wed. And although I'm amused by this conversation, it really must end for she's growing heavier by the second and I don't wish to drop her." He made a move to make it look like his arms were indeed growing weak.

His mother practically jumped out of the way as if he'd really dump Abigail to the floor. He shook his head at her and headed for the stairs. He was further surprised when he saw his mother following closely at his heels like a mother hen protecting her young chick. If he wasn't so irritated by her interference, he'd laugh.

When he reached the top of the landing, his mother skirted around him to open the door to Abigail's bedchamber.

He placed Abigail gently on the bed and watched in amazement as his mother began to fluff the pillows. To his further surprise, she gathered up Abigail's long tresses, and with quick efficiency braided the locks, tying off the single plait with some ribbon she fished out of her pocket. Abigail sighed, burying herself deeper into the blankets.

"She's fine, Mother. I'm glad to see you've taken a liking to my future wife. It's nice to have your approval."

"Approval? I think she's perfect. You chose well, my dear." He thought he noticed tears pooling in her eyes, but she blinked them away so quickly he was not sure. His mother was acting most peculiar. "I'm very proud of you." She tucked a few strands of hair back behind Abigail's ear.

"Thank you. It's really not necessary for you to smother her so." He thought of how he'd tried to do the same to Abigail earlier in the day.

"I'm not smothering. I'm mothering. It's what mother's do. I see nothing wrong with seeing to her comfort. Now out you go. I need to remove her riding habit. You, my dear, are not going to be here when I do."

Jackson gave a laugh and removed himself from the room, but not before he cast one last look at Abigail resting peacefully.

CHAPTER TEN

Abigail awoke the next morning to loud voices and clattering. She didn't remembered coming to her bed and Sophie explained the particulars of how she came to be there. She must have been more tired than she thought. It was just like Jackson *not* to wake her. He was always looking out for her well-being. She was also informed that Lady Hastings had undressed her, plaited her hair, and tucked her in. The thought of her mother doing these tasks for her warmed her. Her mother, the same person Jackson believed to be his mother. *Dear Lord, will this get any easier?* How was she to keep everything straight when everything was turned upside down? She was a ball of nerves.

Stephanie, her biological mother, was kind and seemed more than willing to make up for lost time. Time they would never get back, Abby reminded herself. Meanwhile, Delores Gibbons, the mother who raised her, had yet to learn she didn't have a daughter, but a son. This news would certainly send her to the bottle again, and just when she claimed to finally have full control of her drinking, according to her last letter.

Thinking of letters had Abigail dwelling on the missive her grandfather wrote her. The cryptic words would forever alter her life and Jackson's life.

She heard more orders being issued downstairs, and looked over at the overflowing breakfast tray Sophie brought her. "Perhaps I should go down and help with the preparations." She began to get out of bed when Sophie ceased choosing her outfit for the day and dashed across the room, firmly tucking the blanket back around Abigail's waist. Fixing the pillow behind her head, her maid placed the wooden breakfast tray across her lap.

"The dowager insists you relax today, as does Lady Hastings. There are guests arriving by the cartloads, miss.

Best you eat a hearty meal. I'll get you fixed up right and proper when you finish eating."

Seeing no way out, Abigail took a bite of her toast. "There are many guests here?" She thought their wedding was to be a small, intimate gathering. Delores wasn't even able to attend and the thought saddened her. Biological mother or not, Delores had raised her and thus would always be her mother. There were problems between them because of her mother's drinking, but they loved each other dearly.

Sophie continued to pull some unmentionables from the chest of drawers. "Of course, miss. Lady Waterford does have her fair share of influential friends."

The toast stuck in the back of Abigail's throat. She took a sip of hot tea with cream and swallowed. "Yes, I'm sure she does."

"You should see all the extra help she hired. Your day is sure to be a success. I saw your dress. I must say it's the loveliest gown I've ever laid eyes on."

"It's definitely the grandest one I have ever owned. I can't wait to see how the gown looks once the final alterations are completed."

"I know you'll look exceptional. Now, which do you prefer, the blue or the peach?"

The blue dress had a modest v-neck suitable for daytime wear. Seed pearls edged the neckline, and satin ribbon accentuated the cap sleeves. The dress had flowing skirts, sure to crackle when she walked. The peach dress had a high round neckline edged in cream lace. Little satin bows were affixed to the elbow-length sleeves. The skirts were also flowing but the satin seemed too pumpkin orange. "The blue one, I think, perhaps with matching ribbon interwoven through my hair and those pearl earrings the dowager gave me."

"You have such splendid tastes, miss."

Abigail could have pointed out how Sophie only gave her two dresses to choose from and the choice had really been hers, but her maid would likely not see the humor and return to the wardrobe to offer her more selections. Besides, Abigail would have chosen the blue dress anyway. It was truly lovely.

An hour later, she sat at her dressing mirror worrying her lower lip between her teeth. She felt nervous, dreadfully so. She had to face a house full of strangers, many of whom believed her a bastard.

Remembering that they were here with the purpose of celebrating her nuptials, she prayed all would be well and tried to relax. The dowager would not have invited those who were set on ridicule. Aside from Jackson's support, she knew the dowager, as well as her mother, Lady Hastings, would be by her side.

She convinced herself all was dandy and that her nerves were just getting the better of her. Surely this was how most brides felt the day before their wedding.

Descending the stairs, she saw hordes of colorful, pungent flowers being carried in through the foyer to disappear out onto the verandah at the rear of the house where the wedding reception would take place.

She couldn't help smiling. Tomorrow was her wedding day, the day she and Jackson would vow their love to each other forever. She saw him come out of the parlor looking wonderful as always. The cool, calm smile on his lips never failed to make her breath hitch. *Saints be praised.* She was so thoroughly in love it scared her. At his steady gaze, her nervousness fled like the gypsies in the summer. There wasn't anything she couldn't do with Jackson by her side.

"You look exceptional, my love." He came forward, kissed her cheek, and offered her his arm.

"Thank you." She noticed the throngs of servants moving around the foyer but noted she had yet to see a guest. "I hear we have guests. Where are they hiding?"

"Grandmother has the majority of them ensconced outside on the side patio, away from the chaos. I was waiting for you." Her heart fluttered at the hunger in his eyes. "Would you like to join them?" he asked, pulling her closer. "Or perhaps you and I can escape somewhere more private?"

"As tempting as I find your invitation, my lord..." She batted her eyelashes at him teasingly. "I believe it's best if we go greet our guests."

"Very well." The deflated tone in his voice made her smile.

She began to walk, but she came up short when he didn't budge. "What is it?"

"I think a kiss is very much in order."

Abigail turned into his arms, her hands automatically going up to play with the ends of his hair. "I couldn't agree with you more," she said before his mouth came down upon hers. A moan escaped and he pulled her even closer into his consuming heat. His kisses held the ability to deplete her strength. When he finally backed away, she was unsteady on her feet.

"You're going to be the death of me," he said with a smoldering stare, his forehead coming to rest against hers.

"I certainly hope not, my lord. Although, I have heard it said that the French refer to the pinnacle of pleasure as *le petite mort*."

"Trust me, my love. I will make it far more pleasurable for you than death could ever be. Now shush. I find I can no longer continue this vein of conversation with you. Come, let us greet the guests before I forego my gentleman's promise and steal you away to my room."

Meeting his passion-filled gaze, Abigail flushed and nodded. She was going to see to this man's happiness if it killed her.

The patio was swimming with people, and many more spilled onto the side lawn. Colorfully garbed ladies mingled with richly clad gentlemen of various ages. She recognized some of the dowager's acquaintances who had visited the Waterford home for tea on occasion. She was introduced to a slew of others throughout the long afternoon. Although the guests were all kind and congratulatory to her, she still found herself wishing her mother, Delores, could be with her. She even longed to see her friend Clarissa, but she assumed it was too much for her to hope that Lord Loring would allow her to attend.

Abigail was having a pleasant time conversing with Lady Hastings and many of her close friends when Jackson approached. She wondered where he had disappeared to twenty minutes before and was grateful for his return.

"Excuse me, Mother, ladies; I need a moment with my intended." With a few charming comments, he soon led Abigail away.

"Where are we going, Jackson?"

"I have a surprise for you." He hurried forward and she practically had to jog to keep up with his long strides.

"Really?" Abigail looked at the line of carriages parked next to the stables and the wagons unloading supplies in the front of the house. "And just where is this surprise?"

"I'm right here." Clarissa stepped out from behind a tree bedecked in an amethyst confection covered in layers of flounces. Her sky-blue eyes lit with excitement and something else Abigail could not yet decipher.

"Clarissa," Abigail nearly shouted with glee. "You made it for my wedding. This is the best surprise. I never thought… That is, I'm so happy you are here."

Clarissa gave her an exuberant hug. "We owe my visit all to your persistent fiancé. He convinced Mother that we had to attend. So here we are."

Abigail cast Jackson a blinding smile. He was undoubtedly the most thoughtful man in all of England. "Thank you so much."

He nodded, returning her smile.

"Why don't you come and meet our guests?" Abigail asked.

"I'd prefer not to," Clarissa answered solemnly.

"Why ever not?" Abigail's eyes filled with concern. She knew her friend well enough to know something was bothering her. She turned to find Jackson had wandered a few feet away. "What's wrong?"

Clarissa smacked disgustedly at one of the flounces of her amethyst dress. "I look like the top of some silly cake."

"Not to be rude—I mean the color's lovely on you—but why are you wearing...well, that?" Clarissa didn't need a frilly dress to distract from the classic beauty that she was. The dress was overwhelming.

"Oh this is one of the many dresses my mother had made for my Season."

Abigail couldn't help laughing at Clarissa's abject expression.

"I know! It's ridiculous. I look awful, and you know what is worse?"

Abigail tried to restrain her amusement.

"I now have an entire wardrobe made up of such silly concoctions. This was one of the least offensive."

Both women looked down at the dress, and when their eyes met, they burst into laughter. The dress was truly a nightmare, not at all reflective of Clarissa's refined and elegant sense of style. "I couldn't attend unless I promised my mother I'd wear the dresses she purchased. I don't know how I'm going to survive this catastrophe. As you can see, my mother's tastes are deplorable." Abigail couldn't argue with that. "Nevertheless, I did want to be here, and these dresses..." She smacked down a flounce. "These dresses appear to make my mother happy. Not an easy feat considering she's married to my father."

"So she's here with you?"

"Yes, the dowager took her to her room to rest."

"Well, I don't care what you wear. I'm just happy you are here."

"Me too. So why don't you show me your wedding gown."

"All right, but..." She turned to Jackson, who was smiling. "Would you mind?"

"No, you two enjoy yourselves. I'll go see how my mother's holding up. She tends to overtax herself trying to make sure everyone's happy."

"Then I should go help her," Abigail insisted.

"No, you won't, sweetheart. Go enjoy yourself. I'll assist Mother."

Abby was more than willing to help with the guests, but a part of her really wanted a moment with her friend. "Are you sure?" she asked, and suddenly she found herself physically turned in the direction of the front door.

"I am." He gave her a firm kiss on the lips, turned on his heel, and vanished behind the side of the house.

Clarissa clucked her tongue. "I see he's still a bit overbearing."

"I believe it is just as much a part of him as his head." Abigail linked her arm through Clarissa's and the ladies laughed their way into the house.

Abigail led Clarissa into her dressing room where her gown was hanging.

"Oh, Abby, I love it! Not a flounce or a bow in sight. Simply elegant. It's perfect."

"Thank you. I love it."

Clarissa wandered through her wardrobe, pulling on the skirts of several of her dresses to give them a once over. "Your clothes are spectacular. I never knew you had an eye for fashion."

"I don't; the dowager does. She's been most generous." Abigail longed to tell her friend how she was switched at birth, but she held back. Until she spoke with Jackson, she thought it best not to inform anyone else. They had to get through the wedding first, and there would be plenty of time to tell Clarissa after the honeymoon, but it was hard not to share her news. There wasn't much she kept from her friend. Jackson had informed her that they would be taking a wedding trip when he finished some business in London, an investment he was working on with Alexander, the Earl of Everett. As to their destination, he claimed it was another of his many surprises. She almost guessed the destination to be Cairo. The thought thrilled her. Finally, she'd see Egypt.

"I need to get the dowager together with my mother," said Clarissa. "Perhaps she could explain that bows, pleats, and Saints be praised, ruffles, are not to be borne for a girl over the age of fifteen."

"At least the color is all right."

Clarissa looked down at her amethyst flounced dress. "Yes, it is its only saving grace."

"Well you know you are always welcome to filch anything you wish from my closet."

"Thank you, Abby. I may have to. I swear I have given up on attending any functions dressed as I have to now. I can't tolerate people looking at me with sympathy in their eyes."

"Your clothing is only a small part of who you are. Besides, you're beautiful. With your golden hair and dazzling blue eyes, I believe you could dress in window curtains…"

"Case in point." Clarissa gestured to her own attire.

"I'm telling you a man with a lick of sense won't care how many flounces your mother has sewn to your clothes."

"Speaking of which, where is your mother?" asked Clarissa.

"Oh, she's mingling with the guests." Abigail realized her error as soon as it was out of her mouth. She tried to push her unsettling thoughts from her mind.

"Your mother is here? You must introduce me. I can't wait to meet her."

"I'm sorry, Clarissa. I misspoke. It's Jackson's mother who is doing the mingling. My mother sent a note. She hasn't been feeling well of late. I'm afraid she can't make it. I'm going to visit her soon though. You know she hates to travel." Unfortunately, her mother had never been well enough, or willing for that matter, to leave the confines of her home. She rarely even visited the nearby town not far from where she lived.

Clarissa being Clarissa shrugged. "Then I shall have to go with you the next time you visit her, so we can make sure we describe every detail of your wedding."

"That would be nice. But why don't we go meet your mother." Abigail knew from the many years Clarissa and she had roomed together that Lady Loring was nothing like her narrow-minded husband. Abigail looked forward to meeting her.

***

After a long day of well-wishers and seemingly endless small talk, Abigail found herself peacefully alone in her room. She was excused from any late night entertaining by her mother, who insisted a bride must get a full ten hours of sleep.

Sophie, her maid, was unusually quiet as she went about undressing her. "Are you all right, Sophie?"

"I'm fine, miss." Abigail lifted her arms as her blue dress was pulled over her head and she was left in her chemise.

"Not to pry, Sophie, but you aren't acting like yourself. Why?" Her maid was normally chatty.

"I'm not to bother you, miss." Sophie kept her gaze fixed on the floor.

"I'm asking you to tell me," Abigail pointed out. She truly did want to know why her maid seemed out of sorts.

Taking a deep breath, Sophie exhaled her remark in one long drawn out breath. "The Earl of Waterford has left the estate."

"Jackson has left?" *He knows the truth.*

"I'm afraid so, miss. I'm extremely sorry, miss."

***

Jackson's stallion tore up the ground with rapid strides as he headed for his destination. He would have preferred traveling in the morning, but he feared the trip would take too long, thus causing him to be tardy for his nuptial's—something he wasn't about to let happen.

Thankfully, the moon was high on this almost balmy evening, allowing him to see his way down the well-traveled road, which was blessedly devoid of people this late at night.

After witnessing Abigail's thrill at seeing her friend, he knew what had to be done. He wanted his future wife to have the best wedding day he could provide. To reach this end, he decided to fetch her mother, Delores Gibbons. After all, Delores was the only family Abigail had and he didn't want her regretting that her mother couldn't attend. Abby had suffered through enough difficulties during her life. His goal was to see her happy. He wanted to show her another side to life than the one from which she was ostracized. He wanted to show her she belonged—and so too did her mother.

Abigail belonged with him, always. Their life together would be one filled with joy and acceptance, of passion and heated nights, of sharing and caring. Love. He was completely boots over hat in love. Who would have thought he would have fallen for his grandmother's companion? He was not one to believe in the silly notion of love at first sight, but the moment their eyes met, a special bond existed between them.

Of course, his Abigail wasn't only lovely in the extreme; she was, blessedly, the feistiest woman he had ever met. She even accepted his domineering ways and loved him in spite of them, but he always knew when he stepped over the bounds. His lady could cast an evil eye that threatened to turn a man to cinders at her feet. She also had the kindest heart and a most understanding nature. She took his breath away with her warm innocence. Her courageous ability to adapt to any given situation was remarkable. He admired her strength. They'd be perfect together.

He did wonder what kind of reception he'd receive by his future mother-in-law. Why was the woman so averse to traveling? He stopped at a small town to procure a carriage for her, assuming, that like his fiancée, Mama Gibbons might not be in favor of riding a horse. The carriage would slow their travel, but if they moved quickly, they'd arrive back at the Waterford Estate in the early morning hours. This also meant he'd have to find a place to sleep for the night. He hoped Mama Gibbons was willing to take him in, but if not, he'd circle back to the nearby town to sleep at the inn.

Pulling his horse to a stop in front of a stone cottage with vines climbing up all the sides of the dwelling, he slid out of his saddle. He noticed the small, well-maintained vegetable gardens lining both sides of the walkway. According to his watch fob, it was close to eleven in the evening. He was relieved to see a candle sputtering in the window. At least his future mother-in-law was still awake.

Tying his mount to a nearby tree, he headed toward the door and knocked.

It took a while for someone to answer. He was about to knock again when the door slowly opened and a woman wearing a white kerchief on her head peeked out at him through blue eyes, her hands holding her robe closed at the neck.

She looked confused as her steady gaze looked him over. "Do you know what time it is, sir? What brings you to my door at this hour?"

Jackson put on his most winsome smile; the one he knew made all mothers trust him. "If I may have a word with you, madam."

"What is it you want?" She didn't budge from the door and was clearly not about to allow him entrance. He couldn't blame her. A stranger showing up in the middle of the night was not someone she should allow entrance.

"My name is Jackson Sethos Ramesses Danvers, the Earl of Waterford." He followed this with a formal bow, taking in a whiff of her alcohol-tinged breath.

She eyed him warily. "My daughter's Earl of Waterford?"

"One and the same, madam." She backed up to welcome him inside. A smile lit up her tired face as Jackson entered her residence. "I'm sorry to disturb you at this late hour." He stepped into the cool interior of the main room. The wallpaper adorning the walls was badly frayed and the furniture threadbare, but he noted that the domicile was clean.

"Isn't the wedding tomorrow?" Delores asked, walking across the room to pour herself a large glass of spirits.

"It is," he answered, declining when she offered him a drink. He remembered Abigail's concern over her mother's overindulgence in liquor.

She took a hefty gulp of her drink, seeming to need some kind of restorative because of his appearance at her front door. He saw her hands tremble while she clenched the glass as if her life depended upon it. "Are you all right, madam?"

"You look like someone I used to know, my lord. I'm sorry, but I believe I'm a bit shook up by the similarities." She waved her hand, dismissing her own ramblings as inconsequential. "What brings you to my door?" Panic flashed across her face as she asked. "My daughter isn't ill, is she?"

"She's in fine health, madam. I'm here to collect you."

She laughed, causing some of her drink to spill over the rim of her glass to the floor. She didn't seem to notice. "Collect me, you say?"

"Yes, madam. It is my bride's wish for you to attend our wedding. I'm here to see you do so." Perhaps that came out somewhat domineering, because the woman's back stiffened. He sighed and started again. "It was my hope that I could convince you to travel with me in the morning. It shouldn't take more than a couple of hours, and if you wish, you can be returned after the ceremony."

"My daughter knows I abhor traveling."

"A fact I am well aware of, but I think, this time, you will make an exception. Especially since your attendance will affect the happiness of your daughter."

"Brilliant, my lord. You have added just enough guilt in your demand to make my attendance feasible." She pointed her half-filled glass at him.

He bowed with a smile. "I made myself a promise to do all I can to see to Abigail's happiness. You, madam, are a part of that. I hired a hack in town, a well-sprung vehicle that I think will meet with your approval." He suppressed a groan when the woman tipped more liquor into her mouth. "Perhaps we should discuss all the arrangements in the morning when you are feeling more yourself."

"What you see is what you get," she said, downing the rest of her drink.

Jackson nodded, quickly getting irritated with the drunken woman. "Your daughter needs you, madam, and the least you could do is make an appearance at our wedding."

"The least I could do, young man, is stay put where I belong. Nevertheless, I will consider your offer."

"See that you do." He'd throw the woman on the back of his horse if need be. But hopefully such extreme measures wouldn't be necessary. "Do you perhaps have a place for me to sleep?" He could already envision himself at the inn. He didn't believe she'd allow him to stay. His appearance seemed to upset her, but then it occurred to him that perhaps the woman was always this distressed.

"You wish to stay here?" she all but squeaked.

"If it isn't too much of an inconvenience."

She dismissed his comment with another awkward wave of her hand. He could have sworn he saw tears in her eyes. "You can sleep in Abigail's room. It's the second door down the hall on the right."

Jackson bowed. "Then I'll see you in the morning. Early in the morning, madam."

She sighed as if defeated. "I'll be ready."

Jackson gave her a nod, went outside to see to his horse, and then returned to make his way to Abigail's childhood room. At least Delores was speaking as if she intended to travel with him. He had to fight every instinct he had not to remove the glass of spirits clutched in the lady's hand, but he did wish to start off on the right foot with his mother-in-law.

Tomorrow, Delores would see the end of his tolerance. He wasn't about to bring the mother of his bride to his nuptials smelling like an alehouse.

***

Jackson left Abby's childhood home before dawn, returning by early morning with the carriage he had hired the day before and a driver from town. He entered the house praying Delores had pulled herself out of bed and was ready to depart, but he assumed it would probably take more persuasion on his part to get the woman actually into the vehicle.

What he didn't expect to find was Delores ready with a valise propped by her feet. She was dressed in a smart traveling garment of burgundy that set off her blue eyes and the fading blond strands of her hair she had twisted up onto her head. "You look fetching, madam." Surprisingly, she blushed at his words. *It seems the lady doesn't receive compliments often.* She was an attractive woman and it saddened him to think she wasn't often told.

"Thank you, Jackson. Although, I admit that I'm nervous. I haven't been to a wedding or any kind of social gathering in many years. This isn't what I'm wearing to the wedding. I bought a lovely dress last year. My daughter always insisted I should wear it, even though I have had no place to do so. However, today is a special day. It seems I was saving it for this wondrous occasion. I think my sweet Abigail will be pleased."

"Splendid. We had best be on our way then." He assisted her into the vehicle, nodded to the driver, and swung up onto his horse.

Jackson rode his stallion alongside the carriage, checking his watch. At this rate, they'd make it back with plenty of time to spare before the ceremony. He looked up at the clear blue sky feeling happier than he had ever felt. Today was his wedding day. The weather looked promising; with an outside reception, this was important.

He spoke with Delores on and off throughout the journey. He was delighted to hear stories about his bride as a young girl, but Delores admitted her daughter was often away at school trying to better herself. His sweet Abigail was always trying to find acceptance and better herself in others' eyes.

She was so important to him that his heart squeezed at the years of ostracism she suffered.

When they drew nearer to the Waterford Estate, he noticed a caravan of vehicles sitting in front of the house. Some were being moved to the large expanse of grass next to the stables. Jackson decided to lead them around back to avoid guests, thinking it best to slip Abigail's surprise to her through the servants' entrance.

When they reached the side entrance, he saw Delores pull a silver flask out of her pocket. She was about to put it to her lips when Jackson leaped off his horse and into the driver's perch, shoving the driver aside as he yanked back on the reins.

Delores sputtered on her sip and glared at him as if he'd gone mad. "What is the meaning of this? You darn near choked me to death."

Jackson stepped down and yanked open the vehicle's door. "Give that to me now."

"This?" She held up her flask, and he snatched it from her fingers, causing her to shriek.

With a calm, even voice, he said, "There will be no drinking for you, madam. This is your daughter's special day. You, Mama Gibbons, will refrain from upsetting her with your free flowing spirits."

"How dare you treat me in such a boorish manner!" He could have sworn he saw a smile behind her outrage. *Feigned outrage?* Her peculiar behavior had him baffled, but he didn't have the time or inclination to dwell on such matters at the moment.

"You are to become a part of my family today. As a member of my family, it will behoove you to know that I tend to be most autocratic with those who are a part of my inner circle. I suggest you get used to it. You will refrain from drinking. I promise to be most attentive in order to ensure you achieve this end. Overindulgence is unacceptable, and indulgence of any kind by you is strictly forbidden. Do I make myself clear, madam?" He glared at her and she handed him the cap to her small drinking vial.

"I understand your domineering attitude far too perfectly, my lord. In truth, I admire your fortitude. You have a spine, and I respect your determination." She seemed to be lost in her thoughts for a brief moment, and then she added, "This doesn't mean I agree with your highhanded tactics, but I will hold off from further speculation until I see you with my daughter. Knowing Abigail, I'm sure she has your controlling manner well in hand."

"Indeed she does, madam." Jackson smiled at the woman's keen understanding, relieved she wasn't going to balk any further about him stopping her drinking.

"I like what I see in you, Jackson. Now if you'd be kind enough to show me to my daughter."

"Right this way." He took her hand and helped her out of the vehicle. *It seems I may be having a positive effect on my future mother-in-law.*

He entered the kitchen with Delores clinging tightly to his arm. Whispers surrounded them the moment they crossed the threshold. It seemed the entire household was under the misconception that he had fled to avoid his wedding, which was easily the most ludicrous thing he'd ever heard. He was not about to jeopardize his life with Abigail for anything. When his mother came into the kitchen, her downtrodden face lit up like a child's on Christmas morn. Her relief was obvious. *Bloody hell, I should have left a note explaining my absence.*

"Oh thank heavens!" His mother ran over to hug him, and he let go of Delores. Shooting an evil eye at the servants watching them with curious stares, his mother dutifully turned her attention back to him when they cleared the room. Backing up a few steps, she smacked him hard on the chest. "Where have you been? Your bride has been frantic. I told her you'd be back, but she got it into her head that you were running from her—something about her not being good enough for you. It took all night to get her settled down. I expect an explanation now."

Jackson felt a tinge of anger at his mother's words, for how could Abigail ever believe he would leave her? She needed to trust that his love was true and know that, no matter what happened, he would remain by her side forever. He tried to concentrate on the task at hand. "Mother." Jackson stepped to the side. Delores was practically hiding behind him. "Allow me to introduce Abigail's mother, Miss Delores Gibbons."

Whatever his mother was about to say stopped when she saw Delores. She stared at the woman like she had two heads. Her eyes went from Delores to him and back again numerous times. *What is the matter with her now?* Finally, to Jackson's relief, she smiled.

"Miss Gibbons, it's a pleasure to meet you. I'm Lady Hastings, but you may call me Stephanie."

"Please, call me Delores."

"Very well, Delores. I'm sure Abigail will be thrilled to see you."

"I hope so." Delores looked at Jackson, who was still wondering what had his mother acting peculiar again. "Why are we still dawdling, Jackson? Your mother said Abigail is upset, and so we must go to her at once."

In truth, they had not moved because his mother had yet to get out of their way, but in response to Delores' anxiousness, Jackson took his mother-in-law's arm and they stepped around Stephanie.

"Hurry along, dear. I daresay, just seeing your handsome face will put all her fears to rest," his mother's voice rang out behind them.

Jackson and Delores ascended the stairs arm in arm, turned down a hall, and came to a halt in front of Abigail's room. "Your home is truly lovely, my lord."

"Thank you." Jackson eyed the door. "Allow me to speak with her first before you make your grand entrance."

"I don't know how grand it will be, but I'll be here, my lord." Delores seemed to be enthralled by the expensive flowered wallpaper lining the hall. He watched her run a hand over the smooth surface, so unlike the tattered paper adorning her own walls. An allowance to Abigail's mother would be welcomed and he intended to see she received one. Perhaps then, she could redecorate and buy several of those dresses she saved for special occasions. He already liked the woman. She possessed the same moral fiber he admired in Abigail.

"I'll be back in a moment."

"Take your time, my lord," she stated, ambling down the hall to look at a picture on the far wall.

He shook his head in wonder and pushed open the door to Abigail's room.

CHAPTER ELEVEN

Abigail had one of the worst nights of her life. Sleep had eluded her, and indeed it had taken much convincing by the dowager and Lady Hastings over the course of nearly the entire night before she realized the love of her life would never be so cruel as to leave her. She had hugged this thought to herself while she watched the sunrise and finally closed her eyes for sleep.

Now she sat in front of her window, looking out into the distance but not really seeing much of anything as she prayed for his safe return. She yawned, resting her head against the cool glass. The door opened and she turned to welcome her maid.

Jackson filled the doorway. He stepped in and closed the door behind him. Holding his arms wide, he ordered, "Come here, Abigail."

She didn't hesitate. She leaped from her seat and practically catapulted herself into his comforting embrace. *Jackson is here. He didn't leave me. He loves me.* Tears stung her eyes as she held him in a death grip. "Don't you ever do that to me again! I didn't know what to think. I thought you may have gone for a ride and fallen, or worse. I even tried not to believe you left me, but that was hard." He frowned as she rambled on. "I kept remembering our love and I finally found solace." His beautiful smile reappeared. "Do you know how worried I was? Where on earth have you been? Why didn't you tell me you were leaving?"

His lips stopped her from further query and she melted into his embrace. Eventually he pulled back, a sparkle of mischief dancing in his eyes.

"You're planning something, my lord. I can see it in your eyes. What is it?"

"I have a surprise for you."

"You left to fetch me a surprise?" She blinked, shaking her head in frustration. *Does this man not realize the agony I suffered thinking him dead?* Not that she expected an apology, but it would have been nice. But, he did bring her a surprise and she could hardly be angry at that. *Today is our wedding day.*

"I'm sorry I caused you such worry."

And now all is fine, she thought acerbically, but she held her tongue. His presence lightened her mood considerably.

"You had to know I'd be back, Abigail." He rested is forehead upon hers. "I've been looking forward to this day for weeks now."

"Yes, well, like I said, as the hours passed, I grew increasingly upset, until… Oh, I don't know. You'll think it's silly."

"No I won't. What is it?"

"I was upset until I looked at my ring, your gift to me, your promise to make me happy, and I believed then that all would be well. I fell asleep soon after."

He kissed her. "Good. You can always trust me to be by your side, my sweet, just as I will always trust in you."

She swallowed her guilt at keeping family secrets from him, pushing away any negative thoughts that could tarnish their wedding day. "I love you."

"And I love you." He set her away from him. "Now, if I'm to be freshly bathed and donned in my finest, I had best get to your surprise so we can both ready ourselves. Although, I must say, I find you fetching in your robe." He winked playfully. "How are you holding up?"

"A poor question, my lord, since a few short minutes ago I was worried sick." She cupped his cheek in her hand. "I'm much improved now."

"I'm glad, because your surprise is more than likely growing impatient in the hall." He turned to open the door with a comical flourish.

Abigail's mouth dropped open in joyful surprise as her mother sailed into the room with a bright smile, looking healthy, well, and even happy.

"I certainly couldn't miss my child's special day." Abby found herself enveloped in her mother's embrace, which was something new for her mother was never one for acting syrupy.

Abigail hugged her tightly, breathing in the scent that was uniquely Delores. Her wonderful fiancé brought her mother to her, or rather, his mother. The thoughtfulness of his gesture warmed her heart and proved she was right in loving this man. He was always so good to her.

Jackson cleared his throat, his smile wide as he watched their reunion. "I'll leave you two to your own devices."

"Wait." Abigail stepped out of her mother's arms and dashed across the room to give him a thank you kiss. "Thank you, my love. You are the most thoughtful man on earth. I don't know how you convinced her to come, but it likely wasn't a simple task. She even appears to be in high spirits."

"Seeing your smile is all the thanks I need." He kissed her temple. "I'll see in a couple of hours, my soon-to-be wife." With those parting words, he bowed to her mother and left the room. She knew he felt triumphant with himself.

***

Abigail heard the sound of Jackson whistling and she let out an "isn't it wonderful to be in love" type of sigh.

"That's quite a man you've captured, my dear."

"I think so." Abigail couldn't help grinning. "Did he order you here?" She all but laughed when her mother's face lit up with a telling smile.

"He can obviously be somewhat overbearing when he has his mind set on something," Delores said. "I believe he means well. He certainly cares about you, and that's really all that matters to me. You should have seen him in action though.

He was a man set on doing whatever it took to make his bride happy, a commendable quality to be sure. I daresay he would have dragged me here had I refused, but then, I really did want to be here."

"Why did you tell me in your last letter that you couldn't travel?"

Delores shrugged. "I'm afraid I wasn't feeling well the day I wrote you. Sorry."

Abigail steered from that path. She did not want to hear how her mother drank herself into a sad stupor. "All that matters is you are here now. So, you approve of Jackson?" Not that it mattered, but Abigail was curious about the opinion her mother had formed of the man who would be her husband this day, especially because Jackson was, in actuality, her son.

"It's a bit late for you to be asking my approval, Abby, but yes. I believe Lord Waterford will make you a fine husband."

"Good, because I do too. It's my hope the two of you will grow close." *Like a mother and son should be. Like we are.*

"I'm sure in time we shall. Now why don't you show me your wedding gown."

Abigail opened her dressing room door with an excited flourish. Her dress was hung high in the center of the room where it was less likely to get soiled or wrinkled.

"Oh my word, Abby. It's so lovely."

"I love it." Abigail ran her hand over the satiny pink skirt. "You don't think it overly plain do you? I mean, I refused to allow them to add rosettes along the waistline. Mother, are you crying?"

"I never could fool you." Delores wiped away her tears. "I dreamt of a dress like this when I was young."

"But the man who sired me wasn't the marrying kind?" Abigail hedged a guess. It was like pulling teeth when it came to getting Delores to speak about the man who fathered her child. But now that the child was a male, it was imperative she discover all she could for Jackson's sake. Who was the man who left Delores with no opportunities for a normal life?

"Oh, I heard he married, but recent accounts indicate he's a widower now and has been for many years."

This was the closest Abigail had ever come to finding out the man's identity. Obviously, her mother had kept track of her lost love. "If he favored marriage, why didn't he marry you when he found out you were carrying his child?" Abigail tried to take the sting out of her voice.

"I'm afraid life is never that simple, my dear. He didn't know about you because I never told him. I was only a farmer's daughter, Abby. If we had married, his father would have disowned him and I refused to allow him to give up everything for me."

What about your child? Abigail wanted to ask, but she didn't. Now that her mother was finally talking about the man, she wanted to keep her doing so. Jumping to Jackson's defense wouldn't help, since her mother had no idea he was her offspring. "Am I to assume he's a member of the privileged class?" Abigail asked in a casual manner while she felt along the newly sewn hem of her dress. It was a reasonable assumption to believe him of the upper classes, given what her mother had told her thus far.

"My dear, today is your wedding day. Surely you don't wish to dwell on a past that can't be changed?"

"But the two of you loved each other?"

Her mother hesitated and then nodded. "Hopelessly. For a while, we were each other's worlds, until harsh reality crept in, and I had to banish him from my sight. I wanted him to have the world, and so I gave up mine. This allowed him to enjoy his title, lands, prestige, and all that the wonderful man deserved. He didn't deserve to be cut off without a cent, and we wouldn't have survived together if he had. His father was a powerful man, Abby. He would have never allowed our union." Delores walked over to finger the ribbon on Abigail's wedding slippers. Abigail now knew for certain that, even after all of these years, her mother was still very much in love with Jackson's father. "I'm glad my child will have her happily-ever-after."

Abigail couldn't help herself; she had to ask. "What was his name?"

"It hardly matters, Abby. Best to let sleeping dogs lie."

"But this man's father—is he still alive?"

"No, he passed on about twelve years ago now," Delores said with a shrug.

"And you never contacted the man of your heart?" Abigail couldn't imagine not getting in touch with Jackson, no matter the obstacles.

"I'm sure he has long forgotten me by now." Delores put her fingers to her temples as if warding off a headache. She reached into her pocket and actually smiled when it came out empty. Abigail knew it was her drinking vial she sought, and she briefly wondered where it had gone. But then she smiled, knowing her soon-to-be husband responsible for its disappearance. "Let us forget about him and concentrate on your magical day, all right?"

Abigail knew the discussion would end there. She was still reeling from the fact that Delores had mentioned the man at all. "Very well. Why don't you help me choose some jewelry to match the diamond cross necklace Clarissa loaned me." She linked her arm through Delores' and led her out of the dressing room.

Delores rummaged through Abigail's black lacquered jewelry box as servants began filing into the room to fill her tub with buckets of steamy water. Her mother was right. There would be plenty of time for digging about in the past later. Today was a day of celebration. Abigail wasn't going to allow anything to ruin this joyous day.

***

A steady influx of guests continued downstairs. Many would be staying the night before heading back into town the next day.

When Jackson finally grew tired of being fussed over by his valet, he descended the steps to aid his mother and grandmother while they organized and greeted the new arrivals.

It was only a short ride to the church, and various carriages and phantoms were already lined up in the drive to transport the people to and from the service.

"Jackson, there you are." His mother swooped up behind him bedecked in a sky-blue chiffon gown. She looked exceptionally lovely for his wedding. "You really must do something about your footman."

Jackson cocked an eyebrow. "To which one are you referring?"

"The Herculean one, Simms. The man assisted Mrs. Cartwright and her daughter from their vehicle, and Mrs. Cartwright looked up at his enormous size and fainted. He's scaring our guests with his…his largeness."

Jackson chuckled. "That's why I keep him around."

"All well and good, dear, but perhaps he'd be better off helping behind the scene. I don't have time to be reviving all the female guests."

"I'll see what I can do, Mother. Is there anything else?"

"Enjoy yourself, Jackson. This is going to be a day you will never forget." She spun on her heel, flagged down the housekeeper, and began issuing more orders.

Jackson walked outside in search of Simms, an easy man to find because he stood head and shoulders above the other servants. "Simms, I need a word."

"Yes, my lord. Sorry about the lady fainting earlier. It seems she mistook me for a giant. Women can be fanciful."

"Indeed, but to avoid further silliness, I believe it best if I put you to a different task. It's something very important to me."

"I'd be happy to help in any way I can."

"Good, but you're going to need some extra hands. I want the hunting lodge turned out into a romantic paradise. Do you think you're up to the challenge?"

"Not to boast, my lord, but there's nothing I can't do once I set my mind to it."

"Exactly what I wanted to hear. Now let me tell you what needs to be done." Jackson went on to describe every last detail of what he had envisioned.

***

Abigail tried to remain calm and steady as she stood at the end of the church aisle with all eyes focused on her. She held onto a friend of Jackson's arm, Julian Bancott, Viscount Rathemore, who had happily agreed to accompany her down the aisle, exclaiming it was the closest he'd ever allow himself to get to the marriage alter. At which point, Julian went on to explain how he had once loved and lost, his fiancée having run out on him a few short days before their vows were to be spoken. At Abigail's sigh of understanding, he laughed off his obvious heartbreak with cool nonchalance, as if the event was of no consequence. In truth, it was clear by the look on his face that the loss still bothered him. "She must not have been worthy of your love."

He shrugged. "It's in the past, and right now, we should concentrate on the present." A woman began to strike the keys on a piano. "I believe that is our cue. Are you ready?"

"I've never been more ready for anything in my life." Abigail looked down the bow-bedecked aisle and saw Jackson, glorious in elegant black, come out of the back room to stand in front of the altar. His snowy white cravat was tied fancier than usual, and his hair was slicked back away from his handsome face. His beautiful blue eyes locked with hers. The bishop gave her a nod as he held onto his bible.

She began to walk forward at a rapid pace only to be pulled back to a slower more fluid stride by Julian. "There's no hurry, Abigail. I daresay my friend would wait all day if necessary. Besides, all these people came to witness this spectacular event. It wouldn't do for the bride to rush by them in a blur of pink satin."

She smiled. Julian's words had calmed her nerves a little. Her gaze remained on Jackson as they now *slowly* made their way forward. With a bow, Julian gave her over to Jackson, whose calm smile and soulful gaze put the rest of her nerves at bay.

The bishop's drone filled the church's quaint interior. The tiered candle altarpiece cast light upon the wooden beams above. A short while later, she found herself in Jackson's arms returning his kiss, sealing their fates together. Uproarious applause commenced, and even laughter when Jackson picked her up and carried her out of the church and into an awaiting carriage.

Jackson murmured in her ear as he maneuvered her through the vehicle's door, "You're mine now." A delicious shiver danced up her spine. He deposited her gently on the carriage seat, then climbed in after her, scooped her up into his arms, and rested her on his lap.

She turned to him with possession lodged in her heart. "And now you are mine." He lowered his head to hers and she lifted her chin, allowing him to skim kisses down the side of her neck. "Forever and always."

"Which means I now have every right to do this." His finger slid along the neckline of her wedding gown in a gentle caress, causing her nipples to harden and ache.

"Definitely," she whispered, heat filling her frame, desire rocking through her body.

His hand cupped her breast and she arched into him, wanting more, craving his touch. Soft lips settled on hers, coaxing a soft mewling sound from her throat. And then he lowered the gown so her breasts came to rest on top of the neckline most scandalously. Sexual need clawed at her when he lowered his head and took one of her erect nipples into his heated mouth. Sucking, licking, and tasting her like some sweet delicacy. She moaned, raking her fingers through his hair, pulling him into her chest.

The carriage rolled to a stop, causing Jackson to curse and let out a groan of frustration. Abigail couldn't help but laugh as she hurriedly righted herself. It felt like their desire had been contained forever.

He helped her out of the vehicle. "Just you wait until tonight," he practically growled in her ear.

"Promises, promises," she teased, sauntering into the crowd of well-wishers.

By early evening, the number of guests dwindled. Abigail asked Delores to stay for a couple of days, and to Abby's surprise, she agreed. Unfortunately, Clarissa had already departed, but with the promise, she'd meet up with Abigail in London.

Abigail's feet hurt from being on them all day, and her jaw hurt from her constant smile, but the wedding celebration had been perfect and, all in all, she was quite pleased. She was about to go in search for her husband when he came up behind her, pulling her back against his hard body. She could feel his heat through her many layers of skirts and smiled up at him knowingly.

"We are going."

Abigail leaned further into his body. "Going where, my lord?"

"I have another surprise for you."

She turned into his arms. "At this rate, you shall surely spoil me, husband."

"That is the plan, wife."

"And where's this surprise hiding?"

"In the hunting lodge. You've yet to visit there. It sits on the northern end of the property."

"And you wish to go there now?" She couldn't stop herself from running her hands up the lapels of his elegant black jacket. When he was standing so close, it was easy to forget there were others in the vicinity.

"It's all I've been thinking of since we said 'I do.'"

"Then I'm in favor of saying our good-byes...quickly."

"Let us make a rapid turn about the patio." He took her arm. "I find I'm all tapped out of patience. I need you."

She smiled and kissed him. "Let's hurry." They made their way into a circle of guests when a shrill cry rent the air.

"Oh!" exclaimed Abigail.

"What the...?" Jackson grabbed her hand and they ran into the house, making a speedy search of the rooms they passed. They found Delores on the floor of the blue parlor. Jackson immediately closed the door.

"Mother." Abigail rushed to her mother's side and knelt to examine her. She looked up at Jackson. "I think she fainted."

With an arrogant smile, Jackson reached into his breast pocket to pull out a metal tin of smelling salts. "Here." She cocked an eyebrow in query. "It seemed prudent I carry a vinaigrette when the women around me keep fainting."

She smiled in amusement and passed the open vial beneath her mother's nose. "Mother, can you hear me?"

Delores slowly opened her eyes, confusion evident on her white face.

"Are you all right, Mother? What happened?" Abigail asked. Jackson picked up Delores and laid her on the beige chaise lounge.

"I saw a ghost," Delores said the moment she was seated, her eyes darting around the room as if she expected to find a specter floating in the corner.

"A ghost? Whose ghost?"

"It was his ghost, Abby, your father, the Duke of Salisbury."

Abigail sat back stunned. She now knew Jackson's father's name. Did her mother say the man was a duke? "The Duke of Salisbury is my father?"

"Did you hear what I said, Abby. He's haunting me. He's not even dead, and he's haunting me."

"This is nonsense!" Jackson slammed his hand down on a nearby table. "How much alcohol have you consumed, madam?"

"Now, Jackson, Mother's been very good today." As Abigail tried to defend Delores, the veins at Jackson's temples looked ready to burst.

"Answer me, madam." Jackson's tone was completely accusatory.

Delores glared at him, and then huffed, "I came into the parlor to get away from the crowd." She turned to Abigail. "You know gatherings of such magnitude tend to make me uneasy."

"How much, Delores?"

"Jackson, please," Abigail beseeched.

"How much?" His voice practically shook the rafters.

"I had a small glass of bourbon when I came in here." Delores' shoulders fell in defeat. Abigail fell silent.

"I'm assuming this ghostly apparition came after your restorative?" Jackson asked.

"As a matter of fact it did, but I see no connection between the two."

"Well you'll just have to excuse me if I do."

"Jackson," Abigail scolded, mouthing the words "be nice." At that point, he sighed.

"Come, wife. It's time for us to take our leave."

Abigail crossed the room to stand before her domineering husband. "You will refrain from being a bully, husband. And you will be nice to Delores, understood?" She held her back stiff, wanting him to know she meant what she said.

"You will bid your mother a good evening, Abigail, or else I will toss you over my shoulder and carry you out of the house." His voice was stern, but at the end of his order, he gave her a quick smile, his way of lessening his demands.

"Now see here, Jackson. I will not allow you to order me…"

"Abigail, dear," Delores spoke. "Go with your husband. This is your wedding night."

Jackson raised his hands in victory. "Finally, the woman's making sense."

"Stop it." Abigail smacked him in the chest before walking back to her mother. "Are you truly all right?"

"I'm fine now, dear. Just go."

Jackson opened the door. "You heard her. She's fine. Let's go."

"My lord?" Delores called out to Jackson. "Being that this is my daughter's wedding night. There are a few things I think I should discuss with her before you leave."

"That won't be necessary. I plan to see to her education."

"Yes, well," muttered Delores before falling silent.

Abigail knew her cheeks had turned crimson right along with her mother's. "Jackson will take care of me, Mother. But I need to know you will be well."

Delores patted her hand. "I swear to you, I'm fine. And *sane*, I might add." She practically shouted the word for Jackson's benefit.

"Very good then." Jackson gave an impatient nod toward the open door. "Abigail."

Delores did indeed seem well. It was Jackson's face that was turning a reddish hue. His posture was stiff and militant. But Abigail wanted this night as badly as he did. She kissed her mother on the cheek. "I'll check in on you tomorrow. Lady Hastings and the dowager will see to your comfort."

"I'll be fine, dear. Now go, before one of those throbbing blood vessels in your husband's temple breaks."

"Yes, you're right. Such a lovely day, but a long one for all of us."

"Enjoy your night, my dear."

With a nod, Abigail took Jackson's arm and they left the house, but not before Abigail made sure that Lady Hastings was at Delores' side.

CHAPTER TWELVE

Jackson snatched up the reins on the high sprung phantom and set the horse to a fast clip toward the hunting lodge. He noted that Abigail was extremely quiet, and he assumed she was most likely contemplating the real identity of her father. It wasn't every day a young woman found out she was the daughter of a duke. "I'm sorry if I upset you. Nevertheless, your mother needed to be taken to task, love. I won't allow her alcohol-induced hallucinations to disturb you."

"I know, Jackson. It's just all these years I've tried to squeeze the truth out of her and failed. Do you think she really saw him? I mean…" She worried her bottom lip. "Was the Duke of Salisbury at our wedding?"

Jackson turned down a graveled road leading to the lodge. Evergreens lined the drive and the horse's hooves quieted on fallen pine needles. The air was brisk and refreshing, and Jackson was happy to be putting the wedding, along with the happy guests and cheerful family members, behind him. He was also proud of himself. He did it. He married the love of his life. And although the wedding and reception were above the cuff, he could have done without that last bit in the parlor. Now his wife was thinking about her father instead of the night before them. This was not how he envisioned this moment, but he'd do all he could to help her to cope with this new information. She had told him how she often wondered about her father, and he hoped she'd now feel some peace knowing who the man was. "I'm not rightly sure, love, but I will find out."

"There must be a guest list lying about the house. We should have taken it before we left."

"Can this not wait until tomorrow?" He was willing to do anything for Abigail, including postponing their wedding night if his wife deemed it absolutely necessary, but that didn't mean he wouldn't attempt to talk her out of returning for a guest list. He had far more interesting things on the venue for their wedding night than such considerations, the night for which he had waited with utmost patience.

"Of course this can wait. It has waited this long." She shrugged, moving closer to Jackson's side. He circled his arm around her and she snuggled closer. "I believe for tonight we should just concentrate on ourselves. Don't you think so?"

Every part of his body thought so. He smiled, thinking of the night before them. "I couldn't agree with you more, wife. I promised you a night you won't forget, and I plan to see that promise fulfilled."

"I'm hoping this will be a night you never forget as well, husband."

"I'm not likely to forget the night I made *my* sweet Abigail my own."

"What a possessive man you are, my lord," she teased. He was glad she wasn't going to allow the world to intrude upon them. He was indeed a possessive man where she was concerned.

"Undeniably so, my fair lady." He saw her swallow with difficulty when he addressed her as a lady. She had now soared to the status of a duke's daughter, far surpassing him on the ladder of aristocracy, and he couldn't have been happier for her. She'd always thought herself unworthy of love and respect because of her birth. Hopefully this news would allow her to see herself as he saw her. She was always every inch of a lady, and now there was proof of her stellar bloodlines.

His body came to life when they turned a bend and the lodge came into view. The stone and wood dwelling was nearly surrounded by huge overgrown pines. Near the front porch was a marble birdbath in the semi-kept up front garden, but it was too late in the evening for birds to be flying about. One could hear the soft drone of insects. The scene was peaceful, and more importantly, private.

When the vehicle came to a halt, Simms came out to take the phantom and the horse to a lean-to behind the house. Jackson circled around to carry his bride into their honeymoon hideaway. She giggled when he swept her into his arms. When they crossed over the threshold, the warmth of her body in his arms caused his body to ache with desire too long held in check.

The interior of the hunting lodge was just the way he envisioned. He felt proud when he noticed Abigail's eyes fill with tears. As always, he was touched by her romantic heart.

Roses of every color filled the room to overflowing, their scent wafting through the air as if they had just stepped into a lover's paradise, and indeed they had. Candles were aglow in every corner and on every table. A light repast monopolized the small circular table in the far corner of the room to the left of the roaring fire in the stone hearth. The room was sparsely furnished, but what furniture there was looked rich and heavy.

He placed her on her feet and nodded with a smile at the maid who scurried out of the lodge, closing the door behind her. The twinkle of merriment on the maid's face made him almost laugh with giddiness. Abigail was finally his.

"It's breathtaking, Jackson." He watched her while she traversed the length of the main room, her hand trailing along the smooth expanse of the velvet brown sofa placed in front of the hearth. He noticed how much pleasure she took in touching things, noted that she tended to favor velvet.

"I hoped you'd like it, but don't worry. I still plan to take you on that trip to Egypt." He pulled her into his arms and sank down on the sofa, placing her on his lap. "Are you hungry?"

"No, are you?" She brushed a few hairs back from his brow, running her hand down his cheek.

"Ravenous, but not for food." He ran a finger down her soft cheek, loving the slight blush creeping into her face. He came forward and brushed his lips softly against hers. Tiny kisses meant to entice and hint at the night of pleasure before them. She squirmed on his lap when he deepened the kiss, causing his arousal to jerk in response. "Abigail, love, your wiggling is killing me."

She went to jump up, clearly assuming she was in actuality hurting him, but he grabbed her hips and pushed her down against his erection. "I wasn't being literal, my love. I just want this to be perfect for you. I don't want the race to be over before getting out of the starting gate, so to speak."

She cocked her head sideways, considering his meaning. She cast him a smug and far too sexy smile. "We can't have that." She seemed to enjoy the sexual torment she caused him. *The minx.*

"We have waited so long my body is straining to hold back. To be gentle with you."

"Perhaps…" She slid his elegant coat off his broad shoulders. He leaned forward and she removed the silver waistcoat beneath, discarding them both behind the sofa. Abby then said, "You need to stop thinking so much. I trust you implicitly, husband. I know you wouldn't hurt me."

Just the thought of being inside her was making him sweat. "About that," he paused, realizing he made a mistake in not letting Delores explain what would take place.

She blinked. "There's going to be pain?" She stared down at him for an explanation. She looked surprised by this news. Yes, he really should have allowed the mother and daughter talk.

He groaned. "Some pain is to be expected, so I'm told. Nevertheless, I promise that, after the first time, the pain won't come back."

"And you can guarantee this?"

"I think I can?" *Great job, suave seducer. Nothing like scaring one's wife on your wedding night.*

"You *think* you can?" her voice raised an octave and he chuckled at her look of consternation.

He nuzzled her neck. "I know I can."

"Then where is the pleasure you've been promising me?" She was a complete innocent and he couldn't help smiling at her adoringly. He never loved anyone or anything as he loved Abigail. She was perfection personified.

"I promise you'll experience pleasure many times before the sun rises."

She kissed him then, a deep, heated kiss that seemed to numb his mind. Then she whispered, "All right then, I'm ready."

He gently bit the tendons along her neck, trying to block out the desire she caused to rock through him at her words. His tongue trailed up to her ear, and he whispered, "That's my brave girl."

"And, Jackson?" She held a hand on his chest as she pushed back to look at him.

"Yes, my love."

She gave him an impish grin. "Please don't hold back."

He never answered her plea, his need to have her overriding all thought. He delved his fingers into her hair, sending hairpins flying in various directions, then grasped the sides of her head and pulled her to him, sinking his tongue deep into her mouth, plundering her as if his life depended upon it, and the truth was, he believed it did. She had become as important to him as the air he breathed. Although he wanted to possess her and prove to her just how madly in love he was, he still held back. He would make this special for her. He would hear her beg and plead before he joined their bodies together. She would know she belonged to him mind, body, and soul.

She freed the buttons on his shirt, yanking at his cravat with unskilled fingers and tossing it aside. Her eyes widened in what could only be called sheer delight when she parted the halves of his shirt to run her hands along his chest, combing her fingers through the light smattering of hair covering his chest. Her body moved against him with her manipulations and he groaned. His wife might be an innocent, but her touch sent fire to his loins. She followed his hairline down past his navel and went to work on the buttons of his trousers. His body pressed against her hand and she grasped him through his pants. He throbbed at the contact.

My turn.

His hands traveled up from her hips to trace her silhouette, his fingers skimming along the length of her neckline as he moved them around her lithe form to work on the cloth-covered buttons running down the back of her wedding dress.

With each button he slipped free, his anticipation climbed to even greater heights. He drew the dress down from her shoulders, taking the straps of her pink chemise with it, exposing her glorious breasts for his viewing. Her nipples hardened into tight buds at his close examination. He caressed her, taking one of the rosy nubs between his teeth, and then he laved it with his tongue as she blessedly arched into him.

"Oh, Jackson."

"You like that, my sweet?"

"Umm Hmm." He continued his assault, moving his hands down her waist where her bodice lay scrunched. He stood her up and pushed her garments off her body, gazing at the apex of hair between her shapely thighs with a hunger he didn't know he possessed. She stood before him clad in pink stockings with a lacy white and pink satin garter belt, swaying with desire on her slipper covered feet. Her eyes were heavy with sexual arousal, her black pupils dominating over her golden-rimmed irises.

Giving out a roar like the randy beast he was, he scooped her into his arms and carried her to the bedroom, all the while his wife trailed wet, hot kisses along his heated flesh. She whispered words of love in his ear, and he quickened his pace. Her tongue flicked out to line the curve of his ear, and he practically kicked the door down in his haste to get them inside.

Abigail barely had time to admire the romantic atmosphere of the spacious bedroom before she was tossed none too gently on a rose petal-covered satin bedspread. Her body slid along the satiny surface, scattering the fragrant blooms to the floor. Although she realized this was happening, her gaze never left Jackson's, whose raw hunger made her tingle all over. *Jackson is going to make love to me.* She held out her arms to him. "Come to me." Her voice sounded low and not at all familiar to her ears.

She almost laughed when he began to tug at his boots, hopping on one foot and then repeating the motion as he tugged off the other. She giggled when his fingers shook and he swore when the remaining buttons on his trousers wouldn't surrender. But her laughter died abruptly when he removed his pants, leaving him naked and hard in front of her. She stared with interest and maidenly trepidation at the appendage jutting forth. All of his body was covered in a smattering of hair, except for his man part. She watched it jump upward and noticed his grin when she gasped. Clearly he did it on purpose. She ran her hand over the green satin coverlet in invitation.

"I want you to come to me, Abigail." His voice was low, seductive, and powerful. Clearly her husband wished to be in control, and she decided it was certainly better that way, since she wasn't sure just what it was she was supposed to do, exactly. Soon they would become one, and although she couldn't yet picture how this was to work, her body trembled with anticipation.

She sat up, swinging her legs off the bed to walk toward him. She sashayed forward in a manner she hoped was seductive. Taking her hand, he led her to the side of the bed, indicating for her to sit. She did so, looking over his shoulder at the large mirror which reflected his muscular and very attractive backside. She realized he had positioned them in front of the mirror intentionally and her heart raced. He wanted to watch them worship each other, and as wicked as that image was, she was more than willing to comply.

He undid her garter, tossing it away, before he knelt before her, lifting her leg to rest on his shoulder as he slowly began to peel down her stockings. Her breath hitched at the intimate contact of his fingers on her thighs. She noticed his hands shook as much as hers and was relieved she wasn't the only one so affected. *Dear Lord, I am entirely exposed to him.*

With the task finished, he sat back to look at her nude form. Her legs fell down to the bed, but she shamelessly did not draw her knees together. Glistening beads of sweat formed on his brow. She squirmed with delight when he ran a hand down the hollow of her breasts. He looked her over and with a sigh of what she could only assume was pleasure, and he moved onto the bed to position himself behind her, her head leaned back to rest on his chest, his bare legs encasing hers, and she felt his arousal press into her lower back. To Abigail's surprise, she found herself looking at her naked reflection; her private area exposed, hair mussed, lips kiss swollen. Who was this wanton creature looking back at her? Jackson looked at her reflection in the mirror, slowly taking down the remaining pins securing her hair. He pushed the brown locks over one of her shoulders, raining kisses down her neck, biting and nibbling on her, making her squirm in place.

"You're so lovely, Abigail," he purred in her ear as his hands ran over her arms and then came around behind her to cup both of her breasts. The image embedded in her mind as she leaned into his heat and closed her eyes, encouraging the undeniable power he so easily wove over her.

"Open your eyes, my sweet. I want you to see all the delicious ways I plan to show you my love and devotion." He pinched her nipples and her heart raced as she did what he bid. Slowly her eyes opened and focused on his in the mirror. He grinned wickedly at her, his hand moving over the smooth expanse of her stomach. "What do you feel, Abigail?"

She could feel his erection on the small of her back. She could feel his heat and the hair covering his torso and legs. Her body wanted to melt into him and he actually expected her to speak? *Is he serious?* She could barely gather a coherent thought right now, let alone describe the sensations coursing through her as he thumbed her nipples. "I..." He gently bit her shoulder and she moaned in surrender. "I don't think I can speak," she answered honestly as one of his hands moved lower to the apex between her legs.

"Then just watch." He slid a finger between her silky wet folds and began to fondle her in a way she never imagined. "You're so perfect, Abigail. Open yourself to me, my sweet, I want to see all of you."

Her head rested on his shoulder as she complied. His fingers continued to work their magic as she watched him caress her through the mirror. It was sinful and perfect at the same time. She still couldn't believe that was her reflection. She knew she would never look in a mirror again without remembering this.

"Feel good?"

He opened her legs wider with one hand as the other continued to stroke her with maddening precision. She could feel her dampness on his fingers. Her eyes widened when he drove one of them inside of her. She realized she had not responded to his question, and she pondered it now. *Good* didn't even begin to describe the pleasure he was creating. Her body ached where he touched her, straining to reach a place that only he could take her. Although she didn't know how to react, her body did, of its own accord. Her hips undulated and pushed into his caress.

"That's it, my sweet. Let the pleasure wash over you."

That was a command she happily obeyed. Her head tossed restlessly back and forth, as she fisted the coverlet around her, as she allowed sensation to consume her. "Please, Jackson." She grabbed onto his thighs not knowing what it was she begged for, but she wanted it. As wicked as this seemed, she wanted this. Carnal need clawed through her breast and she began to pant.

"That's my girl, Abigail. Beg for me." As her body tightened, his fingers grew in their frenzy, stroking and entering her until she was hot all over. Her body felt stretched taut. Her mind drifted into a state where only touch and feelings registered. His scent invaded her senses. His body seeped into hers, surrounding her.

"Give yourself to me," he commanded thickly. "Let go, Abigail. Just feel."

His words drove her over the brink of sexual pleasure, and she moaned and convulsed with ecstasy against his hand. Her body shook with the intensity of her first climax. Her mind reeled and her limbs turned to mush. Slowly the waves of pleasure subsided, filling her with a sense of inner peace and completion. She opened her eyes to see his hand still pressed tightly against her, the hunger in his eyes now grown to a level of ardor she had never seen before. "I love you," she said.

"Ah, my beautiful and lovely wife, how happy you make me." He moved from behind her and off the bed to stand between her open legs. Then, to her utter shock, he knelt and placed his mouth at the core of her being.

"What are you..." She didn't get her entire question out before she received her answer. He was showing her how to have pleasure, giving her the lesson he promised her. She was shocked by such flagrant sexual play, but she was also aroused to such a sensual height that she refused to reveal her embarrassment. This was Jackson doing this to her, and she reveled in each new experience.

He flicked his tongue over her folds gently, fondling the nub that fanned her desire. "I'm tasting you, my sweet. It's like heaven," he murmured, briefly gazing at her with hooded eyes. With a heady grin, he plunged his tongue deep inside her, causing her to buck in response. Pleasure began to pool low in her belly again when she shamelessly grasped his head to hold him to her.

With a groan, he spread her legs wide and slid his naked torso up the length of her body. She felt his erection upon her and squirmed to allow him entrance. His chest came down to brush the tops of her sensitized nipples.

Jackson grabbed his cock and rubbed it against her wet heat. She was his. Never in his life had he felt such acute desire for a woman. It took all his control to hold back from entering her. He could taste her on his lips, and he reveled in the possessiveness gripping him. He wanted to enter her now, but he wasn't going to mess this up. He promised to make her beg, and beg she would. He'd make damn sure she never forgot this night, because Lord knew he never would. Just watching her find release was nearly his undoing.

He pushed the head of his cock into her, and she stretched to accommodate him, falling back on the bed in surrender. He moved her backward so their bodies were comfortably on the mattress, and then he inched himself forward again. He made a few shallow thrusts and then pulled himself free.

His arousing wife went to grab him back to her, but he shook his head and lowered himself between her legs.

"Please, Jackson. I want you inside me. I need to feel you."

"Do you like this, Abigail?" He flicked his tongue ruthlessly over her.

"Oh, yes, love…yes."

When her pleas for release became too much for him to endure, he slid back up her body and entered her further, coming to a quick panting stop when he hit her maidenly barrier.

"Kiss me, Abigail," he ordered, and then he plunged his tongue into her mouth as he plunged his cock past the barrier.

He felt her flinch and tighten. Her nails raked his back. He stopped with his full-length embedded deeply inside her. Up on his elbows, he gazed down at her dilated pupils. "Are you all right?"

Her hips undulated beneath him causing him to clench his teeth and hiss. If he wasn't careful, he'd be the one begging. He slid his lips down her neck, gently nipping at the tendons, and then kissing each nibble he took.

"I'm fine, Jackson. Please just move."

He thrust a few more times into her, barely maintaining control. "Are you begging, my sweet?"

She ran a loving finger down his cheek. "Wasn't that your intention, husband?"

"Indeed," he said, removing his cock from her body and moving down to place his mouth upon her again.

She moaned, her head moving back and forth as she begged, her hair fanned across the bed, her nipples hard and erect. He watched her in amazement. She was wonderful. He moved upward again at her frantic pleas, taking a nipple between his teeth, and then he entered her again, pumping himself inside her with the abandon she demanded from him.

She gripped his shoulders, her cries of pleasure pushing him to the brink of his unsteady control. When her body convulsed against him, squeezing his cock, he gave into his own release and spilled himself deep inside of her with a primitive grunt.

Abigail sighed in complete fulfillment. Her body tingled, her thighs twitched, and her head swam in a kind of euphoric amazement. "I love you so much, Jackson."

"And I love you, Abigail." He pulled himself out of her, still dazed by the unbelievable chemistry between them. He lay next to her and smiled when she snuggled into his chest.

She toyed with a few locks of his hair while they gazed lovingly at each other. "Is it always like that?"

"Only with you, my sweet. Only with you."

Abigail smiled, kissed his chest, and curled up for sleep beside him.

CHAPTER THIRTEEN

Abigail must have slept like the dead. She awoke to the smell of breakfast meats, hot chocolate, and some kind of yeasty pastries. She gave a languid stretch. The drapes were partially opened, and by the sun's position, it had to be approaching noon. What a lazy bones she was this morning. *A content, happy, lazy bones.* She moved her vision away from the window and toward the smell of food. Her wonderful husband wasn't there. *A moment to myself.* Time to replay each delicious sensation she experienced during her husband's expert lovemaking. She let out an audible sigh and hugged the Jackson scented pillow to her naked chest, inhaling deeply into the green pillowcase. She had never felt so happy, so alive, and so utterly wonderful.

***

Jackson stood in the threshold between the bathing chamber and the room where he had made Abigail truly his. The bedchamber smelled of sex and he inhaled deeply. His shoulder was leaning on the door's frame as he lazily indulged in watching his wife. She was spectacular. If last night was any indication, he had married a passionate woman. Years of happiness spread out before them.

Abigail's hair was disheveled from their very thorough lovemaking session. She sat on her calves in the middle of the bed with her bare feet tucked beneath her, smelling his pillow. A possessive smile lit his face.

He knew she might feel a little awkward after giving herself so completely last night, and as usual, he couldn't help teasing her a bit.

"There are only a few scents lingering on that pillow, my

love. Which one is it you seek?"

Abigail dropped the pillow and a deep blush filled her cheeks. He swallowed when her breasts bounced with the movement leaving her completely naked before him. His body immediately stirred to life. He had a feeling he'd never get used to the sight of Abigail naked.

"I..." Abigail looked adorable when embarrassed. "What an awful thing to ask, my lord, and entirely wicked."

"Come here, Abigail." He straightened from the door's frame. He was dressed in his burgundy dressing robe and wondered if she'd fetch a wrap before coming to him, but not his darling wife. She didn't hesitate as she got up from the bed with a huge smile and crossed the room to him, nary an ounce of maiden's modesty in her perfect strides. In fact, her eyes held his in a titillating dare as she sauntered forward. *This woman, my wife, is fully aware of the powerful effect she has on me.*

When she reached him, he kissed her fiercely, cupping her face and pressing his aroused body against her naked flesh. Nuzzling her neck, he asked, "You liked my wicked question, didn't you, wife?"

She was breathless now, and his hand sought the soft juncture of curls bellow her satiny smooth stomach. "I did, Jackson." She hid her face in the crook of his neck. "I like all the wicked things you make me feel."

That was all it took. He swept her into his arms and laid her gently on the bed. Dropping his robe on the floor, he joined her.

"What about breakfast?" she asked, moving over to allow him room while staring at his erection. "I'd hate to think you went to so much trouble just for it to grow cold." She reached out and clamped her hand around his cock and his body nearly seized. She had wanted to touch him last night, but he wouldn't let her. He would not stop her explorations this time.

"I didn't make it." He shrugged, taking one of her taut nipples into his mouth to suck. He felt her hand stroke his heated flesh and groaned. "The only thing on my breakfast menu is you, my sweet." He trailed hot kisses along her heated flesh. His hand captured hers to teach her how to give him the most pleasure. Breakfast was long forgotten.

An exhausting hour later, Abigail lay in bed tucked safely in her husband's strong arms and staring at the ceiling. Her lower lip clamped between her teeth as she tried to think of when to tell him the truth. They were so happy.

Selfishly, she wanted to remain ensconced in the hunting lodge for an eternity. She also knew that, the longer she waited, the angrier he may become with her involvement in the secrecy. Besides, the sooner the revelation made and the reaction was over, the sooner they could return to this happiness. Moreover, his actual mother was currently in residence at the Waterford Estate, and knowing her husband, he'd have a slew of questions for Delores.

The feeling she was betraying him was leaving her sick to her stomach. She was just so afraid of his reaction, of what this news would do to them. She had a sinking feeling he'd push her away. Then what would she do? *Saints be praised, we've not yet been wed for twenty-four hours.*

There was also a calmer, more rational voice inside her, reminding her how much Jackson loved her, reminding her of how devoted he was to their future and making her happy. They only needed to make it past this one obstacle. Yes, the truth would be a huge life-altering obstacle. But if they could make it through this, they could make it through anything.

Even if he was recognized by his father, his illegitimacy would disallow him a dukedom. But he'd still have power, prestige, lands to oversee, and many of the other responsibilities and benefits he had as the Earl of Waterford. She pondered how he'd feel about these changes, but was beyond her to imagine it. She had assumed Delores' beloved had been titled, and indeed, Delores indicated as much before the wedding, but never in her wildest dreams did she imagine him a duke. She thought perhaps a baron or even a viscount, but not a duke.

Perhaps Jackson would be thrilled by his leap up the ladder of aristocracy, she reasoned, but in truth, she really wasn't at all sure how he'd react. But didn't she know him well enough to know he'd handle this news as he did every other aspect in his life, with calm, well thought out assertiveness. *Any man would be happy to find himself a duke's son, wouldn't they?* She had a feeling Jackson was the one man who wouldn't see this news of his birth as a boon. He'd most likely dwell on the negatives, on the wrongs dealt to him, on the fact that he was a bastard. She couldn't blame him.

"I think we need to discuss your mother," Jackson stated.

You mean your mother. Good Lord, she couldn't continue with this madness any longer. "Well, I hope you don't believe she's seeing ghosts?"

"I don't." He rested his head on one bent arm behind his head. His other arm was tucked under her neck so she could snuggle into his chest. He too stared at the white ceiling above them at the long, thick brown beams set every few feet.

"And she's not mad either, Jackson. If she said she saw the Duke of Salisbury, then she did."

"Hmm," was all he said.

"Do you know him?" she found herself asking. Was it possible he had actually met and conversed with his own father?

"No, I don't."

Oh, Saints be praised, I have to tell him. But how? Dear God, please help me do this right. "My love," she started out softly, "there's something I need to tell you."

"I know, my sweet; we harmonize in the bedchamber perfectly."

She laughed despite the gravity of the situation. Her stomach churned in nervousness. *Please don't leave me. Let me help you sort through this.* She said, "That's true, but it's not what I was going to say." She kissed his jaw, now lightly covered with coarse hair because he'd yet to shave. She strived for courage as she touched his handsome face.

***

When Abigail's lip slipped inward to be worried between her teeth, Jackson sat up. Something was terribly wrong with his wife. He'd never seen this look before. She was petrified of something. He grabbed her face between his hands forcing her to meet his gaze. "You know you can tell me anything."

She gave him a watery smile. *Good Lord, my wife is going to cry.* His wife never cried. "What, my darling? What is it? Tell me?"

"It's just…so hard. I don't want you to…"

"To what?" *What the hell has happened?* She appeared more than fine fifteen minutes ago. He had half a mind to make love to her again and chase away the hurt look in her eyes.

"To hate me." She gulped and an actual tear slid down her cheek causing him to jerk back in response. His heart lurched. Something had her seriously upset.

"I could never hate you, love. Please don't cry. Nothing can be as bad as to cause tears for my brave girl."

"I'm not feeling all that brave," she whispered, capturing a sob in her throat, which tortured his soul.

Jackson was stupefied. At her hurt expression, a stab of anger surged through him so fiercely it took all his willpower to remain calm. He had to know what was wrong. He had to fix this. He'd do anything to take the dejected look off her pretty face. "Tell me, Abigail," he ordered. He would wait no longer.

She nodded, and her voice took on a resolute tone. "Your grandfather did something a long time ago that was very wrong."

He had no idea what to expect her to say, but mentioning his deceased grandfather might have been the last thing he expected. "My grandfather always did things wrong, Abigail.

He just claimed it for the good and did it. If this is about his adultery, rest assured that I have no intention of sharing myself with anyone but you. His impulses do not extend to his heir."

"And I thank you for that, but this isn't about the Earl of Waterford's carousing."

"All right." He folded his arms over his chest and fixed her with a look that said she better hurry with her explanation. "Pray continue."

"Yes, well, I believe he did what he did because it seemed like the only option—at least to his mind."

Did his wife seriously want to spend their first married day together talking about his egotistical grandfather? He watched her eyes fill up with tears again and silently cursed. He could not imagine anything about the old man upsetting her so. "What did he do, Abigail?"

"He needed an heir, Jackson. He needed you." She cupped his cheek lovingly. The tenderness sent a shiver of fear racing down his erect spine. *What the hell is that supposed to mean? Why are women so bloody confusing?*

Jackson was quickly losing patience. "I know all this, wife."

"I know." Her hand dropped away as she looked down at the sheet draped over her lap. Her breasts moved toward him and back with her sigh of anguish. Whatever she had to tell him was causing her pain, Jackson could not deny that.

***

"What you don't know..." Abigail squeezed her eyes shut tightly. There wasn't a right way to say this. Her body began to tremble and she pulled the sheet up to her chin. Jackson stared back at her in confusion. She could see her delay was making him angry. *You have to tell him. He has to know.* She was really wishing someone else would tell him this news, but the truth was far too important to be left to others. He needed to hear this from the person who loved him the most. Together they were the future. They'd get through this. They had to.

She sat in quiet contemplation. *Now what to say? Jackson, your entire life is based on lies. No, far too cold. How about, Jackson, you're the son of a duke?* No, she had to start at the ugly beginning, at the very first time they met.

"What don't I know? Darling, you're starting to scare me. Come here. You're trembling." Her wonderful man pulled her toward him.

They lay together on the bed facing each other, their legs entwined together amongst the sheet and their hands clasped together in front of the sheet that covered her chest. The arrangement was intimate, and she felt better, but this was far from over.

"Now continue." Jackson's expression was deadly serious. Her husband was running out of his already short supply of patience.

"You and I have met before." He blinked at her, perplexed, and she continued, "We were only babes at the time. I'm so sorry to have to tell you this. Just know I understand some of what you're about to feel."

"Hell's teeth, woman. Say it already!"

"The Earl of Waterford switched me with you when we were babies because he needed you, Jackson."

His head snapped up to smash against the solid wood headboard. She thought the crash accidental until she saw the whites of his eyes. Her husband was furious, and most likely confused and heartbroken as well.

He'd yet to speak when he leaped out of the bed and began to put on his clothing with undue force. She scrambled out of bed and began dressing herself. If he was leaving, she was going with him. She would not allow him to run from her.

When he sat to pull on his boots, he asked with deadly calm, "How long have you kept this information from me, wife?"

"I..." Her throat closed up and she couldn't speak. Her worse fears were coming true. He was going to hate her.

Finally, she was able to choke out, "Only a few days. I'm so sorry. I wanted to tell you sooner, but with the wedding and…"

He stomped out of the room and she ran behind him, combing her fingers through her hair as she went. Her hands were shaking uncontrollably. "Where are we going?" She fastened up the length of her hair with a blue ribbon she used on the bouquet of her wedding flowers, which happened to be on the table near the front door.

"To speak with my grandmother." He stomped out the door and then turned to her with an ugly laugh. "I guess she's your grandmother now, eh?" He walked down the porch steps and she remained right on his heels, struggling as she pulled on her slippers and hopped in his direction. She hurriedly twisted her arms behind her back, hoping she got all the buttons redone on her gown but knowing she hadn't.

She expected this, his anger. Nevertheless, that his ire seemed solely set upon her made her want to cry. "I'm going with you." She had to run to keep up with his strides as he went to the lean-to and harnessed the horse. "Did you hear me, Jackson? I said I'm coming with you."

She suddenly found herself placed none too gently on the horse's bare back, and she let out an "oomph" at impact. Her wedding dress, the only clothing she had found to don before his hurried departure, was rucked up to her thighs. He vaulted up behind her and kicked the horse into action. Abigail clung to the animal's mane for dear life, her knuckles white as she and Jackson rode like a great wind. Her hurriedly tied ribbon came unfastened and whipped off behind them. Hair clung to her face, but she dare not swipe it away for fear of falling off the horse. Jackson was bearing down on the Waterford Estate as if the hounds of hell were after him. Perhaps in her husband's mind, they were. She began to pray.

To her utter consternation, her usually refined husband did not assist her off the horse when the reckless ride finally came to a stop in a flurry of dust. No, her irate husband jumped off and stomped his way into the house, completely ignoring her as she unclenched her tingling fists from the horse's mane.

Abigail sat hugging the horse and looking at the long distance to the ground. If she jumped, she would surely twist an ankle. Why did these confounded animals have to be so large? Searching for help, she found it in the form of Jackson's Herculean footman. What is his name? "Simms!" she hollered, and the horse sidestepped at the sound of her voice, causing her to shriek. Relief filled her when Simms headed quickly in her direction and saved her from the beast.

"Thank you oh so much, Simms."

"You're welcome, milady. Always happy to help."

"Yes, well, thank you." She tried to fix her wedding dress in an effort to gain back a little dignity. She had to get into the house and fast. Lord knew what Jackson would do in his fury, and Delores had yet even to learn the truth. Without another thought, she nodded to Simms, lifted the hem of her skirt from the ground, and dashed into the house.

She found Jackson by way of sound. His shouts of outrage nearly shook the rafters. He had cornered the dowager in her private sitting room, which connected to the woman's bedchamber. Abigail hurried into the room and crossed to sit next to her grandmother. Jackson paced angrily across the expanse of carpet.

"He actually stole another person's child, and he removed your own granddaughter from your home, in turn subjecting her to a life of ostracism. This is unbelievable, and yet so bloody perfect. It's exactly something the conniving man would do. To hell with the consequences! Life had to be his way. He knew best!" Jackson sounded like he was upset on her behalf and his defense warmed her. But it wasn't necessary. All Abigail wanted to do was forget all of this and go back to being happy.

"Jackson, my love..." Abigail flinched when he turned his angry blue eyes upon her. All right, perhaps he wasn't feeling sorry for her plight in all of this.

"I don't want to hear anything from you, Abigail. You betrayed me by withholding the truth. You must be thrilled to find yourself no longer the bastard. The title of *lady* certainly suits you." His evil tone mocked his sincerity.

"I know you're upset." Her eyes filled with tears when he turned away in disgust. Her heart ached for him. He was burning up inside and she couldn't help him. He wouldn't let her in. He had shut himself off from her. The thought tore her up inside. *Please let me in. What about the happiness you promised me?*

"*Upset* does not begin to describe the horror of what I am feeling, *Lady Abigail*," he spat, his face a molten shade of red, the veins along his neck straining with his ire.

"What in blue blazes is all the shouting about?" Lady Hastings walked into the room, and in her astute ladylike manner, she observed the faces around her. Both Abigail and the dowager nodded, and Lady Hastings knew the truth was out.

"Come here, Jackson." Lady Hastings used a stern tone Abigail had never heard before, the same tone a mother took before she scolded the child she loved dearly.

"In case you haven't heard..." Jackson scowled, even swaying a bit on his feet, the lunacy that threatened him now visibly tearing at him. "You are no longer my mother. Delores Gibbons holds that position. As such, I'm no longer required to respond to your demands." Clearly the dowager had told him the identity of his mother for Abigail hadn't gotten that far in her explanation.

Lady Hastings started crying. "You are my son. You will always be my son."

"Then will you respond to me?" Delores stepped into the room, looking the best Abigail had ever seen her, a strength in her posture Abigail had never seen before. Abigail couldn't have been prouder of her. She could tell by Delores' demeanor that she had learned the truth last night. Abigail was relieved Lady Hastings and the dowager had seen to the task.

***

Jackson looked at all the women around the room, noting their tear streaked faces with utter loathing. Then he stomped out of the room as fast as his boots could take him. He had to get away from them. Away from this house! Away from this madness! Away from it all!

He noticed Simms readying a horse for one of the overnight guests. Without a word, he took the mount and turned to find Abigail directly in his path. "Move!" he said from atop the stallion.

"You are not going anywhere without me!" Her hands went to her hips and he nudged the horse closer to her. The stubborn woman didn't budge. Although he knew damn well she was frightened of horses, his brave girl stood there and crossed her arms over her chest in challenge.

She stomped her foot and then jumped back a step when the horse snorted at her. "Jackson, we just married!" she cried out, desperately trying to persuade him. "I'm sorry I didn't tell you sooner. Everyone had thought... It doesn't matter. I should have told you the moment I heard. Please don't leave me."

Thoughts of her betrayal absorbed all his thinking. He didn't want to talk to her. He didn't want to talk to anyone right now. She knew his true identity days ago, and she said nothing. She had plenty of opportunities, so why did she wait until he had a future in sight when she was just going to rip it all away? What kind of heartless monster was she?

"I'm sure you'll find Jackson Sethos Ramesses *Gibbons* has not been wed." With that, he stepped the horse around her, gave his mount a swift kick, and raced past her.

***

Tears fell heavily down Abigail's cheeks as she dropped to her knees in absolute despair. She had lost the love of her life.

Jackson left her. Even worse, he left himself. He no longer thought he knew who he was. Sobs wracked her body as she wept for his sorrow, and then for hers.

Abigail didn't know how long she sat in the dirt-covered drive, her wedding gown ruined beyond repair. Her hands were filthy and she knew her face had to be just as dirty, seeing how she couldn't help herself from wiping at her itchy tears.

Suddenly two loving arms wrapped on each side of her, those of Delores and Lady Hastings, her mothers. More tears came at this thought, that she was lucky enough to have two caring mothers. She left herself solely in their care, having no energy to do otherwise. She was depleted. She'd never felt such despair in her life. Her mothers made shushing sounds as they led her up the stairs. Things like, "don't worry, love," "he'll be back, dear," and "he needs some time" were spoken in whispers.

There was a tub already filled in her room, and they undressed her and she dutifully got in. Soon she was toweled off and placed in a fluffy robe in front of the fire while Delores combed her hair and Lady Hastings went about tidying up her room. Abigail just stared at the flames in the fireplace and prayed for Jackson. She spent a fitful night, and the next day she remained in bed, too disheartened to do anything else.

***

Meanwhile, downstairs in the comfortable atmosphere of the parlor, Lady Hastings, Delores Gibbons, and the Dowager Countess of Waterford tried to come up with a solution to bring their children together again.

All of the overnight guests had left in the morning, all except one man. The Duke of Salisbury remained. Unfortunately, some of the guests were privy to the shouting before they departed. Nevertheless, the dowager was making it her mission to bring society around to accept her family regardless of the circumstances. With that goal in mind, she left the room to begin without delay. The news of Jackson's illegitimacy would spread like a brushfire, and it would take every ounce of influence she had to stem the wagging tongues, and even then, there was no guarantee Abigail and Jackson would be admitted back into society. Nonetheless, she was confident that, with a few whispers in the right ears, everything would work out. Her grandson was the son of a duke, after all.

***

Lady Hastings and Delores refused to sit back and wait. Abigail was in bed, too melancholy to do much more than nod at the questions sent her way, and they were not about to let the chips fall where they may in whatever timeframe Jackson found fitting.

"She refuses to eat," Delores huffed. "I can't stand to see her this way."

"She's a strong woman." Lady Hastings put a comforting hand on Delores. "She'll pull through this. You did a wonderful job raising her." Tears filled Lady Hastings eyes.

"Jackson's a strong man too," Delores stated. "I still can't believe he's mine, or I should say, ours."

"They are both our children."

"So how do we fix this? I can't see an end to this mess when Jackson is nowhere to be found."

"I'm sure he's in London," Lady Hastings stated, her finger tapping her chin while she contemplated what needed to be done.

"This doesn't help, that Abigail won't even get out of bed. I've never seen her like this. She's a fighter and never did allow anyone to get the best of her. It's as if she's given up," Delores said dejectedly.

The dowager returned at that point, having written several correspondences with some of society's leading matrons she considered good friends. "Stuff and applesauce, the poor girl's distraught is all."

"Excuse me, ladies. I'd like a word with Miss Gibbons." The Duke of Salisbury entered the room without an invitation. Even his posture bespoke of his power and authority.

Both Lady Hastings and the dowager turned concerned eyes on Delores, who shuddered at the duke's appearance.

"You need to tell him," Lady Hastings whispered as she stood, the dowager following her lead.

Delores gave a resolute nod.

Both ladies excused themselves from the room with a quick curtsy and a brief "excuse us."

"May I?" The duke indicated the chair across from Delores, and she nodded. He sat. Her mind was filled with images of him in their youth.

He was just as she remembered, though older with gray lining the sides of his still fairly thick blond hair. A few wrinkles gathered near his mouth, and lines fanned out from the corners of his eyes, but all in all, he still possessed the ability to make her heart thump maddeningly. The Duke of Salisbury was a handsome, potent male, so full of strength and mastery—much like their son.

Perhaps she should have told him all those years ago that he fathered a child, but then she knew she would not now be sitting across from the self-assured man he had become. Authority permeated from his rigid posture. As she knew it would, the title fit him like a well-tailored suit. He was the master of his universe.

Suddenly, to her surprise, the austerity of the duke disappeared and he slumped forward to look at her down turned face. This man was her Stephen. "You're as beautiful as the day we first met. You remember that day, don't you, Delores?"

Indeed she did, all too well. "How could I forget?" She laughed. "You were playing in the corn field on Sir Travers' property."

"As were you, if I recall."

"You startled me right out of my quiet place. I had lost

both of my parents and you consoled me."

"And we fell in love."

"I remember." Her voice was hushed. With courage, she lifted her gaze to his.

"As do I." He smiled the same smile she adored as a young girl, his blue eyes crinkling in the corners. She had noticed a resemblance between him and Jackson when she first met the man her daughter was to marry, but seeing him smile just now, she was astonished at how much their son looked like Stephen. "I would have given up all I am to have been with you."

This she knew, and it had haunted her all these years. "I wouldn't have allowed it."

"No, you wouldn't have. And if memory serves, that's precisely why we are separated now. I realized many years later that you instigated that argument to send me on my way. I have two lovely daughters now."

"Yes, I've heard." She smiled. "I'm happy for you."

"Damn it, Delores! I wasn't happy. I tried hard enough to put what we shared behind us, but I was never able to. I took a wife, a nice woman by the name of Victoria. Her father was a friend of my father's. It's been many years since she passed." He ran a hand over his face with a heartfelt sigh. "I never loved her, Delores. I couldn't, not when you held my heart, but Victoria actually understood my plight. I believe she too was in love with another."

"I'm sorry if your life was filled with sorrow. That was never my intent." Did he truly not think she suffered as well? She did what she had to. She did it for him. She had to believe that or she'd break down in a fit of hysterics right now.

"I know what your bloody intent was!" He grew gruff. He was angry with her and she couldn't blame him. She was angry at herself. Her reasons seemed so clear when she was younger, but now she realized she had given up on the two of them, and she felt terrible for it. *Perhaps I made a mistake? No, I did it for him. Look at him now. He's where he belongs.*

Her eyes filled with tears and he passed her his handkerchief. "Don't cry, my love. I don't wish you upset." The handkerchief smelled of him. She smothered a sob with it.

"I'm upset about so much right now. I...I gave you a son, Stephen." She watched him flinch as if he was struck, his hands tightening over the arms of the chair, his knuckles turning white.

"You were with child upon our separation and didn't tell me!" He leaped up from the chair, shaking his fists in the air, ranting curse words under his breath for what seemed to Delores like hours but was only few minutes. He was ferocious in his anger, pacing the room in a rage. Then he stopped to stare at her.

She gulped. "I'm sorry, but I thought..."

"Oh, I know damn well what you thought, Delores. Regardless of the so-called good intentions you thought you had, you kept my first born from me, a son at that. My heir!" he bellowed. Then he began to pace the room again, his hands clasped behind his back.

Of course she could have reminded him that, if he had known, he would have insisted they have a real marriage instead of the farce of a marriage at Gretna Green so many years ago. Then he would have forfeited his inheritance. She loved him too much to allow him to give up so much.

He finally stopped his agitated stomps about the room to look at her. "What is our son's name?"

"Jackson. He has a couple of middle names. I think they refer to some ancient Egyptian king."

"You think?" His face seemed to turn a deep shade of purple. "My God, woman. You aren't sure of our son's name?"

Tears began anew as she shook her head no. Like him, she barely knew her own son and it hurt her heart thinking about it. "His last name is Danvers."

"Not Gibbons?" He sat back down in his chair. Well, actually, it was more like he threw himself into it. The realization of all she told him was leaving him as exhausted as it did her.

"Our son was stolen from me after his birth." She paused, trying to compose herself. She was panting as she continued. "He was switched with a baby girl by the late Earl of Waterford, who was intent on procuring himself an heir."

"But how could this happen? By God, if the old coot were among the living, I'd run Waterford through with my sword!"

"I only found out all of this yesterday. I have tried to remember everything I could about the delivery. It runs through my mind over and over again. It was extremely grueling and I fell into unconsciousness right after I gave birth. I was told I was weak and incoherent for a couple of weeks due to the loss of blood. The late earl must have taken him during that time and switched him with Abigail. In my weakened state, I couldn't prevent it. I did not even know of it." Great heaving sobs erupted from deep within her soul. She had allowed her son to be stolen.

Stephen was out of his chair and pulling her against his strong chest in a matter of seconds. "Hush now, love. It's all right. I knew Waterford my entire life. He'd always been a selfish man. You can't very well blame yourself. I should have been there."

That stopped her tears. The loyal man was trying to take the blame. "You're definitely not to blame. You didn't even know about the babe. Oh dear lord, I'm so sorry to have kept this from you."

The pads of his thumbs brushed away her tears and he nuzzled his face against hers. "You forget, my love. I know why you behaved the way you did. You're a proud woman, Delores. I forgave you for leaving me the moment I saw you yesterday."

She leaned back in amazement, blinking at him with watery eyes. "You forgive me? I don't even forgive me."

"It's easy to forgive the woman I love."

She gulped. Could he really love her after all of these

years? She knew the answer because she had never stopped loving him. Alcohol was her way to cope with the bittersweet memories monopolizing her mind from the moment she woke up until the moment she fell into bed. She cupped his face. She had her Stephen back after all of these years. They deserved some happiness after being separated for so long. "I love you too, Stephen. I've never stopped."

The kiss that ensued was a heated touch of yearning, of years lost to them, of the memories they could have shared if everything would have been different. Theirs was a kiss that said the past no longer matters for we are together now and will remain so. He reached into her heart and she reached out for him with eagerness. Her body swayed into him as one of his hand's held the back of her head, grinding their lips together. When she thought she'd surely swoon if he continued, he broke away and immediately threw himself back into the chair across from her.

"I will, of course, court you properly. You deserve nothing less."

She smiled with overflowing happiness. "I'm looking forward to it."

He gave her a duke-like nod and settled his overpowering gaze on her. She noted that Stephen wore his title proudly, and it gave her heart joy to know he was exactly where an assured, intelligent man like him belonged.

"Jackson was raised by Lady Hastings?"

"Yes. She lost her husband before the children were born, but she, along with the dowager and the now deceased earl, raised Jackson."

"I remember when he died. The old earl had been beside himself when he lost his only son." He rubbed a hand over his face. "So our son is the Earl of Waterford," he said proudly. "I believe I met him a time or two when he was younger."

"Abigail is my daughter." She gave him a hesitant smile. He grinned back at her, seemingly happy by the match between their son and Abigail. She was relieved.

"We've met. Where has the happy couple gone off to celebrate? I think our son will like his wedding present. He's about to become the heir to a dukedom." Stephen appeared jovial at the turn of events.

Delores' brow wrinkled in confusion. "He's not your true heir, Stephen. He can't be because we were never married. Our son's illegitimate."

He came down in front of her, his smile blinding. "We were married, my sweet, at Gretna Green. I remember the day clearly."

"As do I. And you told me the ceremony performed was only practice for the real event, which never took place."

"Would you be upset to learn I told you such a tale to get you to comply?"

Delores' eyes filled with tears of sheer delight. "So we're truly married?"

"We are. Just a matter of fetching the documents from Scotland." He kissed her and then stood with a devastatingly handsome grin.

Stephen was as proud as could be. He now had his heir. She was happy for him. She knew he'd adapt well to being Jackson's father, and she had a feeling Stephen was exactly what her dear boy needed.

"I'm afraid that, when Abigail told him of the treachery of his grandfather, he was understandably upset and…he left. Abigail is upstairs now. She's hurting inside. I want all of this to work out somehow. We could all use some happiness."

"And I intend to see we *all* get it. You and I are off to Gretna Green the moment this conversation is concluded. My son will be legitimate. I'll see it done. He's now the Marquis of Childress and future Duke of Salisbury." Delores nearly gasped at the realization that her Stephen didn't fear society's censure or judgment. He'd see their family through this. "Now are you going to pack or do you plan to just bring the clothes on your back?"

Her heart filled with giddy excitement, flooding her with memories of when they were young. "How long will we be gone?"

"We will be as quick about this business as possible. I plan to find our son and put everything to rights the moment after we say 'I do'."

"Are we to wed again?"

"I'll settle for nothing less." His shoulders stiffened challengingly. "All right then, Delores. Get going, girl." She laughed, and with a kiss to his cheek, left the room.

Delores wasn't going anywhere until she spoke with Abigail.

CHAPTER FOURTEEN

Abigail looked up from glaring at her patterned coverlet to see her mother waltz into her room with the oddest expression on her face. Her eyes were sad and yet her face was flushed and it appeared she was trying to hide a smile.

Delores said nothing when she approached the bed and began straightening the bedding around her. "What's afoot, mother?" She couldn't precisely pinpoint when it happened, but the sadness that engulfed her because of Jackson's departure had turned into an anger so fierce she shook with it. She was in the process of trying to control her rage when Delores entered.

"I do have something to share with you." Delores sat on the edge of the bed and folded her hands in her lap.

"Yes, yes, out with it please." She was frustrated that she was now losing her patience as well as her equanimity. She'd never in her life spent two days wallowing in self-pity. Jackson was in for one hell of a heated discussion when she found him. And find him she would. *How dare he leave me!*

Her mother took a deep breath and spit forth a slew of words. "I'm renewing my marriage to the Duke of Salisbury tonight at Gretna Green."

"Renewing?"

Delores waved a hand through the air. "It's a long story best saved for another time. Let it suffice to say that we were wed when we were young, although I was not aware of this until now. So we are going to Gretna Green to retrieve the papers."

"You're going to Scotland?" *My mother, the one who never travels?*

"Yes. His Grace refuses to wait."

"This is wonderful news." Abby sat up, happy for the first time in days. "You're remarrying the man you love and you're a duchess."

"I am." Tears of joy ran down her mother's cheeks, and Abigail was nearly as happy for her. Delores deserved this happiness. She had suffered enough through the years. Jackson and Abigail deserved some tranquility as well, and Abigail would force-feed it to him if necessary.

"That's not even the best part. Jackson won't only be legitimate but the duke's heir and the Marquis of Childress. Stephen is thrilled to find he has a son after all these years."

Abigail sat back with a thump against the headboard. The duke making Jackson his rightful heir would hopefully help her love overcome all the deceptions played upon him. "This is the best news, Mother."

Abigail tossed back her blankets and swung her legs off the side of the bed. She hugged Delores. "You go and get your happily-ever-after." She kissed her on both cheeks, quickly going to the dressing table to run a brush through her matted hair.

"Where are you going?" Delores stood, watching Abigail rush to the wardrobe.

"I'm going to find my husband. I'm not about to lay about waiting for him to return." She smiled at her mother and shrugged. "It just isn't my way."

"No, it isn't. I'm glad to see that spirit of yours return." Her mother smiled at her warmly.

"Promise to visit us at Waterford Townhouse in London. I'd like to meet this man of yours." She grinned back at her mother.

"He's looking forward to meeting the two of you as well. I'd best be going. My Stephen was never one for waiting. Are you sure you'll be all right?"

Her Stephen was never one for waiting? Does impatience run in one's family? Abigail assumed it must, since Jackson seemed to suffer from the same affliction. "I'll be fine," she said. *The moment I find my errant husband and explain how obtuse he's being.*

"Then I will go happily." Delores turned at the door with her hand upon the crystal knob. "I never thought I would be happy again." And with that, Delores was off on her wedding trip. Abigail was now filled with resolve. She had her own mission to see through.

She yanked the bell cord so hard that the rope dangled in her hand. She tossed it aside as Sophie came rushing in. "Yes, my lady?"

"We're going to London." Abigail kept throwing dresses into the trunk sitting at the foot of her bed. The more she thought about Jackson's absence, the more crazed she became. Where was the happily ever after he promised?

"Sweet Lord, my lady. They'll be a wrinkled mess packing them that way. Here, allow me." Her maid began to pull the dresses back out, folding them with delicate care.

Abigail didn't care what state her wardrobe arrived in. She just wanted to get to London, fast. She was convinced that the sooner she found her wayward husband, the sooner they could set things right.

Lady Hastings walked in with the dowager close behind. "What's the ruckus?"

"I'm off to London," Abigail said from her bent over position. She was rifling through her chest of drawers, tossing various items in Sophie's direction.

"You're going to go to him?" her grandmother asked, nudging Lady Hastings with her elbow. "I told you she was a smart one."

"Yes, you did." Her mother grinned. "I assume you're going to the Waterford townhouse. Would you mind terribly if my husband and I joined you?" This earned Stephanie another elbow from the dowager. "And Lady Waterford, of course."

"That would be lovely, but I'm not willing to wait a moment longer and I really think it would be best if Jackson and I had some alone time."

"We'll follow behind you in a couple of days," the dowager said.

This idea suited Abigail greatly. There was no telling what would happen when she came face to face with Jackson, but she knew this mess, however it might turn out, would be best settled in private. A thought occurred to her. "Grandmother, in the packet of letters you received, was there one for my husband?"

"Yes, dear, and one for Delores, which I gave her last night. I'm sorry we told her before you could, but she was upset and we thought it best she knew everything up front."

Abigail nodded her head in perfect agreement. "You saved me from a task I wasn't looking forward to, and I'm grateful." Abigail sat on the edge of the bed to pull on her traveling shoes. "Would you mind terribly giving Jackson's letter to me?"

"Stuff and applesauce, Abigail. You know I'd be happy to do so." Her grandmother hustled out of the room to retrieve the missive.

"Are you all right, Abigail. You seem…I don't know… different." Lady Hastings made herself useful by rolling up the silk stockings waiting to be packed.

"This is me furious, Mother. I am so angry right now that I could scream. I should never have let him leave. And I certainly shouldn't have withheld the truth from him."

"I'm afraid Jackson can be a bit hardheaded once he sets his mind to something. You couldn't have prevented his flight. If you had told him this news before your wedding, he still would have left. You did what we all thought was best."

"That may very well be true, but I'm not going to lay about waiting for his return when I can go to him. He needs me, whether the obstinate man realizes it or not," she huffed. Then crossed the room to fetch her favorite bonnets, capes, cloaks, and other essentials. For a brief moment, she was amazed by the mass of stuff she had accumulated. With her arms loaded, she dropped her burden on the bed in front of Sophie. *I want my happiness, damn it!* "I won't allow him to run from me."

"An admirable trait in a wife, I should think."

Abigail gave her a firm nod. She scooped up her brush, pins, and her jewelry box.

"I'll see to it that a carriage is made ready for your departure. I'm proud of you, daughter."

As Abigail watched her mother leave the room, a few tears leaked from her eyes and she wiped them angrily away. *The wretched man thinks he doesn't need my help, hah*! He was going to get such an earful that his head would surely ache for a week. She tossed her jewelry in the box, noticing Clarissa's diamond cross. She hadn't seen Clarissa since the wedding reception. This too was something she planned to rectify once she reached London. She wanted to talk with her friend.

"Are we through, Sophie?"

"Almost, my lady. You go downstairs and I'll have Simms carry down the trunks. Am I traveling with you, my lady?"

Abigail hadn't thought about needing her maid, but it would most likely be best if she brought some servants along. "Yes, and inform Simms and my husband's valet that they will be traveling in the luggage vehicle behind us." She smiled, realizing her voice held just the right touch of authority. "That will be all," she added for good measure, and she left the room.

As the vehicles were being loaded, and the servants packed, Abigail decided to seek some nourishment before her departure. She hadn't eaten in two days and she needed all her strength if she was going to bring Jackson back in line.

She ordered tea and sandwiches to be delivered in the parlor, intending to await her mother and grandmother there, but they were already in the room.

"The letter, my dear." The dowager handed her the white missive with Jackson's name inscribed on the front, her late grandfather's unmistakable blue-waxed seal bearing the Waterford's coat of arms, a lone hawk with its wings outstretched.

"Thank you, Grandmother."

The dowager smiled and gave her cheek a loving pat, then went to sit on the sofa.

Lady Hastings took a step toward her. "Are you crying, Mother? It's not like this is goodbye."

"Yes, yes, I know. I just didn't think I would feel this much love for you so quickly." Lady Hastings dabbed at her eyes with a lace hankie.

Abigail's eyes pooled. "I feel exactly the same way, like I have loved you all my life." They embraced as the tea trolley came in bearing Abigail's meal. Her stomach growled as the smell of food awoke her senses.

"Come, come, dear. Sit. You must eat something."

"I am famished," she answered, eyeing the cucumber and ham sandwiches.

Her mother led her to the sofa next to the dowager. She then went over to the small writing desk and pulled out a piece of vellum from the drawer. Lady Hastings dipped a pen in an inkwell and jotted something down, and then she waved the vellum in the air to dry before handing it to Abigail.

"What's this?"

"We won't be far behind you, a few days at the most; but If you should need any assistance before we arrive, the Marchioness of Nottingshire, my husband's sister, will come to your aid."

Abigail hoped she and Jackson could mend the hurt by the time Lady Hastings arrived. She hurriedly polished off a few tiny sandwiches and a cup of tea. "I look forward to your arrival," she said as she swiped the napkin against her mouth. "I should be going if I'm to make London before sundown."

"One more thing, Abigail." Her mother stood. "I like your mother, Delores, and I love the woman you've become, even if it was without my help."

"I'd hoped you'd like Delores, and thank you. I'm partial to you as well."

"Thank you, dear."

"And you too, Grandmother. You mean the world to me."

"Stuff and applesauce, child. Don't get me all blubbery again. Off with you."

Abigail gave her a smile and an enthusiastic nod. She was ready for a showdown with her husband. She walked outside and stepped up into the vehicle, resting her head against the cushiony squabs. "Ready or not, Jackson, here I come."

***

"Wake up, jackass!"

Jackson barely stirred when his friend Alexander kicked his chair again, causing his torso to move back from the place where it draped over the scarred wood table at the Red Robin Tavern. He finally sat up, his gaze slowly meeting his childhood friend's. "Good evening, Alexander."

"Bugger off, Jackson. It's good morning. Do you know how many shit boxes I've been to looking for your mangy ass?"

"Then you bugger off. I never asked you to come along." Jackson raked his fingers through his unkempt hair.

Alexander pulled up a chair and sat, his elbows resting on the table as he relaxed. Then he flexed his fists, continuously, as if readying for a fistfight. "Your mother, or should I say, your mother-in-law, Lady Hastings, left me a cryptic message about your state of mind as a result of recent events. The news of those events, unfortunately, and through no fault of my own, are making the rounds among the higher ends of society…" He looked about the inner sanctum of the dilapidated building in which they sat, then said, "And making the rounds of the lower dregs as well."

Jackson pounded his fist on the table. "Why do you think I'm here? I actually heard myself referred to as a bastard. Trust me, my friend. I have no interest in leaving this table for the rest of my pathetic life."

"And drinking yourself into a bloody stinking stupor helps?"

"Hell yes! It bloody helps! I feel like I got the wind knocked out of me —you know when your body stiffens and you wait for air to fill your starving lungs—and my breath never returns. Jackson poured himself another fortifying glass of bourbon from the half-empty bottle at his elbow. He heard Alexander groan when he downed the contents in one swallow.

"How do you think your abandoned wife feels?" Alexander asked with a sneer.

"Abigail's safe from the gossip in the country," Jackson informed him.

"Certainly, as long as no papers are delivered, and no one comes to visit. I'd hardly call that safe, what with all the servants running about that house with loose lips." After a good two minutes of silence, and evidently trying to dissuade Jackson from his course of drunkenness by giving him a hard stare, Alexander asked, "Are you ready to go?"

"Where?" Jackson asked with a slur. Finally, the alcohol was working.

"Home," Alexander said, as if Jackson really had one.

"No. But I need you to contact my second cousin for me. Tell him I'll set up a meeting with our solicitors and get his inheritance and title properly set up. And tell him congratulations for me. If anyone's to be given my title, I'm glad it's Grayson."

"So you're going to remain here and feel sorry for yourself until when exactly? Your father's a duke, Jackson, a duke," Alexander repeated as if he couldn't believe Jackson's good fortune. "Have you not been informed of this fact? My friend, you should be celebrating, not dwelling on the past. You are now the Marquis of Childress, which is a step or two above the Waterford title, if I must remind you."

Jackson remained silent, knowing Alex would continue his crusade to save him. If the situation were reversed, he was sure he'd do the same. However, Alex couldn't begin to fathom how it felt to have one's life turned upside down. Nor could Alex understand how he felt about his wife keeping something this important from him. *Damn Lord Waterford to hell for the pain he caused. The old man clearly hadn't been happy with the hand fate dealt him. Selfish blighter!*

"I've looked into the Duke of Salisbury's background, Jackson. He has no male heirs and two daughters. He's desperate for an heir, which means you'll inherit everything."

"I'm no longer an only child, but indeed, now have two brand new sisters? Wonderful. Is there anything else? Are they young? Will I need to see to their future come outs? Can we pile on any more dilemmas I must face?"

"Your sarcasm's not helping my temper."

"And again I say bugger off, Alex. Your company's not wanted." Jackson gestured over Alex's shoulder. "Barkeep, another bottle."

Alex's chair slid out and slammed to the floor. His friend was enraged and stomped away. Jackson refilled his glass and settled back into his seat.

***

Alexander refused to allow Jackson to forget the man he was, and still was, regardless of birth, pedigree, or deceptions. Jackson needed to speak with someone who understood what it was like—at least more than he did—to be in his friend's position. He couldn't imagine what he would do in the same situation, but he didn't like the look of defeat in Jackson's eyes. He knew only one person who could fix that.

He was off to fetch Jackson's wife. He would get Abigail's help.

***

Jackson stared into the amber liquid in his glass, wishing it held the answers to straighten out his wreck of a life. Alex didn't understand how he felt. Alex still had his title, and there wasn't a chance in hell he'd be dubbed a bastard. Although his friend's father was deceased, Alex's mother was amongst the living and spoke often of her undying love for her husband.

Even if Jackson was miraculously made legitimate, it wouldn't change the fact that he'd been forced to live in someone else's shoes his entire life. He downed his glass with irritation, enjoying the burning sensation in his gut, and then poured himself another. For three days now he had sat in this hovel of an establishment, taking one of the shabby rooms upstairs for sleep—although he'd yet to make it away from the table. The drink numbed his mind and his soul from all thoughts, a welcome oblivion.

At times, however, drink wasn't enough and his thoughts immediately returned to his wife. How easily Abigail duped him into believing they had a future together. As another day passed, and he'd more time to dwell on the problems plaguing him, he realized she held back the truth due to fear of his reaction, a revelation that only served to aggravate him further.

He was a shell of the man he was only a few days ago. He no longer cared what the fates had in store for him. He was done trying. His entire life he strived to make something of himself, to build a foundation as the Earl of Waterford, to make something of his life and have a voice to be heard and admired. He only longed to be grounded and content, the woman he loved by his side, and he thought he had found what he was searching for in Abigail. But all was for naught. *She'd be far better off married to another.* Without the stigma of her birth, he was sure she'd find herself a better match than the lifeless sod she married.

The thought caused an ache in his chest where his heart used to be. He downed another glass of the mediocre bourbon. *To hell with life, to hell with Abigail, to hell with everything. Christ, I don't even know my own name any longer. I hope the late Earl of Waterford is rotting in his grave.* But he assumed the manipulator was smiling up from his ring of hell due to the havoc he caused Jackson, probably wheeling and dealing his way into some position of power there amongst the others of his ilk.

"Tony, another bottle, if you please."

***

Abigail sprang from the vehicle the moment it came to a halt and bolted up the townhouse steps. She entered the foyer to find the butler and housekeeper bustling out of the kitchen to welcome her. She nodded in their direction and began hollering for Jackson in what she knew was an unladylike manner. At the moment she didn't care about appearances, or indeed if she sounded like a screeching fishwife. The trip to London had taken far too long and her need to reach Jackson was overcoming her good sense.

"His lordship isn't here, my lady. Perhaps you'd like some tea?"

"No time for tea, Mrs. Rhodes. Does my driver know where Jackson's townhouse is located?" Abigail chastised herself. She should have known her husband wouldn't be in the Waterford residence, that indeed it was probably the last place he'd want to be. It had been stupid of her to think otherwise. *I really need to pull myself together if I am going to make this work.*

Mrs. Rhodes peeked out the curtains. "Ah, my lady. Mr. Pickles, your driver, knows where his lordship resides."

Sophie walked in, followed by Simms, who carried her huge trunk over one of his massive shoulders. "Return my luggage to the carriage please, Simms. We aren't staying."

"Yes, my lady." He did as bid and Sophie turned to her with questions hovering on her lips.

"I'm staying at my husband's home, Sophie. We're going there now."

"Yes, my lady." Her maid nodded and returned to the vehicle.

"Mrs. Rhodes, please see that everyone knows where I am staying should I be needed."

"Yes, my lady. And congratulations on your wedding."

Abigail spun around and rushed back to the carriage. "To the Earl of Waterford's house, Mr. Pickles."

"Right away, milady." The carriage lurched into motion. Although it felt like forever, they had actually made great time getting to London and the sun was just beginning to set. She sat looking out the window and then suddenly jumped up to pound on the roof, causing Mr. Pickles to halt.

Clarissa's house sat to her right. "Sophie, I need you to take a message to my friend Clarissa."

"Me, my lady?" Sophie nearly shrieked.

Her maid looked so stricken by the thought of approaching a household she wasn't working for that her hands began to shake. "You can't deliver a simple message?" Abigail couldn't help her tone of frustration.

"My lady, this is the Marquis of Loring's residence. I worked here years ago, but… In truth, my lady, Lord Loring didn't like me much."

"It's my understanding that Lord Loring doesn't like anyone." Abigail huffed and got out of the vehicle. She needed to see her friend, and to hell with how Lord Loring felt about it.

To her utter surprise, the marquis himself answered the door. "My, my, if it isn't the little bastard girl who has turned into a noble overnight."

She put on her winsome smile, refusing to let this man's attempt to belittle her touch her in the slightest. She thought it seemed likely all of London had learned of their plight by now. "Good evening, Lord Loring. May I have a word with Clarissa?"

"No," the man answered with a smug smile.

"Father, please don't give mother any more funds for my wardrobe." Clarissa came into the foyer. "Abigail?"

Oh, thank goodness. "Hello, Clarissa. I'm sorry if I'm disturbing you."

"Saints be praised, Father. Let her in. Can't you see she needs to speak with me?" Clarissa stepped around her father, clearly flummoxed when he grunted, but surprisingly, he left them alone.

"I'm sorry. You're probably getting ready to go out."

Clarissa looked down at her turquoise flounced gown with disgust. "I've pleaded a headache—again. Now come in. We can talk in my mother's sitting room. She went on to the gathering without me."

Abigail followed her friend into a room warmed by a cozy fire from the tiled hearth. Clarissa led her over to sit on an ugly flower-patterned sofa.

"Thankfully this is the only room my father allowed my mother to decorate."

Abigail nodded in agreement—Lady Loring had abysmal taste. The room had bright blue walls with orange and yellow flowered upholstery, which stood out in awful contrast. Lace doilies abounded upon the tabletops, and upon the doilies sat delicate figurines of dancing bears.

"At least we'll be left in private. My father hates this room. He says it gives him a stomachache. Would you care for some tea?"

"I've no time. I need to find Jackson."

"Are all the rumors I keep hearing true?"

Abigail told her friend the entire story as quickly as she could, but at that it took well over an hour, two pots of tea, and many tears from both ladies.

"You know I'll do anything I can to help," Clarissa stated emphatically.

"Believe me, if I thought you could help, I wouldn't hesitate to ask. I still can't believe he left me. He promised never to do so. He promised me so many things. And I want those promises fulfilled. I want my husband back."

"So you've come to the city to achieve that end?"

"Yes. I will pound some sense into him."

"I have absolute faith you'll achieve your goal. I'll come by tomorrow afternoon for the details," Clarissa said with a smile of encouragement.

"I appreciate your support."

Clarissa stood and gave her a needed hug. "You'd do the same for me if the situation called for it. You give that man of yours a lethal tongue-lashing, Abigail. He's sure to realize the life you have together is all that really matters."

"I pray you're right."

Abigail returned to her vehicle, trying not to disturb Sophie in her slumber. But her maid awoke when the carriage lurched forward toward Jackson's residence. She wondered if her husband was angrier about the fact that she withheld information from him or the fact that he had lived his life envisioning himself as the future Earl of Waterford. She prayed it was the latter. She never meant to hurt him let alone betray his trust. She just wanted to love him. The scene in the driveway when they parted, when he seemed to look through her as if she didn't matter, truly scared her.

With each turn of the carriage wheels, her anger returned. She may have withheld a truth from him for a couple of blissful days, but he was the one who walked away from the promises he made her. She understood his sense of feeling lost. She felt like that her entire life. And it wasn't fair he lost his title, wealth, properties, and most likely, many other things. However, he'd gain even more as the duke's son. Jackson was acting like a sulking child. She'd be damned if she let him continue to do so for a moment longer. *Saints be praised, we love each other. When will the stubborn fool realize that was all that mattered.*

She could care less what society made of this entire calamity. It was time for Jackson to realize that none of that was important. It had taken her many years to realize this fact, she had to admit, and still at times, it was difficult to ignore ill treatment. But his circumstances were not exactly hers, those of an utter outcast.

The vehicle stopped, and Abigail looked out at her husband's residence, her new home, which had no ties to the Waterford properties. Jackson had boasted how he purchased the property with his own earnings from some wise investments, but it was hard to see the house in the dark.

Walking up to the porch, she smiled at the brown clay flowerpots, bright with red and white blooms. *Charming.* Without knocking, she walked in. After all, this was her home. The foyer was nicely lit with metal wall sconces. Slate floors with beige walls that glowed in the candlelight surrounded her in a pentagon shaped area. Through an arched cove, she could see a well-stocked library to her left and a spacious parlor done in shades of red to her right. *Quite lovely.*

She was so focused on taking in her surroundings that she didn't notice the butler dressed in black and gold livery until he stepped in front of her to block her from further wandering. This day was really beginning to irk her, fraying further her already frayed temper. Her hands went to her hips and her foot began to tap rapidly on the cool slate. If this servant thought to waylay her from her mission to see her husband, then he was in for a rude awakening. She was in no mood to argue, at least, not with this man.

"His lordship isn't taking callers." The butler remained in her path, crossing his arms over his reed thin chest.

"I am his lordship's wife. And you are?"

She watched the man's face change from red embarrassment to a greenish hue in a matter of seconds. He looked like he was going to be sick. "Preston, my lady."

"Well, Preston, kindly step out of my way." *Or, in the mood I'm in, I'm liable to clobber you in the eye and trample over your body.*

Fortunately for him, Preston leaped to the side and gestured his arms widely. "Yes, my lady. Terribly sorry. We weren't expecting you so soon." He blushed to the roots of his sparse gray hair.

Abigail didn't like the idea of causing the poor man upset, and she smiled to put him at ease. After all, he was now an essential part of her staff. "Where is my husband?"

"I thought him in the country with you, my lady."

"He's not been here?" Then why had this bothersome man insinuated that he was? Men were driving her mad.

"Not in a few weeks, my lady. Would you like me to ready you a room?"

"Yes. Have the master's chambers aired out, or whatever is necessary." She truly had no idea how one went about preparing a room, but she refused to sleep in any room other than her husband's, regardless of what people may deem proper. "My luggage is out front. Simms and my maid Sophie are bringing it in."

"I'll have everything ready in a thrice, my lady. And welcome home." He bowed with a smile, and Abigail acknowledged his comment with a nod.

She marched into the parlor and threw her bonnet off onto a white upholstered chair.

He isn't here.

He isn't here? Where is he if not here? Her anger boiled to the surface in a flash, and then just as quickly sadness engulfed her like a tidal wave, her eyes filling with useless tears. *Saints be praised, will I ever stop this incessant crying?* This too was Jackson's fault. *The bounder!* She planned to strangle him when she found him. She needed to vent her ire, and soon, she was tired of crying.

Even though she wanted to beat him senseless at the moment, she prayed for his safety and his speedy return, and more than anything, for his forgiveness. She picked up her disposed bonnet and made her way to her room. She'd write to a couple of Jackson's closest friends. Perhaps they would have an idea as to her husband's whereabouts. Someone had to know where to find him. Exhaustion took hold of her body, but she knew sleep wouldn't come easily.

Abigail was charmed by the bedchamber. The mammoth four-poster bed had carved spindles that rose to greet her. A writing desk sat against one wall between a matching set of dark wood chest drawers. There were two leather chairs positioned in front of a green marble fireplace, which had already been lit by the obviously competent staff. The room felt masculine and comfortable.

She ordered up a light repast, along with a bath and writing utensils. After sending out her letters and trying to ease her muscles in a hot bath, she crawled beneath the thick feather blankets of her husband's bed. The sheets had been cleaned, but thankfully, the velvet brown coverlet still held his scent, and she inhaled deeply with but one thought filtering through her mind. *I will find my husband.* She ran her hands over the soft velvet until sleep claimed her.

CHAPTER FIFTEEN

Jackson raised his head from where it lay pillowed on his arms on top of the table. Wiping the sleep from his eyes, he looked up at a fancy piece sitting across from him in a form fitting red dress, her breasts spilling over the top of the black lace edging.

"Mornin' guv'nor." The whore smiled, displaying a mouth full of crooked teeth.

Jackson blinked his eyes, trying to recognize his surroundings. *Right. The Red Robin Tavern by the docks.* His head was pounding with the recollection. "I'm not interested in what you're offering. I'm enjoying my solitude," he said gruffly.

She leaned over the table to push the tips of her breasts into the tabletop. "I'm sure I can remedy what ails you, lovey."

Jackson tried not to cringe at the thought. The truth was, since he met Abigail, he no longer gave other women more than a passing glance; but had he never met Abby, he still would not have given this woman a glance. She looked old enough to be his mother. "Not interested," he exclaimed, hollering to the barkeep for a new bottle of spirits.

Her hips swaying in an exaggerated fashion, the whore ambled away from his table, promising he could change his mind at any time and she'd be more than willing. To his growing irritation, she snatched up his bottle of spirits from the waiter and sauntered back over to him. She filled his glass and then produced one from her pocket for herself. Dusting the glass off on her red skirts, she poured herself a libation. "To what are we drinking?"

Jackson fished some coins out of his pocket and placed them in her hand. "*We* aren't drinking to anything. I, on the other hand, wish to be left alone with my sorrows if you don't mind."

At this, she seemed to finally comprehend his desire for solitude for she patted his shoulder in understanding and wandered back up the steps to the rooms above.

Alone with his thoughts, Jackson's mind returned to Abigail, as it had far too often since he left her in tears on the Waterford Estate drive. He missed her. He missed her easy smile and the way she looked at him as if he was her everything. Why would she ever want him now? He felt separated from himself, detached from the life he'd known and thoroughly enjoyed.

Perhaps Alex was right, and he was feeling sorry for himself, but if he didn't mourn all that had changed, who would?"

Abigail, my wife, she would mourn everything with me. God, how he loved her. She understood him in a way he never thought possible. Or at least, she understood the man he was before this news pummeled the life out of him. Could they begin anew? Was it possible to leave the past in the past? At the moment, he felt completely hopeless about the future.

He poured himself another drink, not yet ready for the reality of the new world in which he found himself.

***

Abigail dressed in a lovely sky-blue day dress and pulled her chestnut hair up in a simple ribbon. Her lack of sleep had not helped her temper. She descended the steps to the sound of someone knocking on the front door. Her heart expanded with hope, visions of Jackson filling her mind. These images were quickly vanquished when she realized he would not knock at his own door.

"My lady, the Earl of Everett and Viscount Rathemore are here to see you."

She knew she was now one step closer to finding her husband and smiled at their early morning arrival. "Show them into the parlor, Preston."

"Yes, my lady." She went into the kitchen, surprising the cook when she sat at the servants' table to eat a piece of buttered toast. She couldn't think well on an empty stomach, and she was in no mood to face the dining room alone. Besides, company had arrived, so she only had time for a quick bite.

She walked into the parlor to find two handsome men, men she knew to be her husband's closest confidants. They sat comfortably in the two wing-backed chairs but stood when she entered. She waved them back down.

"It's nice to have you in London, Abigail," Julian commented. The atmosphere in the room was tense, as if no one knew the right words to say. She sensed Jackson's friends were worried about her husband as well.

"Thank you, and thank you both for responding promptly to my plea." She seated herself on the sofa across from them.

"I was going to send for you. I'm glad you're here," Alex said. "Jackson's..." He paused, most likely considering what he should share with her and what was best left unsaid. "He's not in a good state of mind, Abigail. I tried talking to him, but he's not thinking rationally right now. I'm sorry to say I wasn't any help."

Abigail was relieved to hear Alex had spoken with her husband. She nodded solemnly. "Where is he?"

"The Red Robin Tavern, down by the docks."

She stood. She had her destination. "Thank you both for coming. I'm going to retrieve my husband now."

"Hold on." Julian jumped up and blocked her exit.

What is it with men constantly obstructing my way? "Lord Rathemore," she said sternly, "I'm out of patience. As a matter of fact, it's taking every ounce of my ladylike self-control not to find an object to bash you on the head." He actually smiled at her threat. "My husband needs me. I must go to him. Step aside."

Alex came up behind her. "Be reasonable, Abigail. A lady can't just mosey into a tavern, especially one where the dregs of society spend time, and this establishment is indeed one of those. It's not safe."

"You're not going," Julian stated adamantly, crossing his arms over his large chest.

She blinked up at him. The man was as controlling and pompous as Jackson. *God save me from the male species.* "If I must run you down, I will do so," she threatened.

He laughed, but he did not budge from blocking her escape. She let out a sigh of frustration. "Very well, then. You'll both just have to accompany me to this tavern."

"No," both men said in unison, causing her to stomp her foot. Her temper soared. This was ridiculous. Alex had all but said how desperately Jackson needed her.

"No? Perhaps the two of you are failing to forget you have no control over me."

"Listen." Alex placed a hand on her shoulder, but she shrugged it off. "Jackson's angrier than I have ever seen him. He's confused. And if we show up at that…disreputable edifice with his wife in tow…" She could tell he was going to call the tavern something much worse. It dawned on her how low her husband must feel to be at such a place. "Let us just say that he would not want you there and his wrath would be fierce."

Abigail didn't care how angry Jackson became at her appearance. She wanted his anger. They both needed to do some ranting, if only to work through this. "All right. Then what do the two of you propose I do? Shall I sit idly by while he sinks yet lower into his misery?"

"Write him a letter," Julian replied.

Abigail glared at him. "Do you honestly believe I can help my husband by scribbling some words on paper?" Her eyes began to sting. "He needs me. He needs to feel my arms around him, comforting him, assuring him that we will make it through this."

Julian pulled at his neckcloth in discomfort. Both men seemed a bit uncomfortable by her words, most likely because they knew she was right.

Alex was the one to speak. "I'm sorry, but the best we can do is deliver your letter to him. Perhaps you can convince him to come home in writing. I'm sure the rest of what you have to say can wait until he is in a suitable frame of mind. He will not be in said frame of mind if we accompany you to a tavern on the docks."

"And when he refuses?" And she knew he would. If she couldn't stop him from leaving her at the Waterford Estate, she certainly couldn't convince him to return with a few simple words. She wished it were that easy. *Men! They don't understand anything!*

"We will deal with that when and if the time comes."

Abigail tried a different tactic. "You mean to say that you two strong men wouldn't be able to keep me safe for one simple visit to a tavern?" She put on her sweetest smile, but she realized that her ploy wasn't working by the looks of amusement on their faces.

"Nice effort, Abigail." Julian grinned.

Abigail gave them both the meanest look she could muster, then stomped across the room to write her husband a note.

She wanted to tell him what impossible friends he had. Then she wanted to write simply, "Husband, get yourself home, now!" but she settled for something a bit more genteel. Folding the missive, she gave it to Alex, who with a bow, placed it in his coat pocket.

"Ready?" he asked Julian.

"If he's as cantankerous as you say, I highly doubt I'm up for it. However, I want Jackson back as well. He needs to put the past behind him where it belongs. If I can do so, he certainly can." Abigail knew Julian was speaking of his runaway fiancée. She also knew that Julian in no way put all his upset to rest when it came to the woman Abigail believed he still loved. "His focus needs to be on his pretty wife."

"Yes, it does, and thank you," she said. "Now please hurry and bring him back to me."

"So you can slay him?" Alex queried.

"After I tell him I love him." She smiled tightly. "If I seem angry, it's because I'm somewhat overwrought."

"Of course, my lady. Perfectly understandable." Alex gave her a nod of understanding, which was tainted by the fact that he knew Jackson was in for the lecture of a lifetime. Abigail had never cowered, never hidden from anyone. She was not about to let Jackson hide himself away feeling sorry for himself.

When the gentlemen left, she paced the room, wondering how long it would take them to convince Jackson to return home. Likely all day, if one considered how stubborn her husband could be. Could they convince him to return to her? This was the big question. It was something she didn't intend to leave to chance. If they failed to come back with Jackson, she planned to seek out her love and drag him home, be he in a whisky soaked hellhole or the bowels of hell. With that thought, she left the room to put an alternate plan into motion.

***

It was approaching noon when Jackson ordered up another bottle, though the last had dulled his senses and left him in a state of depression. From his place at the table, he could see Julian and Alex coming up the walk through the large glass window. *Now they are doubling up on him. Why can't everyone mind their own bloody business?*

His friends entered the door like men on a mission and walked with purposeful strides in his direction. There were few patrons at this early hour of the day. Two grizzled looking men sat at the bar in soiled clothes. Jackson sat alone amongst the tables.

"You look like hell." Julian turned a chair around and straddled it.

"Bloody hell, Jackson. You need a bath!" Alex scowled as he took seat.

"Ah, my friends. So kind of you to visit me in hell."

"A hell of your own making!" Julian scoffed. "Have you seen yourself?" Everyone knew that Lord Rathemore was known to be a bit of a dandy when it came to his own appearance. It seemed to Jackson he was too unkempt for his friend's refined tastes. But then Julian must not have realized that, right now, Jackson cared not a whit about his appearance.

"And who is it I would see, Julian? Jackson Sethos Ramesses Gibbons Blake? Or some other shit?" he slurred. "A drink?" Both men declined and Jackson gave an ugly laugh. "You're here for intervention? Trust me. I'm not worth the time."

"You're worth a bloody fortune! Christ man, you're the son of a duke. Pull yourself together!" Julian demanded.

Jackson plowed his fingers through his hair, his headache returning with Julian's shouts.

"Listen, Jackson. Your wife has returned to London to find you. We're here at her request." Alex gave the white missive to Jackson. "She wrote you this."

"Delivery made. You can both take your leave now." Jackson tossed the letter to the center of the table as if he didn't care what his wife had to say, when in truth, he found himself wanting to rip it open like a child with a present. His friends stood and he couldn't help asking, "Is Abigail all right?"

Alex nodded. "She is."

"She's at your house, which is where you ass should be," Julian said, and he quit the tavern without looking back at him. Jackson had a feeling his leaving Abigail had Julian reflecting on his own ladylove who left him.

"Your wife needs you." Alex stood and headed for the door, but turned back before exiting to say, "And so do your friends."

Jackson slunk back in his chair the moment his friends left. The white missive seemed to be calling to him. He held it in his hand for several minutes, trying to fathom what his wife would have written. He studied her delicate scrawl, her letters curved and fanciful. Like a fool, he brought the letter to his nose, craving her scent, but he found none. Visions of her smelling his pillow the morning after the best sex of his life filtered through the hazy alcohol-induced fog he was living in.

He flipped open the folds and read the simple lines.

Please talk to me. I love you.

His heart wrenched. His pain was hurting her. He downed another drink, his guilt taking over his mind. *I failed her. I made her promises I didn't keep.* He numbered this among the other miseries he was going to have to deal with. Would this tiresome weight on his shoulders ever lift? Tears leaked out of his eyes, and he put his head down on his folded arms on the table, drink pulling him into slumber.

***

Abigail sat with Clarissa. They were trying to have a normal conversation about the latest fashion trends, a difficult task, considering her mind remained centered on Jackson. She prayed for the millionth time that Alex and Julian would bring him home. She stared down at the gigantic heart-shaped ruby circling her finger, a token of Jackson's unending love. Tears came to the surface of her eyes but she refused to allow them to drop, quickly blinking them away.

"My attempt to keep your mind occupied isn't working, is it? He'll come back, Abby." Clarissa assured her.

Abigail nodded. At the moment, her hopes were meaningless. She had a horrible feeling that her husband would not be back to her any time soon. A pain sliced through her heart at the thought that she could have upset him so much by remaining silent about his parentage. Was it possible he hated her? She couldn't believe such. When Jackson loved, he loved completely. She could feel his love in every touch and in every gaze. When she heard the front door open, she jumped out of her seat to rush to the foyer. Although she had just doubted his return, she couldn't help the excitement leaping in her breast at the thought of him coming home.

Her disappointment was great as she gave a small smile of greeting to Alex and Julian, blinking rapidly to ward off tears. Jackson wasn't with them. She told herself it was expected. Jackson needed time to adjust to the changes that had so upended his life, his notion of who he was, everything. She squeezed her eyes shut and then gestured for Jackson's friends to enter the foyer.

"I'm sorry, Abigail, but he's just not ready," Alex informed her somberly.

Not ready? Anger filled her. She stiffened, and without tears, gave them a nod as if she understood. "I appreciate your efforts."

"Give him a few more days. He's sure to come around," Julian added before the men stepped back onto the porch and Abigail closed the door behind them.

She could hear them outside. Although she shouldn't have remained to listen, she couldn't help wondering if they had other information regarding Jackson that they thought best not to share with her. Could her husband have found solace in the arms of another? She dismissed the thought seconds later. Jackson loved her. He just needed to forgive her.

"Do you think she'll stay put and await his return?" Julian's voice was filled with skepticism. Abigail couldn't help smiling.

The man understood women far better than Alex, for two seconds later she heard Alex answer, "She's an intelligent woman. I'm sure she'll realize she has no choice. A lady can't be seen down by the wharves no matter the reason."

"If you say so." Julian's tone said he thought Alex completely daft. "And what do we do in the meantime? If you ask me, we should physically drag his ass back home to his wife where he belongs."

"I didn't ask. We'll make the rounds at all the influential clubs, spreading the news of Jackson's good fortune." She could picture Alex's devious smile. What they intended to do on Jackson's behalf made her glad they were his friends. *Such loyalty is not easy to find.* "It will help people to know our friend's recent assignation with a ducal title."

"A sound plan," Julian replied.

Abigail moved from the door as Clarissa entered the foyer. Holding on to her composure, she thanked her friend for coming by, insisting she needed time alone. She couldn't tell anyone of her plan for she did not want to give anyone the opportunity to try to talk her out of it. It would only delay her. She came to London to fetch her husband, and fetch him she would. She'd wait for nightfall. As much as she hated to admit it, Alex and Julian were right. It wouldn't do for the future Duchess of Salisbury to be seen traipsing about down by the docks. She would need to hide in the cloak of darkness. With her scheme in mind, she went to find a black bombazine dress and a black hat with veil to hide her features.

***

Hours later, Abigail sat in a hired hack, her spine straight, her mind fixed on one goal: to regain her husband's love and trust.

The lantern light swinging inside the vehicle cast shadows on the opposite seat, and she briefly closed her eyes to ward off a surge of panic. She thought it best not to involve any of the servants in such a private family matter, and so she had traveled alone. As the vehicle clambered over the cobbles, passing numerous warehouses and ambling further off into the still of the night, she looked out at her surroundings and shuddered. She'd never been to London's East End, but she had heard of the poverty. The view out the window was abysmal and sad: dilapidated buildings, children crying, dogs barking, and people arguing, these discordant noises rending the air outside some of the lowly tenements.

She put her head back against the worn squabs of her hired hack. With her veil, she wouldn't be recognized, not that she knew anyone from this area. Nevertheless, dressed in stark black, she appeared to be a woman in mourning. The perfect disguise.

It was a warm, humid evening, and as they neared the Thames, the pungent aroma of what she hoped was only rotting fish filled her nose, which she immediately pinched closed with her fingers. They circled down another road, the smell fading. A few minutes later, the vehicle yanked to a quick stop.

"So sorry, my lady. I thought you said the Gray Goose Tavern, but you didn't, did you?"

Abigail rubbed her temples. If this man had brought her to the wrong place, she was going to scream. She was out of patience. Her nerves were already a mess from being somewhere she knew she shouldn't be. Danger seemed to lurk from every corner. "I'm looking for the Red Robin Tavern."

"Sorry, miss. It's two doors behind us. I can circle back around and drop you off in front. It won't take more than ten minutes." Abigail looked behind them to see the Red Robin Tavern sign a short distance away. She wasn't about to wait a moment longer. The road wasn't wide enough for the driver to maneuver a circle, and ten minutes sounded like an eternity when she was this close. "That's not necessary. I can walk." She paid him from the purse of coins around her wrist. "You can go. Thank you."

"Can't rightly do that, miss. This here's not a nice neighborhood for someone like you." Abigail thought his observation an understatement of large proportions but didn't comment. At present, she'd happily confess she felt like she was a fish out of water in these surroundings. Two drunks passed behind her singing some lewd ballad, causing her to blush beneath her veil.

"I'll be fine, sir. My husband's inside." She was not only trying to reassure the driver but to boost her own confidence that all would be well.

"You go see that husband of yours." The man's voice didn't sound like he approved of Jackson's haunt. "I'll circle around for a while. When I come back, just wave me away if I'm not needed."

She thought that a fine plan, and immediately she felt more at ease. "That's very kind of you, sir." She looked about while he assisted her down from the perch. When her feet hit the wooden walkway, the driver swung back into the vehicle and hurried down the road. She noticed a man standing outside the Gray Goose. Eyes downcast, she walked by him toward the red sign of the Red Robin Tavern. How could her husband want to spend time at such a disgusting and dangerous place? She was so caught up in her own thoughts that she didn't notice the two men in the alley until it was too late. One grabbed her from behind, putting a hand over her breast like a vise, and the other, grabbed her hand, his greedy eyes fixed on her wedding ring while he deftly removed her purse, shoving it into his pants pocket.

She punched, kicked, squirmed, and screamed, but she seemed to afflict little damage to the two mean looking ruffians. She looked about frantically while she clawed at the men, trying to retrieve her arm and make a fist so the one couldn't take her ring. She kicked again and again at the man who held her breast in a meaty fist, but though her heel continued to hit his shin, he didn't flinch. She looked frantically around for help. The man in front of the Gray Goose had disappeared.

Her left arm was suddenly wrenched behind her back and her breath came out in short pants. The man was crushing her ribs with his beefy arms. When she felt her wedding ring begin to slide over her knuckle, she screeched, twisting her head around toward the offender. She found purchase in his arm and sank her teeth into his salty flesh.

The man yelped, leaping back to smack her hard in the face. The blow he dealt her was solid and she staggered with its impact, her veil falling beneath their scuffling feet. Her head swam but she had no time to dwell on pain. The man behind her began to drag her backward.

"Let's get her to the alley. I'd like to taste this feisty morsel."

"The bitch bit me. I say we kill her."

Abigail panicked. They were going to rape and kill her. How was this happening? If they reached the alley, she'd have no chance for rescue. Her eyes blurred with tears, but she would not relinquish her wedding ring.

She lunged forward with all her weight. The monster holding her slammed her into the building and her face smashed up against a window. She struggled as the man cursed and pressed her harder against the glass. She bit into the other assailant's arm finding it her best course of defense. She released the grip her teeth had on his hairy arm and yelped in pain as something pressed into her back, causing such intense agony she screamed, but she did not intend to give up. She clawed for the man's eyes.

***

Jackson's hand shook as he read Abigail's note for the hundredth time. She was right. They needed to talk. Drowning his sorrows wasn't doing either of them a lick of good. But how did a man hold onto something of which he felt himself unworthy? How was he to explain the pain he felt inside? How was he to apologize for leaving her the day after their wedding? Would she ever forgive him for such an error in judgment?

He saw two men through the front window brawling about something. That's how it was around these parts. He'd seen numerous fights and scuffles over the last few days. It was a common enough occurrence, that he dropped his eyes back to his note.

A thud made him look back up and then there she was. He blinked, thinking himself hallucinating in his drunken state. But she was still there. Her face pressed against the glass as two men... *Good God!*

Pushing over his chair, he gave a roar of outrage so loud the barkeep dropped the glass he was polishing. It shattered when it hit the floor.

Jackson tore out the door, his anger boiling to the point of lunacy. How dare these men accost his wife. He'd tear them limb from limb.

He yanked the man who was holding Abigail and planted a facer on him so hard the man went down with a resounding thump and didn't move.

"Jackson," Abigail cried with relief.

He had no time to acknowledge her as the other man who wore a scraggily beard began circling him with a deadly knife. "Now ye done it. I'm going to slice ye to ribbons for hurting poor Ned there. He didn't do ye a bit of harm."

Rage cleared Jackson's mind of the alcohol-induced fog. His eyes fixed on the shiny blade, he darted sideways when the villain lunged forward. The man's momentum carried him forward, and Jackson struck him from behind with a sharp elbow to the back, sending the man sprawling to the ground. The ruffian gained his footing quickly and swung back around to face Jackson. Again the man lunged at him, and this time Jackson grabbed his arm, twisting it behind the man's back. He clutched the man's windpipe with his other hand, adding the right amount of pressure until the knife clattered on the ground as the man's face turned blue from lack of oxygen.

He spun the man around and sent a fist into his face. He heard bone crunch with the impact as blood splattered the ground. The man screamed curses at Jackson about his broken nose, but Jackson was far from ending the man's punishment.

Jackson went to pummel him again but the villain took one look at his comrade lying motionless on the ground and, cradling his own bleeding face, sprinted in the opposite direction.

As much as Jackson wanted to give chase, he needed to assure himself that his wife was indeed unharmed. She leaned against the wall looking completely disheveled but achingly lovely as she took shallow breaths of air. She was pale from her encounter, and he immediately pulled her into his arms.

"Are you all right?" his wife asked, and with no thought for herself, he noted. She clutched him to her and he hoped his presence reassured her. The man at her feet stirred and Jackson found himself wanting to laugh when Abigail kicked the man in the stomach. The man groaned and his head wobbled on the cement, but he remained on the ground moaning in agony.

"I'm fine. Are you sure you're not hurt?" He grasped her head between his hands to look deeply into her eyes. The fight seemed to have been a cure for all his frustrations, for just looking at Abigail made him realize what a fool he'd been.

"Oh, I'm hurt all right, husband. You left me!" she yelled, swaying on her feet. He took her arm to steady her. She had been through a terrible ordeal, which was entirely his fault, and he shook with unspent anger, at these ruffians, at himself, at this woman for taking such a risk. *Damn her brave soul. She could have been killed.*

A hack pulled up alongside the road as if he had hailed one, the same driver who had brought Abigail here doffing his cap in their direction.

"You look pale, Abigail. You should sit. I need to get you home."

"I'm not going anywhere without you," she answered stubbornly, her words broken and soft. He put his arm around her and she flinched. "Ouch!"

Panic filled his voice. "What is it?"

"Something's burning my shoulder. Funny, I didn't notice it before."

Of course she didn't feel her hurts, for fighting for one's life has a way of making one concentrate completely on surviving. "You've had quite a scare." He ran his hand over her shoulders and blanched when one came away covered in blood.

"Can I be of some service?" the driver from the hack asked from his perch.

Abigail must have read the fear on his face for she turned and twisted in an effort to see her shoulder. "What is it? I can't see. Did that man do something to me? Oh, ouch. It really is hurting." She swayed into him again. She was growing weak. Her body was losing too much blood. "Jackson?"

"Yes, love?"

"I hope you are carrying those smelling salts with you." With those words, his wife crumpled in his arms. His heart lurched and began to pound out of control. His entire body trembled with fear as he carried his wife to the hack placed her inside. He gave a shout to the driver, instructing the man to hurry, then climbed inside with her. The vehicle lurched into motion as Jackson arranged Abigail on top of his lap.

With the vehicle moving at a quick pace, Jackson began to undress the upper portion of his wife's body to view her damaged shoulder. To the left of her shoulder blade, blood poured from the knife wound like a fountain. *Far too much blood.* His wife was bleeding to death before his very eyes. She was as white as a sheet. "Faster!" he roared, pounding on the roof, trying to keep his overwhelming emotions at bay. He had to help Abigail. Ripping off his shirt, he balled it up and pressed it hard against the wound to stunt the flow of blood. "You are not dying on me. Do you hear me, wife? I won't allow it."

With one hand holding his makeshift bandage, he pulled her dress up to cover her breasts, his lips pressing kisses to her clammy face. He pushed her hair back from her face, begging her to open her eyes, to speak to him.

Desperate now, he tried to wave the smelling salts he still carried with him beneath her nose, but nothing happened. His wife remained unconscious. He held her to him, tears streaming down his face as he cursed himself. *My wife would never have been hurt if I hadn't felt so damn sorry for myself. If I hadn't hidden myself in such a rotted area where crime is a way of life. I did this to her.* He'd never forgive himself if she died. *Oh Lord, she can't die.* Jackson did something he hadn't done in years, he prayed. He made vows and promises he would definitely keep, as long as God let him keep Abigail.

While murmuring loving and encouraging words in her ear, he noticed the lotus combs in her hair and his chest squeezed tight. If she died, he would go with her. He refused to think of a life without her, for such an existence wasn't possible. She was to be his duchess, his wife, his love, his everything.

CHAPTER SIXTEEN

The hired hack barreled around the corner and came to a speedy halt in front of Jackson's townhouse. Gathering his unconscious wife in his arms, he rushed toward the front door the moment the driver swung the vehicle's door open.

"Fetch me, Dr. Pierson on Water Street. I'll pay you upon your return," Jackson told the driver, hurrying past his wide-eyed butler to take his wife to their room. Jackson's coat was soaked through with her blood. He knew the fear on his face told his servants exactly how serious the situation was. He took the steps two at a time, giving his door a kick to open it. He rushed toward the bed to lay Abigail down.

"My lord?" The butler hustled after him, followed by his distraught housekeeper.

"I need towels, water, bandages, and a sewing kit." He'd sew his wife up himself if the doctor didn't show himself in the next ten minutes. "Be speedy about it, Preston."

"Yes." The butler fled out the door.

"Mrs. Tyler, assist me in removing my wife's garments."

"Yes, my lord." Jackson held Abigail to his chest while he worked with the housekeeper to remove her blood stained clothes. When Mrs. Tyler deftly slipped the buttons free, Jackson eased the garments off, leaving his shirt balled up against the wound as he continually applied pressure.

Resting her back against the pillow so he could sit next to her, he covered her with a sheet. He moved some of her brown tresses away from her pale face to examine the welt on her cheek. She lay limp and still, and he felt tears close his throat. He murmured something wicked in her ear, praying for a reaction, anything that would tell him his wife was going to make it through this. She continued to be still. "Please, love. Wake up for me. I'm so sorry."

"Perhaps you should lie down as well, my lord. I can hold the bandage in place."

"No," Jackson replied with such force his housekeeper jumped. He knew that he really needed to get himself under control. His wife would be fine. She had to be. "My wife is in this condition because of me," he said in way of an explanation for his sharp tone. "I will be the one to see to her recovery."

"Of course, my lord. As you wish. I'll fetch you some clean clothes."

Jackson leaned down to place his cheek against his wife's breast. *Her heart still beats, thank the Lord, but the rhythm is weak.* He'd never felt so utterly helpless.

"Come on, my love. Time to wake up. We're home. Your plan worked, Abigail. I'm exactly where I should be, where I should have been all along, by your side. Oh please wake up, wife. I need to hear your voice." He pleaded, begged, and cried, but it was to no avail. He nuzzled his nose into her chest as tears of agony ripped from his throat.

"Doctor Pierson's here, my lord," Mrs. Tyler announced, ushering the saw bones inside while she deposited Jackson's clean clothing on a nearby chaise.

Doctor Pierson, a bushy browed man with brown eyes and a scarce amount of hair on his head, bowed to Jackson before he came toward the bed.

"Light some more candles, if you please," the doctor instructed the housekeeper, gesturing for Jackson to step away from his patient. "How long has she been senseless?"

Jackson stood, wiping his wife's blood off on his ruined coat. It seemed like she'd been unconscious for many hours, but he knew such wasn't the case. "A half an hour," Jackson answered, pacing the area around the bed. Time seemed to be suspended as he watched Abigail to see if she'd stir at the doctor's manipulations. "She has a knife wound on her left shoulder. There's a welt on her cheek. She's pale, as you can see, and her heart rate's slow. I checked her head…"

"Please sit, my lord," the doctor interrupted. "You look

like you're about to fall over, and I already have my hands full with your wife."

Jackson tried to sit in a chair, but the moment the doctor knelt to remove the cloth covering the wound, he jumped back up again.

"She'll need to be stitched," the doctor informed him. "She's lost a great deal of blood."

Jackson almost groaned in complaint, though he already knew this. The shirt and the coat he was wearing were covered in his wife's vital fluid. "Yes, I know. Will she be all right?" *Please say yes.*

"Hard to say, my lord."

Jackson felt like strangling the man.

"Nevertheless, I'm confident she'll come around once we get her to stop bleeding. You'll need to watch for infection and I can give her laudanum for pain. It should help."

Jackson nodded, and then he sat on the edge of the bed, smoothing back his wife's hair while he held her on her side so the doctor could stitch her up. His wife didn't even wince when the needle was applied to her skin, and her lack of feeling caused an ache to form like a knot in his chest.

For what seemed like an eternity, Jackson watched the doctor cleanse, sew, and apply healing paste before he bandaged her. Slowly Jackson lowered Abigail back onto her back as the doctor wiped his brow with the back of his arm. Reaching into his black bag, the doctor then retrieved a bottle of laudanum and set it on the nightstand. "I'll be back to check on her in the morning." After washing his hands in the table basin, he began to put his medical supplies back in his old leather satchel.

"Thanks, Doctor Pierson." Jackson nodded for his housekeeper to show the doctor out. He was not leaving Abigail's side.

After washing himself and changing out of his soiled clothes, he climbed into bed next to his wife. He needed to feel her close. He wanted to be sure he was there the moment she awoke.

Jackson slid in and out of sleep, checking on Abigail constantly. Countless times, he sat up abruptly in a panic. When she began to moan, he'd lift her head and pour medicine into her mouth, which she thankfully drank without incident. Seeing her do something as mundane as drink from a cup made him believe she'd come through this.

He examined her face. Color was returning to her cheeks, which he knew to be a positive sign. *My brave girl will come back to me. She has to.*

***

The next morning, his eyes heavy, Jackson remained vigilant. But Abigail had yet to open her remarkable eyes for him. He cursed himself for being such a bloody fool.

Not even married twenty-four hours and he walked out on his wife. What the hell was the matter with him? She brought love, laughter, and sunshine into his life, and he had pushed her away. *Hell's teeth, I nearly got her killed, and for what?* So he could sit on his drunken ass feeling sorry for himself? Well he was sorry all right, sorry she got hurt from his reckless behavior. He'd never been so sorry for anything in his life. He wished he could trade places with her. He would willingly give his life for hers.

How could he be so stupid not to realize that what they shared was all he ever needed? He no longer held the title of the Earl of Waterford and was, by recent accounts, the illegitimate son of a duke. But none of that mattered. He no longer cared about money, titles, influence, or society's view of them. And he no longer cared that Abigail withheld the truth from him for a couple of measly days. He knew why she did what she did. On further retrospection, if the situation had been reversed and there had been a chance he couldn't have made her his wife, he too would have lied, and lied, and lied.

"Please, Abigail, awake. I love you so much." His body shook and tears fell down his cheeks. "Please come back to me."

A light knock sounded on the door and Preston stuck his head in. "The Earl of Everett and Viscount Rathemore have come to call on Lady Abigail."

"Is the doctor here?" Jackson swiped at his useless tears.

"Not yet, my lord."

"Well, fetch him, Preston. I want my wife to wake up!"

"Yes, my lord, right away. And your guests?"

He sighed. "Show them to the parlor. I'll be right down. Tell Mrs. Tyler I need her to sit with Abigail for a bit."

"Consider it done, my lord."

Rubbing the back of his fists against his red and swollen eyes, Jackson dressed numbly and went to speak to his friends. Perhaps one of them would be kind enough to shoot him and end his misery.

"Alex, Julian." Jackson entered the parlor, his body not stable on his feet due to his fear for Abigail's health and lack of sleep. His friends' bright smiles told him they were unaware of current events and were happy to see him in residence.

"I'm glad to see you home," Alex said, clapping him on the back.

Julian sniffed the air with disapproval. "How is it you look even worse than you did at the Red Robin Tavern?"

"I'm surprised you're standing, Jackson. I thought that wife of yours would have chewed off your head by now," Alex added.

"Hopefully she'll get a chance to do so. God knows I deserve it." Jackson's voice was heavy with dejection.

Reading his saddened expression, Alex asked, "What happened? You appear more downtrodden than ever."

"My wife was attacked outside the Red Robin Tavern."

"Attacked?" Julian spun on his heel, fixing a pointed look at Alex. "I told you she wouldn't stay put. Women never do!"

"Is she all right?" Alex asked, glaring at Julian as if to say the I-told-you-so could wait.

Jackson ran a trembling hand over his face. "She was stabbed in the shoulder and has yet to wake up."

"Hell and damnation, Jackson! Why didn't you send for us?" Julian questioned.

Jackson shrugged. "There's nothing either of you could do." He sank to the sofa in defeat. "I can't lose her."

Alex nodded. "And you won't, you'll see. Before you know it your wife will be up giving you the tongue lashing of a lifetime."

"I can only hope."

"This is as much our fault," Julian stated. "We should have watched her."

"Knowing Abigail, there was nothing either of you could have done to stop her from finding me. I'm the one at fault."

The room fell into a somber silence, each man lost in his own turbulent thoughts.

"These ruffians, where can they be found?" Alex's fists were clenched. Jackson knew his mind was set on seeing retribution rendered.

"I don't know. I gave their descriptions to my butler, who gave them to the authorities." The truth was Jackson didn't care. All he wanted was his Abigail back in his arms. Even her yelling at him would be a blessing. She would be nowhere near such scoundrels in the future; he planned to see to it.

Julian stepped forward. "Is there anything we can do?"

"Yes. Pray my wife wakes up. And if she doesn't, I'd be more than grateful to have one of you shoot me."

"Enough," Alex scolded. "Your wife is strong, and she'll pull through this."

"He is right. A mere stab wound won't keep a woman like yours down," Julian added.

Jackson nodded solemnly. When he reached his room, he found the doctor listening to what he assured him was the strong, steady beating of Abigail's heart.

"She's doing better, my lord, her heart rate well in the normal range. Continue with the laudanum for pain. The gash seems to be mending well, but if there is a discharge green or a red ring begins to encircle the wound, send for me."

"Thank you," Jackson mumbled before the doctor took his leave. Shedding his clothes, he got back into bed to hold his wife.

***

Abigail was stuck in a repeating dream. No matter how hard she tried, she couldn't awaken. The beginning of the dream was pleasant: she and Jackson holding hands, kissing, making love while he promised her the world. And then she'd be standing in her ruined wedding dress as her husband rode out of her life. If that wasn't a bad enough dream to have over and over, the end of her dream was a hellish nightmare. Two rough looking men wrestled with her for her wedding ring. She kicked at them, screaming and scratching, and then there was a sharp pain and she moaned, still not able to move, afraid the pain would intensify if she did.

It was at this point that someone would pour some kind of wicked brew down her throat and then the dream would start anew.

***

Jackson couldn't take much more of this. His wife's thrashing was making him ill with worry. She mumbled, and he'd lean in closer trying to understand. She'd scream, and he'd rub her brow calming her with his words. She repeatedly called his name as tears leaked out of her closed eyes, each tear a vicious blow to his heart.

He hugged her close, kissing her neck where her pulse beat, encouraging her to open her eyes to see him, to feel his presence and kiss him back. He was eager for any sign at all, the littlest something to prove she'd return to him.

Abigail slept peacefully right now, but he knew it wouldn't last. He got out of bed and went to the basin to splash water on his face.

A knock from the door interrupted his morning ablutions as Preston stepped into the room. "My lord, you have company."

"Who's here," Jackson mumbled, toweling off his face. "I'm not up for company." Due to his constant vigilance at Abigail's side, he lacked sleep. All he wanted to do was crawl back into bed beside her.

"Your family has come to call, my lord."

The only family Jackson wanted to concentrate on was Abigail. He hesitated as he gazed at his overly still wife. There were a number of people who constituted his family these days, and thus he seriously had no clue who might be waiting downstairs.

"What do you wish for me to tell them, my lord?"

He knew he had to tell them about Abigail. They deserved to know what his antics cost them all. A heavy weight settled in his chest. "Tell them I'll be down in a moment. See them made comfortable in the parlor. Have Mrs. Tyler fetch tea." He eyed his butler. "Which of my esteemed relations are downstairs?"

"All of them, my lord, except for your two sisters." Jackson could have sworn he saw Preston smirk. Clearly the man was amused by Jackson's plight, though he could not blame him entirely. He had walked about this house as if he were invulnerable, and now, his entire world was upside down.

"Very well." He realized he had much to say to everyone. His apologies alone could take long into the afternoon; he wasn't very good at them. Abigail learned that much from their first encounter. He missed her so much: her spirit, her wit, and most importantly her love.

Mrs. Tyler cleared her throat at the bedchamber entrance. "Yes, Mrs. Tyler?"

"I thought you might like to have this, my lord." She came across the room to give him a letter addressed to him by his fraudulent grandfather. "I found it in her ladyship's clothing when they were sent to the ragman."

"Thank you," he said, tucking the missive in his pocket.

With her note delivered, Mrs. Tyler quit the room to see to the guests.

Once she left, Jackson sat on the side of the bed, brushing a few wayward hairs away from his wife's face. "I guess you wanted me to read what the devil had to say? Although I'd prefer not to, I shall do so for you."

He withdrew the letter from his pocket, and with uneasiness, broke the wax seal. Nothing the late Earl of Waterford could have written would make up for the lies and treachery he served up to him or Abigail.

My esteemed grandson,

Yes, you are still my grandson, regardless of the circumstances that brought such a miracle about, circumstances I admittedly took advantage of to achieve my ends. I needed you and I like to believe you needed me. I took you from your mother, and I don't regret such a drastic decision. From the day you came home to me, you were my everything, my heir, my protégé.

You're no longer the Earl of Waterford, something I truly do regret, for no one could have been more deserving than you, my boy. When I decided to compose these letters, I took it upon myself to find out your sire's identity. The Duke of Salisbury is a fine man. Incidentally, you are his one sole heir, and it seems he and Delores Gibbons legally wed in secret before you came into this world.

So I guess I raised me a duke and I'm proud it's so. Now you've been hoisted to the ranks of near royalty. With all that I taught you, you're sure to be a powerful influence on society and the political arenas. I wish you well in your new role and count on you to make sure your cousin does well to live up to the title of the Earl of Waterford.

I suppose you hate me, and as such, it is good I'm dead. I wouldn't want to face your wrath. Know that your grandmother and your mother had no knowledge of what I did to assure the future.

Continue to dote on your grandmother. Even if she doesn't share your blood, she and Stephanie love you.

I would apologize, but I feel I gave you a better life than you would have had were you labeled a bastard. Delores would never have been able to see you properly educated. All in all, I think things worked out rather well.

I know this is much to ask of a man who despises me; however, you know I will ask. See it in your heart to give comfort to my true granddaughter, for she is the one I wronged in this, and my actions have affected her deeply.

Thank you for keeping me on my toes and giving me someone to battle with through the years.

Forever your devoted grandfather.

Jackson didn't know what he expected, but nevertheless, for some bizarre reason, the air cleared from his lungs and a deep calm filled him. His grandfather, or at least, the man he strove to impress his entire life, was proud of him. He'd waited many years to hear this news. Regardless of how much pain the old earl caused, that bit of knowledge, along with the fact that Jackson had every intention of seeing to Abigail's happiness, to make up for the wrong her grandfather had done to her if for no other reason, and Lord knew there were a million more reasons, lifted the oppression from him like fog dissipating on a warm sunny morn. He hadn't expected an apology, and he didn't receive one, but at least the old earl felt regret for Abigail's suffering and that would have to be enough. As for being the legitimate heir to the Duke of Salisbury, that was something he would contemplate later.

He kissed Abigail's cheek. "Thank you for this, wife."

He was going to go address their family when he paused. Abigail's lips moved. Her tongue came out to wet them, and then she whispered, "Jackson."

His heart leapt at her movement. "Yes, love. I'm here. I'll always be here." He had heard his name on her lips often in the past couple of days, but she'd never moistened her lips. He gently pushed strands of hair from her face. "Abigail, open your eyes, love."

To his utter joy, her brown eyes rimmed in gold blinked up at him in confusion. "Are you all right, love? How do you feel? No, don't move. Lie still. Your shoulder's hurt." His voice croaked with emotion. Abigail was back. His wife returned to him. The sun sprang free from the clouds; a future was now on the horizon, their future together.

"Are you a dream?" With her uninjured arm, she reached up to cup his stubbly cheek. The groggy haze cleared from her eyes while she examined him, and then she pinched him to make sure he indeed sat next to her.

He kissed her forehead. "I'm real, my love, and I'm not going anywhere, ever."

She gave him a tender sweet smile. "That could get quite tiresome, husband. Your constant vigilance might prove to be more than even *I* can handle."

He laughed at her jest, pressing his lips to hers. He stayed in that position, pressing slow, sweet kisses to her mouth. She finally pushed him back, her eyes telling him she had questions.

"Do you remember what happened?" he asked. Tears filled his eyes when she gave a slow, positive nod.

"You stabbed me." She laughed at his look of disbelief and then winced when the movement caused her shoulder pain.

"I see you still have your humor." He felt elated by her happy demeanor. He had his wife back.

"And I see you haven't been sleeping well. Did I worry you overly?" She traced the dark circles under his sleep-deprived eyes.

"Yes. It was pure torture."

Her chin jutted out in defiance. "Good. It's no more than you deserve for leaving me like that. You should be ashamed! You know I would have dragged you out of the Red Robin Tavern by your mop of blond hair if necessary!"

Jackson smiled at her admonishing tone, completely thrilled to have her back. It would not have been necessary for her to drag him from his own drunken confinement. He realized most of the pain he suffered through the last week was due to his own isolation and avoidance of the woman who held his heart, due to his own foolish doing, in other words. "I would happily follow you anywhere."

"There now," she said with a grin. "That's more like it. And I apologize again for not telling you of your grandfather's secrets sooner. My only excuse is that I love you and wanted to be your wife." She paused, then asked, "And do you have anything else to say about your deplorable behavior?"

"I'm sorry for hurting you and breaking my promises. I willingly admit I've been a fool." He hung his head in true shame and then looked up beneath his lashes to give her a grin.

"Knowing apologies don't come easily for you, I will gracefully accept. Now, kiss me, husband. We are still newlyweds."

And he did give her a kiss, one of longing and promises, which put his life back on track. "I love you, Abigail."

"I love you too, Jackson."

She actually yawned, placing the back of her hand to her mouth as she did so. "Now, what's this I heard about company?"

"You heard that?"

"I've heard many things throughout my ordeal. How long have I been in bed?"

"Two terrifying days."

She smoothed his wrinkled brow with a finger. "I'm sorry to have worried you."

"No you're not," he teased. "This was entirely my fault. You'd never be in this bed if it wasn't for my selfish delusion that I somehow failed as a human being."

"My husband, the man who tends to take the brunt of his family's woes on his shoulders. You are not to blame for two madmen attacking me. Then again, if you wouldn't have bought me such a stunning and expensive wedding ring then…"

"I'm so glad to have you back." Her teasing banter eased his battered soul. Leave it to his brave, intelligent wife to ease his conscience and make him feel on top of the world again.

"I say we stop looking back and concentrate on moving forward with our future together." She held his cheek in the palm of her soft hand as they gazed into each other's eyes in emotion-filled silence, both happy to have found their way back together.

Jackson placed another kiss to her lips. "I don't think I've ever agreed with you more."

"Please don't tell me this is to be a new trend. I won't abide a husband whose views never differ from mine." She laughed playfully, pulling his mouth back down to hers. The kiss that ensued was anything but tender, but a fierce undertaking of love and attraction, of faith and togetherness, of passion and fate. Their tongues melded together, the heat of their bodies merged as he leaned into her.

"Tell our guests to go away," she murmured, sliding her tongue along the muscles of his neck, tenderly biting the tendons.

"I can't love you how I want to, Abigail. You're injured." His hands moved to outline the side of her body in a loving caress.

"You *will* make love to me this evening, husband," she said in a tone that brooked no argument.

His groin tightened with urgency. He grasped her hips and pushed his erection against her thigh. Burying his face in the crook of her neck, he inhaled her, then nibbled her shoulder.

At the sound of her moan of surrender, he jumped from the bed and her face fell into a frown. His breathing labored as he stared down at her passion-filled eyes. Her white dressing gown had come untied during their sweet interlude, and he could see the gentle swells of her breasts push toward the gap of fabric, giving him a tempting view of her cleavage and the hardened nipples visible beneath the soft white fabric. His mouth went dry and he swallowed with difficulty, trying like mad to pull himself under control. "You're hurt and the way I fell right now... Hell's teeth, woman, I don't wish to be gentle." His fists clenched at his sides when his wife allowed one of her perfectly shaped legs to peek out from beneath the bedding. *Sweet Jesus. Her nightrail is rucked up around her waist.* Visions of sliding his hand along the smooth expanse of her thigh had him gritting his teeth. The memory of their wedding night and the passion they had for each other made him groan in frustration.

"Are you telling me my skilled husband can't think of a way to make love to me without further injuring my shoulder?" She acted aghast by the very idea. *The vixen. She dares to taunt me.* He felt barely in control. She pushed the bed coverings further off her body to show both of her legs, and then brazenly, she pulled up her knees. He stared at her in open astonishment, his erection pulsating, begging for release, begging to be buried to the hilt in Abigail's tight, hot... He was clearly losing this battle.

He gave her a wicked smile, his mind coming up with numerous agreeable positions he could use to pleasure his injured wife. "I never said that. As a matter of fact..." He climbed back in bed and she helped him shed his coat with one hand. "I have some ideas I think you'll find most gratifying."

"Perhaps a demonstration is in order." She ran her hand down his chest, giving his nipple a slight pinch through his white shirt. She pressed into his hands with a sigh when he cupped her breasts.

A knock had them both freezing in motion. "Yes?" Jackson called out irritably, slowly removing his exploring hands from her lovely body. Abigail pulled the covers up to her chin. Jackson hid his hardened cock with semi-crossed legs.

Preston poked his head in the room. "Terribly sorry to disturb you, my lord..." The butler's face beamed at his mistress. "Oh, your ladyship, so good to see you awake. His lordship has been at constant vigilance and I'm sure his relief at your recovery is immense. On behalf of the staff, may I say we are happy to have you back."

"Thank you, Preston." Abigail tried to sit up, but her shoulder rebelled at the motion, so she remained reclined.

"The reason for your intrusion, Preston?"

Preston pulled at his collar. "Oh right, my lord. I'm afraid your guests are growing impatient. As a matter of fact…" Preston sputtered as he was pushed aside.

"Where's our daughter?" Both Delores and Stephanie came bustling in the room on each other's heels. The dowager was following at a more sedate pace. Jackson's erection deflated in seconds.

He sat up on the bed to see Lord Hastings enter, and behind him a man who could only be the Duke of Salisbury, his father.

CHAPTER SEVENTEEN

Abigail looked on with sheer delight as their family filled up their bedchamber. After pushing Preston out of the way, both of her mothers and her grandmother rushed the bed to assure themselves that she was well.

"There's really no need for a fuss. I'm perfectly fine. My shoulder hurts, but aside from that, I'm very happy." She grabbed Jackson's hand in hers, giving it a gentle squeeze. He looked at her with such love that she felt the sting of tears. She could see he no longer held onto the demons of the past. He was again happy and carefree. She had her Jackson back. She hugged the thought to herself. They had found their way back to each other's arms.

Delores kissed her cheek and turned to make the appropriate introductions. After all, Jackson had yet to meet his father. "Son, may I introduce you to your father, the Duke of Salisbury." Delores' voice shook with emotion, but she stood proudly with tears in her eyes.

Everyone watched the exchange with mild trepidation and utter gladness to see the biological matters put to rights. Jackson released Abigail's hand and came to his feet at the side of the bed. His eyes fixed on the man who sired him. Abigail looked between the two men, their similarities staggering, from their blue eyes to the stiff posture and sheer power they both emitted with their physically fit frames.

The women watched with smiles when the Duke of Salisbury extended his hand to his son. The duke studied Jackson with a keen intelligence and a wide grin. Abigail looked at Delores who gazed up at her love with a look of utter devotion and joy. The sentiment touched Abigail's heart. How often she had wished to see such a smile of happiness on Delores' face.

The duke smiled down at Abigail. "I'm glad to see you safe, my lady. And I'm proud and honored to have you as part of the family. It seems my son is wise, his decision making nonpareil. I look forward to the day when we can talk at length, Abigail." He leaned down and placed a kiss upon her cheek, then whispered in her ear, "Thank you for making Delores' world have meaning and purpose. You, my dear, are an astonishing blessing." He straightened and turned back to Jackson, clapping him on the back. "Why don't the two of us leave the ladies and his lordship for a time. There's much we need to discuss."

Jackson looked to Abigail as if leaving her for a second wasn't an option. She smiled and placed a kiss on the back of his hand. "Go, my love. I'm certainly not going anywhere. Your father's right. Your conversation is long overdue."

"As always, you are correct, my love." He passed her a wink, and his father made a lighthearted comment about young love, and then they left the room, laughing as they went down the hall.

Abigail laughed. She felt wonderful. She had her husband back. She had her life back.

Before leaving, Lord Hastings placed a kiss on her head. "I'm grateful you are all right, dear. I, too, will always be here if you need me." He kissed his wife before he left. Abigail realized theirs was also a love match; everything seemed so perfect it was scary.

"It's good to see you happy," the dowager, who was now perched on the edge of the bed, said to her.

"I assume the two of you have reconciled?" Lady Hastings asked in reference to Jackson.

Abigail knew she got a silly starry-eyed look upon her face when she thought of her husband, but she didn't care. Love was in the air. "We have. I believe Jackson is ready to accept his new place in the world, and we are both ready to begin anew. Although it's sure to be ages before we can show ourselves in society." Abigail worried her lower lip between her teeth.

"Don't you worry about such things," Delores exclaimed. "The duke has assured me this news won't linger overly long on anyone's lips. My influential and arrogant husband refuses for it to be so."

Abigail hoped she was right, but realistically, she was sure it would take a good twenty years before news of this magnitude was forgotten. "And you, Mother?" She clasped Delores' hand, then asked, "You're happy? The wedding was perfect?"

"How could it not be, my dear. We've loved each other for what seems like forever."

A new feminine voice carried up the stairs from the front hall. "What do you mean, she was stabbed? You're speaking figuratively, I hope." Clarissa Loring's unmistakable voice rose to Abigail's ears, and in less than a minute, she was at Abigail's side. "Saints be praised, Abby, are you all right?"

"I am." Abigail tried not to wince when Clarissa hugged her.

"Watch her shoulder, dear," Lady Hastings said gently.

"Oh, I'm sorry. Are you all right? Did I hurt you?"

"I'm fine." Abigail took one look at Clarissa's orange and white striped dress and laughed. She gazed down at the atrocity of a dress and the shimmering orange slippers beneath. "Your mother's choosing?"

Clarissa let out an unladylike sigh of agitation. "Ugh, yes. Let us try to ignore my attire, shall we?"

"Is such a thing possible?" Abigail teased. She couldn't seem to help herself. "Just teasing. I shall strive to do my best not to notice that glow of your gown."

"My mother's taste has veered from bad to worse. I leave plenty of fashion magazines lying about in the hope that she'll choose to peruse one, but alas, it's been to no avail."

"I'm sorry to hear things haven't improved in that area, but I am glad you're here. I'd like to introduce you to my family." Abigail made the introductions, and then the ladies spoke for a few more minutes after Abigail's retelling of the events, which ended with her current confinement in bed. Clarissa took her leave shortly after, promising to visit again tomorrow.

Delores informed her, "You've had a long day. And although you may not feel like you need more rest, I believe it would be best if you did. The duke and I will be staying down the hall in case you have need of us."

"You don't need to stay here, Mother. You're recently married. I'm sure the duke would prefer to go home. I'm really all right."

Delores' eyes sparkled with mischief, and she had a happy glow to her cheeks as if a joyful light radiated from within to exceed the mere light of living that had been missing all these years. "A word of advice, dear. It's best not to give men everything they wish or they will soon forget how to strive for things they really want and just assume it will always be there."

"Besides," said Delores. "I have little faith that I could get that man to leave here at any rate." The women laughed even harder.

Eventually, the others made their way back downstairs and Abigail found herself alone with Lady Hastings. "Come and sit by me, Mother. Now that we have a moment, I'd like to hear all about your trip to Egypt. It's one place I always dreamed of visiting, and so I insist you don't leave out a single detail."

"Then we'll be sure to take a family trip as soon as you're able." Her new mother kicked off her slippers and got under the covers next to her. For the next hour, they spoke at length about their love of anything Egyptian. The topic eventually turned to Abigail's father, and Stephanie told her all she could about her late husband and how he had always wanted a daughter. They both shed tears for the time they had lost together, but they ended up back on the topic of Egypt. Later, Stephanie helped her bathe and redress into a silk nightrail.

***

Jackson poured his father a drink, passing on the restorative for himself. He had enough alcohol lately to last a lifetime.

He told himself the duke was not at fault for his kidnapping, that the Earl of Waterford could take the blame for such a dastardly deed. He reminded himself that he had a family that loved him unconditionally and that was what mattered. More importantly, he had Abigail, and as much as he was enjoying spending time getting to know the kind of man his father was, it was still going to take time to accustom himself to his new life. Right now, all he wanted to do was make love to his wife. As a matter of fact, the thought was consuming him to such a degree that he was having a hard time following the conversation. What was bizarre was how his father appeared to sense where his thoughts were.

His father told him that he had two sisters who would be officially entering London's social whirl in a few short years. The duke informed him that he expected Jackson's assistance in seeing them properly matched. The thought gave Jackson more than a bit of unease. "That you trust me to see to their futures is an honor, sir." It occurred to him that the Earl of Waterford would never have relinquished so much control to his heir. Jackson resolved that he would try not to be as controlling with his own offspring, and that he'd strive to be more like his father.

Delores walked into the room and Jackson couldn't help noticing the graceful way she moved, the love shining in her eyes when she looked at the duke, and the special smile she seemed to have just for Jackson. Her days with alcohol were obviously in the past. It did his heart good to see her happy.

"I was telling our son how proud we are of the man he has become," the duke informed her. "I also suggested I bring the girls by tomorrow to meet their big brother."

"And their new stepmother," Delores added, sitting on the arm of the cushioned chair beside her husband.

His father brought Delores' hand to his lips. The blush spreading across his mother's cheeks amused Jackson.

"It's a wonderful plan, Your Grace." She patted the duke's hand, now resting on her knee. "Would you mind if I had a moment alone with our son?"

"Are we finished here, son?"

"We are."

The duke walked toward him. "Would you think me a sentimental fool if I were to hug you?"

Jackson chuckled. "I think it's prudent you do so, sir. We've many years to make up for."

The duke held him close, and Jackson felt the rest of his bitterness dissipate like water on a hot day. With a bow to Jackson and a kiss to his new wife, the duke left for the room they were using while staying in Jackson's home. Jackson told his father it wasn't necessary for them to stay, but the duke insisted. Indeed, he was glad to have his parents under his roof.

Delores appeared to be a ball of nerves once the duke left. She looked at Jackson with tear-filled eyes. He imagined she felt terribly guilty for his abduction and he wished he could help her.

"I'm so sorry. I never knew… I…"

Jackson said nothing. He just held out his arms. Delores practically ran into his embrace, and he hugged her close, breathing in her scent and glorifying in the fact that his life was full. He had his family, all of them, and he'd never been happier.

***

"How did everything progress with your father?" Abigail asked. She was semi-reclined in bed and trying to braid her hair when he entered. She stopped and declared it a hopeless cause, quite impossible to do with one hand.

Her heart sped up at her husband's appearance. *Will I ever be able to control myself around him?* She certainly hoped not. Dressed in her silkiest nightrail, she felt decadent and lustful. She wanted to get up and strip off her husband's clothes so she could bask in his beauty.

"Better than I ever imagined. He really is a good man." She watched his manliness prowl the room, and then her breath hitched in her throat when he began to undress casually in front of her greedy eyes. When he pulled off his coat and she noticed his glorious muscles stretched taut beneath his white shirt, she actually trembled with need.

"I'm glad." She tried to sound unflustered. His slow paced disrobing was building up the sexual tension she had coursing inside her. Her anticipation was mounting to wondrous heights. She watched his every move while tingles of pleasure slid along her body.

He continued to shed layers of clothing. When he got down to his small clothes, he climbed into bed, taking her comb. Her mouth went dry. "Here, allow me."

Abigail leaned up as he ran the comb through her long brown tresses with smooth strokes. He combed it away from her face and her neck, and with every stroke, he kissed the skin he revealed. She was melting.

"I like my new family. Thank you, Abigail."

"Thank you for finding me that day at the museum," she murmured.

"Regarding the deceased Earl of Waterford, I read his letter." He began to undo the satiny ties at her shoulders as he spoke, allowing the comb to drop to the floor.

"And?"

"And I accept all he has done. Strangely enough, I find myself, in many ways, grateful." His hands brushed across her shoulders while he nipped at her neck. She noticed how careful he was to avoid her bandage.

"Grateful?" she choked out as her fingers skimmed over her breasts, causing her nipples to extend and ache.

"Without him, I wouldn't have found you."

"Or I you," she purred, finding it difficult to think about anything when his mouth closed over her tightly drawn nipple, taking her into a maelstrom of utter bliss. She arched against him, hissing when her bandage pulled tightly over her injury. He cradled her and laid her back onto the bed from her sitting position.

He pulled her chemise from her body, moving it down her legs to avoid her shoulder. "Do you want me inside you, wife?" he came back up to murmur in her ear, his tongue darting out to caress the outer rim of it.

"I've never wanted anything more," she whispered, running her fingers through the hair on his beautifully sculpted chest. He towered over her, causing her knees to weaken. Her body ached in her most private place, a place she knew was damp with her desire for him.

He flipped on his back and she looked at him with indecision. "Then climb on."

A slow smile edged her mouth as she realized what he was insinuating. With careful movements, she pushed herself on top of him to sit astride his hips. His arousal rubbed against her aching flesh in the most breathtaking manner. She slid her body along his length, wondering how such a position was to work. "All right, husband. Now that I'm up here, why don't you instruct me on how this is done?"

"Gladly, my love, gladly." He gripped her hips and pulled her forward, and grasping his erection, he placed it at her wet center. His muscles clenched as she slowly lowered herself, taking him deep inside her. She sat back with a satisfied smile. She liked this position, relishing the power it allowed her. She was the one in control. She felt heady with excitement as she raised herself and then sank back down, smiling proudly when Jackson's teeth gnashed together in reaction. "Do you like that, Jackson? Do you like me on top of you, forcing you inside me?" Her words seemed to have a profound effect on him, for he grabbed her hips to thrust himself even deeper, a cry of bliss escaping her lips.

When she heard him moan and his eyes fell shut only to reopen and settle upon hers, she continued with her bold words. "Does it feel good with me riding you like a stallion, my love? I'm sure you'll be happy to note that this is one horse I will never fear riding." Her words had an overwhelming effect on her as well. She truly did ride Jackson as if he was a *stallion*, hard, furious, and fast. Then she'd slow, drawing him out almost completely, before she sank back down. Deliberate slowness would take over until she worked them both back up into such a frenzy that coherent thought played no role. Sweat poured from their bodies as Jackson's hips came up to meet hers. He leaned up to take her breast into his mouth. Her body went taut, ready to burst into a whirlwind of intoxicating pleasure.

She'd take them to the brink of ecstasy only to stop and begin again. Eventually, unable to take much more, she tossed her head back and gave into the fire consuming her. Jackson grasped her hips, plunging himself as deep as he could before he gave a guttural groan and found his release. She slid gently off him to snuggle at his side as they both panted and waited for their bodies to calm. Her shoulder stung, but she deemed the pain well worth it.

They lay breathless and spent, whispering their undying words of love. They would never again veer off the path they promised to travel together. Their bond of love was stronger than ever.

A short time later, her husband showed her another new position, taking her to such dizzying heights that Abigail never wanted to leave their room again.

EPILOGUE
Nine months later, at the height of London's Season.

Abigail whirled around on the dance floor, a vision of loveliness. Jackson led her around the high gleaming oak planking beneath the shimmering candles held by the many glittering crystal chandeliers. He watched the light play off the multiple colors of her hair, casting off the streaks in her brunette tresses like a bird taking flight. Candlelight glittered in her bewitching eyes, and a smile seemed affixed to her lovely face. He knew without question that he was the luckiest man on earth. It had taken some getting used to, but he was now comfortable with his new place in the world. He owed all his comfort to his wife, who was devoted in seeing him have the life he enjoyed before they met. Even his second cousin, Grayson, seemed to step easily into his title as the Earl of Waterford, almost as easily as Jackson fit into his title as the Marquis of Childress.

The dowager had happily moved into Lord and Lady Hastings townhouse, while Delores and the duke enjoyed the ducal estate in Surrey with his sisters. They came to visit as often as they could. It seemed Delores had found she actually did like to travel when the duke was with her.

Clarissa Loring was still forced to wear outlandish styles and colors, but she visited with Abigail often, usually to complain about her state of dress, and the two of them together never failed to make Jackson laugh. They were indeed outrageous in their opinions of others, and they enjoyed making up the most entertaining stories of the most gossiped about members of society. Thankfully, he and Abigail were no longer the favorite topic of conversation, due to his father and his grandmother's staunch support. Even his friends relished Jackson's new role. And although he was happy being accepted by the society he enjoyed, he'd throw it all away for Abigail. It had taken his dear wife time to adjust to London's social whirl, but in short time, she had men vying for her attentions—which

Jackson found extremely irritating—but the women also flocked to Abigail's side, hanging on her every word. Even the Mandelin sisters begged Abigail's favor. Being a kind, adaptable, and forgiving person, Abigail did not snub them as they had her. No, not his brave girl. There seemed to be nothing she couldn't handle. Every day with her was magical: her laughter, her considerate viewpoint of people and life in general, her friendship, her love, and even her tolerance for being married to a man as domineering as he could sometimes be. She was his world and he loved her more and more every day.

"You seem to be in a pensive mood this evening, my love. Are you enjoying yourself?" The object of his thoughts peered up at him with her question.

"I am," he answered. "Life seems to have come full circle. I don't think there's anything left that could shock me now."

"No?" Her eyes twinkled up at him in amusement, which should have told him immediately that his wife was going to do exactly that. The music stopped and she placed his hand on the flat of her stomach. "Would it shock you to learn I'm with child?"

His eyes widened in stunned delight. "Truly?"

"Yes." She smiled up adoringly at him, and he placed a kiss on her lips. He pulled her to the center of the dance floor when the music began, then turned to the musicians, indicating with his hands for them to stop playing, which they did. This, in turn, caused all the dancers to stare at Jackson and Abby in disbelief and with curiosity. "What are you doing, Jackson? Lord and Lady Bayberry would not appreciate us interrupting their gathering for a second year in a row, husband."

He pulled her close to him and whispered, "Quiet, wife." Then he declared loudly, "We have an announcement to make."

The End

About the author

Lori Hilden is the author of A Necessary Heir, London's Quest, and six other novels she is working on publishing.

In 1990, Lori read her first Historical Romance novel by one of her favorite authors, Johanna Lindsey. She's been hooked on the Regency Period ever since.

Starving to learn more about history and to capture the authenticity of the time era she loves, Lori attended the University of Michigan, where she earned a Bachelor's in history and a minor in art history. She's been typing away on her computer ever since.

Finding time to write hasn't always been easy for Lori, who has a son 15 months older than her boy/girl twins. She lives in Michigan with her husband, three children, two dogs and three hamsters.

Also by L.A. Hilden:

London's Quest

June 26, 2011
London, England

Her life wasn't over. She had wished for death throughout the last year, but she was still standing. Feeling invigorated by the lack of her nightmares, London Miranda Burton nearly bounced in her heels as she made her way to her favorite pub, the Back Room Tavern, where the fish-n-chips were unreal.

She found herself unable to fight the allure of the place: the food but also the locals who frequented the place had wondrous stories to tell her. Their tales usually revolved around the Back Room Tavern's fascinating history as a meeting place for government spies after its conversion from a coffeehouse to a men-only club in 1817.

According to the locals, the men's club was built by three unforgettable lords, and ladies weren't allowed admittance until 1948. She found it amazing how much had changed for women in just sixty-three years.

"Blimey, look who's back, and aren't you looking spritely today?" Conner, the owner, doorman, and historical curate of the Back Room, gave her a formal bow. "If it isn't the city of London herself," he said with his cool British accent.

Giving him a curtsy for fun since his outfit seemed to call for exactly that, she asked, "What's with the costume?"

"Photo-shoot today for some fancy-pancy singer. The young lady, or should I say, child, is far too indulged. I escaped for a breath of air before the shoot. This costume is a Regency Era special. You like?" Conner asked, puffing out his chest with pride.

London looked from the polished black boots up his skinny legs encased in beige pants, which were mostly covered with a peacock blue waistcoat and a black tailcoat. His upper chest and neck were completely covered with a frilly, fluffy, white confection which, he informed her, was known as a cravat.

"Bollocks! This piece of fluff is tedious," he said. "Took the outfitter nearly twenty minutes to get it like this. The blasted thing nearly suffocates a man." He slipped a finger under the collar to pull at its close fit.

"You look divine, very old-worldly," she complimented him with a nod toward the door. "So which celeb's having her picture taken?"

"Some American girl. They claim she's twenty, but she doesn't act a day over twelve. The names Desirea something," he replied, shooting a glare at the door.

"Desirea Leighton, the singer?"

He gave her a nod in the affirmative while rolling his eyes upward.

"Her song 'Come With Me' has topped the billboard chart for weeks now. At least it was number one according to Ryan Seacrest the last time I was home. She had a hit TV series with Disney when she was younger, and I've heard she's a fine opera singer."

"I'm sure she is a…precocious child."

London laughed. "For crying out loud, Conner. She's twenty and so hardly a child."

A wail came from inside the tavern and Conner cringed at the sound.

"What was that?" London asked, glancing at the door.

"The hardly-a-child creature to whom you refer," Conner responded in clear frustration while holding the door open. "After you, London, but you enter at your own risk."

Curious, London moved inside the vast entryway. The welcoming feeling of belonging enveloped her, as always seemed to happen whenever she ventured inside the inviting warmth of the pub. The smell of wood cleaner penetrated the air over the scent of stale tobacco and ale. Looking into the main salon with its beautiful draperies, she noticed the large incongruous mountain of beach sand covering the floor in the center of the room. Cameras, lights, and various photography equipment littered the area. The starlet Desirea Leighton had her arms crossed over her ample bosom, and she was stomping her foot into the sand in an obvious display of temper.

"Unfrikkenbelievable!" the young blond hollered. "You expect me to pose with a model in a string bikini while I wear this silly Regency dress. You must be out of your ever-loving mind. Where's my agent? I want to speak to him now!"

"Desirea, if you'd just give me a moment…" A short man in khaki pants and a white shirt with rolled sleeves shifted on his feet in obvious nervousness as he tried to placate the star.

"Give you a moment?" Desirea screeched. "I won't be outshined in my own frikken photo-shoot. And why the hell am I dressed like this in a bar with frikken sand on the floor? This entire theme is beyond ridiculous. I've had enough! I'm going outside for some air. When I return, have her dressed in something more appropriate or have her gone!"

Desirea Leighton stormed past London and slammed the door.

"Ah bloody hell. That's what I get for trying to make some extra blunt. I need this photo-shoot over already. My customers are not going to want to set their barstools in sand." Conner threw up his hands in aggravation. "I have to talk to the wanker who can hurry this damn thing along. Make yourself at home, London."

London nodded as Conner walked into another room yelling for some guy named Howard. Looking from the sand-covered floor to the door out which Desirea fled, London decided to lend a hand. After all, Conner claimed Desirea had the manners of a child, and Lord knew, as a former first grade teacher, London had a vast amount of experience dealing with six-year-olds.

She squeezed her eyes shut trying to prevent the sting of tears. She had left the job she once loved when she realized she couldn't watch other people's children grow and play and learn, without thinking of her own precious Noah and what he'd be able to do now, a year later. How big would he be? She couldn't continue to teach her class with tears in her eyes. It wasn't fair to her students, and so she quit. Without any family holding her to the city she had come to despise, she left, escaping in the hope of saving herself from wallowing in despair forever.

London sighed as sadness washed over her like an ocean tide. Pushing away her grief, she stepped through the sand and toward the door. Desirea was right. A beach inside a historical landmark was absurd.

She didn't have to go far to find Miss Leighton. The young starlet sat at the end of the building on an outcropping of stone that jutted out from the structure. The girl's fingers moved rapidly as she punched in a text message on her Blackberry. She was a very pretty girl, with bright blue eyes and long lashes.

"Miss Leighton, my name is London Burton. I thought perhaps I could be of assistance."

"Do you have a Cat-in-the-Hat super vacuum that will suck up five hundred pounds of sand and my manager? If not, I'm afraid you can't help."

Desirea looked up, her intention, London assumed, to give her a look of dismissal, but instead the young lady's face dropped and she turned a stark shade of white. London watched Desirea tighten her grip on her phone. The whites in Desirea's eyes enlarged.

"What is it?" London asked in concern, the hair on the back of her neck standing on end. She abruptly spun around to see what had put such a horrified expression on the young lady's face.

"It's him," Desirea hissed as her body visibly began to shake and she dropped her phone to the pavement.

This reaction sent shivers of warning up London's spine. "Him? Him who?" London couldn't see anyone close enough to warrant such fear. But she spun around and looked harder at everyone in sight.

"Marvin Travers, my stalker," murmured the girl.

"Is he dangerous?" London asked, although she assumed the man had to be considering Desirea's fear. Besides, weren't all stalkers dangerous?

"Shhh, or he'll hear you. I don't think he saw me. He's behind the building now." The girl's wide blue eyes looked quickly around their surroundings. "Oh my god, you have to hide me."

"Hide you? Really? Is that necessary? I mean, he's a fan, right?"

"A crazed fan." Desirea grabbed London's arm. "Please," the girl begged, shaking in fear.

This is what I get for trying to help, pulled into someone else's nightmare. "Okay, okay. Let me think." She looked around at the people walking by, her gaze dismissing a dark alley. Now where was a safe place to hide? Thinking it best to hide where people would hear their shouts, London grabbed Desirea's arm and hurried them back toward the pub. She ushered the singer through the door and into the back parlor. She had hoped to find help, but the crew and Conner were nowhere in sight.

London looked around frantically for a hiding place. Her gaze came to rest on a closed paneled door. At least, she thought, it was a door. The entry did match all the other rectangular recesses along the wall, but she remembered Conner once telling her a story about the hidden niche. She pushed at the panel and it opened toward her. "Hurry. In here." She grabbed the girl, ordering her inside the hidden closet.

Desirea stepped inside. "Wait," she exclaimed. "It's too dark. You have to come too." The girl would not release London's arm. "Come on, before he sees me."

"There's not enough room in there for the two of us." Truthfully, there was more than enough room, but seriously, London was not about to hide in a closet, especially when she didn't have to.

"The hell there isn't." Desirea yanked her closer.

"Don't be silly," London said in a placating tone, trying to remove her arm from this girl's surprisingly strong grip. "I'll get rid of him and then let you know when it's safe to come out."

"I'm not hiding in here by myself," the girl said, keeping her firm hold on London's arm.

Enough was enough. "Well, I'm afraid you're just going to have to…"

Desirea suddenly tugged with all her might. Not able to break her fall, London landed right on top of her. The celeb yelped in pain when her head connected with the back wall. The crash caused the back panel of the closet to open, revealing a secret passageway.

"A hidden passage," Desirea said in a voice filled with awe, as if she and London were explorers. The girl sat on the ground, eyeing the passage and rubbing her head. Then she slowly got to her feet, which had been holding the closet door open as she sat upon the floor.

London whirled around in protest as the door slammed shut, sealing them inside. "Look what you've done," she groaned, looking back at Desirea in the shadows. The cement and wood tunnel held a hazy illuminating glow that prevented them from being cloaked in utter darkness. She had no idea of the eerie light's source, but she was grateful for any illumination. The coldness of the tunnel sent goose bumps skidding across her flesh. She turned back toward the door. "There's no latch on this side. We're stuck." London felt around the edges of the door, feeling panic slam into her chest. She began to shake and a tingling heat filled the top half of her body, increasing her panic.

"Hello," a male voice called from the other side of the door.

"We're…" A hand clamped over London's mouth.

"Shut up! It's Marvin," Desirea hissed in her ear.

By this point, London was beyond being slightly irritated with the girl. But when Desirea brushed against her, London could feel that she was shaking uncontrollably and decided to remain silent. Desirea was obviously truly terrified of this Marvin person, which told London she'd be wise to fear the man as well.

The closet was darker than the tunnel and the smell of old wood permeated the small space. Footsteps came nearer as Marvin continued to call out for Desirea in the tavern.

"Desirea. It's Marvin. Now where ya hiding, my pretty? Bet you didn't expect to see me on this side of the Atlantic. Come on out now, so we can talk. It wasn't nice of you to sic the cops on me. You didn't think a restraining order and a stint in prison would keep me away, did you?" he bellowed in anger.

Desirea whimpered behind her.

"No one will stop your most devoted fan from paying you homage."

A chill passed through London at Marvin's words. His voice held a crazed quality. London had no idea what this man had done to instill such fear in the singer, nor did she want to find out. Reaching into the semi-dark, she grabbed Desirea's trembling fingers. "Come on," London whispered, guiding the girl through the hidden door and into the foggy, cold passageway.

Here the walls were even closer, so with hands clasped together, they hurried quietly sideways through the tunnel. London continually tried to will her rapidly beating heart to slow down, but without success. Panic filled her very being, at the darkness, the closeness of the space, the angry man on the other side of the wall behind them. She knew there had to be an exit door at the other end. She groped forward in the gloom with her free hand, unhappy to realize that she clearly suffered from a mild case of claustrophobia. As they edged further forward, the wall dipped toward them and was now a mere two inches from her face. She felt like she was breathing in the old cement of the wall. If the wall came any closer, they would have to turn back.

Beams began to creak and moan overhead, showering them with dust. They both screamed and stumbled forward. Thankfully, the corridor widened, but only slightly. All London could think was that, if the ceiling caved, they were doomed. But the beams settled, and a whooshing outrush of breath from both of them echoed through the space, but the relief that washed over them was momentary.

A few seconds later, noise drowned out anything they might have said to each other. The corridor filled with a buzzing so deafening that Desirea screamed and bumped into London. Smoke began to fill the air, causing them to hack and cough.

"What's happening?" Desirea asked between pants for air. They both struggled for oxygen as they continued forward.

"I don't know," London replied, fear gripping her as she thought they might die in some hidden corridor and never be found. The cloying smoke brought back images of the car crash that took her son's life, and her heart now raced madly. She swallowed a scream, and the taste of smoke in her mouth made her gag. Her head bobbed and she grew dizzy.

"You okay?" asked Desirea. "The smoke's making me ill."

"Me too," London choked out as they trudged forward.

The moaning and creaking of the beams roared to life, sending forth a rush of air that whistled through the semi-dark stealing their breath but also the smoke. Both women shook and let out silent screams as the wind grew stronger, pushing at their backs and throwing them forward like a kite in a hurricane. At one point, London was completely lifted her off her feet.

Then the wind stopped.

The sound of male voices filtered into the settled space. The air, now void of smoke, was crisp and London could smell coffee and masculine cologne.

"What happened?" Desirea questioned.

London couldn't possibly explain the feeling of crossing into the Twilight Zone. Frustrated by the trouble she was going through on this girl's behalf, she snapped," How should I know?" She still felt dizzy and she was swaying where she stood. "Damn it," she cursed. She felt like vomiting. Her mouth watered and she swallowed.

"This must be our stop," said Desirea, and she was right, thought London, because she was not about to go back through that scary-ass corridor.

They stared at the wooden door before them, which was identical to the one they used to escape the tavern. Laughter filtered through the door, and light shone through the crack at the bottom, casting a tiny speck of illumination into the wooden closet area.

London was fearful to open it, to see who was on the other side.

"Is there a latch?" Desirea asked.

"No," London replied, slowly moving her fingers around the door's edges. She wondered why her dizziness wasn't going away.

"Well then give it a shove, girlfriend. I want the hell out of here."

London was gripped in panic. Something had happened when they crossed over the threshold from the tavern and into the corridor, but her reason could not tell her what. She had merely sensed the change, a shift in the atmosphere that filled her with something like horror mixed with dread. She truly didn't want to open the door and find herself in even more danger, but now she couldn't seem to focus. She tried to blink away her dizziness.

"Oh, come on, already! Get out of the way." Desirea moved around her.

The girl turned sideways, and with all her might, shoved the door with her shoulder. The door flew open and Desirea's screech echoed through the passageway as she pitched forward.

London looked down to see Desirea on the floor, her voluminous skirts billowing around her. London then scanned the room to find an unbelievably beautiful man glaring at her, but her vision blurred and the handsome stranger grew fuzzy. Black spots swam before her eyes.

"Holy hell," London whispered, no longer able to fight her wooziness. Her legs crumbled and she fainted. Her last thought was of the panel door slamming shut behind them, closing the passageway.